The Third Leonaur Book of Great Ghost and Horror Stories

The Third Leonaur Book of Great Ghost and Horror Stories

Sixteen Spine Chilling and Strange Tales
Including 'The Last Lords of Gardonal', 'The Ship
That Saw a Ghost', 'The Temple', 'A Strange
Goldfield', and 'When I Was Dead'

Compiled by

Eunice Hetherington

LEONAUR

The Third Leonaur Book of
Great Ghost and Horror Stories
Sixteen Spine Chilling and Strange Tales Including 'The Last Lords of
Gardonal', 'The Ship That Saw a Ghost', 'The Temple', 'A Strange Goldfield', and
'When I Was Dead'
Compiled by Eunice Hetherington

Leonaur is an imprint of Oakpast Ltd

ISBN: 978-1-78282-894-5 (hardcover)
ISBN: 978-1-78282-895-2 (softcover)

http://www.leonaur.com

Publisher's Notes

Contents

A Bottomless Grave   7
Ambrose Bierce

The Feather Pillow   15
Horacio Quiroga

The Last Lords of Gardonal   19
William Gilbert

The Man-Eating Tree   53
Phil Robinson

The Ship That Saw a Ghost   61
Frank Norris

The Stone Chamber   75
H. B. Marriott Watson

The Temple   107
Edward Benson

Let Loose   123
Mary Cholmondeley

Haunted by Spirits   139
George Manville Fenn

A Strange Goldfield   147
Guy Boothby

Aylmer Vance and the Vampire   155
Alice and Claude Askew

Ken's Mystery   173
Julian Hawthorne

The Vampire Maid   193
Hume Nisbet

When I Was Dead   199
Vincent James O'Sullivan

A Mystery of the Campagna   203
Von Degen (Anne Crawford)

The Red Hand   233
Arthur Machen

A Bottomless Grave

Ambrose Bierce

My name is John Brenwalter. My father, a drunkard, had a patent
for an invention, for making coffee-berries out of clay; but he was an
honest man and would not himself engage in the manufacture. He
was, therefore, only moderately wealthy, his royalties from his really
valuable invention bringing him hardly enough to pay his expenses
of litigation with rogues guilty of infringement. So, I lacked many
advantages enjoyed by the children of unscrupulous and dishonour-
able parents, and had it not been for a noble and devoted mother, who
neglected all my brothers and sisters and personally supervised my
education, should have grown up in ignorance and been compelled
to teach school. To be the favourite child of a good woman is better
than gold.

When I was nineteen years of age my father had the misfortune
to die. He had always had perfect health, and his death, which occurred at the dinner table without a moment's warning, surprised no
one more than himself. He had that very morning been notified that
a patent had been granted him for a device to burst open safes by
hydraulic pressure, without noise. The Commissioner of Patents had
pronounced it the most ingenious, effective and generally meritori-
ous invention that had ever been submitted to him, and my father
had naturally looked forward to an old age of prosperity and honour.
His sudden death was, therefore, a deep disappointment to him; but
my mother, whose piety and resignation to the will of Heaven were
conspicuous virtues of her character, was apparently less affected. At
the close of the meal, when my poor father's body had been removed
from the floor, she called us all into an adjoining room and addressed
us as follows:

"My children, the uncommon occurrence that you have just wit-

7

nessed is one of the most disagreeable incidents in a good man's life, and one in which I take little pleasure, I assure you. I beg you to believe that I had no hand in bringing it about. Of course," she added, after a pause, during which her eyes were cast down in deep thought, "of course it is better that he is dead."

She uttered this with so evident a sense of its obviousness as a self-evident truth that none of us had the courage to brave her surprise by asking an explanation. My mother's air of surprise when any of us went wrong in any way was very terrible to us. One day, when in a fit of peevish temper, I had taken the liberty to cut off the baby's ear, her simple words, "John, you surprise me!" appeared to me so sharp a reproof that after a sleepless night I went to her in tears, and throwing myself at her feet, exclaimed: "Mother, forgive me for surprising you." So now we all—including the one-eared baby—felt that it would keep matters smoother to accept without question the statement that it was better, somehow, for our dear father to be dead. My mother continued:

"I must tell you, my children, that in a case of sudden and mysterious death the law requires the Coroner to come and cut the body into pieces and submit them to a number of men who, having inspected them, pronounce the person dead. For this the Coroner gets a large sum of money. I wish to avoid that painful formality in this instance; it is one which never had the approval of—of the remains. John"—here my mother turned her angel face to me-"you are an educated lad, and very discreet. You have now an opportunity to show your gratitude for all the sacrifices that your education has entailed upon the rest of us. John, go and remove the Coroner."

Inexpressibly delighted by this proof of my mother's confidence, and by the chance to distinguish myself by an act that squared with my natural disposition, I knelt before her, carried her hand to my lips and bathed it with tears of sensibility. Before five o'clock that afternoon I had removed the Coroner.

I was immediately arrested and thrown into jail, where I passed a most uncomfortable night, being unable to sleep because of the profanity of my fellow-prisoners, two clergymen, whose theological training had given them a fertility of impious ideas and a command of blasphemous language altogether unparalleled. But along toward morning the jailer, who, sleeping in an adjoining room, had been equally disturbed, entered the cell and with a fearful oath warned the reverend gentlemen that if he heard any more swearing their sacred calling would not prevent him from turning them into the street. After that they moderated their objectionable conversation, substituting an accordion, and I slept the peaceful and refreshing sleep of youth and innocence.

The next morning, I was taken before the Superior Judge, sitting as a committing magistrate, and put upon my preliminary examination. I pleaded not guilty, adding that the man whom I had murdered was a notorious Democrat. (My good mother was a Republican, and from early childhood I had been carefully instructed by her in the principles of honest government and the necessity of suppressing factional opposition.) The Judge, elected by a Republican ballot-box with a sliding bottom, was visibly impressed by the cogency of my plea and offered me a cigarette.

"May it please your Honour," began the District Attorney, "I do not deem it necessary to submit any evidence in this case. Under the law of the land you sit here as a committing magistrate. It is therefore your duty to commit. Testimony and argument alike would imply a doubt that your Honour means to perform your sworn duty. That is my case."

My counsel, a brother of the deceased Coroner, rose and said: "May it please the Court, my learned friend on the other side has so well and eloquently stated the law governing in this case that it only remains for me to inquire to what extent it has been already complied with. It is true, your Honour is a committing magistrate, and as such it is your duty to commit — what? That is a matter which the law has wisely and justly left to your own discretion, and wisely you have discharged already every obligation that the law imposes. Since I have known your Honour you have done nothing but commit. You have committed embracery, theft, arson, perjury, adultery, murder — every crime in the calendar and every excess known to the sensual and depraved, including my learned friend, the District Attorney. You have done your whole duty as a committing magistrate, and as there is no evidence against this worthy young man, my client, I move that he be discharged."

An impressive silence ensued. The Judge arose, put on the black cap and in a voice trembling with emotion sentenced me to life and liberty. Then turning to my counsel, he said, coldly but significantly:

"I will see you later."

The next morning the lawyer who had so conscientiously defended me against a charge of murdering his own brother—with whom he had a quarrel about some land—had disappeared and his fate is to this day unknown.

In the meantime, my poor father's body had been secretly buried at midnight in the back yard of his late residence, with his late boots on and the contents of his late stomach unanalysed. "He was opposed to display," said my dear mother, as she finished tamping down the earth above him and assisted the children to litter the place with straw; "his instincts were all domestic and he loved a quiet life."

My mother's application for letters of administration stated that she had good reason to believe that the deceased was dead, for he had not come home to his meals for several days; but the Judge of the Crowbait Court—as she ever afterward contemptuously called it—decided that the proof of death was insufficient, and put the estate into the hands of the Public Administrator, who was his son-in-law. It was found that the liabilities were exactly balanced by the assets; there was left only the patent for the device for bursting open safes without noise, by hydraulic pressure and this had passed into the ownership of the Probate Judge and the Public Administrator—as my dear mother preferred to spell it. Thus, within a few brief months a worthy and respectable family was reduced from prosperity to crime; necessity compelled us to go to work.

In the selection of occupations, we were governed by a variety of considerations, such as personal fitness, inclination, and so forth. My mother opened a select private school for instruction in the art of changing the spots upon leopard-skin rugs; my eldest brother, George Henry, who had a turn for music, became a bugler in a neighbouring asylum for deaf mutes; my sister, Mary Maria, took orders for Professor Pumpernickel's Essence of Latchkeys for flavouring mineral springs, and I set up as an adjuster and gilder of crossbeams for gibbets. The other children, too young for labour, continued to steal small articles exposed in front of shops, as they had been taught.

In our intervals of leisure, we decoyed travellers into our house and buried the bodies in a cellar.

In one part of this cellar we kept wines, liquors and provisions. From the rapidity of their disappearance we acquired the superstitious belief that the spirits of the persons buried there came at dead of night and held a festival. It was at least certain that frequently of a morning we would discover fragments of pickled meats, canned goods and such debris, littering the place, although it had been securely locked and barred against human intrusion. It was proposed to remove the provisions and store them elsewhere, but our dear mother, always generous and hospitable, said it was better to endure the loss than risk exposure: if the ghosts were denied this trifling gratification they might set on foot an investigation, which would overthrow our scheme of the division of labour, by diverting the energies of the whole family into the single industry pursued by me—we might all decorate the cross-beams of gibbets. We accepted her decision with filial submission, due to our reverence for her worldly wisdom and the purity of her character.

One night while we were all in the cellar—none dared to enter it alone—engaged in bestowing upon the mayor of an adjoining town the solemn offices of Christian burial, my mother and the younger children, holding a candle each, while George Henry and I laboured with a spade and pick, my sister Mary Maria uttered a shriek and covered her eyes with her hands. We were all dreadfully startled and the mayor's obsequies were instantly suspended, while with pale faces and in trembling tones we begged her to say what had alarmed her. The younger children were so agitated that they held their candles unsteadily, and the waving shadows of our figures danced with uncouth and grotesque movements on the walls and flung themselves into the most uncanny attitudes.

The face of the dead man, now gleaming ghastly in the light, and now extinguished by some floating shadow, appeared at each emergence to have taken on a new and more forbidding expression, a maligner menace. Frightened even more than ourselves by the girl's scream, rats raced in multitudes about the place, squeaking shrilly, or starred the black opacity of some distant corner with steadfast eyes, mere points of green light, matching the faint phosphorescence of decay that filled the half-dug grave and seemed the visible manifestation of that faint odour of mortality which tainted the unwholesome air. The children now sobbed and clung about the limbs of their elders, dropping their candles, and we were near being left in total darkness, except for that sinister light, which slowly welled upward from the disturbed earth and overflowed the edges of the grave like a fountain.

Meanwhile my sister, crouching in the earth that had been thrown out of the excavation, had removed her hands from her face and was staring with expanded eyes into an obscure space between two wine casks.

"There it is!—there it is!" she shrieked, pointing; "God in heaven! can't you see it?"

11

And there indeed it was!—a human figure, dimly discernible in the gloom—a figure that wavered from side to side as if about to fall, clutching at the wine-casks for support, had stepped unsteadily forward and for one moment stood revealed in the light of our remaining candles; then it surged heavily and fell prone upon the earth. In that moment we had all recognized the figure, the face and bearing of our father—dead these ten months and buried by our own hands!—our father indubitably risen and ghastly drunk!

On the incidents of our precipitate flight from that horrible place—on the extinction of all human sentiment in that tumultuous, mad scramble up the damp and mouldy stairs—slipping, falling, pulling one another down and clambering over one another's back—the lights extinguished, babes trampled beneath the feet of their strong brothers and hurled backward to death by a mother's arm!—on all this I do not dare to dwell. My mother, my eldest brother and sister and I escaped; the others remained below, to perish of their wounds, or of their terror—some, perhaps, by flame. For within an hour we four, hastily gathering together what money and jewels we had and what clothing we could carry, fired the dwelling and fled by its light into the hills. We did not even pause to collect the insurance, and my dear mother said on her death-bed, years afterward in a distant land, that this was the only sin of omission that lay upon her conscience. Her confessor, a holy man, assured her that under the circumstances Heaven would pardon the neglect.

About ten years after our removal from the scenes of my childhood I, then a prosperous forger, returned in disguise to the spot with a view to obtaining, if possible, some treasure belonging to us, which had been buried in the cellar. I may say that I was unsuccessful: the discovery of many human bones in the ruins had set the authorities digging for more. They had found the treasure and had kept it for their honesty. The house had not been rebuilt; the whole suburb was, in fact, a desolation. So many unearthly sights and sounds had been reported thereabout that nobody would live there. As there was none to question nor molest, I resolved to gratify my filial piety by gazing once more upon the face of my beloved father, if indeed our eyes had deceived us and he was still in his grave. I remembered, too, that he had always worn an enormous diamond ring, and never having seen it nor heard of it since his death, I had reason to think he might have been buried in it. Procuring a spade, I soon located the grave in what had been the backyard and began digging. When I had got down about four feet the whole bottom fell out of the grave and I was precipitated into a large drain, falling through a long hole in its crumbling arch. There was no body, nor any vestige of one.

Unable to get out of the excavation, I crept through the drain, and having with some difficulty removed a mass of charred rubbish and blackened masonry that choked it, emerged into what had been that fateful cellar.

All was clear. My father, whatever had caused him to be "taken bad" at his meal (and I think my sainted mother could have thrown some light upon that matter) had indubitably been buried alive. The grave having been accidentally dug above the forgotten drain, and down almost to the crown of its arch, and no coffin having been used, his struggles on reviving had broken the rotten masonry and he had fallen through, escaping finally into the cellar. Feeling that he was not welcome in his own house, yet having no other, he had lived in subterranean seclusion, a witness to our thrift and a pensioner on our providence. It was he who had eaten our food; it was he who had drunk our wine—he was no better than a thief! In a moment of intoxication, and feeling, no doubt, that need of companionship which is the one sympathetic link between a drunken man and his race, he had left his place of concealment at a strangely inopportune time, entailing the most deplorable consequences upon those nearest and dearest to him—a blunder that had almost the dignity of crime.

The Feather Pillow

Horacio Quiroga

Alicia's entire honeymoon gave her hot and cold shivers. A blonde, angelic, and timid young girl, the childish fancies she had dreamed about being a bride had been chilled by her husband's rough character. She loved him very much, nonetheless, although sometimes she gave a light shudder when, as they returned home through the streets together at night, she cast a furtive glance at the impressive stature of her Jordan, who had been silent for an hour. He, for his part, loved her profoundly but never let it be seen.

For three months—they had been married in April—they lived in a special kind of bliss.

Doubtless she would have wished less severity in the rigorous sky of love, more expansive and less cautious tenderness, but her husband's impassive manner always restrained her.

The house in which they lived influenced her chills and shuddering to no small degree. The whiteness of the silent patio—friezes, columns, and marble statues—produced the wintry impression of an enchanted palace. Inside the glacial brilliance of stucco, the completely bare walls, affirmed the sensation of unpleasant coldness. As one crossed from one room to another, the echo of his steps reverberated throughout the house, as if long abandonment had sensitized its resonance.

Alicia passed the autumn in this strange love nest. She had determined, however, to cast a veil over her former dreams and live like a sleeping beauty in the hostile house, trying not to think about anything until her husband arrived each evening.

It is not strange that she grew thin. She had a light attack of influenza that dragged on insidiously for days and days: after that Alicia's health never returned. Finally, one afternoon she was able to go into the garden, supported on her husband's arm. She looked around listlessly.

15

Suddenly Jordan, with deep tenderness, ran his hand very slowly over her head, and Alicia instantly burst into sobs, throwing her arms around his neck. For a long time, she cried out all the fears she had kept silent, redoubling her weeping at Jordan's slightest caress. Then her sobs subsided, and she stood a long while, her face hidden in the hollow of his neck, not moving or speaking a word.

This was the last day Alicia was well enough to be up. On the following day she awakened feeling faint. Jordan's doctor examined her with minute attention, prescribing calm and absolute rest.

'I don't know,' he said to Jordan at the street door. 'She has a great weakness that I am unable to explain. And with no vomiting, nothing…if she wakes tomorrow as she did today, call me at once.'

When she awakened the following day, Alicia was worse. There was a consultation. It was agreed there was an anaemia of incredible progression, completely inexplicable. Alicia had no more fainting spells, but she was visibly moving toward death. The lights were lighted all day long in her bedroom, and there was complete silence. Hours went by without the slightest sound.

Alicia dozed. Jordan virtually lived in the drawing room, which was also always lighted. With tireless persistence he paced ceaselessly from one end of the room to the other. The carpet swallowed his steps. At times he entered the bedroom and continued his silent pacing back and forth alongside the bed, stopping for an instant at each end to regard his wife.

Suddenly Alicia began to have hallucinations, vague images, at first seeming to float in the air, then descending to floor level. Her eyes excessively wide, she stared continuously at the carpet on either side of the head of her bed. One night she suddenly focused on one spot. Then she opened her mouth to scream, and pearls of sweat suddenly beaded her nose and lips.

'Jordan! Jordan!' she clamoured, rigid with fright, still staring at the carpet.

Jordan ran to the bedroom, and, when she saw him appear, Alicia screamed with terror.

'It's I, Alicia, it's I!'

Alicia looked at him confusedly; she looked at the carpet; she looked at him once again; and after a long moment of stupefied confrontation, she regained her senses. She smiled and took her husband's hand in hers, caressing it, trembling, for half an hour.

Among her most persistent hallucinations was that of an anthropoid poised on his fingertips on the carpet, staring at her.

The doctors returned, but to no avail. They saw before them a diminishing life, a life bleeding away day by day, hour by hour, absolutely without their knowing why. During their last consultation Alicia lay in a stupor while they took her pulse, passing her inert wrist from one to another. They observed her a long time in silence and then moved into the dining room.

'Phew'...The discouraged chief physician shrugged his shoulders. 'It is an inexplicable case. There is little we can do. . . .'

'That's my last hope!' Jordan groaned. And he staggered blindly against the table.

Alicia's life was fading away in the subdelirium of anaemia, a delirium which grew worse through the evening hours but which let up somewhat after dawn. The illness never worsened during the daytime, but each morning she awakened pale as death, almost in a swoon. It seemed only at night that her life drained out of her in new waves of blood. Always when she awakened, she had the sensation of lying collapsed in the bed with a million-pound weight on top of her.

Following the third day of this relapse she never left her bed again. She could scarcely move her head. She did not want her bed to be touched, not even to have her bedcovers arranged. Her crepuscular terrors advanced now in the form of monsters that dragged themselves toward the bed and laboriously climbed upon the bedspread.

Then she lost consciousness. The final two days she raved ceaselessly in a weak voice. The lights funereally illuminated the bedroom and drawing room. In the deathly silence of the house the only sound was the monotonous delirium from the bedroom and the dull echoes of Jordan's eternal pacing.

Finally, Alicia died. The servant, when she came in afterward to strip the now empty bed, stared wonderingly for a moment at the pillow.

'Sir!' she called Jordan in a low voice. 'There are stains on the pillow that look like blood.'

Jordan approached rapidly and bent over the pillow. Truly, on the case, on both sides of the hollow left by Alicia's head, were two small dark spots.

'They look like punctures,' the servant murmured after a moment of motionless observation.

'Hold it up to the light,' Jordan told her.

The servant raised the pillow but immediately dropped it and stood staring at it, livid and trembling. Without knowing why, Jordan felt the hair rise on the back of his neck.

'What is it?' he murmured in a hoarse voice.

'It's very heavy,' the servant whispered, still trembling.

Jordan picked it up; it was extraordinarily heavy. He carried it out of the room, and on the dining room table he ripped open the case and the ticking with a slash. The top feathers floated away, and the servant, her mouth opened wide, gave a scream of horror and covered her face with her clenched fists: in the bottom of the pillowcase, among the feathers, slowly moving its hairy legs, was a monstrous animal, a living, viscous ball. It was so swollen one could scarcely make out its mouth.

Night after night, since Alicia had taken to her bed, this abomination had stealthily applied its mouth—its proboscis one might better say—to the girl's temples, sucking her blood. The puncture was scarcely perceptible. The daily plumping of the pillow had doubtlessly at first impeded its progress, but as soon as the girl could no longer move, the suction became vertiginous. In five days, in five nights, the monster had drained Alicia's life away.

These parasites of feathered creatures, diminutive in their habitual environment, reach enormous proportions under certain conditions. Human blood seems particularly favourable to them, and it is not rare to encounter them in feather pillows.

The Last Lords of Gardonal

William Gilbert

CHAPTER 1

One of the most picturesque objects of the valley of the Engadin is the ruined castle of Gardonal, near the village of Madaline. In the feudal times it was the seat of a family of barons, who possessed as their patrimony the whole of the valley, which with the castle had descended from father to son for many generations. The two last of the race were brothers; handsome, well-made, fine-looking young men, but in nature they more resembled fiends than human beings—so cruel, rapacious, and tyrannical were they. During the earlier part of his life their father had been careful of his patrimony. He had also been unusually just to the serfs on his estates, and in consequence they had attained to such a condition of comfort and prosperity as was rarely met with among those in the power of the feudal lords of the country; most of whom were arbitrary and exacting in the extreme.

For several years in the latter part of his life he had been subject to a severe illness, which had confined him to the castle, and the management of his possessions and the government of his serfs had thus fallen into the hands of his sons. Although the old baron had placed so much power in their hands; still he was far from resigning his own authority. He exacted a strict account from them of the manner in which they performed the different duties he had intrusted to them; and having a strong suspicion of their character, and the probability of their endeavouring to conceal their misdoings, he caused agents to watch them secretly, and to report to him as to the correctness of the statements they gave. These agents possibly knowing that the old man had but a short time to live invariably gave a most favourable description of the conduct of the two young nobles, which, it must be admitted, was not, during their father's lifetime, particularly reprehensible on the whole. Still, they frequently showed as much of the cloven foot as to prove to the tenants what they had to expect at no distant day.

At the old baron's death, Conrad, the elder, inherited as his portion the castle of Gardonal, and the whole valley of Engadin; while to Hermann, the younger, was assigned some immense estates belong to his father in the Bresciano district; for even in those early days, there was considerable intercourse between the inhabitants of that northern portion of Italy and those of the valley of the Engadin. The old baron had also willed, that should either of his sons die without children his estates should go to the survivor.

Conrad accordingly now took possession of the castle and its territory, and Hermann of the estates on the southern side of the Alps which, although much smaller than those left to his elder brother, were still of great value. Notwithstanding the disparity in the worth of the legacies bequeathed to the two brothers, a perfectly good feeling existed between them, which promised to continue, their tastes being the same, while the mountains which divided them tended to the continuance of peace.

Conrad had hardly been one single week feudal lord of the Engadin before the inhabitants found, to their sorrow, how great was the difference between him and the old baron. Instead of the score of armed retainers his father had kept, Conrad increased the number to three hundred men, none of whom were natives of the valley. They had been chosen with great care from a body of Bohemian, German, and Italian outlaws, who at that time infested the borders of the Grisons, or had found refuge in the fastnesses of the mountains—men capable of any atrocity and to whom pity was unknown. From these miscreants the baron especially chose for his body-guard those who were ignorant of the language spoken by the peasantry of the Engadin, as they would be less likely to be influenced by any supplications or excuses which might be made to them when in the performance of their duty.

Although the keeping of so numerous a body of armed retainers might naturally be considered to have entailed great expense, such a conclusion would be most erroneous, at least as far as regarded the present baron, who was as avaricious as he was despotic. He contrived to support his soldiers by imposing a most onerous tax on his tenants, irrespective of his ordinary feudal imposts; and woe to the unfortunate villagers who from inability, or from a sense of the injustice inflicted on them, did not contribute to the uttermost farthing the amount levied on them. In such a case a party of soldiers was immediately sent off to the defaulting village to collect the tax, with permission to live at free quarters till the money was paid; and they knew their duty too well to return home till they had succeeded in their errand.

In doing this they were frequently merciless in the extreme, exacting the money by torture or any other means they pleased; and when they had been successful in obtaining the baron's dues, by way of further punishment they generally robbed the poor peasantry of everything they had which was worth the trouble of carrying away, and not unfrequently, from a spirit of sheer mischief, they spoiled all that remained. Many were the complaints which reached the ears of the baron of the cruel behaviour of his retainers; but in no case did they receive any redress; the baron making it a portion of his policy that no crimes committed by those under his command should be invested, so long as those crimes took place when employed in collecting taxes which he had imposed, and which had remained unpaid.

But the depredations and cruelties of the Baron Conrad were not confined solely to the valley of the Engadin. Frequently in the summer-time when the snows had melted on the mountains, so as to make the road practicable for his soldiers and their plunder, he would make a raid on the Italian side of the Alps. There they would rob and commit every sort of atrocity with impunity; and when they had collected sufficient booty, they returned with it to the castle. Loud indeed were the complaints which reached the authorities of Milan. With routine tardiness, the government never took any energetic steps to punish the offenders until the winter had set in; and to cross the mountains in that season would have been almost an impossibility, at all events for an army.

When the spring returned, more prudential reasons prevailed, and the matter, gradually diminishing in interest, was at last allowed to die out without any active measures being taken. Again, the districts in which the atrocities had been committed were hardly looked upon by the Milanese government as being Italian. The people themselves were beginning to be infected by a heresy which approached closely to the Protestantism of the present day; nor was their language that of Italy, but a *patois* of their own. Thus, the government began to consider it unadvisable to attempt to punish the baron, richly as he deserved it, on behalf of those who after all were little worthy of the protection they demanded. The only real step they took to chastise him was to get him excommunicated by the Pope; which, as the baron and his followers professed no religion at all, was treated by them with ridicule.

It happened that in one of his marauding expeditions in the Valteline the baron, when near Bormio, saw a young girl of extraordinary beauty. He was only attended at the time by two followers, else it is more than probable he would have made her a prisoner and carried her off to Gardonal. As it was, he would probably have made the attempt had she not been surrounded by a number of peasants, who were working in some fields belonging to her father. The baron was also aware that the militia of the town, who had been expecting his visit were under arms, and on an alarm being given could be on the spot in a few minutes. Now as the baron combined with his despotism a considerable amount of cunning, he merely attempted to enter into conversation with the girl. Finding his advances coldly received, he contented himself with inquiring of one of the peasants the girl's name and place of abode. He received for reply that her name was Teresa Biffi, and that she was the daughter of a substantial farmer, who with his wife and four children (of whom Teresa was the eldest) lived in a house at the extremity of the land he occupied.

As soon as the baron had received this information, he left the spot and proceeded to the farmer's house, which he inspected externally with great care. He found it was of considerable size, strongly built of stone, with iron bars to the lower windows, and a strong well-made oaken door which could be securely fastened from the inside. After having made the round of the house (which he did alone), he returned to his two men, whom, in order to avoid suspicion, he had placed at a short distance from the building, in a spot where they could not easily be seen.

"Ludovico," he said to one of them who was his lieutenant and invariably accompanied him in all his expeditions, "mark well that house; for some day, or more probably night, you may have to pay it a visit."

Ludovico merely said in reply that he would be always ready and willing to perform any order his master might honour him with, and the baron, with his men, then left the spot.

The hold the beauty of Teresa Biffi had taken upon the imagination of the baron actually looked like enchantment. His love for her, instead of diminishing by time, seemed to increase daily. At last he resolved on making her his wife; and about a month after he had seen her, he commissioned his lieutenant Ludovico to carry to Biffi an offer of marriage with his daughter; not dreaming, at the moment, of the possibility of a refusal. Ludovico immediately started on his mission and in due time arrived at the farmer's house and delivered the baron's message. To Ludovico's intense surprise, however, he received from Biffi a positive refusal. Not daring to take back so uncourteous a reply to his master, Ludovico went on to describe the great advantage which would accrue to the farmer and his family if the baron's proposal were accepted. Not only, he said, would Teresa be a lady of the highest rank, and in possession of enormous wealth both in gold and jewels, but that the other members of her family would also be ennobled, and each of them, as they grew up, would receive appointments under the baron, besides having large estates allotted to them in the Engadin Valley.

The farmer listened with patience to Ludovico, and when he had concluded, he replied—

"Tell your master I have received his message, and that I am ready to admit that great personal advantages might accrue to me and my family by accepting his offer. Say, that although I am neither noble nor rich, that yet at the same time I am not poor; but were I as poor as the blind mendicant whom you passed on the road in coming hither, I would spurn such an offer from so infamous a wretch as the baron. You say truly that he is well known for his power and his wealth; but the latter has been obtained by robbing both rich and poor, who had not the means to resist him, and his power has been greatly strengthened by engaging in his service a numerous band of robbers and cutthroats, who are ready and willing to murder any one at his bidding. You have my answer, and the sooner you quit this neighbourhood the better, for I can assure you that any one known to be in the service of the Baron Conrad is likely to meet with a most unfavourable reception from those who live around us."

"Then you positively refuse his offer?" said Ludovico.

"Positively, and without the slightest reservation," was the farmer's reply.

"And you wish me to give him the message in the terms you have made use of?"

"Without omitting a word," was the farmer's reply. "At the same time, you may add to it as many of the same description as you please."

"Take care," said Ludovico. "There is yet time for you to reconsider your decision. If you insist on my taking your message to the baron, I must of course do so; but in that case make your peace with heaven as soon as you can, for the baron is not a man to let such an insult pass. Follow my advice, and accept his offer ere it is too late."

"I have no other answer to give you," said Biffi.

"I am sorry for it," said Ludovico, heaving a deep sigh; "I have now no alternative," and mounting his horse he rode away.

Now it must not be imagined that the advice Ludovico gave the farmer, and the urgent requests and arguments he offered, were altogether the genuine effusions of his heart. On the contrary, Ludovico had easily perceived, on hearing the farmer's first refusal, that there was no chance of the proposal being accepted. He had therefore occupied his time during the remaining portion of the interview in carefully examining the premises, and mentally taking note of the manner in which they could be most easily entered, as he judged rightly enough, that before long he might be sent to the house on a far less peaceable mission.

Nothing could exceed the rage of the baron when he heard the farmer's message.

"You cowardly villain!" he said to Ludovico, "did you allow the wretch to live who could send such a message to your master?"

"So please you," said Ludovico. "What could I do?"

"You could have struck him to the heart with your dagger, could you not?" said the baron. "I have known you do such a thing to an old woman for half the provocation. Had it been Biffi's wife instead you might have shown more courage."

"Had I followed my own inclination," said Ludovico, "I would have killed the fellow on the spot; but then I could not have brought away the young lady with me, for there were too many persons about the house and in the fields at the time. So, I thought, before acting further, I had better let you hear his answer. One favour I hope your excellency will grant me, that if the fellow is to be punished you will allow me to inflict it as a reward for the skill, I showed in keeping my temper when I heard the message."

"Perhaps you have acted wisely, Ludovico," said the baron, after a few moments' silence. "At present my mind is too much ruffled by the villain's impertinence to think calmly on the subject. Tomorrow we will speak of it again."

Next day the baron sent for his lieutenant, and said to him—

"Ludovico, I have now a commission for you to execute which I think will be exactly to your taste. Take with you six men whom you can trust, and start this afternoon for Bormio. Sleep at some village on the road, but let not one word escape you as to your errand. Tomorrow morning leave the village—but separately—so that you may not be seen together, as It is better to avoid suspicion. Meet again near the farmer's house, and arrive there, if possible, before evening has set in, for in all probability you will have to make an attack upon the house, and you may thus become well acquainted with the locality before doing so; but keep yourselves concealed, otherwise you will spoil all.

"After you have done this, retire some distance, and remain concealed till midnight, as then all the family will be in their first sleep, and you will experience less difficulty than if you began later. I particularly wish you to enter the house without using force, but if you cannot do so, break into it in any way you consider best. Bring out the girl and do her no harm. If any resistance is made by her father, kill him; but not unless you are compelled, as I do not wish to enrage his daughter against me. However, let nothing prevent you from securing her. Burn the house down or anything you please, but bring her here. If you execute your mission promptly and to my satisfaction, I promise you and those with you a most liberal reward. Now go and get ready to depart as speedily as you can."

Ludovico promised to execute the baron's mission to the letter, and shortly afterwards left the castle accompanied by six of the greatest ruffians he could find among the men-at-arms.

Although on the spur of the moment Biffi had sent so defiant a message to the baron, he afterwards felt considerable uneasiness as to the manner in which it would be received. He did not repent having refused the proposal, but he knew that the baron was a man of the most cruel and vindictive disposition, and would in all probability seek some means to be avenged. The only defence he could adopt was to make the fastenings of his house as secure as possible, and to keep at least one of his labourers about him whom he could send as a messenger to Bormio for assistance, and to arouse the inhabitants in the immediate vicinity, in case of his being attacked. Without any hesitation all promised to aid Biffi in every way in their power, for he had acquired great renown among the inhabitants of the place for the courage he had shown in refusing so indignantly the baron's offer of marriage for his daughter.

About midnight, on the day after Ludovico's departure from the castle, Biffi was aroused by someone knocking at the door of his house, and demanding admission. It was Ludovico, for after attempting in vain to enter the house secretly, he had concealed his men, determining to try the effect of treachery before using force. On the inquiry being made as to who the stranger was, he replied that he was a poor traveller who had lost his way, and begged that he might be allowed a night's lodging, as he was so weary, he could not go a step further.

"I am sorry for you," said Biffi, "but I cannot allow you to enter this house before daylight. As the night is fine and warm you can easily sleep on the straw under the windows, and in the morning, I will let you in and give you a good breakfast."

Again, and again did Ludovico plead to be admitted, but in vain; Biffi would not be moved from his resolution. At last, however, the bravo's patience got exhausted, and suddenly changing his manner he roared out in a threatening tone, "If you don't let me in, you villain, I will burn your house over your head. I have here, as you may see, plenty of men to help me to put my threat into execution," he continued, pointing to the men, who had now come up, "so you had better let me in at once."

In a moment Biffi comprehended the character of the person he had to deal with; so, instead of returning any answer, he retired from the window and alarmed the inmates of the house. He also told the labourer whom he had engaged to sleep there to drop from a window at the back and run as fast as he could to arouse the inhabitants in the vicinity, and tell them that his house was attacked by the baron and his men. He was to beg them to arm themselves and come to his aid as quickly as possible, and having done this, he was to go on to Bormio on the same errand. The poor fellow attempted to carry out his master's orders; but in dropping from the window he fell with such force on the ground that he could only move with difficulty, and in trying to crawl away he was observed by some of the baron's men, who immediately set on him and killed him.

Ludovico, finding that he could not enter the house either secretly or by threatenings, attempted to force open the door, but it was so firmly barricaded from within that he did not succeed; while in the meantime Biffi and his family employed themselves in placing wooden faggots and heavy articles of furniture against it, thus making it stronger than ever. Ludovico, finding he could not gain an entrance by the door, told his men to look around in search of a ladder, so that they might get to the windows on the first floor, as those on the ground floor were all small, high up, and well barricaded, as was common in Italian houses of the time; but in spite of all their efforts no ladder could be found.

He now deliberated what step he should next take. As it was getting late, he saw that if they did not succeed in effecting an entrance quickly the dawn would break upon them, and the labourers going to their work would raise an alarm. At last one man suggested that as abundance of fuel could be obtained from the stacks at the back of the house they might place a quantity of it against the door and set fire to it; adding that the sight of the flames would soon make the occupants glad to effect their escape by the first-floor windows.

The suggestion was no sooner made than acted upon. A quantity of dry fuel was piled up against the house door to the height of many feet, and a light having been procured by striking a flint stone against the hilt of a sword over some dried leaves, fire was set to the pile. From the dry nature of the fuel, the whole mass was in a blaze in a few moments. But the scheme did not have the effect Ludovico had anticipated. True, the family rushed towards the windows in the front of the house, but when they saw the flames rising so fiercely, they retreated in the utmost alarm. Meanwhile the screams from the women and children—who had now lost all self-control—mingled with the roar of the blazing element which, besides having set fire to the faggots and furniture placed within the door, had now reached a quantity of fodder and Indian corn stored on the ground floor.

Ludovico soon perceived that the whole house was in flames, and that the case was becoming desperate. Not only was there the danger of the fire alarming the inhabitants in the vicinity by the light it shed around, but he also reflected what would be the rage of his master if the girl should perish in the flames, and the consequent punishment which would be inflicted on him and those under his command if he returned empty-handed. He now called out to Biffi and his family to throw themselves out of the window, and that he and his men would save them. It was some time before he was understood, but at last Biffi brought the two younger children to the window, and, lowering them as far as he could, he let them fall into the arms of Ludovico and his men, and they reached the ground in safety.

Biffi now returned for the others, and saw Teresa standing at a short distance behind him. He took her by the hand to bring her forward, and they had nearly reached the window, when she heard a scream from her mother, who being an incurable invalid was confined to her bed. Without a moment's hesitation, the girl turned back to assist her, and the men below, who thought that the prey they wanted was all but in their hands, and cared little about the fate of the rest of the family, were thus disappointed. Ludovico now anxiously awaited the reappearance of Teresa—but he waited in vain. The flames had gained entire mastery, and even the roof had taken fire. The screams of the inmates were now no longer heard, for if not stifled in the smoke they were lost in the roar of the fire; whilst the glare which arose from it illumined the landscape far and near.

It so happened that a peasant, who resided about a quarter of a mile from Biffi's house, had to go a long distance to his work, and having risen at an unusually early hour, he saw the flames, and aroused the inmates of the other cottages in the village, who immediately armed themselves and started off to the scene of the disaster, imagining, but too certainly, that it was the work of an incendiary. The alarm was also communicated to another village, and from thence to Bormio, and in a short time a strong band of armed men had collected, and proceeded together to assist in extinguishing the flames. On their arrival at the house, they found the place one immense heap of ashes—not a soul was to be seen, for Ludovico and his men had already decamped.

The dawn now broke, and the assembled peasantry made some attempt to account for the fire. At first, they were induced to attribute it to accident, but on searching around they found the dead body of the murdered peasant, and afterwards the two children who had escaped, and who in their terror had rushed into a thick copse to conceal themselves. With great difficulty they gathered from them sufficient to show that the fire had been caused by a band of robbers who had come for the purpose of plundering the house; and their suspicion fell immediately on Baron Conrad, without any better proof than his infamous reputation.

As soon as Ludovico found that an alarm had been given, he and his men started off to find their horses, which they had hidden among some trees about a mile distant from Biffi's house. The daylight was just breaking, and objects around them began to be visible, but not so clearly as to allow them to see for any distance. Suddenly one of the men pointed to an indistinct figure in white some little way in advance of them. Ludovico halted for a moment to see what it might be, and, with his men, watched it attentively as it appeared to fly from them.

"It is the young girl herself," said one of the men. "She has escaped from the fire; and that was exactly as she appeared in her white dress with her father at the window. I saw her well, and am sure I am not mistaken."

"It is indeed the girl," said another. "I also saw her."

"I hope you are right," said Ludovico; "and if so, it will be fortunate indeed, for should we return without her we may receive but a rude reception from the baron."

They now quickened their pace, but, fast as they walked, the figure in white walked quite as rapidly. Ludovico, who of course began to suspect that it was Teresa attempting to escape from them, commanded his men to run as fast as they could in order to reach her. Although they tried their utmost, the figure, however, still kept the same distance before them. Another singularity about it was, that as daylight advanced the figure appeared to become less distinct, and ere they had reached their horses it seemed to have melted away.

CHAPTER 2

Before mounting their horses, Ludovico held a consultation with his men as to what course they had better adopt; whether they should depart at once or search the neighbourhood for the girl. Both suggestions seemed to be attended with danger. If they delayed their departure, they might be attacked by the peasantry, who by this time were doubtless in hot pursuit of them; and if they returned to the baron without Teresa, they were almost certain to receive a severe punishment for failing in their enterprise. At last the idea struck Ludovico that a good round lie might possibly succeed with the baron and do something to avert his anger, while there was little hope of its in the slightest manner availing with the enraged peasantry.

He therefore gave the order for his men to mount their horses, resolving to tell the baron that Teresa had escaped from the flames, and had begged their assistance, but a number of armed inhabitants of Bormio chancing to approach, she had sought their protection. A great portion of this statement could be substantiated by his men, as they still fully believed that the figure in white which they had so indistinctly seen was the girl herself. Ludovico and his men during their homeward journey had great difficulty in crossing the mountains, in consequence of a heavy fall of snow (for it was now late in the autumn). Next day they arrived at the castle of Gardonal.

It would be difficult to describe the rage of the baron when he heard that his retainers had been unsuccessful in their mission. He ordered Ludovico to be thrown into a dungeon, where he remained for more than a month, and was only then liberated in consequence of the baron needing his services for some expedition requiring special skill and courage. The other men were also punished, though less severely than their leader, on whom, of course, they laid all the blame.

For some time after Ludovico's return, the baron occupied himself in concocting schemes, not only to secure the girl Teresa (for he fully believed the account Ludovico had given of her escape), but to revenge himself on the inhabitants of Bormio for the part they had taken in the affair; and it was to carry out these schemes that he liberated Ludovico from prison.

The winter had passed, and the spring sun was rapidly melting the snows on the mountains, when one morning three travel-stained men, having the appearance of respectable *burghers*, arrived at the Hospice, and requested to be allowed an interview with the *Innominato*. A messenger was despatched to the castle, who shortly afterwards returned, saying that his master desired the visitors should immediately be admitted into his presence. When they arrived at the castle, they found him fully prepared to receive them, a handsome repast being spread out for their refreshment. At first the travellers seemed under some restraint; but this was soon dispelled by the friendly courtesy of the astrologer. After partaking of the viands which had been set before them, the *Innominato* inquired the object of their visit. One of them who had been evidently chosen as spokesman, then rose from his chair and addressed their host as follows:

"We have been sent to your excellency by the inhabitants of Bormio as a deputation, to ask your advice and assistance in a strait we are in at present. Late in the autumn of last year, the Baron Conrad, feudal lord of the Engadin, was on some not very honest expedition in our neighbourhood, when by chance he saw a very beautiful girl, of the name of Teresa Biffi, whose father occupied a large farm about half a league from the town. The baron, it appears, became so deeply enamoured of the girl that he afterwards sent a messenger to her father with an offer of marriage for his daughter. Biffi, knowing full well the infamous reputation of the baron, unhesitatingly declined his proposal and in such indignant terms as to arouse the tyrant's anger to the highest pitch. Determining not only to possess himself of the girl, but to avenge the insult he had received, he sent a body of armed retainers, who in the night attacked the farmer's house, and endeavoured to effect an entrance by breaking open the door.

"Finding they could not succeed, and after murdering one of the servants who had been sent to a neighbouring village to give the alarm, they set fire to the house, and with the exception of two children who contrived to escape, the whole family, including the young girl herself, perished in the flames. It appears, however, that the baron (doubtless through his agents) received a false report that the young girl had escaped, and was taken under the protection of some of the inhabitants of Bormio. In consequence, he sent another body of armed men, who arrived in the night at the house of the *podesta*, and contrived to make his only son, a boy of about fifteen years old, a prisoner, bearing him off to the baron's castle. They left word, that unless Teresa Biffi was placed in their power before the first day of May, not only would the youth be put to death, but the baron would also wreak vengeance on the whole town.

"On the perpetration of this last atrocity, we again applied to the government of Milan for protection; but although our reception was most courteous, and we were promised assistance, we have too good reason to doubt our receiving it. Certainly, up to the present time no steps have been taken in the matter, nor has a single soldier been sent, although the time named for the death of the child has nearly expired. The townsmen therefore, having heard of your great wisdom and power, your willingness to help those who are in distress, as well as to protect the weak and oppressed, have sent us to ask you to take them under your protection; is the baron is not a man to scruple at putting such a threat into execution."

The *Innominato*, who had listened to the delegate with great patience and attention, told him that he had no soldiers or retainers at his orders; while the baron, whose wicked life was known to him, had many.

"But your excellency has great wisdom, and from all we have heard, we feel certain that you could protect us."

"Your case," said the *Innominato*, "is a very sad one, I admit, and you certainly ought to be protected from the baron's machinations. I will not disguise from you that I have the power to help you. Tell the unhappy *podesta* that he need be under no alarm as to his son's safety, and that I will oblige the baron to release him. My art tells me that the boy is still alive, though confined in prison. As for your friends who sent you to me, tell them that the baron shall do them no harm. All you have to do is, to contrive some means by which the baron may hear that the girl Teresa Biffi has been placed by me where he will never find her without my permission."

"But Teresa Biffi," said the delegate, "perished with her father; and the baron will wreak his vengeance both on you and us, when he finds you cannot place the girl in his power."

"Fear nothing, but obey my orders," said the *Innominato*. "Do what I have told you, and I promise you shall have nothing to dread from him. The sooner you carry out my directions the better."

The deputation now returned to Bormio, and related all that had taken place at their interview with the *Innominato*. Although the result of their mission was scarcely considered satisfactory, they determined, after much consideration, to act on the astrologer's advice. But how to carry it out was a very difficult matter. This was, however, overcome by one of the chief inhabitants of the town—a man of most determined courage—offering himself as a delegate to the baron, to convey to him the *Innominato's* message. Without hesitation the offer was gratefully accepted, and the next day he started on his journey. No sooner had he arrived at the castle of Gardonal, and explained the object of his mission, than he was ushered into the presence of the baron, whom he found in the great hall, surrounded by a numerous body of armed men.

"Well," said the baron, as soon as the delegate had entered, "have your townspeople come to their senses at last, and sent me the girl Teresa?"

"No, they have not, baron," was the reply, "for she is not in their custody. All they can do is to inform you where you may possibly receive some information about her."

"And where may that be?"

"The only person who knows where she may be found is the celebrated astrologer who lives in a castle near Lecco."

"Ah now, you are trifling with me," said the baron sternly. "You must be a great fool or a very bold man to try such an experiment as that."

"I am neither the one nor the other, your excellency; nor am I trifling with you. What I have told you is the simple truth."

"And how did you learn it?"

"From the *Innominato's* own lips."

"Then you applied to him for assistance against me," said the baron, furiously.

"That is hardly correct, your excellency," said the delegate. "It is true we applied to him for advice as to the manner in which we should act in case you should attack us, and put your threat into execution respecting the son of the *podesta*."

"And what answer did he give you?"

"Just what I have told you—that he alone knows where Teresa Biffi is to be found, and that you could not remove her from the protection she is under without his permission."

"Did he send that message to me in defiance?" said the baron.

"I have no reason to believe so, your excellency."

The baron was silent for some time; he then inquired of the delegate how many armed retainers the *Innominato* kept.

"None, I believe," was the reply. "At any rate, there were none to be seen when the deputation from the town visited him."

The baron was again silent for some moments, and seemed deeply absorbed in thought. He would rather have met with any other opponent than the *Innominato*, whose reputation was well known to him, and whose learning he dreaded more than the power of any nobleman—no matter how many armed retainers he could bring against him.

"I very much suspect," he said at last, "that some deception is being practised on me. But should my suspicion be correct I shall exact terrible vengeance. I shall detain you," he continued, turning abruptly and fiercely on the delegate, "as a hostage while I visit the *Innominato*; and if I do not succeed with him, you shall die on the same scaffold as the son of your *podesta*."

It was in vain that the delegate protested against being detained as a prisoner, saying that it was against all rules of knightly usage; but the baron would not listen to reason, and the unfortunate man was immediately hurried out of the hall and imprisoned.

Although the baron by no means liked the idea of an interview with the *Innominato*, he immediately made preparations to visit him, and the day after the delegate's arrival he set out on his journey, attended by only four of his retainers. It should here be mentioned, that it is more than probable the baron would have avoided meeting the *Innominato* on any other occasion whatever, so great was the dislike he had to him. He seemed to be acting under some fatality; some power seemed to impel him in his endeavours to obtain Teresa which it was impossible to account for.

The road chosen by the baron to reach the castle of the *Innominato* was rather a circuitous one. In the first place, he did not consider it prudent to pass through the Valteline; and in the second, he thought that by visiting his brother on his way he might be able to obtain some particulars as to the character of the mysterious individual whom he was about to see, as his reputation would probably be better known among the inhabitants of the Bergamo district than by those in the valley of the Engadin.

The baron arrived safely at his brother's castle, where the reports which had hitherto indistinctly reached him of the wonderful power and skill of the astrologer were fully confirmed. After remaining a day with his brother, the baron started for Lecco. Under an assumed name he stayed here for two days, in order that he might receive the report of one of his men, whom he had sent forward to ascertain whether the *Innominato* had any armed men in his castle; for, being capable of any act of treachery himself, he naturally suspected treason in others. The man in due time returned, and reported that, although he had taken great pains to find out the truth, he was fully convinced, that not only were there no soldiers in the castle, but that it did not, to the best of his belief, contain an arm of any kind—the *Innominato* relying solely on his occult power for his defence.

Perfectly assured that he had no danger to apprehend, the baron left Lecco, attended by his retainers, and in a few hours afterwards he arrived at the Hospice, where his wish for an interview was conveyed to the astrologer. After some delay a reply was sent that the *Innominato* was willing to receive the baron on condition that he came alone, as his retainers would not be allowed to enter the castle. The baron hesitated for some moments, not liking to place himself in the power of a man who, after all, might prove a very dangerous adversary, and who might even use treacherous means. His love for Teresa Biffi, however, urged him to accept the invitation, and he accompanied the messenger to the castle.

The *Innominato* received his guest with stern courtesy; and, without even asking him to be seated, requested to know the object of his visit.

"Perhaps I am not altogether unknown to you," said the baron. "I am lord of the Engadin."

"Frankly," said the *Innominato*, "your name and reputation are both well known to me. It would give me great satisfaction were they less so."

"I regret to hear you speak in that tone," said the baron, evidently making great efforts to repress his rising passion. "A person in my position is not likely to be without enemies, but it rather surprises me to find a man of your reputation so prejudiced against me without having investigated the accusations laid to my charge."

"You judge wrongly if you imagine that I am so," said the *Innomi-*

nato. "But once more, will you tell me the object of your visit?"

"I understood," said the baron, "by a message sent to me by the insolent inhabitants of Bormio, that you know the person with whom a young girl, named Teresa Biffi, is at present residing. Might I ask if that statement is correct?"

"I hardly sent it in those words," said the *Innominato.* "But admitting it to be so, I must first ask your reason for inquiring."

"I have not the slightest objection to inform you," said the baron. "I have nothing to conceal. I wish to make her my wife."

"On those terms I am willing to assist you," said the astrologer. "But only on the condition that you immediately release the messenger you have most unjustly confined in one of your dungeons, as well as the young son of the *podesta*, and that you grant them a safe escort back to Bormio; and further, that you promise to cease annoying the people of that district. Do all this, and I am willing to promise you that Teresa Biffi shall not only become your wife, but shall bring with her a dowry and wedding outfit sufficiently magnificent even for the exalted position to which you propose to raise her."

"I solemnly promise you," said the baron, "that the moment the wedding is over, the delegate from Bormio and the son of the *podesta* shall both leave my castle perfectly free and unhampered with any conditions; and moreover that I will send a strong escort with them to protect them on their road."

"I see you are already meditating treachery," said the *Innominato.* "But I will not, in any manner, alter my offer. The day week after their safe return to Bormio Teresa Biffi shall arrive at the castle of Gardonal for the wedding ceremony. Now you distinctly know my conditions, and I demand from you an unequivocal acceptance or refusal."

"What security shall I have that the bargain will be kept on your side?" said the baron.

"My word, and no other."

The baron remained silent for a moment, and then said—

"I accept your offer. But clearly understand me in my turn, sir astrologer. Fail to keep your promise, and had you ten times the power you have I will take my revenge on you; and I am not a man to threaten such a thing without doing it."

"All that I am ready to allow," said the *Innominato*, with great coolness; "that is to say, in case you have the power to carry out your threat, which in the present instance you have not. Do not imagine that because I am not surrounded by a band of armed cut-throats and miscreants, I am not the stronger of the two. You little dream how powerless you are in my hands. You see this bird," he continued, taking down a common sparrow in a wooden cage from a nail in the wall on which it hung,—"it is not more helpless in my hands than you are; nay more, I will now give the bird far greater power over you than I possess over it."

As he spoke, he unfastened the door of the cage, and the sparrow darted from it through the window into the air, and in a moment afterwards was lost to sight.

"That bird," the astrologer went on to say, "will follow you till I deprive it of the power. I bear you no malice for doubting my veracity. Falsehood is too much a portion of your nature for you to disbelieve its existence in others. I will not seek to punish you for the treachery which I am perfectly sure you will soon be imagining against me without giving you fair warning; for, a traitor yourself, you naturally suspect treason in others. As soon as you entertain a thought of evading your promise to release your prisoners, or conceive any treason or ill feeling against me, that sparrow will appear to you. If you instantly abandon the thought no harm will follow; but if you do not a terrible punishment will soon fall upon you. In whatever position you may find yourself at the moment, the bird will be near you, and no skill of yours will be able to harm it."

The baron now left the *Innominato*, and returned with his men to Lecco, where he employed himself for the remainder of the day in making preparations for his homeward journey. To return by the circuitous route he had taken in going to Lecco would have occupied too much time, as he was anxious to arrive at his castle, that he might without delay release the prisoners and make preparations for his wedding with Teresa Biffi. To pass the Valteline openly with his retainers—which was by far the shortest road—would have exposed him to too much danger; he therefore resolved to divide his party and send three men back by his brother's castle, so that they could return the horses they had borrowed.

Then he would disguise himself and the fourth man (a German who could not speak a word of Italian, and from whom he had nothing therefore to fear on the score of treachery) as two Tyrolese merchants returning to their own country. He also purchased two mules and some provisions for the journey, so that they need not be obliged to rest in any of the villages they passed through, where possibly they might be detected, and probably maltreated.

Next morning the baron and his servant, together with the two mules, went on board a large bark which was manned by six men, and which he had hired for the occasion, and in it they started for Colico. At the commencement of their voyage they kept along the eastern side of the lake, but after advancing a few miles the wind, which had hitherto been moderate, now became so strong as to cause much fatigue to the rowers, and the captain of the bark determined on crossing the lake, so as to be under the lee of the mountains on the other side. When half way across they came in view of the turrets of the castle of the *Innominato*. The sight of the castle brought to the baron's mind his interview with its owner, and the defiant manner in which he had been treated by him. The longer he gazed the stronger became his anger against the *Innominato*, and at last it rose to such a point that he exclaimed aloud, to the great surprise of the men in the boat, "Someday I will meet thee again, thou insolent villain, and I will then take signal vengeance on thee for the insult offered me yesterday."

The words had hardly been uttered when a sparrow, apparently driven from the shore by the wind, settled on the bark for a moment, and then flew away. The baron instantly remembered what the *Innominato* had said to him, and also the warning the bird was to give. With a sensation closely resembling fear, he tried to change the current of his thoughts, and was on the point of turning his head from the castle, when the rowers in the boat simultaneously set up a loud shout of warning, and the baron then perceived that a heavily-laden vessel, four times the size of his own, and with a huge sail set, was running before the wind with great velocity, threatening the next moment to strike his boat on the beam; in which case both he and the men would undoubtedly be drowned. Fortunately, the captain of the strange bark had heard the cry of the rowers, and by rapidly putting down his helm saved their lives; though the baron's boat was struck with so much violence on the quarter that she nearly sank.

The Baron Conrad had now received an earnest that the threat of the *Innominato* was not a vain one, and feeling that he was entirely in his power, resolved if possible, not to offend him again. The boat continued on her voyage, and late in the evening arrived safely at Colico, where the baron, with his servant and the mules, disembarked, and without delay proceeded on their journey. They continued on their road till nightfall, when they began to consider how they should pass the night. They looked around them, but they could perceive no habitation or shelter of any kind, and it was now raining heavily. They continued their journey onwards, and had almost come to the conclusion that they should be obliged to pass the night in the open air, when a short distance before them they saw a low cottage, the door of which was open, showing the dim light of a fire burning within. The baron now determined to ask the owner of the cottage for permission to remain there for the night; but to be certain that no danger could arise, he sent forward his man to discover whether it was a house standing by itself, or one of a village; as in the latter case he would have to use great caution to avoid being detected.

His servant accordingly left him to obey orders, and shortly afterwards returned with the news that the house was a solitary one, and that he could not distinguish a trace of any other in the neighbourhood. Satisfied with this information, the baron proceeded to the cottage door, and begged the inmates to afford him shelter for the night, assuring them that the next morning he would remunerate them handsomely. The peasant and his wife—a sickly-looking, emaciated old couple—gladly offered them all the accommodation the wretched cabin could afford. After fastening up the mules at the back of the house, and bringing in the baggage and some dry fodder to form a bed for the baron and his servant, they prepared some of the food their guests had brought with them for supper, and shortly afterwards the baron and his servant were fast asleep.

Next morning, they rose early and continued on their journey. After they had been some hours on the road, the baron, who had before been conversing with his retainer, suddenly became silent and absorbed in thought. He rode on a few paces in advance of the man, thinking over the conditions made by the *Innominato*, when the idea struck him whether it would not be possible in some way to evade them. He had hardly entertained the thought, when the sparrow flew rapidly before his mule's head, and then instantly afterwards his servant, who had ridden up to him, touched him on the shoulder and pointed to a body of eight or ten armed men about a quarter of a mile distant, who were advancing towards them.

The baron, fearing lest they might be some of the armed inhabitants of the neighbourhood who were banded together against him, and seeing that no time was to be lost, immediately plunged, with his servant, into a thick copse where, without being seen, he could command a view of the advancing soldiers as they passed. He perceived that when they came near the place where he was concealed, they halted, and evidently set about examining the traces of the footsteps of the mules. They communed together for some time as if in doubt what course they should adopt, and finally, the leader giving the order, they continued their march onwards, and the baron shortly afterwards left his place of concealment.

Nothing further worthy of notice occurred that day; and late at night they passed through Bormio, fortunately without being observed. They afterwards arrived safely at the foot of the mountain pass, and at dawn began the ascent. The day was fine and calm, and the sun shone magnificently. The baron, who now calculated that the dangers of his journey were over, was in high spirits, and familiarly conversed with his retainer. When they had reached a considerable elevation, the path narrowed, so that the two could not ride abreast, and the baron went in advance. He now became very silent and thoughtful, all his thoughts being fixed on the approaching wedding, and in speculations as to how short a time it would take for the delegate and the youth to reach Bormio. Suddenly the thought occurred to him, whether the men whom he should send to escort the hostages back, could not, when they had completed their business, remain concealed in the immediate neighbourhood till after the celebration of the wedding, and then bring back with them some other hostage, and thus enable him to make further demands for compensation for the insult he considered had been offered him.

Although the idea had only been vaguely formed, and possibly with but little intention of carrying it out, he had an immediate proof that the power of the astrologer was following him. A sparrow settled on the ground before him, and did not move until his mule was close to it, when it rose in the air right before his face. He continued to follow its course with his eyes, and as it rose higher, he thought he perceived a tremulous movement in an immense mass of snow, which had accumulated at the base of one of the mountain peaks. All thought of treachery immediately vanished. He gave a cry of alarm to his servant, and they both hurried onwards, thus barely escaping being buried in an avalanche, which the moment afterwards overwhelmed the path they had crossed.

The baron was now more convinced than ever of the tremendous power of the *Innominato*, and so great was his fear of him, that he resolved for the future not to contemplate any treachery against him, or entertain any thoughts of revenge.

The day after the baron's arrival at the castle of Gardonal, he ordered the delegate and the *podesta's* son to be brought into his presence. Assuming a tone of much mildness and courtesy, he told them he much regretted the inconvenience they had been put to, but that the behaviour of the inhabitants of Bormio had left him no alternative. He was ready to admit that the delegate had told him the truth, although from the interview he had with the *Innominato*, he was by no means certain that the inhabitants of their town had acted in a friendly manner towards him, or were without blame in the matter. Still he did not wish to be harsh, and was willing for the future to be on friendly terms with them if they promised to cease insulting him—what possible affront they could have offered him it would be difficult to say. "At the same time, in justice to myself," he continued (his natural cupidity gaining the ascendant at the moment), "I hardly think I ought to allow you to return without the payment of some fair ransom."

He had scarcely uttered these words when a sparrow flew in at the window, and darting wildly two or three times across the hall, left by the same window through which it had entered. Those present who noticed the bird looked at it with an eye of indifference—but not so the baron. He knew perfectly well that it was a warning from the astrologer, and he looked around him to see what accident might have befallen him had he continued the train of thought. Nothing of an extraordinary nature followed the disappearance of the bird. The baron now changed the conversation, and told his prisoners that they were at liberty to depart as soon as they pleased; and that to prevent any misfortune befalling them on the road, he would send four of his retainers to protect them. In this he kept his promise to the letter, and a few days afterwards the men returned, reporting that the delegate and the son of the *podesta* had both arrived safely at their destination.

Chapter 3

Immediately after the departure of his prisoners, the baron began to make preparations for his wedding, for although he detested the *Innominato* in his heart, he had still the fullest reliance on his fulfilling the promise he had made. His assurance was further confirmed by a messenger from the astrologer to inform him that on the next Wednesday the affianced bride would arrive with her suite, and that he (the *Innominato*) had given this notice, that all things might be in readiness for the ceremony.

Neither expense nor exertion was spared by the baron to make his nuptials imposing and magnificent. The chapel belonging to the castle, which had been allowed to fall into a most neglected condition, was put into order, the altar redecorated, and the walls hung with tapestry. Preparations were made in the inner hall for a banquet on the grandest scale, which was to be given after the ceremony; and on a dais in the main hall into which the bride was to be conducted on her arrival were placed two chairs of state, where the baron and his bride were to be seated.

When the day arrived for the wedding, everything was prepared for the reception of the bride. As no hour had been named for her arrival, all persons who were to be engaged in the ceremony were ready in the castle by break of day; and the baron, in a state of great excitement, mounted to the top of the watch-tower, that he might be able to give orders to the rest the moment her cavalcade appeared in sight. Hour after hour passed, but still Teresa did not make her appearance, and at last the baron began to feel considerable anxiety on the subject.

At last a mist, which had been over a part of the valley, cleared up, and all the anxiety of the baron was dispelled; for in the distance he perceived a group of travellers approaching the castle, some mounted on horseback and some on foot. In front rode the bride on a superb white palfrey, her face covered with a thick veil. On each side of her rode an esquire magnificently dressed. Behind her were a waiting woman on horseback and two men-servants; and in the rear were several led mules laden with packages. The baron now quitted his position in the tower and descended to the castle gates to receive his bride. When he arrived there, he found one of the esquires, who had ridden forward at the desire of his mistress, waiting to speak to him.

"I have been ordered," he said to the baron, "by the Lady Teresa, to request that you will be good enough to allow her to change her dress before she meets you."

The baron of course willingly assented, and then retired into the hall destined for the reception ceremony. Shortly afterwards Teresa arrived at the castle, and being helped from her palfrey, she proceeded with her lady in waiting and a female attendant (who had been engaged by the baron) into her private apartment, while two of the muleteers brought up a large trunk containing her wedding dress.

In less than an hour Teresa left her room to be introduced to the baron, and was conducted into his presence by one of the esquires. As soon as she entered the hall, a cry of admiration arose from all present—so extraordinary was her beauty. The baron, in a state of breathless emotion, advanced to meet her, but before he had reached her she bent on her knee, and remained in that position till he had raised her up. "Kneel not to me, thou lovely one," he said. "It is for all present to kneel to thee in adoration of thy wonderful beauty, rather than for thee to bend to anyone." So saying, and holding her hand, he led her to one of the seats on the *daïs*, and then, seating himself by her side, gave orders for the ceremony of introduction to begin. One by one the different persons to be presented were led up to her, all of whom she received with a grace and amiability which raised her very high in their estimation.

When the ceremony of introduction was over the baron ordered that the procession should be formed, and then, taking Teresa by the hand, he led her into the chapel, followed by the others. When all were arranged in their proper places the marriage ceremony was performed by the priest, and the newly-married couple, with the retainers and guests, entered into the banqueting hall. Splendid as was the repast which had been prepared for the company, their attention seemed for some time more drawn to the baron and his bride than to the duties of the feast. A handsomer couple it would have been impossible to find. The baron himself, as has been stated already, had no lack of manly beauty either in face or form; while the loveliness of his bride appeared almost more than mortal. Even their splendid attire seemed to attract little notice when compared with their personal beauty.

After the surprise and admiration had somewhat abated, the feast progressed most satisfactorily. All were in high spirits, and good humour and conviviality reigned throughout the hall. Even on the baron it seemed to produce a kindly effect, so that few who could have seen him at that moment would have imagined him to be the stern, cold-blooded tyrant he really was. His countenance was lighted up with good humour and friendliness. Much as his attention was occupied with his bride, he had still a little to bestow on his guests, and he rose many times from his seat to request the attention of the servants to their wants. At last he cast his eye over the tables as if searching for some person whom he could not see, and he then beckoned to the *major domo*, who, staff of office in hand, advanced to receive his orders.

"I do not see the esquires of the Lady Teresa in the room," said the baron.

"Your excellency," said the man, "they are not here."

"How is that?" said the baron, with some impatience. "You ought to have found room for them in the hall. Where are they?"

"Your excellency," said the *major domo*, who from the expression of the baron's countenance evidently expected a storm, "they are not here. The whole of the suite left the castle immediately after the mules were unladen and her ladyship had left her room. I was inspecting the places which I had prepared for them, when a servant came forward and told me that the esquires and attendants had left the castle. I at once hurried after them and begged they would return, as I was sure your excellency would feel hurt if they did not stay to the banquet. But they told me they had received express orders to leave the castle directly after they had seen the Lady Teresa lodged safely in it. I again entreated them to stay, but it was useless. They hurried on their way, and I returned by myself."

"The ill-bred hounds!" said the baron, in anger. "A sound scourging would have taught them better manners."

"Do not be angry with them," said Teresa, laying her hand gently on that of her husband's; "they did but obey their master's orders."

"Someday, I swear," said the baron, "I will be revenged on their master for this insult, miserable churl that he is!"

He had no sooner uttered these words than he looked round him for the sparrow, but the bird did not make its appearance. Possibly its absence alarmed him even more than its presence would have done, for he began to dread lest the vengeance of the astrologer was about to fall on him, without giving him the usual notice. Teresa, perceiving the expression of his countenance, did all in her power to calm him, but for some time she but partially succeeded. He continued to glance anxiously about him, to ascertain, if possible, from which side the blow might come. He was just on the point of raising a goblet to his lips, when the idea seized him that the wine might be poisoned. He declined to touch food for the same reason. The idea of being struck with death when at the height of his happiness seemed to overwhelm him. Thanks, however, to the kind soothing of Teresa, as well as the absence of any visible effects of the *Innominato's* anger, he at last became completely reassured, and the feast proceeded.

Long before the banquet had concluded the baron and his wife quitted the hall and retired through their private apartments to the terrace of the castle. The evening, which was now rapidly advancing, was warm and genial, and not a cloud was to be seen in the atmosphere. For some time, they walked together up and down on the terrace; and afterwards they seated themselves on a bench. There, with his arm round her waist and her head leaning on his shoulder, they watched the sun in all his magnificence sinking behind the mountains. The sun had almost disappeared, when the baron took his wife's hand in his.

"How cold thou art, my dear!" he said to her. "Let us go in."

Teresa made no answer, but rising from her seat was conducted by her husband into the room which opened on to the terrace, and which was lighted by a large brass lamp which hung by a chain from the ceiling. When they were nearly under the lamp, whose light increased as the daylight declined, Conrad again cast his arm round his wife, and fondly pressed her head to his breast. They remained thus for some moments, entranced in their happiness.

"Dost thou really love me, Teresa!" asked the baron.

"Love you?" said Teresa, now burying her face in his bosom. "Love you? Yes, dearer than all the world. My very existence hangs on your life. When that ceases my existence ends."

When she had uttered these words, Conrad, in a state of intense happiness, said to her—

"Kiss me, my beloved."

Teresa still kept her face pressed on his bosom; and Conrad, to overcome her coyness, placed his hand on her head and gently pressed it backwards, so that he might kiss her.

He stood motionless, aghast with horror, for the light of the lamp above their heads showed him no longer the angelic features of Teresa but the hideous face of a corpse that had remained sometime in the tomb, and whose only sign of vitality was a horrible phosphoric light which shone in its eyes. Conrad now tried to rush from the room, and to scream for assistance—but in vain. With one arm she clasped him tightly round the waist, and raising the other, she placed her clammy hand upon his mouth, and threw him with great force upon the floor. Then seizing the side of his neck with her lips, she deliberately and slowly sucked from him his life's blood; while he, utterly incapable either of moving or crying, was yet perfectly conscious of the awful fate that was awaiting him.

In this manner Conrad remained for some hours in the arms of his vampire wife. At last faintness came over him, and he grew insensible. The sun had risen some hours before consciousness returned. He rose from the ground horror-stricken and pallid, and glanced fearfully around him to see if Teresa were still there; but he found himself alone in the room. For some minutes he remained undecided what step to take. At last he rose from his chair to leave the apartment, but he was so weak he could scarcely drag himself along. When he left the room, he bent his steps towards the courtyard.

Each person he met saluted him with the most profound respect, while on the countenance of each was visible an expression of intense surprise, so altered was he from the athletic young man they had seen him the day before. Presently he heard the merry laughter of a number of children, and immediately hastened to the spot from whence the noise came. To his surprise he found his wife Teresa, in full possession of her beauty, playing with several children, whose mothers had brought them to see her, and who stood delighted with the condescending kindness of the baroness towards their little ones.

Conrad remained motionless for some moments, gazing with intense surprise at his wife, and the idea occurred to him that the events of the last night must have been a terrible dream and nothing more. But he was at a loss how to account for his bodily weakness? Teresa, in the midst of her gambols with the children, accidentally raised her head and perceived her husband. She uttered a slight cry of pleasure when she saw him, and snatching up in her arms a beautiful child she had been playing with, she rushed towards him, exclaiming—

"Look, dear Conrad, what a little beauty this is! Is he not a little cherub?"

The baron gazed wildly at his wife for a few moments, but said nothing.

"My dearest husband, what ails you?" said Teresa. "Are you not well?"

Conrad made no answer, but turning suddenly round staggered hurriedly away, while Teresa, with an expression of alarm and anxiety on her face, followed him with her eyes as he went. He still hurried on till he reached the small sitting-room from which he was accustomed each morning to issue his orders to his dependants, and seated himself in a chair to recover if possible, from the bewilderment he was in. Presently Ludovico, whose duty it was to attend on his master every morning for instructions, entered the room, and bowing respectfully to the baron, stood silently aside, waiting till he should be spoken to, but during the time marking the baron's altered appearance with the most intense curiosity. After some moments the baron asked him what he saw to make him stare in that manner.

"Pardon my boldness, your excellency," said Ludovico, "but I was afraid you might be ill. I trust I am in error."

"What should make you think I am unwell?" inquired the baron.

"Your highness's countenance is far paler than usual, and there is a small wound on the side of your throat. I hope you have not injured yourself."

The last remark of Ludovico decided the baron that the events of the evening had been no hallucination. What stronger proof could be required than the marks of his vampire wife's teeth still upon him? He perceived that some course of action must be at once decided upon, and the urgency of his position aided him to concentrate his thoughts. He determined on visiting a celebrated anchorite who lived in the mountains about four leagues distant, and who was famous not only for the piety of his life, but for his power in exorcising evil spirits. Having come to this resolution, he desired Ludovico immediately to saddle for him a sure-footed mule, as the path to the anchorite's dwelling was not only difficult but dangerous.

Ludovico bowed, and after having been informed that there were no other orders, he left the room, wondering in his mind what could be the reason for his master's wishing a mule saddled, when he generally rode only the highest-spirited horses. The conclusion he came to was, that the baron must have been attacked with some serious illness, and was about to proceed to some skilful leech.

As soon as Ludovico had left the room, the baron called to one of the servants whom he saw passing, and ordered breakfast to be brought to him immediately, hoping that by a hearty meal he should recover sufficient strength for the journey he was about to undertake. To a certain extent he succeeded, though possibly it was from the quantity of wine he drank, rather than from any other cause, for he had no appetite and had eaten but little.

He now descended into the courtyard of the castle, cautiously avoiding his wife. Finding the mule in readiness, he mounted it and started on his journey. For some time, he went along quietly and slowly, for he still felt weak and languid, but as he attained a higher elevation of the mountains, the cold breeze seemed to invigorate him. He now began to consider how he could rid himself of the horrible vampire he had married, and of whose real nature he had no longer any doubt. Speculations on this subject occupied him till he had entered on a narrow path on the slope of an exceedingly high mountain.

It was difficult to keep footing, and it required all his caution to prevent himself from falling. Of fear, however, the baron had none, and his thoughts continued to run on the possibility of separating himself from Teresa, and on what vengeance he would take on the *Innominato* for the treachery he had practised on him, as soon as he should be fairly freed. The more he dwelt on his revenge, the more excited he became, till a last he exclaimed aloud, "Infamous wretch! Let me be but once fairly released from the execrable fiend you have imposed upon me, and I swear I will burn thee alive in thy castle, as a fitting punishment for the sorcery thou hast practised."

Conrad had hardly uttered these words, when the pathway upon which he was riding gave way beneath him, and glided down the incline into a tremendous precipice below. He succeeded in throwing himself from his mule, which, with the debris of the rocks, was hurried over the precipice, while he clutched with the energy of despair at each object, he saw likely to give him a moment's support. But everything he touched gave way, and he gradually sank and sank towards the verge of the precipice, his efforts to save himself becoming more violent the nearer he approached to what appeared certain death. Down he sank, till his legs actually hung over the precipice, when he succeeded in grasping a stone somewhat firmer than the others, thus retarding his fall for a moment. In horror he now glanced at the terrible chasm beneath him, when suddenly different objects came before his mind with fearful reality. There was an unhappy peasant, who had without permission killed a head of game, hanging from the branch of a tree still struggling in the agonies of death, while his wife and children were in vain imploring the baron's clemency.

This vanished and he saw a boy with a knife in his hand, stabbing at his own mother for some slight offence she had given him.

This passed, and he found himself in a small village, the inhabitants of which were all dead within their houses; for at the approach of winter he had, in a fit of ill-temper, ordered his retainers to take from them all their provisions; and a snowstorm coming on immediately afterwards, they were blocked up in their dwellings, and all perished.

Again, his thoughts reverted to the position he was in, and his eye glanced over the terrible precipice that yawned beneath him, when he saw, as if in a dream, the house of Biffi the farmer, with his wife and children around him, apparently contented and happy.

As soon as he had realised the idea, the stone which he had clutched began to give way, and all seemed lost to him, when a sparrow suddenly flew on the earth a short distance from him, and immediately afterwards darted away "Save but my life!" screamed the baron, "and I swear I will keep all secret."

The words had hardly been uttered, when a goatherd with a long staff in his hand appeared on the incline above him. The man perceiving the imminent peril of the baron, with great caution, and yet with great activity, descended to assist him. He succeeded in reaching a ledge of rock a few feet above, and rather to the side of the baron, to whom he stretched forth the long mountain staff in his hand. The baron clutched it with such energy as would certainly have drawn the goatherd over with him, had it not been that the latter was a remarkably powerful man. With some difficulty the baron reached the ledge of the rock, and the goatherd then ascended to a higher position, and in like manner drew the baron on, till at last he had contrived to get him to a place of safety. As soon as Conrad found himself out of danger, he gazed wildly around him for a moment, then dizziness came over him, and he sank fainting on the ground.

When the baron had recovered his senses, he found himself so weak that it would have been impossible for him to have reached the castle that evening. He therefore willingly accompanied the goatherd to his hut in the mountains, where he proposed to pass the night. The man made what provision he could for his illustrious guest, and prepared him a supper of the best his hut afforded; but had the latter been composed of the most exquisite delicacies, it would have been equally tasteless; for Conrad had not the slightest appetite. Evening was now rapidly approaching, and the goatherd prepared a bed of leaves, over which he threw a cloak, and the baron, utterly exhausted, reposed on it for the night, without anything occurring to disturb his rest.

Next morning, he found himself somewhat refreshed by his night's rest, and he prepared to return to the castle, assisted by the goatherd, to whom he had promised a handsome reward. He had now given up all idea of visiting the anchorite, dreading that by so doing he might excite the animosity of the *Innominato*, of whose tremendous power he had lately received more than ample proof. In due time he reached home in safety, and the goatherd was dismissed after having received the promised reward. On entering the castle-yard the baron found his wife in a state of great alarm and sorrow, and surrounded by the retainers. No sooner did she perceive her husband, than, uttering a cry of delight and surprise, she rushed forward to clasp him in her arms; but the baron pushed her rudely away, and hurrying forwards, directed his steps to the room in which he was accustomed to issue his orders. Ludovico, having heard of the arrival of his master, immediately waited on him.

"Ludovico," said the baron, as soon as he saw him, "I want you to execute an order for me with great promptitude and secrecy. Go below, and prepare two good horses for a journey; one for you, the other for myself. See that we take with us provisions and equipments for two or three days. As soon as they are in readiness, leave the castle with them without speaking to any one, and wait for me about a league up the mountain, where in less than two hours I will join you. Now see that you faithfully carry out my orders, and if you do so, I assure you, you will lose nothing by your obedience."

Ludovico left the baron's presence to execute his order, when immediately afterwards a servant came into the room, and inquired if the Lady Teresa might enter.

"Tell your mistress," said the baron, in a tone of great courtesy and kindness, "that I hope she will excuse me for the moment, as I am deeply engaged in affairs of importance; but I shall await her visit with great impatience in the afternoon."

The baron now left to himself, began to draw out more fully the plan for his future operations. He resolved to visit his brother Hermann, and consult him as to what steps he ought to take in this horrible emergency; and in case no better means presented themselves, he determined on offering to give up to Hermann the castle of Gardonal and the whole valley of the Engadin, on condition of receiving from him an annuity sufficient to support him in the position he had always been accustomed to maintain. He then intended to retire to some distant country, where there would be no probability of his being followed by the horrible monster whom he had accepted as his wife. Of course, he had no intention of receiving Teresa in the afternoon, and he had merely put off her visit the purpose of allowing himself to escape with greater convenience from the castle.

About an hour after Ludovico had left him, the baron quitted the castle by a postern, with as much haste as his enfeebled strength would allow, and hurried after his retainer, whom he found awaiting him with the horses. The baron immediately mounted one, and followed by Ludovico, took the road to his brother's, where in three days he arrived in safety. Hermann received his brother with great pleasure, though much surprised at the alteration in his appearance.

"My dear Conrad," he said to him, "what can possibly have occurred to you? You look very pale, weak, and haggard. Have you been ill?"

"Worse, a thousand times worse," said Conrad. "Let us go where we may be by ourselves, and I will tell you all."

Hermann led his brother into a private room, where Conrad explained to him the terrible misfortune which had befallen him. Hermann listened attentively, and for some time could not help doubting whether his brother's mind was not affected; but Conrad explained everything in so circumstantial and lucid a manner as to dispel that idea. To the proposition which Conrad made, to make over the territory of the Engadin Valley for an annuity, Hermann promised to give full consideration. At the same time, before any further steps were taken in the matter, he advised Conrad to visit a villa he had, on the sea-shore, about ten miles distant from Genoa; where, in quiet and seclusion, he would be able to recover his energies.

Conrad thanked his brother for his advice, and willingly accepted the offer. Two days afterwards he started on the journey, and by the end of the week arrived safely, and without difficulty, at the villa.

On the evening of his arrival, Conrad, who had employed himself during the afternoon in visiting the different apartments as well as the grounds surrounding the villa, was seated at a window overlooking the sea. The evening was deliciously calm, and he felt such ease and security as he had not enjoyed for some time past. The sun was sinking in the ocean, and the moon began to appear, and the stars one by one to shine in the cloudless heavens. The thought crossed Conrad's mind that the sight of the sun sinking in the waters strongly resembled his own position when he fell over the precipice. The thought had hardly been conceived when someone touched him on the shoulder. He turned round, and saw standing before him, in the full majesty of her beauty—his wife Teresa!

"My dearest Conrad," she said, with much affection in her tone, "why have you treated me in this cruel manner? It was most unkind of you to leave me suddenly without giving the slightest hint of your intentions."

"Execrable fiend," said Conrad, springing from his chair, "leave me! Why do you haunt me in this manner?"

"Do not speak so harshly to me, my dear husband," said Teresa. "To oblige you I was taken from my grave; and on you now my very existence depends."

"Rather my death," said Conrad. "One night more such as we passed, and I should be a corpse."

"Nay, dear Conrad," said Teresa; "I have the power of indefinitely prolonging your life. Drink but of this," she continued, taking from the table behind her a silver goblet, "and tomorrow all ill effects will have passed away."

Conrad mechanically took the goblet from her hand, and was on

50

the point of raising it to his lips when he suddenly stopped, and with a shudder replaced it again on the table.

"It is blood," he said.

"True, my dear husband," said Teresa; "what else could it be? My life is dependent on your life's blood, and when that ceases so does my life. Drink then, I implore you," she continued, again offering him the goblet. "Look, the sun has already sunk beneath the wave; a minute more and daylight will have gone. Drink, Conrad, I implore you, or this night will be your last."

Conrad again took the goblet from her hand to raise it to his lips; but it was impossible, and he placed it on the table. A ray of pure moonlight now penetrated the room, as if to prove that the light of day had fled. Teresa, again transformed into a horrible vampire, flew at her husband, and throwing him on the floor, fastened her teeth on the half-healed wound in his throat. The next morning, when the servants entered the room, they found the baron a corpse on the floor; but Teresa was nowhere to be seen, nor was she ever heard of afterwards.

Little more remains to be told. Hermann took possession of the castle of Gardonal and the Valley of the Engadin, and treated his vassals with even more despotism than his brother had done before him. At last, driven to desperation, they rose against him and slew him; and the valley afterwards became absorbed into the Canton of the Grisons.

The Man-Eating Tree

Phil Robinson

(Before committing this paper to the ridicule of the Great Mediocre—for many, I fear, will be inclined to regard this story as
incredible—I would venture on the expression of an opinion
regarding credulity, which I do not remember to have met before. It is this. Placing supreme Wisdom and supreme Unwisdom at the two extremes, and myself in the exact mean between
them, I am surprised to find that whether I travel towards the
one extreme or the other, the credulity of those I meet in-
creases. To put it as a paradox—*whether a man be foolisher or wiser
than I am, he is more credulous.* I make this remark to point out to
those of the Great Mediocre whose notice it may have escaped,
that credulity is not of itself shameful or contemptible, and that
it depends upon the manner rather than the matter of their
belief, whether they gravitate towards the sage or the reverse
way. According, therefore, to the incredibility found in the following, the reader may measure, as pleases him, his wisdom or
his unwisdom.—Z. Oriel)

Peregrine Oriel, my maternal uncle, was a great traveller, as his
prophetical sponsors at the font seemed to have guessed he would
be. Indeed, he had rummaged in the garrets and cellars of the earth
with something more than ordinary diligence. But in the narrative of
his travels he did not, unfortunately, preserve the judicious caution of
Xenophon between 'the thing seen' and 'the thing heard', and thus it
came about that the town-councillors of Brunsbüttel (to whom he
had shown a duck-billed platypus, caught alive by him in Australia,
and who had him posted for 'an importer of artificial vermin') were
not alone in their scepticism of some of the old man's tales.

Thus, for instance, who could hear and believe the tale of the man-sucking tree from which he had barely escaped with life? He called it himself 'more terrible than the Upas'—'This awful plant, that rears its splendid death-shade in the central solitude of a Nubian fern forest, sickens by its unwholesome humours all vegetation from its immediate vicinity, and feeds upon the wild beasts that, in the terror of the chase, or the heat of noon, seek the thick shelter of its boughs; upon the birds that, flitting across the open space, come within the charmed circle of its power, or innocently refresh themselves from the cups of its great waxen flowers; upon even man himself when, an infrequent prey, the savage seeks its asylum in the storm, or turns from the harsh foot-wounding sword-grass of the glade, to pluck the wondrous fruit that hang plumb down among the wondrous foliage'.

And such fruit!—'glorious golden ovals, great honey-drops, swelling by their own weight into pear-shaped translucencies. The foliage glistens with a strange dew, that all day long drips on to the ground below, nurturing a rank growth of grasses, which shoot up in places so high that their spikes of fierce blood-fed green show far up among the deep-tinted foliage of the terrible tree, and, like a jealous body-guard, keep concealed the fearful secret of the charnel-house within, and draw round the black roots of the murderous plant a decent screen of living green.'

Such was his description of the plant; and the other day, looking up in a botanical dictionary I find that there is really known to naturalists a family of carnivorous plants; but I see that they are most of them very small, and prey upon little insects only. My maternal uncle, however, knew nothing of this, for he died before the days of the discovery of the sun dew and pitcher plants, and grounding his knowledge of the man-sucking tree simply on his own terrible experience of it, explained its existence by theories of his own. Denying the fixity of all the laws of nature except one, that the stronger shall endeavour to consume the weaker, and 'holding even this fixity to be itself only a means to a greater general changefulness', he argued that—since any partial distribution of the faculty of self-defence would presume an unworthy partiality in the Creator and since the sensual instincts of beast and vegetable and manifestly analogous—'the world must be as percipient as sentient throughout.'

Carrying on his theory (for it was something more than 'hypothesis' with him) a stage or two further, he arrived at the belief that, 'given the necessity of any imminent danger or urgent self-interest, every animal or vegetable could eventually revolutionise its nature, the wolf feeding on grass or nesting in trees, and the violet arming herself with thorns or entrapping insects.'

'How?' he would ask, 'can we claim for man the consequence of perceptions to sensations, and yet deny to beasts that hear, see, feel, smell, and taste, a percipient principle co-existent with their senses? And if in the whole range of the "animate" world there is this gift of self-defence against extirpation and offence against weakness, why is the "inanimate" world, holding as fierce a struggle for existence as the other, to be left defenceless and unarmed? And I deny that it is. The Brazilian epiphyte strangles the tree and sucks out its juices. The tree, again, to starve off its vampire parasite, withdraws its juices into its roots, and piercing the ground in some new place, turns the current of its sap into other growths. The epiphyte then drops off the dead boughs on to the fresh green sprouts springing from the ground beneath it—and so the fight goes on. Again, look at the Indian peepul tree; in what does the fierce yearning of its roots towards the distant well differ from the sad struggling of the camel to the oasis or of Sennacherib s army to the saving Nile?

'Is the sensitive plant unconscious! I have walked for miles through Plains of it, and watched, till the watching almost made me afraid lest the plants should pluck up courage and turn upon me, the green carpet paling into silver grey before my feet, and fainting away all round me I walked. So strangely did I feel the influence of this universal aversion, that I would have argued with the plant; but what was the use? If only I stretched out my hands, the mere shadow of the limb terrified the vegetable to sickness; shrubs crumbled up at every commencement of my speech; and at my periods great sturdy-looking bushes, to whose robustness I had foolishly appealed, sank in pallid supplication. Not a leaf would keep me company.

'A breath went forth from me that sickened life. My mere presence paralyzed life, and I was glad at last to come out among a less timid vegetation, and to feel the resentful spear-grass retaliating on the heedlessness that would have crushed it. The vegetable world, however, has its revenges. You may keep the guinea-pig in a hutch, but how will you pet the basilisk? The little sensitive plant in your garden amuses your children (who will find pleasure also in seeing cockchafers spin round on a pin), but how could you transplant a vegetable that seizes the running deer, strikes down the passing bird, and once taking hold of him, sucks the carcase of man himself, till his matter becomes as vague as his mind, and all his "animate" capabilities cannot snatch him from the terrible embrace of—God help him!—an "inanimate" tree?

'Many years ago,' said my uncle, 'I turned my restless steps towards Central Africa, and made the journey from where the Senegal empties itself into the Atlantic to the Nile, skirting the Great Desert, and reaching Nubia on my way to the eastern coast. I had with me then three native attendants, two of them brothers, the third, Otona, a young savage from the Gaboon uplands, a mere lad in his teens; and one day, leaving my mule with the two men, who were pitching my tent for the night, I went on with my gun, the boy accompanying me, towards a fern forest, which I saw in the near distance. As I approached it, I found the forest was cut into two by a wide glade, and seeing a small herd of the common antelope, an excellent beast in the pot, browsing their way along the shaded side, I crept after them.

'Though ignorant of their real danger, the herd was suspicious, and slowly trotting along before me, enticed me for a mile or more along the verge of the fern growths. Turning a corner, I suddenly became aware of a solitary tree growing in the middle of the glade—one tree alone. It struck me at once that I had never seen a tree exactly like it before; but being intent upon venison for my supper, I looked at it only long enough to satisfy my first surprise at seeing a single plant of such rich growth flourishing luxuriantly in a spot where only the harsh fern-canes seemed to thrive. The deer meanwhile were midway between me and the tree, and looking at them I saw they were going to cross the glade. Exactly opposite them was an opening in the forest, in which I should certainly have lost my supper; so, I fired into the middle of the family as they were filing before me.

'I hit a young fawn, and the rest of the herd, wheeling round in their sudden terror, made off in the direction of the tree, leaving the fawn struggling on the ground. Otona, the boy, ran forward at my order to secure it, but the little creature seeing him coming, attempted to follow its comrades, and at a fair pace held on their course. The herd had meanwhile reached the tree, but suddenly, instead of passing under it, swerved in their career, and swept round it at some yards distance. *Was I mad? or did the plant really try to catch the deer?* On a sudden I saw, or thought I saw, the tree violently agitated, and while the ferns all round were standing motionless in the dead evening air, its boughs were swayed by some sudden gust towards the herd, and swept in the force of their impulse almost to the ground. I drew my hand across my eyes, closed them for a moment, and looked again.

'The tree was as motionless as myself! Towards it, and now close to it, the boy was running in excited pursuit of the fawn. He stretched out his hands to catch it. It bounded from his eager grasp. Again, he reached forward, and again it escaped him. There was another rush forward, and the next instant boy and deer were beneath the tree.

'And now there was no mistaking what I saw.

'The tree was convulsed with motion, leaned forward, swept its thick foliaged boughs to the ground, and enveloped from my sight the pursuer and the pursued! I was within a hundred yards, and the cry of Otona from the midst of the tree came to me in all the clearness of its agony. There was then one stifled, strangling scream, and except for the agitation of the leaves where they had closed upon the boy, there was not a sign of life! I called out "Otona"! No answer came. I tried to call out again, but my utterance was like that of some wild beast smitten at once with sudden terror and its death wound. I stood there, changed from all semblance of a human being. Not all the terrors of earth together could have made me take my eye from the awful plant, or my foot off the ground. I must have stood thus for at least an hour, for the shadows had crept out from the forest half across the glade before that hideous paroxysm of fear left me.

'My first impulse then was to creep stealthily away lest the tree should perceive me, but my returning reason bade me approach it. The boy might have fallen into the lair of some beast of prey, or perhaps the terrible life in the tree was that of some great serpent among its branches. Preparing to defend myself, I approached the silent tree— the harsh grass crisping beneath my feet with a strange loudness—the cicadas in the forest shrilling till the air seemed throbbing round me with waves of sound. The terrible truth was soon before rue in all its awful novelty. The vegetable first discovered my presence at about fifty yards distance. I then became aware of a stealthy motion among the thick-lipped leaves, reminding me of some wild beast slowly gathering itself up from long sleep, a vast coil of snakes in restless motion.

'Have you ever seen bees hanging from a bough—a great cluster of bodies, bee clinging to bee—and by striking the bough, or agitating the air, caused that massed life to begin sulkily to disintegrate, each insect asserting its individual right to move? And do you remember how, without one bee leaving the pensile cluster, the whole became gradually instinct with sullen life and horrid with a multitudinous motion?

'I came within twenty yards of it. The tree was quivering through every branch, muttering for blood, and, helpless with rooted feet, yearning with every branch towards me. It was that Terror of the Deep Sea which the men of the northern fjords dread, and which, anchored upon some sunken rock, stretches into vain space its longing arms, pellucid as the sea itself, and as relentless—maimed Polypheme groping for his victims.

'Each separate leaf was agitated and hungry. Like hands they fumbled together, their fleshy palms curling upon themselves and again unfolding, closing on each other and falling apart again, thick, helpless, fingerless hands—rather lips or tongues than hands—dimpled closely with little cup—like hollows. I approached nearer and nearer, step by step, till I saw that these soft horrors were all of them in motion, opening and closing incessantly.

'I was now within ten yards of the farthest reaching bough. Every part of it was hysterical with excitement. The agitation of its members was awful—sickening yet fascinating. In an ecstasy of eagerness for the food so near them, the leaves turned upon each other. Two meeting would suck together face to face, with a force that compressed their joint thickness to a half, thinning the two leaves into one, now grappling in a volute like a double shell, writhing like some green worm, and at last faint with the violence of the paroxysm, would slowly separate, falling apart as leeches gorged drop off the limbs. A sticky dew glistened in the dimples, welled over, and trickled down the leaf. The sound of it dripping from leaf to leaf made it seem as if the tree was muttering to itself. The beautiful golden fruit as they swung here and there were clutched now by one leaf, and now by another, held for a moment close enfolded from the sight, and then as suddenly released. Here a large leaf, vampire-like, had sucked out the juices of a smaller one. It hung limp and bloodless, like a carcase of which the weasel has tired.

'I watched the terrible struggle till my starting eyes, strained by intense attention, refused their office, and I can hardly say what I saw. But the tree before me seemed to have become a live beast. Above me I felt conscious was a great limb, and each of its thousand clammy hands reached downwards towards me, fumbling. It strained, shivered, rocked, and heaved. It flung itself about in despair. The boughs, tantalized to madness with the presence of flesh, were tossed to this side and to that, in the agony of a frantic desire. The leaves were wrung together as the hands of one driven to madness by sudden misery. I felt the vile dew spurting from the tense veins fall upon me. My clothes began to give out a strange odour. The ground I stood on glistened with animal juices.

'Was I bewildered by terror? Had my senses abandoned me in my need? I know not—but the tree seemed to me to be alive. Leaning over towards me, it seemed to be pulling up its roots from the softened ground, and to be moving towards me. A mountainous monster, with myriad lips, mumbling together for my life, was upon me! Like one who desperately defends himself from imminent death, I made an effort for life, and fired my gun at the approaching horror. To my dizzied senses the sound seemed far off, but the shock of the recoil partially recalled me to myself, and starting back I reloaded. The shots had torn their way into the soft body of the great thing. The trunk as it received the wound shuddered, and the whole tree was struck with a sudden quiver. A fruit fell down—slipping from the leaves, now rigid with swollen veins, as from carven foliage.

'Then I saw a large arm slowly droop, and without a sound it was severed from the juice-fattened bole, and sank down softly, noiselessly, through the glistening leaves. I fired again, and another vile fragment was powerless—dead. At each discharge the terrible vegetable yielded a life. Piecemeal I attacked it, killing here a leaf and there a branch. My fury increased with the slaughter till, when my ammunition was exhausted, the splendid giant was left a wreck—as if some hurricane had torn through it. On the ground lay heaped together the fragments, struggling, rising and falling, gasping. Over them drooped in dying languor a few stricken boughs, while upright in the midst stood, dripping at every joint, the glistening trunk. My continued firing had brought up one of my men on my mule. He dared not, so he told me, come near me, thinking me mad.

'I had now drawn my hunting-knife, and with this was fighting—with the leaves. Yes—but each leaf was instinct with a horrid life; and more than once I felt my hand entangled for a moment and seized as if by sharp lips. Ignorant of the presence of my companion I made a rush forward over the fallen foliage, and with a last paroxysm of frenzy drove my knife up to the handle into the soft bole, and, slipping on the fast congealing sap, fell, exhausted and unconscious, among the still panting leaves. My companions carried me back to the camp, and after vainly searching for Otona awaited my return to consciousness. Two or three hours elapsed before I could speak, and several days before I could approach the terrible thing. My men would not go near it. It was quite dead; for as we came up a great-billed bird with gaudy plumage that had been securely feasting on the decaying fruit, flew up from the wreck. We removed the rotting foliage, and there, among the dead leaves still limp with juices, and piled round the roots, we found the ghastly relics of many former meals, and—its last nourishment—the corpse of little Otona. To have removed the leaves would have taken too long, so we buried the body as it was with a hundred vampire leaves still clinging to it.'

Such, as nearly as I remember it, was my uncle's story of the Man-eating Tree

The Ship That Saw a Ghost

Frank Norris

Very much of this story must remain untold, for the reason that if it were definitely known what business I had aboard the tramp steam-freighter *Glarus*, three hundred miles off the South American coast on a certain summer's day, some few years ago, I would very likely be obliged to answer a great many personal and direct questions put by fussy and impertinent experts in maritime law—who are paid to be inquisitive. Also, I would get "Ally Bazan," Strokher and Hardenberg into trouble.

Suppose on that certain summer's day, you had asked of Lloyds' agency where the *Glarus* was, and what was her destination and cargo. You would have been told that she was twenty days out from Callao, bound north to San Francisco in ballast; that she had been spoken by the bark *Medea* and the steamer *Benevento*; that she was reported to have blown out a cylinder head, but being manageable was proceeding on her way under sail.

That is what Lloyds would have answered.

If you know something of the ways of ships and what is expected of them, you will understand that the *Glarus*, to be some half a dozen hundred miles south of where Lloyds' would have her, and to be still going south, under full steam, was a scandal that would have made her brothers and sisters ostracize her finally and forever.

And that is curious, too. Humans may indulge in vagaries innumerable, and may go far afield in the way of lying; but a ship may not so much as quibble without suspicion. The least lapse of "regularity," the least difficulty in squaring performance with intuition, and behold she is on the black list, and her captain, owners, officers, agents and consignors, and even supercargoes, are asked to explain.

And the *Glarus* was already on the black list. From the beginning

61

her stars had been malign. As the *Breda*, she had first lost her reputation, seduced into a filibustering escapade down the South American coast, where in the end a plain-clothes United States detective—that is to say, a revenue cutter—arrested her off Buenos Ayres and brought her home, a prodigal daughter, besmirched and disgraced.

After that she was in some dreadful black-birding business in a far quarter of the South Pacific; and after that—her name changed finally to the *Glarus*—poached seals for a syndicate of Dutchmen who lived in Tacoma, and who afterward built a club-house out of what she earned.

And after that we got her.

We got her, I say, through Ryder's South Pacific Exploitation Company. The "President" had picked out a lovely little deal for Hardenberg, Strokher and Ally Bazan (the Three Black Crows), which he swore would make them "independent rich" the rest of their respective lives. It is a promising deal (B. 300 it is on Ryder's map), and if you want to know more about it you may write to ask Ryder what B. 300 is. If he chooses to tell you, that is his affair.

For B. 300—let us confess it—is, as Hardenberg puts it, as crooked as a dog's hind leg. It is as risky as barratry. If you pull it off you may— after paying Ryder his share—divide sixty-five, or possibly sixty-seven, thousand dollars between you and your associates. If you fail, and you are perilously like to fail, you will be sure to have a man or two of your companions shot, maybe yourself obliged to pistol certain people, and in the end fetch up at Tahiti, prisoner in a French patrol-boat.

Observe that B. 300 is spoken of as still open. It is so, for the reason that the Three Black Crows did not pull it off. It still stands marked up in red ink on the map that hangs over Ryder's desk in the San Francisco office; and any one can have a chance at it who will meet Cyrus Ryder's terms. Only he can't get the *Glarus* for the attempt.

For the trip to the island after B. 300 was the last occasion on which the *Glarus* will smell blue water or taste the trades. She will never clear again. She is lumber.

And yet the *Glarus* on this very blessed day of 1902 is riding to her buoys off Sausalito in San Francisco Bay, complete in every detail (bar a broken propeller shaft), not a rope missing, not a screw loose, not a plank started—a perfectly equipped steam-freighter.

But you may go along the "Front" in San Francisco from Fisherman's Wharf to the China steamships' docks and shake your dollars under the seamen's noses, and if you so much as whisper *Glarus* they will edge suddenly off and look at you with scared suspicion, and then, as like as not, walk away without another word. No pilot will take the *Glarus* out; no captain will navigate her; no stoker will feed her fires; no sailor will walk her decks. The *Glarus* is suspect. She has seen a ghost.

★★★★★★

It happened on our voyage to the island after this same B. 300. We had stood well off from shore for day after day, and Hardenberg had shaped our course so far from the track of navigation that since the *Benevento* had hulled down and vanished over the horizon no stitch of canvas nor smudge of smoke had we seen. We had passed the equator long since, and would fetch a long circuit to the southard, and bear up against the island by a circuitous route. This to avoid being spoken. It was tremendously essential that the *Glarus* should not be spoken.

I suppose, no doubt, that it was the knowledge of our isolation that impressed me with the dreadful remoteness of our position. Certainly, the sea in itself looks no different at a thousand than at a hundred miles from shore. But as day after day I came out on deck at noon, after ascertaining our position on the chart (a mere pin-point in a reach of empty paper), the sight of the ocean weighed down upon me with an infinitely great awesomeness—and I was no new hand to the high seas even then.

But at such times the *Glarus* seemed to me to be threading a loneliness beyond all worlds and beyond all conception desolate. Even in more populous waters, when no sail notches the line of the horizon, the propinquity of one's kind is nevertheless a thing understood, and to an unappreciated degree comforting. Here, however, I knew we were out, far out in the desert. Never a keel for years upon years before us had parted these waters; never a sail had bellied to these winds. Perfunctorily, day in and day out we turned our eyes through long habit toward the horizon. But we knew, before the look, that the searching would be bootless. Forever and forever, under the pitiless sun and cold blue sky stretched the indigo of the ocean floor. The ether between the planets can be no less empty, no less void.

I never, till that moment, could have so much as conceived the imagination of such loneliness, such utter stagnant abomination of desolation. In an open boat, bereft of comrades, I should have gone mad in thirty minutes.

I remember to have approximated the impression of such empty immensity only once before, in my younger days, when I lay on my

63

back on a treeless, bushless mountainside and stared up into the sky for the better part of an hour.

You probably know the trick. If you do not, you must understand that if you look up at the blue long enough, the flatness of the thing begins little by little to expand, to give here and there; and the eye travels on and on and up and up, till at length (well for you that it lasts but the fraction of a second), you all at once see space. You generally stop there and cry out, and—your hands over your eyes—are only too glad to grovel close to the good old solid earth again. Just as I, so often on short voyage, was glad to wrench my eyes away from that horrid vacancy, to fasten them upon our sailless masts and stack, or to lay my grip upon the sooty smudged taffrail of the only thing that stood between me and the Outer Dark.

For we had come at last to that region of the Great Seas where no ship goes, the silent sea of Coleridge and the Ancient One, the unplumbed, untracked, uncharted Dreadfulness, primordial, hushed, and we were as much alone as a grain of star-dust whirling in the empty space beyond Uranus and the ken of the greater telescopes.

So, the *Glarus* plodded and churned her way onward. Every day and all day the same pale-blue sky and the unwinking sun bent over that moving speck. Every day and all day the same black-blue water-world, untouched by any known wind, smooth as a slab of syenite, colourful as an opal, stretched out and around and beyond and before and behind us, forever, illimitable, empty. Every day the smoke of our fires veiled the streaked whiteness of our wake. Every day Hardenberg (our skipper) at noon pricked a pin-hole in the chart that hung in the wheel-house, and that showed we were so much farther into the wilderness. Every day the world of men, of civilization, of newspapers, policemen and street-railways receded, and we steamed on alone, lost and forgotten in that silent sea.

"Jolly lot o' room to turn raound in," observed Ally Bazan, the colonial, "withaout steppin' on y'r neighbour's toes."

"We're clean, clean out o' the track o' navigation," Hardenberg told him. "An' a blessed good thing for us, too. Nobody ever comes down into these waters. Ye couldn't pick no course here. Everything leads to nowhere."

"Might as well be in a bally balloon," said Strokher.

I shall not tell of the nature of the venture on which the *Glarus* was bound, further than to say it was not legitimate. It had to do with an ill thing done more than two centuries ago. There was money in the venture, but it was not to be gained by a violation of metes and bounds which are better left intact.

The island toward which we were heading is associated in the minds of men with a Horror.

A ship had called there once, two hundred years in advance of the *Glarus*—a ship not much unlike the crank high-prowed caravel of Hudson, and her company had landed, and having accomplished the evil they had set out to do, made shift to sail away. And then, just after the palms of the island had sunk from sight below the water's edge, the unspeakable had happened. The Death that was not Death had arisen from out the sea and stood before the ship, and over it, and the blight of the thing lay along the decks like mould, and the ship sweated in the terror of that which is yet without a name.

Twenty men died in the first week, all but six in the second. These six, with the shadow of insanity upon them, made out to launch a boat, returned to the island and died there, after leaving a record of what had happened.

The six left the ship exactly as she was, sails all set, lanterns all lit—left her in the shadow of the Death that was not Death.

She stood there, becalmed, and watched them go. She was never heard of again.

Or was she—well, that's as may be.

But the main point of the whole affair, to my notion, has always been this. The ship was the last friend of those six poor wretches who made back for the island with their poor chests of plunder. She was their guardian, as it were, would have defended and befriended them to the last; and also we, the Three Black Crows and myself, had no right under heaven, nor before the law of men, to come prying and peeping into this business—into this affair of the dead and buried past. There was sacrilege in it. We were no better than body-snatchers.

★★★★★★

When I heard the others complaining of the loneliness of our surroundings, I said nothing at first. I was no sailor man, and I was on board only by tolerance. But I looked again at the maddening sameness of the horizon—the same vacant, void horizon that we had seen now for sixteen days on end, and felt in my wits and in my nerves that same formless rebellion and protest such as comes when the same note is reiterated over and over again.

It may seem a little thing that the mere fact of meeting with no other ship should have ground down the edge of the spirit. But let the incredulous—bound upon such a hazard as ours—sail straight into nothingness for sixteen days on end, seeing nothing but the sun, hearing nothing but the thresh of his own screw, and then put the question.

And yet, of all things, we desired no company. Stealth was our one great aim. But I think there were moments—toward the last—when the Three Crows would have welcomed even a cruiser.

Besides, there was more cause for depression, after all, than mere isolation.

On the seventh day Hardenberg and I were forward by the cathead, adjusting the grain with some half-formed intent of spearing the porpoises that of late had begun to appear under our bows, and Hardenberg had been computing the number of days we were yet to run.

"We are some five hundred odd miles off that island by now," he said, "and she's doing her thirteen knots handsome. All's well so far—but do you know, I'd just as soon raise that point o' land as soon as convenient."

"How so?" said I, bending on the line. "Expect some weather?"

"Mr. Dixon," said he, giving me a curious glance, "the sea is a queer proposition, put it any ways. I've been a seafarin' man since I was big as a minute, and I know the sea, and what's more, the Feel o' the sea. Now, look out yonder. Nothin', hey? Nothin' but the same ol' skyline we've watched all the way out. The glass is as steady as a steeple, and this ol' hooker, I reckon, is as sound as the day she went off the ways. But just the same if I were to home now, a-foolin' about Gloucester way in my little dough-dish—d'ye know what? I'd put into port. I sure would. Because why? Because I got the Feel o' the Sea, Mr. Dixon. I got the Feel o' the Sea."

I had heard old skippers say something of this before, and I cited to Hardenberg the experience of a skipper captain I once knew who had turned turtle in a calm sea off Trincomalee. I ask him what this Feel of the Sea was warning him against just now (for on the high sea any premonition is a premonition of evil, not of good). But he was not explicit.

"I don't know," he answered moodily, and as if in great perplexity, coiling the rope as he spoke. "I don't know. There's some blame thing or other close to us, I'll bet a hat. I don't know the name of it, but there's a big bird in the air, just out of sight som'eres, and," he suddenly exclaimed, smacking his knee and leaning forward, "I—don't—like—it—one—dam'—bit."

The same thing came up in our talk in the cabin that night, after the dinner was taken off and we settled down to tobacco. Only, at this time, Hardenberg was on duty on the bridge. It was Ally Bazan who spoke instead.

"Seems to me," he hazarded, "as haow they's somethin' or other a-goin' to bump up pretty blyme soon. I shouldn't be surprised, naow, y'know, if we piled her up on some bally uncharted reef along o' tonight and went strite daown afore we'd had a bloomin' charnce to s'y 'So long, gen'lemen all.'"

He laughed as he spoke, but when, just at that moment, a pan clattered in the galley, he jumped suddenly with an oath, and looked hard about the cabin.

Then Strokher confessed to a sense of distress also. He'd been having it since day before yesterday, it seemed.

"And I put it to you the glass is lovely," he said, "so it's no blow. I guess," he continued, "we're all a bit seedy and ship-sore."

And whether or not this talk worked upon my own nerves, or whether in very truth the Feel of the Sea had found me also, I do not know; but I do know that after dinner that night, just before going to bed, a queer sense of apprehension came upon me, and that when I had come to my stateroom, after my turn upon deck, I became furiously angry with nobody in particular, because I could not at once find the matches. But here was a difference. The other man had been merely vaguely uncomfortable.

I could put a name to my uneasiness. I felt that we were being watched.

★★★★★★

It was a strange ship's company we made after that. I speak only of the Crows and myself. We carried a scant crew of stokers, and there was also a chief engineer. But we saw so little of him that he did not count. The Crows and I gloomed on the quarterdeck from dawn to dark, silent, irritable, working upon each other's nerves till the creak of a block would make a man jump like cold steel laid to his flesh. We quarrelled over absolute nothings, glowered at each other for half a word, and each one of us, at different times, was at some pains to declare that never in the course of his career had he been associated with such a disagreeable trio of brutes. Yet we were always together, and sought each other's company with painful insistence.

Only once were we all agreed, and that was when the cook, a Chinaman, spoiled a certain batch of biscuits. Unanimously we fell foul of the creature with so much vociferation as fishwives till he fled the cabin in actual fear of mishandling, leaving us suddenly seized with noisy hilarity—for the first time in a week. Hardenberg proposed a round of drinks from our single remaining case of beer. We stood up and formed an Elk's chain and then drained our glasses to each other's health with profound seriousness.

That same evening, I remember, we all sat on the quarterdeck till late and—oddly enough—related each one his life's history up to date; and then went down to the cabin for a game of euchre before turning in.

We had left Strokher on the bridge—it was his watch—and had forgotten all about him in the interest of the game, when—I suppose it was about one in the morning—I heard him whistle long and shrill. I laid down my cards and said:

"Hark!"

In the silence that followed we heard at first only the muffled lope of our engines, the cadenced snorting of the exhaust, and the ticking of Hardenberg's big watch in his waistcoat that he had hung by the arm-hole to the back of his chair. Then from the bridge, above our deck, prolonged, intoned—a wailing cry in the night—came Strokher's voice:

"Sail oh-h-h."

And the cards fell from our hands, and, like men turned to stone, we sat looking at each other across the soiled red cloth for what seemed an immeasurably long minute.

Then stumbling and swearing, in a hysteria of hurry, we gained the deck.

There was a moon, very low and reddish, but no wind. The sea beyond the taffrail was as smooth as lava, and so still that the swells from the cutwater of the *Glarus* did not break as they rolled away from the bows.

I remember that I stood staring and blinking at the empty ocean—where the moonlight lay like a painted stripe reaching to the horizon—stupid and frowning, till Hardenberg, who had gone on ahead, cried:

"Not here—on the bridge!"

We joined Strokher, and as I came up the others were asking:
"Where? Where?"

And there, before he had pointed, I saw—we all of us saw—And I heard Hardenberg's teeth come together like a spring trap, while Ally

Bazan ducked as though to a blow, muttering:

"Gord 'a' mercy, what nyme do ye put to' a ship like that?"

And after that no one spoke for a long minute, and we stood there, moveless black shadows, huddled together for the sake of the blessed elbow touch that means so incalculably much, looking off over our port quarter.

For the ship that we saw there—oh, she was not a half-mile distant—was unlike any ship known to present day construction.

She was short, and high-pooped, and her stern, which was turned a little toward us, we could see, was set with curious windows, not unlike a house. And on either side of this stern were two great iron cressets such as once were used to burn signal-fires in. She had three masts with mighty yards swung 'thwart ship, but bare of all sails save a few rotting streamers. Here and there about her a tangled mass of rigging drooped and sagged.

And there she lay, in the red eye of the setting moon, in that solitary ocean, shadowy, antique, forlorn, a thing the most abandoned, the most sinister I ever remember to have seen.

Then Strokher began to explain volubly and with many repetitions.

"A derelict, of course. I was asleep; yes, I was asleep. Gross neglect of duty. I say I was asleep—on watch. And we worked up to her. When I woke, why—you see, when I woke, there she was," he gave a weak little laugh, "and—and now, why, there she is, you see. I turned around and saw her sudden like—when I woke up, that is."

He laughed again, and as he laughed the engines far below our feet gave a sudden hiccough. Something crashed and struck the ship's sides till we lurched as we stood. There was a shriek of steam, a shout—and then silence.

The noise of the machinery ceased; the *Glarus* slid through the still water, moving only by her own decreasing momentum.

Hardenberg sang, "Stand by!" and called down the tube to the engine-room.

"What's up?"

I was standing close enough to him to hear the answer in a small, faint voice:

"Shaft gone, sir."

"Broke?"

"Yes, sir."

Hardenberg faced about.

69

"Come below. We must talk." I do not think any of us cast a glance at the Other Ship again. Certainly, I kept my eyes away from her. But as we started down the companion-way I laid my hand on Strokher's shoulder. The rest were ahead. I looked him straight between the eyes as I asked:

"Were you asleep? Is that why you saw her so suddenly?"

It is now five years since I asked the question. I am still waiting for Strokher's answer.

Well, our shaft was broken. That was flat. We went down into the engine-room and saw the jagged fracture that was the symbol of our broken hopes. And in the course of the next five minutes' conversation with the chief we found that, as we had not provided against such a contingency, there was to be no mending of it. We said nothing about the mishap coinciding with the appearance of the Other Ship. But I know we did not consider the break with any degree of surprise after a few moments.

We came up from the engine-room and sat down to the cabin table.

"Now what?" said Hardenberg, by way of beginning.

Nobody answered at first.

It was by now three in the morning. I recall it all perfectly. The ports opposite where I sat were open and I could see. The moon was all but full set. The dawn was coming up with a copper murkiness over the edge of the world. All the stars were yet out. The sea, for all the red moon and copper dawn, was grey, and there, less than half a mile away, still lay our consort. I could see her through the portholes with each slow careening of the *Glarus*.

"I vote for the island," cried Ally Bazan, "shaft or no shaft. We rigs a bit o' syle, y'know——" and thereat the discussion began.

For upward of two hours it raged, with loud words and shaken forefingers, and great noisy bangings of the table, and how it would have ended I do not know, but at last—it was then maybe five in the morning—the lookout passed word down to the cabin:

"Will you come on deck, gentlemen?" It was the mate who spoke, and the man was shaken—I could see that—to the very vitals of him. We started and stared at one another, and I watched little Ally Bazan go slowly white to the lips. And even then, no word of the ship, except as it might be this from Hardenberg:

"What is it? Good God Almighty, I'm no coward, but this thing is getting one too many for me."

Then without further speech he went on deck.

The air was cool. The sun was not yet up. It was that strange, queer mid-period between dark and dawn, when the night is over and the day not yet come, just the grey that is neither light nor dark, the dim dead blink as of the refracted light from extinct worlds.

We stood at the rail. We did not speak; we stood watching. It was so still that the drip of steam from some loosened pipe far below was plainly audible, and it sounded in that lifeless, silent greyness like— God knows what—a death tick.

"You see," said the mate, speaking just above a whisper, "there's no mistake about it. She is moving—this way."

"Oh, a current, of course," Strokher tried to say cheerfully, "sets her toward us."

Would the morning never come?

Ally Bazan—his parents were Catholic—began to mutter to himself.

Then Hardenberg spoke aloud.

"I particularly don't want—that—out—there—to cross our bows. I don't want it to come to that. We must get some sails on her."

"And I put it to you as man to man," said Strokher, "where might be your wind."

He was right. The *Glarus* floated in absolute calm. On all that slab of ocean nothing moved but the Dead Ship.

She came on slowly; her bows, the high, clumsy bows pointed toward us, the water turning from her forefoot. She came on; she was near at hand. We saw her plainly—saw the rotted planks, the crumbling rigging, the rust-corroded metal-work, the broken rail, the gaping deck, and I could imagine that the clean water broke away from her sides in refluent wavelets as though in recoil from a thing unclean. She made no sound. No single thing stirred aboard the hulk of her— but she moved.

We were helpless. The *Glarus* could stir no boat in any direction; we were chained to the spot. Nobody had thought to put out our lights, and they still burned on through the dawn, strangely out of place in their red-and-green garishness, like maskers surprised by daylight.

And in the silence of that empty ocean, in that queer half-light between dawn and day, at six o'clock, silent as the settling of the dead to the bottomless bottom of the ocean, grey as fog, lonely, blind, soulless, voiceless, the Dead Ship crossed our bows.

I do not know how long after this the ship disappeared, or what was the time of day when we at last pulled ourselves together. But we came to some sort of decision at last. This was to go on—under sail. We were too close to the island now to turn back for—for a broken shaft.

The afternoon was spent fitting on the sails to her, and when after nightfall the wind at length came up fresh and favourable, I believe we all felt heartened and a deal more hardy—until the last canvas went aloft, and Hardenberg took the wheel.

We had drifted a good deal since the morning, and the bows of the *Glarus* were pointed homeward, but as soon as the breeze blew strong enough to get steerageway Hardenberg put the wheel over and, as the booms swung across the deck, headed for the island again.

We had not gone on this course half an hour—no, not twenty minutes—before the wind shifted a whole quarter of the compass and took the *Glarus* square in the teeth, so that there was nothing for it but to tack. And then the strangest thing befell.

I will make allowance for the fact that there was no centre-board nor keel to speak of to the *Glarus*. I will admit that the sails upon a nine-hundred-ton freighter are not calculated to speed her, nor steady her. I will even admit the possibility of a current that set from the island toward us. All this may be true, yet the *Glarus* should have advanced. We should have made a wake.

And instead of this, our stolid, steady, trusty old boat was—what shall I say?

I will say that no man may thoroughly understand a ship—after all. I will say that new ships are cranky and unsteady; that old and seasoned ships have their little crotchets, their little fussinesses that their skippers must learn and humour if they are to get anything out of them; that even the best ships may sulk at times, shirk their work, grow unstable, perverse, and refuse to answer helm and handling. And I will say that some ships that for years have sailed blue water as soberly and as docilely as a street-car horse has plodded the treadmill of the 'tween-tracks, have been known to balk, as stubbornly and as conclusively as any old Bay Billy that ever wore a bell. I know this has happened, because I have seen it. I saw, for instance, the *Glarus* do it.

Quite literally and truly we could do nothing with her. We will say, if you like, that that great jar and wrench when the shaft gave way shook her and crippled her. It is true, however, that whatever the cause may have been, we could not force her toward the island. Of course, we all said "current"; but why didn't the log-line trail?

For three days and three nights we tried it. And the *Glarus* heaved and plunged and shook herself just as you have seen a horse plunge and rear when his rider tries to force him at the steam-roller.

I tell you I could feel the fabric of her tremble and shudder from bow to stern-post, as though she were in a storm; I tell you she fell off from the wind, and broad-on drifted back from her course till the sensation of her shrinking was as plain as her own staring lights and a thing pitiful to see.

We rowelled her, and we crowded sail upon her, and we coaxed and bullied and humoured her, till the Three Crows, their fortune only a plain sail two days ahead, raved and swore like insensate brutes, or shall we say like *mahouts* trying to drive their stricken elephant upon the tiger—and all to no purpose. "Damn the damned current and the damned luck and the damned shaft and all," Hardenberg would exclaim, as from the wheel he would catch the *Glarus* falling off. "Go on, you old hooker—you tub of junk! My God, you'd think she was scared!"

Perhaps the *Glarus* was scared, perhaps not; that point is debatable. But it was beyond doubt of debate that Hardenberg was scared.

A ship that will not obey is only one degree less terrible than a mutinous crew. And we were in a fair way to have both. The stokers, whom we had impressed into duty as A.B.'s, were of course superstitious; and they knew how the *Glarus* was acting, and it was only a question of time before they got out of hand.

That was the end. We held a final conference in the cabin and decided that there was no help for it—we must turn back.

And back we accordingly turned, and at once the wind followed us, and the "current" helped us, and the water churned under the forefoot of the *Glarus*, and the wake whitened under her stern, and the log-line ran out from the trail and strained back as the ship worked homeward.

We had never a mishap from the time we finally swung her about; and, considering the circumstances, the voyage back to San Francisco was propitious.

But an incident happened just after we had started back. We were perhaps some five miles on the homeward track. It was early evening and Strokher had the watch. At about seven o'clock he called me up on the bridge.

"See her?" he said.

And there, far behind us, in the shadow of the twilight, loomed the other ship again, desolate, lonely beyond words. We were leaving her rapidly astern. Strokher and I stood looking at her till she dwindled to a dot. Then Strokher said:

"She's on post again."

And when months afterward we limped into the Golden Gate and cast anchor off the "Front" our crew went ashore as soon as discharged, and in half a dozen hours the legend was in every sailors' boarding-house and in every seaman's dive, from Barbary Coast to Black Tom's.

It is still there, and that is why no pilot will take the *Glarus* out, no captain will navigate her, no stoker feed her fires, no sailor walk her decks. The *Glarus* is suspect. She will never smell blue water again, nor taste the trades. She has seen a Ghost.

The Stone Chamber

H. B. Marriott Watson

It was not until early summer that Warrington took possession of Marvyn Abbey. He had bought the property in the preceding autumn, but the place had so fallen into decay through the disorders of time that more than six months elapsed ere it was inhabitable. The delay, however, fell out conveniently for Warrington; for the Bosanquets spent the winter abroad, and nothing must suit but he must spend it with them. There was never a man who pursued his passion with such ardour. He was ever at Miss Bosanquet's skirts, and bade fair to make her as steadfast a husband as he was attached a lover. Thus, it was not until after his return from that prolonged exile that he had the opportunity of inspecting the repairs discharged by his architect. He was nothing out of the common in character, but was full of kindly impulses and a fellow of impetuous blood.

When he called upon me in my chambers he spoke with some excitement of his abbey, as also of his approaching marriage; and finally, breaking into an exhibition of genuine affection, declared that we had been so long and so continuously intimate that I, and none other, must help him warm his house and marry his bride. It had indeed been always understood between us that I should serve him at the ceremony, but now it appeared that I must start my duties even earlier. The prospect of a summer holiday in Utterbourne pleased me. It was a charming village, set upon the slope of a wooded hill and within call of the sea. I had a slight knowledge of the district from a riding excursion taken through that part of Devonshire; and years before, and ere Warrington had come into his money, had viewed the abbey ruins from a distance with the polite curiosity of a passing tourist.

I examined them now with new eyes as we drove up the avenue. The face which the ancient building presented to the valley was of magnificent design, but now much worn and battered.

Part of it, the right wing, I judged to be long past the uses of a dwelling, for the walls had crumbled away, huge gaps opened in the foundations, and the roof was quite dismantled.

Warrington had very wisely left this portion to its own sinister decay; it was the left wing which had been restored, and which we were to inhabit. The entrance, I will confess, was a little mean, for the large doorway had been bricked up and an ordinary modern door gave upon the spacious terrace and the winding gardens. But apart from this, the work of restoration had been undertaken with skill and piety, and the interior had retained its native dignity, while resuming an air of proper comfort. The old oak had been repaired congruous with the original designs, and the great rooms had been as little altered as was requisite to adapt them for daily use.

Warrington passed quickly from chamber to chamber in evident delight, directing my attention upon this and upon that, and eagerly requiring my congratulations and approval. My comments must have satisfied him, for the place attracted me vastly. The only criticism I ventured was to remark upon the size of the rooms and to question if they might dwarf the insignificant human figures they were to entertain.

He laughed. "Not a bit," said he. "Roaring fires in winter in those fine old fireplaces; and as for summer, the more space the better. We shall be jolly."

I followed him along the noble hall, and we stopped before a small door of very black oak.

"The bedrooms," he explained, as he turned the key, "are all upstairs, but mine is not ready yet.

"And besides, I am reserving it; I won't sleep in it till—you understand," he concluded, with a smiling suggestion of embarrassment.

I understood very well. He threw the door open.

"I am going to use this in the meantime," he continued. "Queer little room, isn't it? It used to be a sort of library. How do you think it looks?"

We had entered as he spoke, and stood, distributing our glances in that vague and general way in which a room is surveyed. It was a chamber of much smaller proportions than the rest, and was dimly lighted by two long narrow windows sunk in the great walls. The bed and the modern fittings looked strangely out of keeping with its ancient privacy. The walls were rudely distempered with barbaric frescos, dating, I conjectured, from the fourteenth century; and the floor was of stone, worn into grooves and hollows with the feet of many generations. As I was taking in these facts, there came over me a sudden curiosity as to those dead Marvyns who had held the abbey for so long. This silent chamber seemed to suggest questions of their history; it spoke eloquently of past ages and past deeds, fallen now into oblivion. Here, within these thick walls, no echo from the outer world might carry, no sound would ring within its solitary seclusion. Even the silence seemed to confer with one upon the ancient transactions of that extinct House.

Warrington stirred, and turned suddenly to me. "I hope it's not damp," said he, with a slight shiver. "It looks rather solemn. I thought furniture would brighten it up."

"I should think it would be very comfortable," said I. "You will never be disturbed by any sounds at any rate."

"No," he answered, hesitatingly; and then, quickly, on one of his impulses: "Hang it, Heywood, there's too much silence here for me." Then he laughed. "Oh, I shall do very well for a month or two." And with that appeared to return to his former placid cheerfulness.

The train of thought started in that sombre chamber served to entertain me several times that day. I questioned Warrington at dinner, which we took in one of the smaller rooms, commanding a lovely prospect of dale and sea. He shook his head. Archaeological lore, as indeed anything else out of the borders of actual life, held very little interest for him.

"The Marvyns died out in 1714, I believe," he said, indifferently; "someone told me that—the man I bought it from, I think. They might just as well have kept the place up since; but I think it has been only occupied twice between then and now, and the last time was forty years ago. It would have rotted to pieces if I hadn't taken it. Perhaps Mrs Batty could tell you. She's lived in these parts almost all her life."

To humour me, and affected, I doubt not, by a certain pride in his new possession, he put the query to his housekeeper upon her appearance subsequently; but it seemed that her knowledge was little fuller than his own, though she had gathered some vague traditions of the countryside.

The Marvyns had not left a reputable name, if rumour spoke truly; theirs was a family to which black deeds had been credited. They were ill-starred also in their fortunes, and had become extinct suddenly; but for the rest, the events had fallen too many generations ago to be current now between the memories of the village.

Warrington, who was more eager to discuss the future than to recall the past, was vastly excited by his anticipations. St Pharamond, Sir William Bosanquet's house, lay across the valley, barely five miles away; and as the family had now returned, it was easy to forgive Warrington's elation.

"What do you think?" he said, late that evening; and clapping me upon the shoulder, "You have seen Marion; here is the house. Am I not lucky? Damn it, Heywood, I'm not pious, but I am disposed to thank God! I'm not a bad fellow, but I'm no saint; it's fortunate that it's not only the virtuous that are rewarded. In fact, it's usually contrariwise. I owe this to—Lord, I don't know what I owe it to. Is it my money? Of course, Marion doesn't care a rap for that; but then, you see, I mightn't have known her without it. Of course, there's the house, too. I'm thankful I have money. At any rate, here's my new life. Just look about and take it in, old fellow. If you knew how a man may be ashamed of himself! But there, I've done. You know I'm decent at heart—you must count my life from today." And with this outbreak he lifted the glass between fingers that trembled with the warmth of his emotions, and tossed off his wine.

He did himself but justice when he claimed to be a good fellow; and, in truth, I was myself somewhat moved by his obvious feeling. I remember that we shook hands very affectionately, and my sympathy was the prelude to a long and confidential talk, which lasted until quite a late hour.

At the foot of the staircase, where we parted, he detained me.

"This is the last of my wayward days," he said, with a smile. "Late hours—liquor—all go. You shall see. Goodnight. You know your room. I shall be up long before you." And with that he vanished briskly into the darkness that hung about the lower parts of the passage.

I watched him go, and it struck me quite vaguely what a slight impression his candle made upon that channel of opaque gloom. It seemed merely as a thread of light that illumined nothing. Warrington himself was rapt into the prevalent blackness; but long afterwards, and even when his footsteps had died away upon the heavy carpet, the tiny beam was visible, advancing and flickering in the distance.

My window, which was modern, opened upon a little balcony, where, as the night was warm and I was indisposed for sleep, I spent half an hour enjoying the air. I was in a sentimental mood, and my thoughts turned upon the suggestions which Warrington's conversation had induced. It was not until I was in bed, and had blown out the light, that they settled upon the square, dark chamber in which my host was to pass the night. As I have said, I was wakeful, owing, no doubt, to the high pitch of the emotions which we had encouraged; but presently my fancies became inarticulate and incoherent, and then I was overtaken by profound sleep.

Warrington was up before me, as he had predicted, and met me in the breakfast-room.

"What a beggar you are to sleep!" he said, with a smile. "I've hammered at your door for half an hour."

I apologized for myself, alleging the rich country air in my defence, and mentioned that I had had some difficulty in getting to sleep.

"So, had I," he remarked, as we sat down to the table. "We got very excited, I suppose. Just see what you have there, Heywood. Eggs? Oh, damn it, one can have too much of eggs!" He frowned, and lifted a third cover. "Why in the name of common sense can't Mrs Batty give us more variety?" he asked, impatiently.

I deprecated his displeasure, suggesting that we should do very well; indeed, his discontent seemed to me quite unnecessary. But I supposed Warrington had been rather spoiled by many years of club life.

He settled himself without replying, and began to pick over his plate in a gingerly manner.

"There's one thing I will have here, Heywood," he observed. "I will have things well appointed."

"I'm not going to let life in the country mean an uncomfortable life. A man can't change the habits of a lifetime."

In contrast with his exhilarated professions of the previous evening, this struck me with a sense of amusement at the moment; and the incongruity may have occurred to him, for he went on:

"Marion's not over strong, you know, and must have things *comme il faut*. She shan't decline upon a lower level. The worst of these rustics is that they have no imagination." He held up a piece of bacon on his fork, and surveyed it with disgust. "Now, look at that! Why the devil don't they take tips from civilized people like the French?"

It was so unlike him to exhibit this petulance that I put it down to a bad night, and without discovering the connection of my thoughts, asked him how he liked his bedroom.

"Oh, pretty well, pretty well," he said, indifferently. "It's not so cold as I thought. But I slept badly. I always do in a strange bed;" and pushing aside his plate, he lit a cigarette. "When you've finished that garbage, Heywood, we'll have a stroll round the abbey," he said.

His good temper returned during our walk, and he indicated to me various improvements which he contemplated, with something of his old ardour. The left wing of the house, as I have said, was entire, but a little apart were the ruins of a chapel. Surrounded by a low mossgrown wall, it was full of picturesque charm; the roofless chancel was spread with ivy, but the aisles were intact. Grass grew between the stones and the floor, and many creepers had strayed through chinks in the wall into those sacred precincts. The solemn quietude of the ruin, maintained under the spell of death, awed me a little, but upon Warrington apparently it made no impression. He was only zealous that I should properly appreciate the distinction of such a property. I stooped and drew the weeds away from one of the slabs in the aisle, and was able to trace upon it the relics of lettering, well-nigh obliterated under the corrosion of time.

"There are tombs," said I.

"Oh, yes," he answered, with a certain relish. "I understand the Marvyns used it as a mausoleum. They are all buried here. Some good brasses, I am told."

The associations of the place engaged me; the aspect of the abbey faced the past; it seemed to refuse communion with the present; and somehow the thought of those two decent humdrum lives which should be spent within its shelter savoured of the incongruous. The white-capped maids and the emblazoned butlers that should tread these halls offered a ridiculous appearance beside my fancies of the ancient building. For all that, I envied Warrington his home, and so I told him, with a humorous hint that I was fitter to appreciate its glories than himself.

He laughed. "Oh, I don't know," said he. "I like the old-world look as much as you do. I have always had a notion of something venerable. It seems to serve you for ancestors." And he was undoubtedly delighted with my enthusiasm.

But at lunch again he chopped round to his previous irritation, only now quite another matter provoked his anger. He had received a letter by the second post from Miss Bosanquet, which, if I may judge from his perplexity, must have been unusually confused. He read and re-read it, his brow lowering.

"What the deuce does she mean?" he asked, testily. "She first makes an arrangement for us to ride over today, and now I can't make out whether we are to go to St Pharamond, or they are coming to us. Just look at it, will you, Heywood?"

I glanced through the note, but could offer no final solution, whereupon he broke out again:

"That's just like women—they never can say anything straight-forwardly. Why, in the name of goodness, couldn't she leave things as they were? You see," he observed, rather in answer, as I fancied, to my silence, "we don't know what to do now; if we stay here, they mayn't come, and if we go probably, we shall cross them." And he snapped his fingers in annoyance.

I was cheerful enough, perhaps because the responsibility was not mine, and ventured to suggest that we might ride over, and return if we missed them. But he dismissed the subject sharply by saying:

"No, I'll stay. I'm not going on a fool's errand," and drew my attention to some point in the decoration of the room.

The Bosanquets did not arrive during the afternoon, and Warrington's ill-humour increased.

His love-sick state pleaded in excuse of him, but he was certainly not a pleasant companion. He was sour and snappish, and one could introduce no statement to which he would not find a contradiction. So unamiable did he grow that at last I discovered a pretext to leave him, and rambled to the back of the abbey into the precincts of the old chapel. The day was falling, and the summer sun flared through the western windows upon the bare aisle. The creepers rustled upon the gaping walls, and the tall grasses waved in shadows over the bodies of the forgotten dead. As I stood contemplating the effect, and meditating greatly upon the anterior fortunes of the abbey, my attention fell upon a huge slab of marble, upon which the yellow light struck sharply. The faded lettering rose into greater definition before my eyes and I read slowly:

"Here lyeth the body of Sir Rupert Marvyn."

Beyond a date, very difficult to decipher, there was nothing more; of eulogy, of style, of record, of pious considerations such as were usual to the period, not a word. I read the numerals variously as 1723 and 1745; but however, they ran it was probable that the stone covered the resting-place of the last Marvyn. The history of this futile house interested me not a little, partly for Warrington's sake, and in part from a natural bent towards ancient records; and I made a mental note of the name and date.

When I returned Warrington's surliness had entirely vanished, and had given place to an effusion of boisterous spirits. He apologized jovially for his bad temper.

"It was the disappointment of not seeing Marion," he said. "You will understand that some day, old fellow. But, anyhow, we'll go over tomorrow," and forthwith proceeded to enliven the dinner with an ostentation of good-fellowship I had seldom witnessed in him. I began to suspect that he had heard again from St Pharamond, though he chose to conceal the fact from me. The wine was admirable; though Warrington himself was no great judge, he had entrusted the selection to a good palate. We had a merry meal, drank a little more than was prudent, and smoked our cigars upon the terrace in the fresh air. Warrington was restless. He pushed his glass from him. "I'll tell you what, old chap," he broke out, "I'll give you a game of billiards. I've got a decent table."

I demurred. The air was too delicious, and I was in no humour for a sharp use of my wits. He laughed, though he seemed rather disappointed.

"It's almost sacrilege to play billiards in an abbey," I said, whimsically. "What would the ghosts of the old Marvyns think?"

"Oh, hang the Marvyns!" he rejoined, crossly. "You're always talking of them."

He rose and entered the house, returning presently with a flagon of whisky and some glasses.

"Try this," he said. "We've had no liqueurs," and pouring out some spirit he swallowed it raw.

I stared, for Warrington rarely took spirits, being more of a wine drinker; moreover, he must have taken nearly the quarter of a tumbler. But he did not notice my surprise, and, seating himself, lit another cigar.

"I don't mean to have things quiet here," he observed, reflectively. "I don't believe in your stagnant rustic life. What I intend to do is to keep the place warm—plenty of house parties, things going on all the year. I shall expect you down for the shooting, Ned. The coverts promise well this year."

I assented willingly enough, and he rambled on again.

"I don't know that I shall use the abbey so much. I think I'll live in town a good deal. It's brighter there. I don't know though. I like the place. Hang it, it's a rattling good shop, there's no mistake about it. Look here," he broke off, abruptly, "bring your glass in, and I'll show

82

you something."

I was little inclined to move, but he was so peremptory that I followed him with a sigh. We entered one of the smaller rooms which overlooked the terrace, and had been diverted into a comfortable library. He flung back the windows.

"There's air for you," he cried. "Now, sit down," and walking to a cupboard produced a second flagon of whisky. "Irish!" he ejaculated, clumping it on the table. "Take your choice," and turning again to the cupboard, presently sat down with his hands under the table. "Now, then, Ned," he said, with a short laugh. "Fill up, and we'll have some fun," with which he suddenly threw a pack of cards upon the board.

I opened my eyes, for I do not suppose Warrington had touched cards since his college days; but, interpreting my look in his own way, he cried:

"Oh, I'm not married yet. Warrington's his own man still. Poker? Eh?"

"Anything you like," said I, with resignation.

A peculiar expression of delight gleamed in his eyes, and he shuffled the cards feverishly.

"Cut," said he, and helped himself to more whisky.

It was shameful to be playing there with that beautiful night without, but there seemed no help for it. Warrington had a run of luck, though he played with little skill; and his excitement grew as he won.

"Let us make it ten shillings," he suggested.

I shook my head. "You forget I'm not a millionaire," I replied. "Bah!" he cried. "I like a game worth the victory. Well, fire away." His eyes gloated upon the cards, and he fingered them with unctuous affection. The behaviour of the man amazed me. I began to win.

Warrington's face slowly assumed a dull, lowering expression; he played eagerly, avariciously; he disputed my points, and was querulous.

"Oh, we've had enough!" I cried in distaste.

"By Jove, you don't!" he exclaimed, jumping to his feet. "You're the winner, Heywood, and I'll see you damned before I let you off my revenge!"

The words startled me no less than the fury which rang in his accents. I gazed at him in stupefaction. The whites of his eyes showed wildly, and a sullen, angry look determined his face.

Suddenly I was arrested by the suspicion of something upon his neck.

"What's that?" I asked. "You've cut yourself."

He put his hand to his face. "Nonsense," he replied, in a surly fashion.

I looked closer, and then I saw my mistake. It was a round, faint red mark, the size of a florin, upon the column of his throat, and I set it down to the accidental pressure of some button.

"Come on!" he insisted, impatiently.

"Bah! Warrington," I said, for I imagined that he had been overexcited by the whisky he had taken. "It's only a matter of a few pounds. Why make a fuss? Tomorrow will serve."

After a moment his eyes fell, and he gave an awkward laugh. "Oh, well, that'll do," said he.

"But I got so infernally excited."

"Whisky," said I, sententiously.

He glanced at the bottle. "How many glasses have I had?" and he whistled. "By Jove, Ned, this won't do! I must turn over a new leaf. Come on; let's look at the night."

I was only too glad to get away from the table, and we were soon upon the terrace again.

Warrington was silent, and his gaze went constantly across the valley, where the moon was rising, and in the direction in which, as he had indicated to me, St Pharamond lay. When he said goodnight, he was still pre-occupied.

"I hope you will sleep better," he said.

"And you, too," I added.

He smiled. "I don't suppose I shall wake the whole night through," he said; and then, as I was turning to go, he caught me quickly by the arm.

"Ned," he said, impulsively and very earnestly, "don't let me make a fool of myself again. I know it's the excitement of everything. But I want to be as good as I can for her."

I pressed his hand. "All right, old fellow," I said; and we parted.

I think I have never enjoyed sounder slumber than that night. The first thing I was aware of was the singing of thrushes outside my window. I rose and looked forth, and the sun was hanging high in the eastern sky, the grass and the young green of the trees were shining with dew. With an uncomfortable feeling that I was very late I hastily dressed and went downstairs. Warrington was waiting for me in the breakfast-room, as upon the previous morning, and when he turned from the window at my approach, the sight of his face startled me. It was drawn and haggard, and his eyes were shot with blood; it was a face broken and savage with dissipation. He made no answer to my questioning, but seated himself with a morose air.

"Now you have come," he said, sullenly, "we may as well begin. But it's not my fault if the coffee's cold."

I examined him critically, and passed some comment upon his appearance.

"You don't look up to much," I said. "Another bad night?"

"No; I slept well enough," he responded, ungraciously; and then, after a pause: "I'll tell you what, Heywood. You shall give me my revenge after breakfast."

"Nonsense," I said, after a momentary silence. "You're going over to St Pharamond."

"Hang it!" was his retort, "one can't be always bothering about women. You seem mightily indisposed to meet me again."

"I certainly won't this morning," I answered, rather sharply, for the man's manner grated upon me. "This evening, if you like; and then the silly business shall end."

He said something in an undertone of grumble, and the rest of the meal passed in silence. But I entertained an uneasy suspicion of him, and after all he was my friend, with whom I was under obligations not to quarrel; and so when we rose, I approached him.

"Look here, Warrington," I said. "What's the matter with you? Have you been drinking?

"Remember what you asked me last night."

"Hold your damned row!" was all the answer he vouchsafed, as he whirled away from me, but with an embarrassed display of shame.

But I was not to be put off in that way, and I spoke somewhat more sharply.

"We're going to have this out, Warrington," I said. "If you are ill, let us understand that; but I'm not going to stay here with you in this cantankerous spirit."

"I'm not ill," he replied testily.

"Look at yourself," I cried, and turned him about to the mirror over the mantelpiece.

He started a little, and a frown of perplexity gathered on his forehead.

"Good Lord! I'm not like that, Ned," he said, in a different voice. "I must have been drunk last night." And with a sort of groan, he directed a piteous look at me.

"Come," I was constrained to answer, "pull yourself together. The ride will do you good. And no more whisky."

"No, by Heaven, no!" he cried vehemently, and seemed to shiver; but then, suddenly taking my arm, he walked out of the room.

The morning lay still and golden. Warrington's eyes went forth across the valley.

"Come round to the stables, Ned," he said, impulsively. "You shall choose you own nag."

I shook my head. "I'll choose yours," said I, "but I am not going with you." He looked surprised.

"No, ride by yourself. You don't want a companion on such an errand. I'll stay here, and pursue my investigations into the Marvyns."

A scowl crossed his face, but only for an instant, and then he answered: "All right, old chap; do as you like. Anyway, I'm off at once." And presently, when his horse was brought, he was laughing merrily.

"You'll have a dull day, Ned; but it's your own fault, you duffer. You'll have to lunch by yourself, as I shan't be back till late." And, gaily flourishing his whip, he trotted down the drive.

It was some relief to me to be rid of him, for, in truth, his moods had worn my nerves, and I had not looked for a holiday of this disquieting nature. When he returned, I had no doubt it would be with quite another face, and meanwhile I was excellent company for myself. After lunch I amused myself for half an hour with idle tricks upon the billiard-table, and, tiring of my pastime, fell upon the housekeeper as I returned along the corridor. She was a woman nearer to sixty than fifty, with a comfortable, portly figure, and an amiable expression. Her eyes invited me ever so respectfully to conversation, and stopping, I entered into talk. She inquired if I liked my room and how I slept.

"'Tis a nice look-out you have, Sir," said she. "That was where old Lady Martin slept."

It appeared that she had served as kitchen-maid to the previous tenants of the abbey, nearly fifty years before.

"Oh, I know the old house in and out," she asserted; "and I arranged the rooms with Mr Warrington."

We were standing opposite the low doorway which gave entrance to Warrington's bedroom, and my eyes unconsciously shot in that direction. Mrs Batty followed my glance.

"I didn't want him to have that," she said; "but he was set upon it. It's smallish for a bedroom, and in my opinion isn't fit for more than a lumber-room. That's what Sir William used it for."

I pushed open the door and stepped over the threshold, and the housekeeper followed me.

"No," she said, glancing round; "and it's in my mind that it's damp, Sir."

Again I had a curious feeling that the silence was speaking in my ear; the atmosphere was thick and heavy, and a musty smell, as of faded draperies, penetrated my nostrils. The whole room looked indescribably dingy, despite the new hangings. I went over to the narrow window and peered through the diamond panes. Outside, but seen dimly through that ancient and discoloured glass, the ruins of the chapel confronted me, bare and stark, in the yellow sunlight. I turned.

"There are no ghosts in the abbey, I suppose, Mrs Batty?" I asked, whimsically.

But she took my inquiry very gravely. "I have never heard tell of one, Sir," she protested; "and if there was such a thing, I should have known it."

As I was rejoining her a strange low whirring was audible, and looking up I saw in a corner of the high-arched roof a horrible face watching me out of black narrow eyes. I confess that I was very much startled at the apparition, but the next moment realized what it was. The creature hung with its ugly fleshy wings extended over a grotesque stone head that leered down upon me, its evil-looking snout projecting into the room; it lay perfectly still, returning me glance for glance, until moved by the repulsion of its presence I clapped my hands, and cried loudly; then, slowly flitting in a circle round the roof, it vanished with a flapping of wings into some darker corner of the rafters. Mrs Batty was astounded, and expressed surprise that it had managed to conceal itself for so long.

"Oh, bats live in holes," I answered. "Probably there is some small access through the masonry." But the incident had sent an uncomfortable shiver through me all the same.

Later that day I began to recognise that, short of an abrupt return to town, my time was not likely to be spent very pleasantly. But it was the personal problem so far as it concerned Warrington himself that distressed me even more. He came back from St Pharamond in a morose and ugly temper, quite alien to his kindly nature. It seems that he had quarrelled bitterly with Miss Bosanquet, but upon what I could not determine, nor did I press him for an explanation. But the fumes of his anger were still rising when we met, and our dinner was a most depressing meal.

He was in a degree of irritation which rendered it impossible to address him, and I soon withdrew into my thoughts. I saw, however, that he was drinking far too much, as, indeed, was plain subsequently when he invited me into the library. Once more he produced the hateful cards, and I was compelled to play, as he reminded me somewhat churlishly that I had promised him his revenge.

"Understand, Warrington," I said, firmly, "I play tonight, but never again, whatever the result. In fact, I am in half the mind to return to town tomorrow."

He gave me a look as he sat down, but said nothing, and the game began. He lost heavily from the first, and as nothing would content him but we must constantly raise the stakes, in a shore time I had won several hundred pounds. He bore the reverses very ill, breaking out from time to time into some angry exclamation, now petulantly questioning my playing, and muttering oaths under his breath. But I was resolved that he should have no cause of complaint against me for this one night, and disregarding his insane fits of temper, I played steadily and silently. As the tally of my gains mounted, he changed colour slowly, his face assuming a ghastly expression, and his eyes suspiciously denoting my actions. At length he rose, and throwing himself quickly across the table, seized my hand ferociously as I dealt a couple of cards.

"Damn you! I see your tricks," he cried, in frenzied passion. "Drop that hand, do you hear?"

"Drop that hand, or by—"

But he got no further, for, rising myself, I wrenched my hand from his grasp, and turned upon him, in almost as great a passion as himself. But suddenly, and even as I opened my mouth to speak, I stopped short with a cry of horror. His face was livid to the lips, his eyes were cast with blood, and upon the dirty white of his flesh, right in the centre of his throat, the round red scar, flaming and ugly as a wound, stared upon me.

"Warrington" I cried, "what is this? What have you?—" And I pointed in alarm to the spot.

"Mind your own business," he said, with a sneer. "It is well to try and draw off attention from your knavery. But that trick won't answer with me."

Without another word I flung the IOU's upon the table, and turning on my heel, left the room. I was furious with him, and fully resolved to leave the abbey in the morning. I made my way upstairs to my room, and then, seating myself upon the balcony, endeavoured to recover my self-possession.

The more I considered, the more unaccountable was Warrington's behaviour. He had always been a perfectly courteous man, with a great lump of kindness in his nature; whereas these last few days he had been nothing other than a savage. It seemed certain that he must be ill or going mad; and as I reflected upon this the conjecture struck me with a sense of pity. If it was that he was losing his senses, how horrible was the tragedy in face of the new and lovely prospects opening in his life. Stimulated by this growing conviction, I resolved to go down and see him, more particularly as I now recalled his pleading voice that I should help him, on the previous evening. Was it not possible that this pathetic appeal derived from the instinct of the insane to protect themselves?

I found him still in the library; his head had fallen upon the table, and the state of the whisky bottle by his arm showed only too clearly his condition. I shook him vigorously, and he opened his eyes.

"Warrington, you must go to bed," I said.

He smiled, and greeted me quite affectionately. Obviously, he was not so drunk as I had supposed.

"What is the time, Ned?" he asked.

I told him it was one o'clock, at which he rose briskly.

"Lord, I've been asleep," he said. "Help me, Ned. I don't think I'm sober. Where have you been?"

I assisted him to his room, and he undressed slowly, and with an effort. Somehow, as I stood watching him, I yielded to an unknown impulse and said, suddenly:

"Warrington, don't sleep here. Come and share my room."

"My dear fellow," he replied, with a foolish laugh, "yours is not the only room in the house. I can use half-a-dozen if I like."

"Well, use one of them," I answered.

He shook his head. "I'm going to sleep here," he returned, obstinately.

I made no further effort to influence him, for, after all, now that the words were out, I had absolutely no reason to give him or myself for my proposition. And so, I left him. When I had closed the door, and was turning to go along the passage, I heard very clearly, as it seemed to me, a plaintive cry, muffled and faint, but very disturbing, which sounded from the room.

Instantly I opened the door again. Warrington was in bed, and the heavy sound of his breathing told me that he was asleep. It was impossible that he could have uttered the cry. A night-light was burning by his bedside, shedding a strong illumination over the immediate vicinity, and throwing antic shadows on the walls.

As I turned to go, there was a whirring of wings, a brief flap behind me, and the room was plunged in darkness. The obscene creature that lived in the recesses of the roof must have knocked out the tiny light with its wings. Then Warrington's breathing ceased, and there was no sound at all. And then once more the silence seemed to gather round me slowly and heavily, and whisper to me. I had a vague sense of being prevailed upon, of being enticed and lured by something in the surrounding air; a sort of horror circumscribed me, and I broke from the invisible ring and rushed from the room. The door clanged behind me, and as I hastened along the hail, once more there seemed to ring in my ears the faint and melancholy cry.

I awoke, in the sombre twilight that precedes the dawn, from a sleep troubled and encumbered with evil dreams. The birds had not yet begun their day, and a vast silence brooded over the abbey gardens. Looking out of my window, I caught sight of a dark figure stealing cautiously round the corner of the ruined chapel. The furtive gait, as well as the appearance of a man at that early hour, struck me with surprise; and hastily throwing on some clothes, I ran downstairs, and, opening the hall-door, went out. When I reached the porch which gave entrance to the aisle I stopped suddenly, for there before me, with his head to the ground, and peering among the tall grasses, was the object of my pursuit. Then I stepped quickly forward and laid a hand upon his shoulder. It was Warrington.

"What are you doing here?" I asked.

He turned and looked at me in bewilderment. His eyes wore a dazed expression, and he blinked in perplexity before he replied.

"It's you, is it?" he said weakly. "I thought—" and then paused. "What is it?" he asked.

"I followed you here," I explained. "I only saw your figure, and thought it might be some intruder."

He avoided my eyes. "I thought I heard a cry out here," he answered.

"Warrington," I said, with some earnestness, "come back to bed."

He made no answer, and slipping my arm in his, I led him away. On the doorstep he stopped, and lifted his face to me.

"Do you think it's possible—" he began, as if to inquire of me, and then again paused. With a slight shiver he proceeded to his room, while I followed him. He sat down upon his bed, and his eyes strayed to the barred window absently. The black shadow of the chapel was visible through the panes.

"Don't say anything about this," he said, suddenly. "Don't let Marion know."

I laughed, but it was an awkward laugh.

"Why, that you were alarmed by a cry for help, and went in search like a gentleman?" I asked, jestingly.

"You heard it, then?" he said, eagerly.

I shook my head, for I was not going to encourage his fancies. "You had better go to sleep," I replied, "and get rid of these nightmares."

He sighed and lay back upon his pillow, dressed as he was. Ere I left him he had fallen into a profound slumber.

If I had expected a surly mood in him at breakfast, I was much mistaken. There was not a trace of his nocturnal dissipations; he did not seem even to remember them, and he made no allusion whatever to our adventure in the dawn. He perused a letter carefully, and threw it over to me with a grin.

"Lor, what queer sheep women are!" he exclaimed, with rather a coarse laugh.

I glanced at the letter without thinking, but ere I had read half of it I put it aside. It was certainly not meant for my eyes, and I marvelled at Warrington's indelicacy in making public, as it were, that very private matter. The note was from Miss Bosanquet, and was clearly designed for his own heart, couched as it was in the terms of warm and fond affection. No man should see such letters save he for whom they are written.

"You see, they're coming over to dine," he remarked, carelessly. "Trust a girl to make it up if you let her alone long enough."

I made no answer; but though Warrington's grossness irritated me, I reflected with satisfaction upon his return to good humour, which I attributed to the reconciliation.

When I moved out upon the terrace the maid had entered to remove the breakfast things. I was conscious of a slight exclamation behind me, and Warrington joined me presently, with a loud guffaw.

"That's a damned pretty girl!" he said, with unction. "I'm glad Mrs Batty got her. I like to have good-looking servants."

I suddenly interpreted the incident, and shrugged my shoulders.

"You're a perfect boor this morning, Warrington," I exclaimed, irritably.

He only laughed. "You're a dull dog of a saint, Heywood," he retorted. "Come along," and dragged me out in no amiable spirit.

I had forgotten how perfect a host Warrington could be, but that evening he was displayed at his best. The Bosanquets arrived early. Sir William was an easy-going man, fond of books and of wine, and I now guessed at the taste which had decided Warrington's cellar. Miss Bosanquet was as charming as I remembered her to be; and if any objection might be taken to Warrington himself by my anxious eyes it was merely that he seemed a trifle excited, a fault which, in the circumstances, I was able to condone. Sir William hung about the table, sipping his wine.

Warrington, who had been very abstemious, grew restless, and, finally apologizing in his graceful way, left me to keep the baronet company. I was the less disinclined to do so as I was anxious not to intrude upon the lovers, and Sir William was discussing the history of the abbey.

He had an old volume somewhere in his library which related to it, and, seeing that I was interested, invited me to look it up.

We sat long, and it was not until later that the horrible affair which I must narrate occurred.

The evening was close and oppressive, owing to the thunder, which already rumbled far away in the south. When we rose, we found that Warrington and Miss Bosanquet were in the garden, and thither we followed. As at first, we did not find them, Sir William, who had noted the approaching storm with some uneasiness, left me to make arrangements for his return; and I strolled along the paths by myself, enjoying a cigarette. I had reached the shrubbery upon the further side of the chapel, when I heard the sound of voices—a man's rough and rasping, a woman's pleading and informed with fear. A sharp cry ensued, and without hesitation I plunged through the thicket in the direction of the speakers. The sight that met me appalled me for the moment. Darkness was falling, lit with ominous flashes; and the two figures stood out distinctly in the bushes, in an attitude of struggle.

I could not mistake the voices now. I heard Warrington's, brusque with anger, and almost savage in its tones, crying, "You shall!" and there followed a murmur from the girl, a little sob, and then a piercing cry. I sprang forward and seized Warrington by the arm; when, to my horror, I perceived that he had taken her wrist in both hands and was roughly twisting it, after the cruel habit of schoolboys. The malevolent cruelty of the action so astounded me that for an instant I remained motionless; I almost heard the bones in the frail wrist cracking; and then, in a second, I had seized Warrington's hands in a grip of iron, and flung him violently to the ground. The girl fell with him, and as I picked her up he rose too, and, clenching his fists, made as though to come at me, but instead turned and went sullenly, and with a ferocious look of hate upon his face, out of the thicket.

Miss Bosanquet came to very shortly, and though the agony of the pain must have been considerable to a delicate girl, I believe it was rather the incredible horror of the act under which she swooned. For my part I had nothing to say: not one word relative to the incident dared pass my lips. I inquired if she was better, and then, putting her arm in mine, led her gently towards the house. Her heart beat hard against me, and she breathed heavily, leaning on me for support. At the chapel I stopped, feeling suddenly that I dare not let her be seen in this condition, and bewildered greatly by the whole atrocious business.

"Come and rest in here," I suggested, and we entered the chapel.

I set her on a slab of marble, and stood waiting by her side. I talked fluently about anything; for lack of a subject, upon the state of the chapel and the curious tomb I had discovered. Recovering a little, she joined presently in my remarks. It was plain that she was putting a severe restraint upon herself. I moved aside the grasses, and read aloud the inscription on Sir Rupert's grave-piece, and turning to the next, which was rankly overgrown, feigned to search further.

As I was bending there, suddenly, and by what thread of thought I know not, I identified the spot with that upon which I had found Warrington stooping that morning. With a sweep of my hand I brushed back the weeds, uprooting some with my fingers, and kneeling in the twilight, pored over the monument. Suddenly a wild flare of light streamed down the sky, and a great crash of thunder followed. Miss Bosanquet started to her feet and I to mine. The heaven was lit up, as it were, with sunlight, and, as I turned, my eyes fell upon the now uncovered stone. Plainly the lettering flashed in my eyes:

"Priscilla, Lady Marvyn."

Then the clouds opened, and the rain fell in spouts, shouting and dancing upon the ancient roof overhead.

We were under a very precarious shelter, and I was uneasy that Miss Bosanquet should run the risk of that flimsy, ravaged edifice; and so, in a momentary lull I managed to get her to the house.

I found Sir William in a restless state of nerves. He was a timorous man, and the thunder had upset him, more particularly as he and his daughter were now storm-bound for some time. There was no possibility of venturing into those rude elements for an hour or more. Warrington was not inside, and no one had seen him. In the light Miss Bosanquet's face frightened me; her eyes were large and scared, and her colour very dead white. Clearly, she was very near a breakdown. I found Mrs Batty, and told her that the young lady had been severely shaken by the storm, suggesting that she had better lie down for a little. Returning with me, the housekeeper led off the unfortunate girl, and Sir William and I were left together. He paced the room impatiently, and constantly inquired if there were any signs of improvement in the weather. He also asked for Warrington, irritably. The burden of the whole dreadful night seemed fallen upon me. Passing through the hall I met Mrs Batty again. Her usually placid features were disturbed and aghast.

"What is the matter?" I asked. "Is Miss Bosanquet—"

"No, Sir; I think she's sleeping," she replied. "She's in—she is in Mr Warrington's room."

I started. "Are there no other rooms?" I asked, abruptly.

"There are none ready, Sir, except yours," she answered, "and I thought—"

"You should have taken her there," I said, sharply. The woman looked at me and opened her mouth. "Good heavens!" I said, irritably, "what is the matter? Everyone is mad tonight."

"Alice is gone, Sir," she blurted forth.

Alice, I remembered, was the name of one of her maids.

"What do you mean?" I asked, for her air of panic betokened something graver than her words.

The thunder broke over the house and drowned her voice.

"She can't be out in this storm—she must have taken refuge somewhere," I said.

At that the strings of her tongue loosened, and she burst forth with her tale. It was an abominable narrative.

"Where is Mr Warrington?" I asked; but she shook her head.

There was a moment's silence between us, and we eyed each other aghast. "She will be all right," I said at last, as if dismissing the subject.

The housekeeper wrung her hands. "I never would have thought it!" she repeated, dismally. "I never would have thought it!"

"There is some mistake," I said; but, somehow, I knew better. Indeed, I felt now that I had almost been prepared for it.

"She ran towards the village," whispered Mrs Batty. "God knows where she was going! The river lies that way."

"Pooh!" I exclaimed. "Don't talk nonsense. It is all a mistake. Come, have you any brandy?" Brought back to the material round of her duties she bustled away with a sort of briskness, and returned with a flagon and glasses. I took a strong nip, and went back to Sir William. He was feverish, and declaimed against the weather unceasingly. I had to listen to the string of misfortunes which he recounted in the season's crops. It seemed all so futile, with his daughter involved in her horrid tragedy in a neighbouring room. He was better after some brandy, and grew more cheerful, but assiduously wondered about Warrington.

"Oh, he's been caught in the storm and taken refuge somewhere," I explained, vainly. I wondered if the next day would ever dawn.

By degrees that thunder rolled slowly into the northern parts of the sky, and only fitful flashes seamed the heavens. It had lasted now more than two hours. Sir William declared his intention of starting, and asked for his daughter. I rang for Mrs Batty, and sent her to rouse Miss Bosanquet.

Almost immediately there was a knock upon the door, and the housekeeper was in the doorway, with an agitated expression, demanding to see me. Sir William was looking out of the window, and fortunately did not see her.

"Please come to Miss Bosanquet, Sir," she cried, very scared. "Please come at once."

In alarm I hastily ran down the corridor and entered Warrington's room. The girl was lying upon the bed, her hair flowing upon the pillow; her eyes, wide open and filled with terror, stared at the ceiling, and her hands clutched and twined in the coverlet as if in an agony of pain. A gasping sound issued from her, as though she were struggling for breath under suffocation. Her whole appearance was as of one in the murderous grasp of an assailant.

I bent over. "Throw the light, quick," I called to Mrs Batty; and as I put my hand on her shoulder to lift her, the creature that lived in the chamber rose suddenly from the shadow upon the further side of the bed, and sailed with a flapping noise up to the cornice. With an exclamation of horror, I pulled the girl's head forward, and the candle-light glowed on her pallid face. Upon the soft flesh of the slender throat was a round red mark, the size of a florin.

At the sight I almost let her fall upon the pillow again; but, commanding my nerves, I put my arms round her, and, lifting her bodily from the bed, carried her from the room. Mrs Batty followed.

"What shall we do?" she asked, in a low voice.

"Take her away from this damned chamber!" I cried. "Anywhere—the hall, the kitchen rather."

I laid my burden upon a sofa in the dining-room, and despatching Mrs Batty for the brandy, gave Miss Bosanquet a draught. Slowly the horror faded from her eyes; they closed, and then she looked at me.

"What have you?—where am I?" she asked.

"You have been unwell," I said. "Pray don't disturb yourself yet."

She shuddered, and closed her eyes again.

Very little more was said. Sir William pressed for his horses, and as the sky was clearing, I made no attempt to detain him, more particularly as the sooner Miss Bosanquet left the abbey the better for herself. In half an hour she recovered sufficiently to go, and I helped her into the carriage. She never referred to her seizure, but thanked me for my kindness. That was all. No one asked after Warrington—not even Sir William. He had forgotten everything, save his anxiety to get back. As the carriage turned from the steps, I saw the mark upon the girl's throat, now grown fainter.

I waited up till late into the morning, but there was no sign of Warrington when I went to bed.

Nor had he made his appearance when I descended to breakfast. A letter in his handwriting, however, and with the London postmark, awaited me. It was a pitiful scrawl, in the very penmanship of which one might trace the desperate emotions by which he was torn. He implored my forgiveness. "Am I a devil?" he asked. "Am I mad? It was not I! It was not I!" he repeated, underlining the sentence with impetuous dashes. "You know," he wrote; "and you know, therefore, that everything is at an end for me. I am going abroad today. I shall never see the abbey again."

It was well that he had gone, as I hardly think that I could have faced him; and yet I was loth myself to leave the matter in this horrible tangle. I felt that it was enjoined upon me to meet the problems, and I endeavoured to do so as best I might. Mrs Batty gave me news of the girl Alice.

It was bad enough, though not so bad as both of us had feared. I was able to make arrangements on the instant, which I hoped might bury that lamentable affair for the time. There remained Miss Bosanquet; but that difficulty seemed beyond me. I could see no avenue out of the tragedy. I heard nothing save that she was ill—an illness attributed upon all hands to the shock of exposure to the thunderstorm. Only I knew better, and a vague disinclination to fly from the responsibilities of the position kept me hanging on at Utterbourne.

It was in those days before my visit to St Pharamond that I turned my attention more particularly to the thing which had forced itself relentlessly upon me. I was never a superstitious man; the gossip of old wives interested me merely as a curious and unsympathetic observer.

And yet I was vaguely discomfited by the transaction in the abbey, and it was with some reluctance that I decided to make a further test of Warrington's bedroom. Mrs Batty received my determination to change my room easily enough, but with a protest as to the dampness of the Stone Chamber. It was plain that her suspicions had not marched with mine. On the second night after Warrington's departure I occupied the room for the first time.

I lay awake for a couple of hours, with a reading lamp by my bed, and a volume of travels in my hand, and then, feeling very tired, put out the light and went to sleep. Nothing distracted me that night; indeed, I slept more soundly and peaceably than before in that house. I rose, too, experiencing quite an exhilaration, and it was not until I was dressing before the glass that I remembered the circumstances of my mission; but then I was at once pulled up, startled swiftly out of my cheerful temper.

Faintly visible upon my throat was the same round mark which I had already seen stamped upon Warrington and Miss Bosanquet. With that, all my former doubts returned in force, augmented and militant. My mind recurred to the bat, and tales of bloodsucking by those evil creatures revived in my memory. But when I had remembered that these were of foreign beasts, and that I was in England, I dismissed them lightly enough. Still, the impress of that mark remained, and alarmed me. It could not come by accident; to suppose so manifold a coincidence was absurd. The puzzle dwelt with me, unsolved, and the fingers of dread slowly crept over me.

Yet I slept again in the room. Having but myself for company, and being somewhat bored and dull, I fear I took more spirit than was my custom, and the result was that I again slept profoundly. I awoke about three in the morning, and was surprised to find the lamp still burning.

I had forgotten it in my stupid state of somnolence. As I turned to put it out, the bat swept by me and circled for an instant above my head. So overpowered with torpor was I that I scarcely noticed it, and my head was no sooner at rest than I was once more unconscious. The red mark was stronger next morning, though, as on the previous day, it wore off with the fall of evening.

But I merely observed the fact without any concern; indeed, now the matter of my investigation seemed to have drawn very remote. I was growing indifferent, I supposed, through familiarity.

But the solitude was palling upon me, and I spent a very restless day. A sharp ride I took in the afternoon was the one agreeable experience of the day. I reflected that if this burden were to continue, I must hasten up to town. I had no desire to tie myself to Warrington's apron, in his interest. So dreary was the evening, that after I had strolled round the grounds and into the chapel by moonlight, I returned to the library and endeavoured to pass the time with Warrington's cards.

But it was poor fun with no antagonist to pit myself against; and I was throwing down the pack in disgust when one of the manservants entered with the whisky.

It was not until long afterwards that I fully realized the course of my action; but even at the time I was aware of a curious sub-feeling of shamefacedness. I am sure that the thing fell naturally, and that there was no awkwardness in my approaching him. Nor, after the first surprise, did he offer any objection. Later he was hardly expected to do so, seeing that he was winning very quickly. The reason of that I guessed afterwards, but during the play I was amazed to note at intervals how strangely my irritation was aroused. Finally, I swept the cards to the floor, and rose, the man, with a smile in which triumph blended with uneasiness, rose also.

"Damn you, get away!" I said, angrily.

True to his traditions to the close, he answered me with respect, and obeyed; and I sat staring at the table. With a sudden flush, the grotesque folly of the night's business came to me, and my eyes fell on the whisky bottle. It was nearly empty. Then I went to bed.

Voices cried all night in that chamber—soft, pleading voices. There was nothing to alarm in them; they seemed in a manner to coo me to sleep. But presently a sharper cry roused me from my semi-slumber; and getting up, I flung open the window. The wind rushed round the abbey, sweeping with noises against the corners and gables. The black chapel lay still in the moonlight, and drew my eyes. But, resisting a strange, unaccountable impulse to go further, I went back to bed.

The events of the following day are better related without comment.

At breakfast I found a letter from Sir William Bosanquet, inviting me to come over to St Pharamond. I was at once conscious of an eager desire to do so: it seemed somehow as though I had been waiting for this. The visit assumed preposterous proportions, and I was impatient for the afternoon.

Sir William was polite, but not, as I thought, cordial. He never alluded to Warrington, from which I guessed that he had been informed of the breach, and I conjectured also that the invitation extended to me was rather an act of courtesy to a solitary stranger than due to a desire for my company. Nevertheless, when he presently suggested that I should stay to dinner, I accepted promptly. For, to say the truth, I had not yet seen Miss Bosanquet, and I experienced a strange curiosity to do so. When at last she made her appearance, I was struck, almost for the first time, by her beauty. She was certainly a handsome girl, though she had a delicate air of ill-health.

After dinner Sir William remembered by accident the book on the abbey which he had promised to show me, and after a brief hunt in the library we found it. Shortly afterwards he was called away, and with an apology left me. With a curious eagerness I turned the pages of the volume and settled down to read.

It was published early in the century, and purported to relate the history of the abbey and its owners. But it was one chapter which specially drew my interest—that which recounted the fate of the last Marvyn. The family had become extinct through a bloody tragedy; that fact held me.

The bare narrative, long since passed from the memory of tradition, was here set forth in the baldest statements. The names of Sir Rupert Marvyn and Priscilla, Lady Marvyn, shook me strangely, but particularly the latter. Some links of connection with those gravestones lying in the abbey chapel constrained me intimately. The history of that evil race was stained and discoloured with blood, and the end was in fitting harmony—a lurid holocaust of crime. There had been two brothers, but it was hard to choose between the foulness of their lives. If either, the younger, William, was the worse; so at least the narrative would have it. The details of his excesses had not survived, but it was abundantly plain that they were both notorious gamblers.

The story of their deaths was wrapt in doubt, the theme of conjecture only, and probability; for none was by to observe save the three veritable actors—who were at once involved together in a bloody dissolution. Priscilla, the wife of Sir Rupert, was suspected of an intrigue with her brother-in-law. She would seem to have been tainted with the corruption of the family into which she had married. But according to a second rumour, chronicled by the author, there was some doubt if the woman were not the worst of the three. Nothing was known of her parentage; she had returned with the passionate Sir Rupert to the abbey after one of his prolonged absences, and was accepted as his legal wife. This was the woman whose infamous beauty had brought a terrible sin between the brothers.

Upon the night which witnessed the extinction of this miserable family, the two brothers had been gambling together. It was known from the high voices that they had quarrelled, and it is supposed that, heated with wine and with the lust of play, the younger had thrown some taunt at Sir Rupert in respect to his wife. Whereupon—but this is all conjecture—the elder stabbed him to death. At least, it was understood that at this point the sounds of a struggle were heard, and a bitter cry. The report of the servants ran that upon this noise Lady Marvyn rushed into the room and locked the door behind her. Fright was busy with those servants, long used to the savage manners of the house. According to witnesses, no further sound was heard subsequently to Lady Marvyn's entrance; yet when the doors were at last broken open by the authorities, the three bodies were discovered upon the floor.

How Sir Rupert and his wife met their deaths there was no record. "This tragedy," proceeded the scribe, "took place in the Stone Chamber underneath the stairway."

I had got so far when the entrance of Miss Bosanquet disturbed me. I remember rising in a dazed condition—the room swung about me. A conviction, hitherto resisted and stealthily entertained upon compulsion, now overpowered me.

"I thought my father was here," explained Miss Bosanquet, with a quick glance round the room.

I explained the circumstances, and she hesitated in my neighbourhood with a slight air of embarrassment.

"I have not thanked you properly, Mr Heywood," she said presently, in a low voice, scarcely articulate. "You have been very considerate and kind. Let me thank you now." And ended with a tiny spasmodic sob.

Somehow, an impulse overmastered my tongue. Fresh from the perusal of that chapter, queer possibilities crowded in my mind, odd considerations urged me.

"Miss Bosanquet," said I, abruptly, "let me speak of that a little. I will not touch on details."

"Please," she cried, with a shrinking notion as of one that would retreat in very alarm.

"Nay," said I, eagerly; "hear me. It is no wantonness that would press the memory upon you."

"You have been a witness to distressful acts; you have seen a man under the influence of temporary madness. Nay, even yourself, you have been a victim to the same unaccountable phenomena."

"What do you mean?" she cried, tensely.

"I will say no more," said I. "I should incur your laughter. No, you would not laugh, but my dim suspicions would leave you still incredulous. But if this were so, and if these were the phenomena of a brief madness, surely you would make your memory a grave to bury the past."

"I cannot do that," said she, in low tones.

"What!" I asked. "Would you turn from your lover, aye, even from a friend, because he was smitten with disease? Consider; if your dearest upon earth tossed in a fever upon his bed, and denied you in his ravings, using you despitefully, it would not be he that entreated you so. When he was quit of his madness and returned to his proper person, would you not forget—would you not rather recall his insanity with the pity of affection?"

"I do not understand you," she whispered.

"You read your Bible," said I. "You have wondered at the evil spirits that possessed poor victims. Why should you decide that these things have ceased? We are too dogmatic in our modern world. Who can say under what malign influence a soul may pass, and out of its own custody?"

She looked at me earnestly, searching my eyes.

"You hint at strange things," said she, very low.

But somehow, even as I met her eyes, the spirit of my mission failed me. My gaze, I felt, devoured her ruthlessly. The light shone on her pale and comely features; they burned me with an irresistible attraction. I put forth my hand and took hers gently. It was passive to my touch, as though in acknowledgment of my kindly offices. All the while I experienced a sense of fierce elation. In my blood ran, as it had been fire, a horrible incentive, and I knew that I was holding her hand very tightly. She herself seemed to grow conscious of this, for she made an effort to withdraw her fingers, at which, the passion rushing through my body, I clutched them closer, laughing aloud. I saw a wondering look dawn in her eyes, and her bosom thinly veiled, heaved with a tiny tremor. I was aware that I was drawing her steadily to me. Suddenly her bewildered eyes, dropping from my face, lit with a flare of terror, and, wrenching her hand away, she fell back with a cry, her gaze riveted upon my throat.

"That accursed mark! What is it? What is it?—" she cried, shivering from head to foot.

In an instant, the wild blood singing in my head, I sprang towards her. What would have followed I know not, but at that moment the door opened and Sir William returned. He regarded us with consternation; but Miss Bosanquet had fainted, and the next moment he was at her side. I stood near, watching her come to with a certain nameless fury, as of a beast cheated of its prey.

Sir William turned to me, and in his most courteous manner begged me to excuse the untoward scene. His daughter, he said, was not at all strong, and he ended by suggesting that I should leave them for a time.

Reluctantly I obeyed, but when I was out of the house, I took a sudden panic. The demoniac possession lifted, and in a craven state of trembling I saddled my horse, and rode for the abbey as if my life depended upon my speed.

I arrived at about ten o'clock, and immediately gave orders to have my bed prepared in my old room. In my shaken condition the sinister influences of that stone chamber terrified me; and it was not until I had drunk deeply that I regained my composure.

But I was destined to get little sleep. I had steadily resolved to keep my thoughts off the matter until the morning, but the spell of the chamber was strong upon me. I awoke after midnight with an irresistible feeling drawing me to the room. I was conscious of the impulse, and combated it, but in the end succumbed; and throwing on my clothes, took a light and went downstairs. I flung wide the door of the room and peered in, listening, as though for some voice of welcome. It was as silent as a sepulchre; but directly I crossed the threshold voices seemed to surround and coax me. I stood wavering, with a curious fascination upon me. I knew I could not return to my own room, and I now had no desire to do so.

As I stood, my candle flaring solemnly against the darkness, I noticed upon the floor in an alcove bare of carpet, a large black mark, which appeared to be a stain. Bending down, I examined it, passing my fingers over the stone. It moved to my touch. Setting the candle upon the floor, I put my fingertips to the edges, and pulled hard. As I did so the sounds that were ringing in my ears died instantaneously;

the next moment the slab turned with a crash, and discovered a gaping hole of impenetrable blackness.

The patch of chasm thus opened to my eyes was near a yard square. The candle held to it shed a dim light upon a stone step a foot or two below, and it was clear to me that a stairway communicated with the depths. Whether it had been used as a cellar in times gone by I could not divine, but I was soon to determine this doubt; for, stirred by a strange eagerness, I slipped my legs through the hole, and let myself cautiously down with the light in my hand. There were a dozen steps to descend ere I reached the floor and what turned out to be a narrow passage. The vault ran forward straight as an arrow before my eyes, and slowly I moved on.

Dank and chill was the air in those close confines, and the sound of my feet returned from those walls dull and sullen. But I kept on, and, with infinite care, must have penetrated quite a hundred yards along that musty corridor ere I came out upon an ampler chamber. Here the air was freer, and I could perceive with the aid of my light that the dimensions of the place were lofty. Above, a solitary ray of moonlight, sliding through a crack, informed me that I was not far from the level of the earth. It fell upon a block of stone, which rose in the middle of the vault, and which I now inspected with interest. As the candle threw its flickering beams upon this I realized where I was.

I scarcely needed the rude lettering upon the coffins to acquaint me that here was the family vault of the Marvyns. And now I began to perceive upon all sides whereon my feeble light fell the crumbling relics of the forgotten dead—coffins fallen into decay, bones and grinning skulls resting in corners, disposed by the hand of chance and time. This formidable array of the mortal remains of that poor family moved me to a shudder. I turned from those ugly memorials once more to the central altar where the two coffins rested in this sombre silence. The lid had fallen from the one, disclosing to my sight the grisly skeleton of a man, that mocked and leered at me.

It seemed in a manner to my fascinated eyes to challenge my mortality, inviting me too to the rude and grotesque sleep of death. I knew, as by an instinct, that I was standing by the bones of Sir Rupert Marvyn, the protagonist in that terrible crime which had locked three souls in eternal ruin. The consideration of this miserable spectacle held me motionless for some moments, and then I moved a step closer and cast my light upon the second coffin.

As I did so I was aware of a change within myself. The grave and

103

melancholy thoughts which I had entertained, the sober bent of my solemn reflections, gave place instantly to a strange exultation, an unholy sense of elation. My pulse swung feverishly, and, while my eyes were riveted upon the tarnished silver of the plate, I stretched forth a tremulously eager hand and touched the lid. It rattled gently under my fingers.

Disturbed by the noise, I hastily withdrew them; but whether it was the impetus offered by my touch, or through some horrible and nameless circumstance—God knows—slowly and softly a gap opened between the lid and the body of the coffin! Before my startled eyes the awful thing happened, and yet I was conscious of no terror, merely of surprise and—it seems terrible to admit—of a feeling of eager expectancy.

The lid rose slowly on the one side, and as it lifted the dark space between it and the coffin grew gently charged with light. At that moment my feeble candle, which had been gradually diminishing, guttered and flickered. I seemed to catch a glimpse of something, as it were, of white and shining raiment inside the coffin; and then came a rush of wings and a whirring sound within the vault. I gave a cry, and stepping back missed my foothold; the guttering candle was jerked from my grasp, and I fell prone to the floor in darkness. The next moment a sheet of flame flashed in the chamber and lit up the grotesque skeletons about me; and at the same time a piercing cry rang forth. Jumping to my feet, I gave a dazed glance at the conflagration.

The whole vault was in flames. Dazed and horror-struck, I rushed blindly to the entrance; but as I did so the horrible cry pierced my ears again, and I saw the bat swoop round and circle swiftly into the flames. Then, finding the exit, I dashed with all the speed of terror down the passage, groping my way along the walls, and striking myself a dozen times in my terrified flight.

Arrived in my room, I pushed over the stone and listened. Not a sound was audible. With a white face and a body torn and bleeding I rushed from the room, and locking the door behind me, made my way upstairs to my bedroom. Here I poured myself out a stiff glass of brandy.

It was six months later ere Warrington returned. In the meantime, he had sold the abbey. It was inevitable that he should do so; and yet the new owner, I believe, has found no drawback in his property, and the Stone Chamber is still used for a bedroom upon occasions, being considered very old-fashioned. But there are some facts against which no appeal is possible, and so it was in his case. In my relation of the tragedy I have made no attempt at explanation, hardly even to myself; and it appears now for the first time in print, of course with suppositious names.

The Temple

Edward Benson

Frank Ingleton and I had left London early in July with the intention of spending a couple of months at least in Cornwall. This sojourn was not by any means to be a complete holiday, for he was a student of those remains of prehistoric civilisation which are found in such mysterious abundance in the ancient county, and I was employed on a book which should have already been approaching completion, but which was still lamentably far from its consummation. Naturally there was to be a little golf and a little sea-bathing for relaxation, but we were both keen on our work and meant to have gathered in a respectable harvest of industry before we returned.

The village of St. Caradoc, from all accounts, seemed likely to be favourable to our projects, for there were remains in the neighbourhood which had never been thoroughly investigated by any archaeologist, and its position on the map, remote from any of the more celebrated holiday centres, promised a reasonable tranquillity. It supplied also the desirable relaxations the club-house of a pleasantly hazardous golf-course, stood at the bottom of the hotel garden, and five minutes' walk across the sand-dunes among which the holes were placed, led to the beach. The hotel was comfortable, and at present half-empty, and fortune seemed to smile on our undertakings. We settled down, therefore without further plans. Frank meant, before he left, to visit other parts of the county, but here, within a mile of the hotel, was that curious circle of monoliths, like some Stonehenge in miniature, known as the "Council of Penruth." It had always been supposed, so Frank told me, that it was some place of Druidical worship, but he distrusted the conclusion and wanted to study it minutely on the spot.

I went there with him by way of an evening saunter on the second day after our arrival. The shortest way was along the sand-dunes, and thence up a steep, grassy slope on to the ploughed stretches of the uplands. In that warm, soft climate the wheat was in full ear, and beginning already to turn ripe and tawny. A very narrow path led across these cornfields to our destination, and from far off one could see the circle of stones, four to five feet high, standing there, black and austere, against the yellowing grain. Though all the country round was in cultivation no plough had furrowed the interior of the circle, and inside was the ancient turf of the downs, short and velvety, with patches of thyme and hare-bells. It seemed odd a plough could have passed backwards and forwards between the monoliths and a half-acre of land have been made fruitful.

"But why isn't it ploughed?" I asked.

"Oh, you're in the land of superstitions and ancient sorceries," he said. "These circles are never touched or made use of. And do you see, the path across the fields by which we have come passes round it, it doesn't run across it. There it goes again on the far side, pursuing the same line, after making the detour."

He laughed.

"The farmer of the land was up here this morning when I was making some measurements," he said. "He went round it, I noticed, and when his dog came inside after some interesting smell, he called it back, and cuffed it, and rapped out: 'Come out of that there and never do you go within again.'"

"But what's the idea?" I asked.

"Something clings to it, some curse, some abomination. They think no doubt, just as the archaeologists do, that the place has been a Druidical temple, where dreadful rites were performed and human sacrifices made. But they are all wrong this was never a temple at all, it was a Council Chamber, and the very name of it, the 'Council of Penruth,' confirms that. No doubt there was a temple somewhere about dearly should I like to find it."

It had been hot work climbing up that steep, slippery hillside from the village, and we sat down within the circle, leaning our backs against two adjacent stones, and as we sat and rested Frank explained to me the grounds of his belief.

"If you care to count them," he said, "you'll find there are twenty-one of these monoliths, against two of which you and I are leaning, and if you care to measure the distances between them you will find that they are all equal. Each stone, in fact, represents the seat of a member of the council of twenty-one. But if the place had been a temple there would have been a larger gap between two of the stones towards the east, where the gate of the temple was, facing the rising sun, and somewhere within the circle, probably exactly in the middle, there would have been a large, flat stone, which was the stone of sacrifice, where no doubt human victims were offered. Or, if the stone had disappeared, there would have been a depression where it once was. Those are the distinguishing marks of a temple, and this place lacks them. It has always been assumed that it was a temple, and it has been described as such. But I am sure I am right about it."

"But there is a temple somewhere about?" I asked.

"Certain to be. If any of these prehistoric settlements was large enough to have a council hall, it would certainly have had a temple, though the remains of it have very likely disappeared. When the country was Christianised, the old religion—if you can call it a religion—was reckoned an abomination, and the places of worship were destroyed, just as the Israelites destroyed the groves of Baal, But I mean to explore very thoroughly here: there may be remains in some of those woods down there. This is just the sort of remote place where the temple might have escaped destruction."

"And what was the ancient religion?" I asked,

"Very little is known about it. It certainly was a religion not of love but fear. The gods were the blind powers of nature, manifesting themselves in storms and destruction and plague, and had to be propitiated with human sacrifices. And the priests, of course, dealt in magic and sorcery. They were the governing class, and kept their power alive by terror. If you offended them, as likely as not you would be sent for and told that the gods required your eldest son as a blood-offering next mid-summer day at sunrise when the first beams of morning shone through the eastern gate of the temple. It was wise to be a good churchman in those days."

"It looks a kindly country nowadays," I said. "The temples of the old gods are empty."

"Yes, but it's extraordinary how old superstitions linger. It isn't a year ago that there was a witch-craft trial in Penzance. The cattle belonging to some farmer near here began to pine and die, and he went to an old woman who said that a spell had been cast on them, and that if he paid her, she could remove it. He went on paying and paying, and at last got tired of that and prosecuted her instead."

He looked at his watch.

"Let's take a stroll before dinner," he said. "Instead of going back the way we came, we might make a ramble down the hillside in front and through the woods. They look rather attractive."

"And may conceal a pagan temple," said I, getting up.

We skirted the harvest fields, and found a path leading through a big fir-wood that climbed up the hillside. The trees were of no great growth as regards height, and the prevalent wind from the south-west, to which they stood exposed, had combed and pressed their branches landwards. But the foliage of the tree-tops was very dense, making a curious sombre twilight as we penetrated deeper into the wood. There was no undergrowth whatever below them, the ground was spread thick and smooth with fallen pine needles, and with the tree trunks rising straight and column-like and that thick roof of branches above, the place looked like some great hall of nature's building.

No whisper of wind moved overhead, and so dark and still was it that you might easily have conceived yourself to be walking up the aisle of some walled-in place. The smell of the firs was thick in the air like incense, and the foot went noiselessly as over spread carpets. No birds flitted between the tree trunks or called to each other, the only noise was the murmurous buzz of flies, which sounded like some long-held organ note.

It had been hot enough outside in the fresh draught off the sea, but here where no breeze winnowed the air it was stiflingly close, and as we plunged deeper into the dimness, I was conscious of some gathering oppression of the spirit. It was an uncomfortable place, it seemed thick with unseen presences. And the same notion must have struck Frank as well.

"I feel as if we were being watched," he said. "here are eyes peeping at us from behind the trunks, and they don't like us. Now what makes so silly an idea enter my head?"

"A grove of Baal is it?" I suggested. "One that has escaped destruction and is full of the spirits of murderous priests."

"I wish it was," he said. "Then we could inquire the way to the temple."

Suddenly he pointed ahead.

"Hullo, what's that?" he said.

I followed the direction of his finger, and for one half-second thought I saw the glimmer of something white moving among the trees. But before I could focus it, it was gone. Somehow, the heat and the oppression had got on my nerves,

"Well, it's not our wood," I said. "I suppose other people have just as much right to walk here. But I've had enough of tree-trunks, I should like to have done with the wood."

Even as I spoke, I saw it was getting lighter in front of us glimmers of day began to show between the thick-set trunks, and presently we found ourselves threading the last row of the trees. The light of day poured in again and the stir of the sea breeze it was like coming out of some crowded and airless building into the open air.

We emerged into a delectable place a broad stretch of downland turf was spread in front of us, smooth and ancient turf like that in the circle, jewelled with thyme and centaury and bugloss. The path we had been following lay straight across this, and dipping down over the edge of it we came suddenly on the most enchanting little house, low and two-storied, standing in a small enclosure of lawn and garden beds. The hill behind it had evidently once been quarried, but long ago, for now the sheer sides of it were overgrown with a tangle of ivy and briony, and at their base lay a pool of water. Beyond and bordering the lawn was a copse of birches and hornbeams, which half encircled the clearing in which stood house and garden.

The house itself, smothered in honeysuckle and climbing fuchsia seemed unoccupied, for the chimneys were smokeless and the blinds drawn down over the windows. As we turned the corner of its low fence and came on to the front of it, the impression was verified, for there by the gate was a notice proclaiming that it was to be let furnished, and directing that application should be made to a house agent in St. Caradoc's.

"But it's a pocket Paradise," said I. "Why shouldn't we—"

Frank interrupted me.

"Of course, there's no reason why we shouldn't," he said. "In fact, there's every reason why we should. The manager at the hotel told me they were filling up next week and wanted to know for how long we should stop. We'll make inquiries tomorrow morning, and find the agent and the keys."

The keys next morning revealed a charm within that came up to the promise of what we had seen without, and, what was as wonderful, the agent could provide our staff as well. This consisted of a rotund and capable Cornishwoman who, with her daughter to help her, would arrive early every morning, and remain till she had served our dinner, and then go back to her cottage in St. Caradoc's. If that would suffice us, she was ready to be in charge as soon as we settled to take the little house it must be understood, however, that she would not sleep there. Without making any further inquiries, the assurance that she was a clean and capable cook and competent in every way was enough, and two days afterwards we entered into possession. The rent asked was extraordinarily low, and my suspicious mind, as we went through the house, visualised an absence of water-supply or a kitchen range that, while getting red hot, left its ovens as in the chill of an Arctic night. But no such dispiriting discoveries awaited us Mrs. Fennell turned taps and manipulated dampers, and, scouring capably through the house, pronounced on her solemn guarantee that we should be very comfortable. "But I go back to my own house at night, gentlemen," she said, "and I promise you the water will be hot and your breakfast ready for you by eight in the morning."

We entered that afternoon our luggage had been sent up an hour before, and when we arrived the portmanteaux were already unpacked and clothes bestowed in their drawers, and tea ready in the sitting-room. It and its adjoining dining-room with a small parqueted hall, formed the ground floor accommodation. Beyond the dining-room was the kitchen, the convenience of which had already satisfied Mrs. Fennell. Upstairs there were two good bedrooms, and above the kitchen two smaller servants' rooms, which, by our arrangement, would be unoccupied. There was a bathroom between the two bedrooms with a door into it from each for two friends occupying the house nothing could have been more exactly what was wanted with nothing to spare. Mrs. Fennell gave us an admirable plain dinner, and by nine o'clock she had locked the outer kitchen door and left us.

Before going to bed we wandered out into the garden, marvelling at our luck. The hotel, as the manager had told us, was already beginning to fill up, the dining-room tonight would have been a cackle of voices, the sitting-room crowded, and surely it was a wonderfully good exchange to be housed in this commodious little tranquillity of a place, with our own unobtrusive establishment that came at dawn and left at night. It remained only to see if this paragon who was so proficient in her kitchen would be as punctual in the morning.

"But I wonder why she and her daughter would not establish themselves here?" said Frank. "They live alone down in the village. You'd have thought that they would have shut their cottage up, and saved themselves a morning and evening tramp."

"Gregariousness," said I. "They like to know that there are people, just people, close at hand and to right and left. I like to know that there are not."

As I spoke we turned at the garden gate, where the notice that the house was to let had been, and my eyes, quite idly, travelled across the space of open downland to the black fringe of the wood that stood above it, and for a moment, bright, and then quenched again like the line of fire made by a match that has been struck and has not flared, I saw a light there. It was only for a second that it was visible, but it must have been somewhere inside the wood, for against that luminous streak I saw the shape of the fir trunks.

"Did you see that?" I said to Frank.

"A light in the wood?" he asked. "Yes, it has appeared there several times. Just for a moment and then disappearing again. Some farmer, perhaps, finding his way home."

That was a very sensible conclusion, and, for some reason that I did not trouble to probe, my mind hastened to adopt it. After all, who was more likely to be passing through the wood than men from the upland farms going home at closing time from the Red Lion at St. Caradoc's?

I was roused next morning out of very deep sleep by the entry of Mrs. Fennell with hot water it was a struggle to join myself up with the waking world again. I had the impression of having dreamed very vividly of things dark and dim, and of perilous places, and though I had certainly slept for something like eight hours at a stretch I felt curiously unrefreshed.

At breakfast Frank was more silent than his wont, but presently we were making plans for the day. He proposed to explore the wood again, while I was busy with my work in the afternoon a round of golf would bring us to teatime. Before he started and I settled down, we strolled about the garden that dozed tranquilly in the hot morning sun, and again congratulated ourselves on our exchange from the hotel. We went down to the pool below the quarried cliff, and there I left him to return to the house, while he, in order to start exploring at once, followed an overgrown path that led into the copse of birch and hornbeam of which I have spoken. But I had not crossed the lawn before I heard myself called.

"Come here a minute," he shouted, "I've found something interesting." I retraced my steps, and pushing through the trees found him standing by a tall, black granite stone that pushed its moss-green head above the undergrowth.

"It's a monolith," he said excitedly. "It's like one of those stones in the circle. Perhaps there has been another circle here, or, perhaps, it's a stone of the temple. It's deep in the earth, it looks as if it was in place. Let's see if we can find another in this copse."

He pushed on into the thick growing trees to the right of the path, and I, infected with his enthusiasm, made an exploration to the left. Before long I came upon another stone of the same character as the first, and my shout of discovery was echoed by his. Yet another rewarded his hunting, and as I emerged from the copse on the edge of the quarry pool, I found a fifth, standing but fallen forward in a bed of rushes that fringed the water.

In the excitement of this find, my planned studiousness was, of course, abandoned so, too, when we had eaten a hearty lunch, was the projected game of golf, and before evening we had arrived at a rough scheme of the entire place. Most of the stones were in the belt of copse that half-encircled the house, and with a tape-measure we found that these were set at uniform intervals from each other except that exactly twice that interval separated the two stones that lay due east of the circle. In the bank that lay to the south of the house several were missing, but in each case, by digging at the proper intervals, we found fragments of granite grassed over in the soil, which indicated that these stones had been broken up and used, probably, for building materials, and this conjecture of Frank's was confirmed by the discovery of pieces of granite built into the walls of the house we occupied.

He had jotted down the approximate position of the stones, and passed over to me the paper on which he had drawn his plan.

"Without doubt it's a temple," he said, "there's the double interval at the east, which I told you about, and which was the gate into it."

I looked at what he had drawn.

"Then our house stands just in the centre of it," I said.

"Yes, what vandals they were to build it just there," said he. "Probably the stone of sacrifice lies somewhere below it. Good Lord, dinner ready, Mrs. Fennell? I had no idea it was so late."

The sky had clouded over during the afternoon, and while we sat at dinner, a windless and heavy rain began to fall and thunder to mutter over the sea. Mrs. Fennell came in to enquire into our tastes for tomorrow, and as there was every appearance of a violent storm approaching, I asked her whether she and her girl would not stop here for the night and save themselves a wetting.

"No, I'll be off now, sir, thank you," she said. "We don't mind a wetting in Cornwall."

"But not very good for your rheumatism," I said. She had mentioned that she was a sufferer in this respect.

A blink of lightning flashed rather vividly across the uncurtained windows, and the rain hissed more heavily.

"No, I'll be off now," she said, "for it's late already. Goodnight, gentlemen."

We heard her turn the key in the kitchen door, and presently the figures of herself and her girl passed the window.

"Not even umbrellas," said Frank. "They'll be drenched before they get down."

"I wonder why they wouldn't stop," said I.

Frank was soon employed on preparations for a plan to scale that he was meaning to make tomorrow, and he began putting in the house, which he had ascertained stood just in the centre of the temple. The size of the ground plan of it was all he required on the scale he intended for the complete plan, and after measuring the sitting-room, passage, and dining-room, he went through into the kitchen. Meanwhile, I had settled down to the work I had intended to do this morning, and proposed to get a couple of solid hours at it before I went to bed. It was rather hard to get the thread of it again, and for some time I floundered with false starts and erased sentences, but before long I got into better form, and was already happily absorbed in it when he called me from the kitchen.

"Oh, I can't come," I said, "I'm busy."

"Just a moment, please," he shouted.

I laid down my pen and went to him. He had moved the kitchen table aside and turned up the drugget that covered the floor.

"Look there!" he said.

The floor was paved with stone of the district, very likely from the quarry just outside. But in the centre was an oblong slab of granite, some six feet by four in dimensions.

"That's a whacking big stone," I said. "Odd of them to have been at the trouble of putting that there."

"They didn't," said he. "I'll bet it was there when they laid the floor!"

Then I understood.

"The stone of sacrifice?" I asked.

"Rather. Granite and just in the centre of the temple. It can't be anything else."

Some sudden thrill of horror seized me. It was on that stone that young boys and maidens, torn from their mother's arms and bound hand and foot, were laid, while the priest, with one hand over the victim's eyes, plunged the flint knife into the smooth, white throat, sawing through the tissue till the blood spurted from the severed artery. . . . In the flickering light of the candle Frank carried the stone seemed wet and darkly glistening, and was that noise only the rain volleying on the roof, or the beating of drums to drown the cries of the victim? , . .

"It's terrible," I said, "I wish you hadn't found it."

Frank was on his knees by it, examining the surface of it. "I can't say I agree with you," he said. "It just puts the final touch of certainty on my discovery. Besides, whether I had found it or not, it would have been there just the same,"

"Well, I'm going on with my work," I said. "It's more cheerful than stones of sacrifice."

He laughed.

"I hope it's as interesting," he said.

It appeared, when I went back to it, that it was not, and try as I would I could not recapture the interest which is necessary to production of any kind. Even my eye wandered from the words I wrote, as for my mind, it would give only the most cursory glance at that for which I demanded its fixed attention. It was busy elsewhere. I found myself, at its bidding, scrutinising the shadowy corners of the room, but there was nothing there, and all the time some strange darkness, blacker than that which pressed in upon the house, began to grow upon my spirit. There was fear mingled with it, though I did not know what I was afraid of, but chiefly it was some sort of despair and depression, distant as yet and undefined, but quietly closing in upon me. . . . As I sat with my pen still in my hand, trying to analyse these perturbed and troubled sensations, I heard Frank call out sharply from the kitchen, the door of which, on my return, I had left open.

"Hullo!" he cried. "What's that? Is anyone there?"

I jumped from my seat and went to join him. He was standing close to the stove, holding his candle above his head, and looking at the door into the garden, which Mrs, Fennell had locked on her departure.

"What's the matter?" I asked.

He looked round at me, startled by the sound of my voice.

"Curious," he said, "I was just measuring the stone, when out of the corner of my eye I thought I saw that door open. But it's locked, isn't it?"

He tried the handle, but sure enough it was locked. "Optical delusion," he said. "Well, I've finished here for the present. But what a night! Frightfully oppressive, isn't it? And not a breath of air stirring."

We went back to the sitting-room. I put away my laboured manuscript and we got out the cards for a game of piquet. But after one *partie*, he rose with a yawn.

"I really don't think I could keep awake for another," he said, "I'm heavy with sleep. Let's have a breath of air, the rain seems to have stopped, and go to bed. Or are you going to sit up and work?"

I had not meant to do so, but his suggestion made me determine to have another try. There was certainly some mysterious pall of depression on me, and the wisest thing to do was to fight it.

"I shall try for half an hour," I said, "and see how it goes," and I followed him to the front door of the house. The rain, as he said, had ceased, but the darkness was impenetrable, and shuffling with our feet, we took a few steps along the gravel path to the corner of the house. There the light from the sitting-room windows cast a circle of illumination, and one could see the flower-beds glistening with the wet. Though it was night, the air was still so hot that the gravel path was steaming. Beyond that nothing was visible of the lawn or the hill that sloped up to the fir-wood. But, as we stood there, I saw, as last night, a light moving up there. Now, however, it seemed to be outside the wood, for its progress was not interrupted by the tree-trunks.

Frank saw it too, and pointed at it.

"It's too wet tonight," he said, "but tomorrow evening, I vote we go up there, and see who these nightly wanderers are. It's coming closer, and there's another of them."

Even as we looked a third light sprang up, and in another moment all had vanished again.

I carried out my intention of trying to work, but I could make nothing of it, and presently I found myself nodding over a page that contained nothing but erasures. With head bent forward, I drifted into a doze and from dozing into sleep, and when I woke, I found the lamp burning low and the wick smouldering. I seemed to have come back from some very distant place, and, only half awake, I lit a candle and quenched the lamp and went to the windows to bolt them. And then my heart stood still, for I thought I saw someone standing outside and looking in through the intervening glass. But it must have been a sleepy fancy, for now, broad awake again, I was staring at my own reflection cast by the candle on the window. I told myself that what

I had seen was no more than that, but as I creaked my way upstairs I found myself asking if I really believed that. . . .

As I dressed next morning, after another long but unrefreshing night, I began puzzling over a lost memory to which I had tried to find the clue yesterday. There was a bookcase in the sitting-room with some two or three dozen volumes in it, and opening one or two of these I had found the name Samuel Townwick inscribed in them. I knew I had seen that name not so many months ago in the daily Press, but I could not recapture the connection in which I had read it but from the recurrence of it in these books it was reasonable to conjecture that he was the owner of the house we occupied. In taking it, his name had not come up the house agent had plenary powers, and our deposit of a fortnight's rent clinched the contract. But this morning the name still haunted me, and since I had other small businesses in St. Caradoc's, I settled to walk down there and make some definite inquiry at the agent's. Frank was too busy with his plan to accompany me, and I set out alone.

The feeling of depression and vague foreboding was more leaden than ever this morning, and I was aware by that sixth sense, which needs no speech or language, that he was a prey to the same causeless weight. But I had not gone fifty yards from the house when the burden of it was lifted from me, and I knew again the exhilaration proper to such a morning. The rain of last evening had cleared the air, the sea breeze drew lightly landwards, and, as if I had come out of some tunnel, I rejoiced in the morning splendour. The village hummed with holiday: Mr. Cranston received me with polite enquiries as to our comfort and Mrs. Fennell's capability, and having assured him on that score, I approached my point.

"Mr. Samuel Townwick is the owner, is he not?" I asked.

The agent's smile faded a little.

"He was, sir," he said. "I act for the executors."

Suddenly, in a flash, some of what I had been groping for came back to me. "I begin to remember," I said. "He died suddenly there was an inquest, I want to know the rest. Hadn't you better tell me?"

He shifted his glance and came back to me again.

"It was a painful affair," he said. "The executors naturally do not want it talked about."

Another glimpse of what I had forgotten blinked on my memory.

"Suicide," I said. "The usual verdict of unsound mind was brought in. And—and is that why Mrs. Fennell won't sleep in the house? She left last night in a deluge of rain."

I readily gave him my promise of secrecy, for I had not the slightest desire to tell Frank, and he told me the rest. Mr, Townwick had been for some days in a very depressed state of mind, and one morning the servants coming down had found him lying underneath the kitchen table with his throat cut. Beside him was a sharp, curiously-shaped fragment of flint covered with blood. The jagged nature of the wound had confirmed the idea that he had sawn at his throat till he had severed the jugular vein. Murder was ruled out, for he was a strong man, and there were no marks on his body or about the room of there having been any struggle, nor any sign of an assailant having entered. Both kitchen doors were locked on the inside, his valuables were untouched, and from the position of the body the only reasonable inference was that he had laid down under the table, and there deliberately done himself to death. . . . I repeated my assurance of silence and went out.

I knew now what the source of my nameless horror and depression had been. It was no haunting spectre of Townwick that I feared it was the power, whatever that was, which had driven him to kill himself on the stone of sacrifice.

I went back up the hill: there was the garden blazing in the July noon, and the sweet tranquillity of the place was spread abroad in the air. But I had no sooner passed the copse and come within the circle than the dead weight of something unseen began to lay its burden on me again. There was something here, horrible and menacing and potent

I found Frank in the sitting-room. His head was bent over his plan, and he started as I entered.

"Hullo!" he said. "I've made all my measurements and I want to sit tight and finish my plan today. I don't know why, but I feel I must hurry about it and get it done. And I've got the most awful fit of the blues. I can't account for it, but anyhow, occupation is the best thing. Go into lunch, will you, I don't want any."

I looked at him and saw some indefinable change had come over his face. There was terror in his eyes that came from within I can express it in no other way than that.

"Anything wrong?" I asked.

"No just blues. I want to go on working. This evening, you know, we have to see where those lights come from."

All afternoon he sat close over his work, and it was not till the day was fading that he got up.

"That's done," he said. "Good Lord, we have found a temple and a half! And I'm horribly tired. I shall have a snooze till dinner."

The invasion of fear beleaguered me, it seemed to pour in through the open windows in the gathering dusk, it gathered its reinforcements outside, ready to support the onrush of it. And yet how childish it was to yield to it. By now we were alone in the house, for we had told Mrs. Fennell that a cold meal would serve us in this heat, and while Frank slept, I had heard the lock of the outside kitchen door turn and she and the girl went by the window.

Presently he stirred and awoke. I had lit the lamp, and I saw his hand feel in his waistcoat pocket, and he drew out a small object which he held out to me.

"A flint knife," he said. "I picked it up in the garden this morning. It's got a fine edge to it."

At that I felt a prickle of terror run through the hair of my head, and I jumped up.

"Look here," I said, "you've had no walk today, and that always gives you the blues. Let's go down and dine at the hotel."

His head was outside the illumination of the lamp, and from the dimness there came a curious cackle of laughter.

"But I can't," he said. "How strange that you don't know that I can't. They've surrounded the place, and there's no way out. Listen! Can't you hear the drums and the squeal of their pipes? And their hands are about me. Christ! It's terrible to die."

He got up and began to move with curious little shuffling steps towards the kitchen. I had laid the flint knife down on the table and he snatched it up. The horror of presences unseen and multitudinous closed in round me, but I knew they were concentrated not on me, but on him. They poured in, not through the window alone but through the solid walls of the house outside on the lawn there were lights moving, slow and orderly.

I had still control of my mind, the awfulness and the imminence of what so closely beset us gave me the courage and clearness of despair. I darted from my chair and stood with my back to the kitchen door.

"You're not to go in there," I said. "You must come away with me out of this. Pull yourself together, Frank. We'll get through yet once outside the garden we're safe."

He paid no attention to what I said it was as if he did not hear me. He laid his hand on my shoulder, and I felt his fingers press through the muscles and grind like points of steel on the underlying bone. Some maniac force possessed them, and he pulled me aside as if I had been a feather.

There was one thing only to be done. With my disengaged arm I hit him full on the chin, and he fell like a log across the floor. Without pausing for a second I gripped him round the knees and began dragging him senseless and inert towards the door.

It is difficult to state in words what those next few minutes held. I saw nothing, I heard nothing. I felt no touch of invisible hands upon me, but I can imagine no grinding agony of pain that wrenches body and soul asunder to equal that war of the evil and the unseen that raged about me. I struggled against no visible adversary, and there was the horror of it, for I am sure that no phantom of the dead that die not could have evoked so unnerving a terror.

Before those intangible hosts had fully closed in round me and my unconscious burden, I had got him on to the lawn, and it was then that the full stress of their beleaguering might poured in upon me. Strange fugitive lights wavered round me and muttered voices filled the air, and as I dragged Frank over the grass his weight seemed to grow till it was not a man's body that I was pulling along, but something well-nigh immovable, so that I had to tug and pant for breath and tug again.

"God help us both," I heard myself muttering. "Deliver us from our ghostly enemies . . ." and again I tugged and panted for breath. Close at hand now was the ring of enclosing copse, where the stones of the circle stood, and I made one final effort of concentration, for I knew that my spirit was spent, and soon there would be no power of fight left in me at all.

"In the name of the Holiest, and by the power of the Highest," I cried aloud, and waited for a moment, gathering what dregs of strength were still left in me. And then I leaned forward, and the strained sinews of my legs were slackened as the weight of Frank's body moved after me, and I made another step, and yet another, and we had passed beyond the copse, and out of the accursed precinct.

I knew no more after that. I had fallen forwards half across him, and when I regained my senses he was stirring, and the dew of the grass was on my face. There stood the house, with the lamp still burning in the window of the sitting-room, and the quiet night was around us, with a clear and starry heaven.

Let Loose

Mary Cholmondeley

The dead abide with us! Though stark and cold
Earth seems to grip them, they are with us still.

Some years ago, I took up architecture, and made a tour through
Holland, studying the buildings of that interesting country. I was not
then aware that it is not enough to take up art. Art must take you up,
too. I never doubted but that my passing enthusiasm for her would be
returned. When I discovered that she was a stern mistress, who did not
immediately respond to my attentions, I naturally transferred them to
another shrine. There are other things in the world besides art. I am
now a landscape gardener.

But at the time of which I write I was engaged in a violent flirta-
tion with architecture. I had one companion on this expedition, who
has since become one of the leading architects of the day. He was
a thin, determined-looking man with a screwed-up face and heavy
jaw, slow of speech, and absorbed in his work to a degree which I
quickly found tiresome. He was possessed of a certain quiet power of
overcoming obstacles which I have rarely seen equalled. He has since
become my brother-in-law, so I ought to know; for my parents did
not like him much and opposed the marriage, and my sister did not
like him at all, and refused him over and over again; but, nevertheless,
he eventually married her.

I have thought since that one of his reasons for choosing me as his
travelling companion on this occasion was because he was getting up
steam for what he subsequently termed 'an alliance with my family',
but the idea never entered my head at the time. A more careless man
as to dress I have rarely met, and yet, in all the heat of July in Holland,
I noticed that he never appeared without a high, starched collar, which

had not even fashion to commend it at that time.

I often chaffed him about his splendid collars, and asked him why he wore them, but without eliciting any response. One evening, as we were walking back to our lodgings in Middeburg, I attacked him for about the thirtieth time on the subject.

'Why on earth do you wear them?' I said.

'You have, I believe, asked me that question many times,' he replied, in his slow, precise utterance; 'but always on occasions when I was occupied. I am now at leisure, and I will tell you.'

And he did.

I have put down what he said, as nearly in his own words as I can remember them.

Ten years ago, I was asked to read a paper on English Frescoes at the Institute of British Architects. I was determined to make the paper as good as I could, down to the slightest details, and I consulted many books on the subject, and studied every fresco I could find. My father, who had been an architect, had left me, at his death, all his papers and note-books on the subject of architecture. I searched them diligently, and found in one of them a slight unfinished sketch of nearly fifty years ago that specially interested me. Underneath was noted, in his clear, small hand—Frescoed east wall of crypt. Parish Church. Wet Waste-on-the-Wolds, Yorkshire (*via* Pickering).

The sketch had such a fascination for me that I decided to go there and see the fresco for myself. I had only a very vague idea as to where Wet Waste-on-the-Wolds was, but I was ambitious for the success of my paper; it was hot in London, and I set off on my long journey not without a certain degree of pleasure, with my dog Brian, a large nondescript brindled creature, as my only companion.

I reached Pickering, in Yorkshire, in the course of the afternoon, and then began a series of experiments on local lines which ended, after several hours, in my finding myself deposited at a little out-of-the-world station within nine or ten miles of Wet Waste. As no conveyance of any kind was to be had, I shouldered my portmanteau, and set out on a long white road that stretched away into the distance over the bare, treeless wold. I must have walked for several hours, over a waste of moorland patched with heather, when a doctor passed me, and gave me a lift to within a mile of my destination. The mile was a long one, and it was quite dark by the time I saw the feeble glimmer of lights in front of me, and found that I had reached Wet Waste. I had considerable difficulty in getting any one to take me in; but at last I persuaded the owner of the public-house to give me a bed, and, quite tired out, I got into it as soon as possible, for fear he should change his mind, and fell asleep to the sound of a little stream below my window.

I was up early next morning, and inquired directly after breakfast the way to the clergyman's house, which I found was close at hand. At Wet Waste everything was close at hand. The whole village seemed composed of a straggling row of one-storeyed grey stone houses, the same colour as the stone walls that separated the few fields enclosed from the surrounding waste, and as the little bridges over the beck that ran down one side of the grey wide street. Everything was grey.

The church, the low tower of which I could see at a little distance, seemed to have been built of the same stone; so was the parsonage when I came up to it, accompanied on my way by a mob of rough, uncouth children, who eyed me and Brian with half-defiant curiosity.

The clergyman was at home, and after a short delay I was admitted. Leaving Brian in charge of my drawing materials, I followed the serv-ant into a low panelled room, in which, at a latticed window, a very old man was sitting. The morning light fell on his white head bent low over a litter of papers and books.

'Mr er—?' he said, looking up slowly, with one finger keeping his place in a book.

'Blake.'

'Blake,' he repeated after me, and was silent.

I told him that I was an architect; that I had come to study a fresco in the crypt of his church, and asked for the keys.

'The crypt,' he said, pushing up his spectacles and peering hard at me. 'The crypt has been closed for thirty years. Ever since—' and he stopped short.

'I should be much obliged for the keys,' I said again.

He shook his head.

'No,' he said. 'No one goes in there now.'

'It is a pity,' I remarked, 'for I have come a long way with that one object'; and I told him about the paper I had been asked to read, and the trouble I was taking with it.

He became interested. 'Ah!' he said, laying down his pen, and re-moving his finger from the page before him, 'I can understand that. I also was young once, and fired with ambition. The lines have fallen to me in somewhat lonely places, and for forty years I have held the cure of souls in this place, where, truly, I have seen but little of the world, though I myself may be not unknown in the paths of literature. Possibly you may have read a pamphlet, written by myself, on the Syrian version of the Three Authentic Epistles of Ignatius?'

'Sir,' I said, 'I am ashamed to confess that I have not time to read even the most celebrated books. My one object in life is my art. *Ars longa, vita brevis*, you know.'

'You are right, my son,' said the old man, evidently disappointed, but looking at me kindly.

'There are diversities of gifts, and if the Lord has entrusted you with a talent, look to it. Lay it not up in a napkin.'

I said I would not do so if he would lend me the keys of the crypt. He seemed startled by my recurrence to the subject and looked undecided.

'Why not?' he murmured to himself. 'The youth appears a good youth. And superstition! What is it but distrust in God!'

He got up slowly, and taking a large bunch of keys out of his pocket, opened with one of them an oak cupboard in the corner of the room.

'They should be here,' he muttered, peering in; 'but the dust of many years deceives the eye.

See, my son, if among these parchments there be two keys; one of iron and very large, and the other steel, and of a long thin appearance.'

I went eagerly to help him, and presently found in a back drawer two keys tied together, which he recognised at once.

'Those are they,' he said. 'The long one opens the first door at the bottom of the steps which go down against the outside wall of the church hard by the sword graven in the wall. The second opens (but it is hard of opening and of shutting) the iron door within the passage leading to the crypt itself. My son, is it necessary to your treatise that you should enter this crypt?'

I replied that it was absolutely necessary.

'Then take them,' he said, 'and in the evening you will bring them to me again.'

I said I might want to go several days running, and asked if he would not allow me to keep them till I had finished my work; but on that point he was firm.

'Likewise,' he added, 'be careful that you lock the first door at the foot of the steps before you unlock the second, and lock the second also while you are within. Furthermore, when you come out lock the iron inner door as well as the wooden one.'

I promised I would do so, and, after thanking him, hurried away, delighted at my success in obtaining the keys. Finding Brian and my sketching materials waiting for me in the porch, I eluded the vigilance of my escort of children by taking the narrow private path between the parsonage and the church which was close at hand, standing in a quadrangle of ancient yews.

The church itself was interesting, and I noticed that it must have arisen out of the ruins of a previous building, judging from the number of fragments of stone caps and arches, bearing traces of very early carving, now built into the walls. There were incised crosses, too, in some places, and one especially caught my attention, being flanked by a large sword. It was in trying to get a nearer look at this that I stumbled, and, looking down, saw at my feet a flight of narrow stone steps green with moss and mildew. Evidently this was the entrance to the crypt. I at once descended the steps, taking care of my footing, for they were damp and slippery in the extreme.

Brian accompanied me, as nothing would induce him to remain behind. By the time I had reached the bottom of the stairs, I found myself almost in darkness, and I had to strike a light before I could find the keyhole and the proper key to fit into it. The door, which was of wood, opened inwards fairly easily, although an accumulation of mould and rubbish on the ground outside showed it had not been used for many years. Having got through it, which was not altogether an easy matter, as nothing would induce it to open more than about eighteen inches, I carefully locked it behind me, although I should have preferred to leave it open, as there is to some minds an unpleasant feeling in being locked in anywhere, in case of a sudden exit seeming advisable.

I kept my candle alight with some difficulty, and after groping my way down a low and of course exceedingly dank passage, came to another door. A toad was squatting against it, who looked as if he had been sitting there about a hundred years. As I lowered the candle to the floor, he gazed at the light with unblinking eyes, and then retreated slowly into a crevice in the wall, leaving against the door a small cavity in the dry mud which had gradually silted up round his person. I noticed that this door was of iron, and had a long bolt, which, however, was broken.

Without delay, I fitted the second key into the lock, and pushing the door open after considerable difficulty, I felt the cold breath of the crypt upon my face. I must own I experienced a momentary regret at locking the second door again as soon as I was well inside, but I felt it my duty to do so. Then, leaving the key in the lock, I seized my candle and looked round. I was standing in a low vaulted chamber with groined roof, cut out of the solid rock. It was difficult to see where the crypt ended, as further light thrown on any point only showed other rough archways or openings, cut in the rock, which had probably served at one time for family vaults.

A peculiarity of the Wet Waste crypt, which I had not noticed in other places of that description, was the tasteful arrangement of skulls and bones which were packed about four feet high on either side. The skulls were symmetrically built up to within a few inches of the top of the low archway on my left, and the shin bones were arranged in the same manner on my right. But the fresco! I looked round for it in vain. Perceiving at the further end of the crypt a very low and very massive archway, the entrance to which was not filled up with bones, I passed under it, and found myself in a second smaller chamber. Holding my candle above my head, the first object its light fell upon was— the fresco, and at a glance I saw that it was unique.

Setting down some of my things with a trembling hand on a rough stone shelf hard by, which had evidently been a credence table, I examined the work more closely. It was a reredos over what had probably been the altar at the time the priests were proscribed. The fresco belonged to the earliest part of the fifteenth century, and was so perfectly preserved that I could almost trace the limits of each day's work in the plaster, as the artist had dashed it on and smoothed it out with his trowel. The subject was the Ascension, gloriously treated. I can hardly describe my elation as I stood and looked at it, and reflected that this magnificent specimen of English fresco painting would be made known to the world by myself. Recollecting myself at last, I opened my sketching bag, and, lighting all the candles I had brought with me, set to work.

Brian walked about near me, and though I was not otherwise than glad of his company in my rather lonely position, I wished several times I had left him behind. He seemed restless, and even the sight of so many bones appeared to exercise no soothing effect upon him. At last, however, after repeated commands, he lay down, watchful but motionless, on the stone floor.

I must have worked for several hours, and I was pausing to rest my eyes and hands, when I noticed for the first time the intense stillness that surrounded me. No sound from me reached the outer world. The church clock which had clanged out so loud and ponderously as I went down the steps, had not since sent the faintest whisper of its iron tongue down to me below. All was silent as the grave. This was the grave. Those who had come here had indeed gone down into silence. I repeated the words to myself, or rather they repeated themselves to me.

Gone down into silence.

I was awakened from my reverie by a faint sound. I sat still and listened. Bats occasionally frequent vaults and underground places.

The sound continued, a faint, stealthy, rather unpleasant sound. I do not know what kinds of sounds bats make, whether pleasant or otherwise. Suddenly there was a noise as of something falling, a momentary pause—and then—an almost imperceptible but distant jangle as of a key.

I had left the key in the lock after I had turned it, and I now regretted having done so. I got up, took one of the candles, and went back into the larger crypt—for though I trust I am not so effeminate as to be rendered nervous by hearing a noise for which I cannot instantly account; still, on occasions of this kind, I must honestly say I should prefer that they did not occur. As I came towards the iron door, there was another distinct (I had almost said hurried) sound. The impression on my mind was one of great haste. When I reached the door, and held the candle near the lock to take out the key, I perceived that the other one, which hung by a short string to its fellow, was vibrating slightly. I should have preferred not to find it vibrating, as there seemed no occasion for such a course; but I put them both into my pocket, and turned to go back to my work.

As I turned, I saw on the ground what had occasioned the louder noise I had heard, namely, a skull which had evidently just slipped from its place on the top of one of the walls of bones, and had rolled almost to my feet. There, disclosing a few more inches of the top of an archway behind, was the place from which it had been dislodged. I stooped to pick it up, but fearing to displace any more skulls by meddling with the pile, and not liking to gather up its scattered teeth, I let it lie, and went back to my work, in which I was soon so completely absorbed that I was only roused at last by my candles beginning to burn low and go out one after another.

Then, with a sigh of regret, for I had not nearly finished, I turned to go. Poor Brian, who had never quite reconciled himself to the place, was beside himself with delight. As I opened the iron door he pushed past me, and a moment later I heard him whining and scratching, and I had almost added, beating, against the wooden one. I locked the iron door, and hurried down the passage as quickly as I could, and almost before I had got the other one ajar there seemed to be a rush past me into the open air, and Brian was bounding up the steps and out of sight. As I stopped to take out the key, I felt quite deserted and left behind. When I came out once more into the sunlight, there was a vague sensation all about me in the air of exultant freedom.

It was already late in the afternoon, and after I had sauntered back to the parsonage to give up the keys, I persuaded the people of the public-house to let me join in the family meal, which was spread out in the kitchen. The inhabitants of Wet Waste were primitive people, with the frank, unabashed manner that flourishes still in lonely places, especially in the wilds of Yorkshire; but I had no idea that in these days of penny posts and cheap newspapers such entire ignorance of the outer world could have existed in any corner, however remote, of Great Britain.

When I took one of the neighbour's children on my knee—a pretty little girl with the palest aureole of flaxen hair I had ever seen—and began to draw pictures for her of the birds and beasts of other countries, I was instantly surrounded by a crowd of children, and even grown-up people, while others came to their doorways and looked on from a distance, calling to each other in the strident unknown tongue which I have since discovered goes by the name of 'Broad Yorkshire'.

The following morning, as I came out of my room, I perceived that something was amiss in the village. A buzz of voices reached me as I passed the bar, and in the next house I could hear through the open window a high-pitched wail of lamentation.

The woman who brought me my breakfast was in tears, and in answer to my questions, told me that the neighbour's child, the little girl whom I had taken on my knee the evening before, had died in the night.

I felt sorry for the general grief that the little creature's death seemed to arouse, and the uncontrolled wailing of the poor mother took my appetite away.

I hurried off early to my work, calling on my way for the keys, and with Brian for my companion descended once more into the crypt, and drew and measured with an absorption that gave me no time that day to listen for sounds real or fancied. Brian, too, on this occasion seemed quite content, and slept peacefully beside me on the stone floor. When I had worked as long as I could, I put away my books with regret that even then I had not quite finished, as I had hoped to do. It would be necessary to come again for a short time on the morrow. When I returned the keys late that afternoon, the old clergyman met me at the door, and asked me to come in and have tea with him.

'And has the work prospered?' he asked, as we sat down in the long, low room, into which I had just been ushered, and where he seemed to live entirely.

I told him it had, and showed it to him.

'You have seen the original, of course?' I said.

'Once,' he replied, gazing fixedly at it. He evidently did not care to be communicative, so I turned the conversation to the age of the church.

'All here is old,' he said. 'When I was young, forty years ago, and came here because I had no means of mine own, and was much moved to marry at that time, I felt oppressed that all was so old; and that this place was so far removed from the world, for which I had at times longings grievous to be borne; but I had chosen my lot, and with it I was forced to be content. My son, marry not in youth, for love, which truly in that season is a mighty power, turns away the heart from study, and young children break the back of ambition. Neither marry in middle life, when a woman is seen to be but a woman and her talk a weariness, so you will not be burdened with a wife in your old age.

I had my own views on the subject of marriage, for I am of opinion that a well-chosen companion of domestic tastes and docile and devoted temperament may be of material assistance to a professional man. But my opinions once formulated, it is not of moment to me to discuss them with others, so I changed the subject, and asked if the neighbouring villages were as antiquated as Wet Waste 'Yes, all about here is old,' he repeated. 'The paved road leading to Dyke Fens is an ancient pack road, made even in the time of the Romans. Dyke Fens, which is very near here, a matter of but four or five miles, is likewise old, and forgotten by the world.

'The Reformation never reached it. It stopped here. And at Dyke Fens they still have a priest and a bell, and bow down before the saints. It is a damnable heresy, and weekly I expound it as such to my people, showing them true doctrines; and I have heard that this same priest has so far yielded himself to the Evil One that he has preached against me as withholding gospel truths from my flock; but I take no heed of it, neither of his pamphlet touching the Clementine Homilies, in which he vainly contradicts that which I have plainly set forth and proven beyond doubt, concerning the word Asaph.'

The old man was fairly off on his favourite subject, and it was some time before I could get away. As it was, he followed me to the door, and I only escaped because the old clerk hobbled up at that moment, and claimed his attention.

The following morning, I went for the keys for the third and last time. I had decided to leave early the next day. I was tired of Wet Waste, and a certain gloom seemed to my fancy to be gathering over the place. There was a sensation of trouble in the air, as if, although the day was bright and clear, a storm were coming.

This morning, to my astonishment, the keys were refused to me when I asked for them. I did not, however, take the refusal as, final—I make it a rule never to take a refusal as final—and after a short delay I was shown into the room where, as usual, the clergyman was sitting, or rather, on this occasion, was walking up and down.

'My son,' he said with vehemence, 'I know wherefore you have come, but it is of no avail. I cannot lend the keys again.'

I replied that, on the contrary, I hoped he would give them to me at once.

'It is impossible,' he repeated. 'I did wrong, exceeding wrong. I will never part with them again.'

'Why not?'

He hesitated, and then said slowly:

'The old clerk, Abraham Kelly, died last night.' He paused, and then went on: 'The doctor has just been here to tell me of that which is a mystery to him. I do not wish the people of the place to know it, and only to me he has mentioned it, but he has discovered plainly on the throat of the old man, and also, but more faintly on the child's, marks as of strangulation. None but he has observed it, and he is at a loss how to account for it. I, alas! can account for it but in one way, but in one way!'

I did not see what all this had to do with the crypt, but to humour the old man, I asked what that way was.

'It is a long story, and, haply, to a stranger it may appear but foolishness, but I will even tell it; for I perceive that unless I furnish a reason for withholding the keys, you will not cease to entreat mc for them.

'I told you at first when you inquired of me concerning the crypt, that it had been closed these thirty years, and so it was. Thirty years ago, a certain Sir Roger Despard departed this life, even the Lord of the manor of Wet Waste and Dyke Fens, the last of his family, which is now, thank the Lord, extinct. He was a man of a vile life, neither fearing God nor regarding man, nor having compassion on innocence, and the Lord appeared to have given him over to the tormentors even in this world, for he suffered many things of his vices, more especially from drunkenness, in which seasons, and they were many, he was as one possessed by seven devils, being an abomination to his household and a root of bitterness to all, both high and low.

'And, at last, the cup of his iniquity being full to the brim, he came to die, and I went to exhort him on his deathbed; for I heard that terror had come upon him, and that evil imaginations encompassed him so thick on every side, that few of them that were with him could abide in his presence. But when I saw him, I perceived that there was no place of repentance left for him, and he scoffed at me and my superstition, even as he lay dying, and swore there was no God and no angel, and all were damned even as he was. And the next day, towards evening, the pains of death came upon him, and he raved the more exceedingly, inasmuch as he said he was being strangled by the Evil One.

'Now on his table was his hunting knife, and with his last strength he crept and laid hold upon it, no man withstanding him, and swore a great oath that if he went down to burn in hell, he would leave one of his hands behind on earth, and that it would never rest until it had drawn blood from the throat of another and strangled him, even as he himself was being strangled. And he cut off his own right hand at the wrist, and no man dared go near him to stop him, and the blood went through the floor, even down to the ceiling of the room below, and thereupon he died.

'And they called me in the night, and told me of his oath, and I for I thought it better he should take it with him, so that he might have it, I counselled that no man should speak of it, and I took the dead hand, which none had ventured to touch, and I laid it beside him in his coffin; if haply some day after much tribulation he should perchance be moved to stretch forth his hands towards God. But the story got spread about, and the people were affrighted, so, when he came to be buried in the place of his fathers, he being the last of his family, and the crypt likewise full, I had it closed, and kept the keys myself, and suffered no man to enter therein anymore; for truly he was a man of an evil life, and the devil is not yet wholly overcome, nor cast chained into the lake of fire.

'So, in time the story died out, for in thirty years much is forgotten. And when you came and asked me for the keys, I was at the first minded to withhold them; but I thought it was a vain superstition, and I perceived that you do but ask a second time for what is first refused;

so I let you have them, seeing it was not an idle curiosity, but a desire to improve the talent committed to you, that led you to require them.'

The old man stopped, and I remained silent, wondering what would be the best way to get them just once more.

'Surely, sir,' I said at last, 'one so cultivated and deeply read as yourself cannot be biased by an idle superstition.'

'I trust not,' he replied, 'and yet—it is a strange thing that since the crypt was opened two people have died, and the mark is plain upon the throat of the old man and visible on the young child. No blood was drawn, but the second time the grip was stronger than the first. The third time, perchance—'

'Superstition such as that,' I said with authority, 'is an entire want of faith in God. You once said so yourself.'

I took a high moral tone which is often efficacious with conscientious, humble-minded people.

He agreed, and accused himself of not having faith as a grain of mustard seed; but even when I had got him so far as that, I had a severe struggle for the keys. It was only when I finally explained to him that if any malign influence had been let loose the first day, at any rate, it was out now for good or evil, and no further going or coming of mine could make any difference, that I finally gained my point. I was young, and he was old; and, being much shaken by what had occurred, he gave way at last, and I wrested the keys from him.

I will not deny that I went down the steps that day with a vague, indefinable repugnance, which was only accentuated by the closing of the two doors behind me. I remembered then, for the first time, the faint jangling of the key and other sounds which I had noticed the first day, and how one of the skulls had fallen. I went to the place where it still lay. I have already said these walls of skulls were built up so high as to be within a few inches of the top of the low archways that led into more distant portions of the vault. The displacement of the skull in question had left a small hole just large enough for me to put my hand through.

I noticed for the first time, over the archway above it, a carved coat-of-arms, and the name, now almost obliterated, of Despard. This, no doubt, was the Despard vault. I could not resist moving a few more skulls and looking in, holding my candle as near the aperture as I could. The vault was full. Piled high, one upon another, were old coffins, and remnants of coffins, and strewn bones. I attribute my present determination to be cremated to the painful impression produced on me by this spectacle. The coffin nearest the archway alone was intact, save for a large crack across the lid. I could not get a ray from my candle to fall on the brass plates, but I felt no doubt this was the coffin of the wicked Sir Roger. I put back the skulls, including the one which had rolled down, and carefully finished my work. I was not there much more than an hour, but I was glad to get away.

If I could have left Wet Waste at once I should have done so, for I had a totally unreasonable longing to leave the place; but I found that only one train stopped during the day at the station from which I had come, and that it would not be possible to be in time for it that day.

Accordingly, I submitted to the inevitable, and wandered about with Brian for the remainder of the afternoon and until late in the evening, sketching and smoking. The day was oppressively hot, and even after the sun had set across the burnt stretches of the Wolds, it seemed to grow very little cooler. Not a breath stirred. In the evening, when I was tired of loitering in the lanes, I went up to my own room, and after contemplating afresh my finished study of the fresco, I suddenly set to work to write the part of my paper bearing upon it. As a rule, I write with difficulty, but that evening words came to me with winged speed, and with them a hovering impression that I must make haste, that I was much pressed for time. I wrote and wrote, until my candles guttered out and left me trying to finish by the moonlight, which, until I endeavoured to write by it, seemed as clear as day.

I had to put away my MS., and, feeling it was too early to go to bed, for the church clock was just counting out ten, I sat down by the open window and leaned out to try and catch a breath of air. It was a night of exceptional beauty; and as I looked out my nervous haste and hurry of mind were allayed. The moon, a perfect circle, was—if so poetic an expression be permissible—as it were, sailing across a calm sky. Every detail of the little village was as clearly illuminated by its beams as if it were broad day; so, also, was the adjacent church with its primeval yews, while even the Wolds beyond were dimly indicated, as if through tracing paper.

I sat a long time leaning against the window-sill. The heat was still intense. I am not, as a rule, easily elated or readily cast down; but as I sat that light in the lonely village on the moors, with Brian's head against my knee, how, or why, I know not, a great depression gradually came upon me.

My mind went back to the crypt and the countless dead who had been laid there. The sight of the goal to which all human life, and strength, and beauty, travel in the end, had not affected me at the time, but now the very air about me seemed heavy with death.

What was the good, I asked myself, of working and toiling, and grinding down my heart and youth in the mill of long and strenuous effort, seeing that in the grave folly and talent, idleness and labour lie together, and are alike forgotten? Labour seemed to stretch before me till my heart ached to think of it, to stretch before me even to the end of life, and then came, as the recompense of my labour—the grave. Even if I succeeded, if, after wearing my life threadbare with toil, I succeeded, what remained to me in the end? The grave. A little sooner, while the hands and eyes were still strong to labour, or a little later, when all power and vision had been taken from them; sooner or later only—the grave.

I do not apologise for the excessively morbid tenor of these reflections, as I hold that they were caused by the lunar effects which I have endeavoured to transcribe. The moon in its various quarterings has always exerted a marked influence on what I may call the subdominant, namely, the poetic side of my nature.

I roused myself at last, when the moon came to look ill upon me where I sat, and, leaving the window open, I pulled myself together and went to bed.

I fell asleep almost immediately, but I do not fancy I could have been asleep very long when I was wakened by Brian. He was growling in a low, muffled tone, as he sometimes did in his sleep, when his nose was buried in his rug. I called out to him to shut up; and as he did not do so, turned in bed to find my match box or something to throw at him. The moonlight was still in the room, and as I looked at him, I saw him raise his head and evidently wake up. I admonished him, and was just on the point of falling asleep when he began to growl again in a low, savage manner that waked me most effectually.

Presently he shook himself and got up, and began prowling about the room. I sat up in bed and called to him, but he paid no attention. Suddenly I saw him stop short in the moonlight; he showed his teeth, and crouched down, his eyes following something in the air. I looked at him in horror. Was he going mad? His eyes were glaring, and his head moved slightly as if he were following the rapid movements of an enemy.

Then, with a furious snarl, he suddenly sprang from the ground, and rushed in great leaps across the room towards me, dashing himself against the furniture, his eyes rolling, snatching and tearing wildly in the air with his teeth. I saw he had gone mad. I leaped out of bed, and rushing at him, caught him by the throat. The moon had gone behind a cloud; but in the darkness I felt him turn upon me, felt him rise up, and his teeth close in my throat. I was being strangled. With all the strength of despair, I kept my grip of his neck, and, dragging him across the room, tried to crush in his head against the iron rail of my bedstead. It was my only chance. I felt the blood running down my neck. I was suffocating. After one moment of frightful struggle, I beat his head against the bar and heard his skull give way. I felt him give one strong shudder, a groan, and then I fainted away.

When I came to myself, I was lying on the floor, surrounded by the people of the house, my reddened hands still clutching Brian's throat. Someone was holding a candle towards me, and the draught from the window made it flare and waver. I looked at Brian. He was stone dead. The blood from his battered head was trickling slowly over my hands. His great jaw was fixed in something that—in the uncertain light—I could not see.

They turned the light a little.

'Oh, God!' I shrieked. 'There! Look! Look!'

'He's off his head,' said someone, and I fainted again.

I was ill for about a fortnight without regaining consciousness, a waste of time of which even now I cannot think without poignant regret. When I did recover consciousness, I found I was being carefully nursed by the old clergyman and the people of the house. I have often heard the unkindness of the world in general inveighed against, but for my part I can honestly say that I have received many more kindnesses than I have time to repay. Country people especially are remarkably attentive to strangers in illness.

I could not rest until I had seen the doctor who attended me, and had received his assurance that I should be equal to reading my paper on the appointed day. This pressing anxiety removed, I told him of what I had seen before I fainted the second time. He listened attentively, and then assured me, in a manner that was intended to be soothing, that I was suffering from an hallucination, due, no doubt, to the shock of my dog's sudden madness.

'Did you see the dog after it was dead?' I asked.

He said he did. The whole jaw was covered with blood and foam; the teeth certainly seemed convulsively fixed, but the case being evidently one of extraordinarily virulent hydrophobia, owing to the intense heat, he had had the body buried immediately.

My companion stopped speaking as we reached our lodgings, and went upstairs. Then, lighting a candle, he slowly turned down his collar.

'You see I have the marks still,' he said, 'but I have no fear of dying of hydrophobia. I am told such peculiar scars could not have been made by the teeth of a dog. If you look closely you see the pressure of the five fingers. That is the reason why I wear high collars.'

Haunted by Spirits

George Manville Fenn

"But what an out-of-the-way place to get to," I said, after being most cordially received by my old school fellow and his wife, one bitter night after a long ride. "But you really are glad to see me, eh?"

"Now, hold your tongue, do," cried Ned and his wife in a breath. "You won't get away again under a month, so don't think it. But where we are going to put you I don't know," said Ned.

"Oh, I can sleep anywhere, chairs, table, anything you like; only make me welcome. Fine old house this seems, but however came you to take it?"

"Got it cheap, my boy. Been shut up for twenty years. It's haunted, and no one will live in it. But I have it full for this Christmas, at all events, and what's more I have some potent spirits in the place too, but they are all corked down tightly, so there is no fear at present. But I say, Lilly," cried Ned, addressing his wife, "why we shall have to go into the haunted room and give him our place."

"That you won't," I said. "I came down here on purpose to take you by surprise, and to beg for a snack of dinner on Christmas-Day; and now you are going to give me about the greatest treat possible, a bed in a haunted room. What kind of a ghost is it?"

"You mustn't laugh," said Ned, trying to appear very serious; "for there is not a soul living within ten miles of this place, that would not give you a long account of the horrors of the Red Chamber: of spots of blood upon the bedclothes coming down in a regular rain; noises; clashing of swords; shrieks and groans; skeletons or transparent bodies. Oh, my dear fellow, you needn't grin, for it's all gospel truth about here, and if we did not keep that room screwed up, not a servant would stay in the house."

"Wish I could buy it and take it away," I said.

"I wish you could, indeed," cried Ned, cordially.

Half an hour after Ned and I were busy with screwdriver and candle busy in the large corridors, turning the rusty screws which held a large door at the extreme end of the house. First one and then another was twirled out till nothing held the door but the lock; the key for which Ned Harrington now produced from his pocket—an old, many-warded, rusty key, at least a couple of hundred years old.

"Hold the candle a little lower," said Ned, "here's something in the keyhole," when pulling out his knife, he picked out a quantity of paper, evidently very recently stuffed in. He then inserted the key, and after a good deal of effort it turned, and the lock shot back with a harsh, grating noise. Ned then tried the handle, but the door remained fast; and though he tugged and tugged, it still stuck, till I put one hand to help him, when our united efforts made it come open with a rush, knocking over the candle, and there we were standing upon the portal of the haunted room in the dark.

"I'll fetch a light in a moment out of the hall," said Ned, and he slipped off, while I must confess to a certain feeling of trepidation on being left alone, listening to a moaning, whistling noise, which I knew to be the wind, but which had all the same a most dismal effect upon my nerves, which, in spite of my eagerness to be the inmate of the closed room, began to whisper very strongly that they did not like it at all. But the next minute Ned was beside me with the light, and we entered the gloomy dusty old chamber—a bedchamber furnished after the fashion of the past century. The great four-post bedstead looked heavy and gloomy, and when we drew back the curtains, I half expected to see a body lying in state, but no, all was very dusty, very gloomy, and soul chilling, but nothing more.

"Come, there's plenty of room for a roaring fire," said Ned, "and I think after all we had better come here ourselves, and let you have our room."

"That you will not," I said, determinedly. "Order them to light a fire, and have some well-aired things put upon that bed, and it will be a clever ghost that wakes me tonight, for I'm as tired as a dog."

"Here, Mary," shouted Ned to one of the maids, "coals and wood here, and a broom."

We waited about, peering here and there at the old toilet-ware and stands, the old chest of drawers and armoire, old chairs and paintings, for all seemed as if the room had been suddenly quitted; while inside a huge cupboard beside the fireplace hung a dusty horseman's cloak, and in the corner were a long thin rapier and a quaint old-fashioned firelock.

"Strikes chilly and damp," said I, snuffing the smell of old boots and fine dust.

"Ah, but we'll soon drive that out," said Ned. "But you'd better give in, my boy. 'Pon my word, I'm ashamed to let you come in here."

"Pooh! nonsense!" I said. "Give me a roaring fire, and that's all I want."

"Ah!" cried Ned. "But what a while that girl is;" and then he stepped out into the passage. "Why, what are you standing there for?" he cried. "Come and light this fire."

"Plee', sir, I dussent," said the maid.

"Here, give me hold," cried Ned, in a pet; "and send your mistress here;" and then he made his appearance with a coal-scuttle, paper, and wood; when between us we soon had a fire alight and roaring up the huge chimney, while the bright flames flickered and danced, and gave quite a cheerful aspect to the place.

"Well," cried Mrs Harrington, who now appeared, "how are you getting on?" but neither Ned's wife nor her sister stood looking, for, in spite of all protestations, dressed as they were, they set to sweeping, dusting, airing linen, bed, mattress, *etcetera*, we helping to the best of our ability—for no maid, either by threats or persuasion, would enter the place—and at last we made the place look, if not comfortable, at all events less dismal than before we entered. The old blinds came down like so much tinder when touched, while, as to the curtains, the first attempt to draw them brought down such a cloud of dust, that they were left alone, though Mrs Harrington promised that the place should be thoroughly seen to in the morning.

Returning to the drawing-room, the remainder of the evening was most agreeably spent; while the cause of my host and hostess's prolonged absence produced endless comments and anecdotes respecting the Red Chamber—some of them being so encouraging in their nature that Ned Harrington, out of sheer compassion, changed the conversation.

"Well, my boy," said Ned, when the ladies had all retired for the night, "you shan't go to bed till the witching hour is past;" so he kept me chatting over old times, till the clock had gone one—the big old turret-clock, whose notes flew booming away upon the frosty air. "Christmas-Eve tomorrow, so we'll have a tramp on the moors after the wild ducks—plenty out here. I say, my boy, I believe this is the original Moated Grange, so don't be alarmed if you hear the mice."

"There's only one thing I care for," I said, "and that is anything in the shape of a practical joke."

"Honour bright! my boy," said Ned; "you need fear nothing of that kind;" and then I was alone in the Haunted Chamber, having locked myself in.

My first proceeding was to give the large fire an extra poke, which sent a flood of light across the room, and the flames gushing up the chimney; my next, to take one of the candles and make a tour of my bedroom, during which I looked under the bed, behind the curtains, and into armoire and cupboard, but discovered nothing. Next thing I tried the windows, through which I could just dimly see the snow-white country, but they were fast and blackened with dirt. The chimney-glass, too, was so injured by damp, that the dim reflection given back was something startling, being more like a bad photograph of life-size than anything else; and at length, having fully made up my mind that I was alone, and that, as far as I could make out, there were neither trap-doors nor secret passages in the wall, I undressed, put out the candles, and plunged into bed.

But I was wrong in what I had said to my host about sleeping, for I never felt more wakeful in my life. I watched the blaze of the fire sink down to a ruddy glow, the glow turn blacker and blacker till at last the fire was all but extinct, while the room was dark as could be. But my eyesight was painfully acute, while my hearing seemed strained to catch the slightest passing sound. The wind roared and rumbled in the great chimney, and swept sighing past the windows; and, though it had a strange, wild sound with it, yet I had heard the wind before, and therefore paid but little heed to its moans.

All at once the fire seemed to fall together with a tinkling sound, a bright flame leaped up, illumining the room for a moment, then becoming extinct, and leaving all in darkness; but there was light for a long enough interval for me to see, or fancy I saw, the cupboard door open and the great horseman's cloak stand out in a weird-like manner before me, as though covering the shoulders of some invisible figure.

I felt warm—then hot—then in a profuse perspiration, but I told myself it was fancy, punched my pillow, and turned over upon the other side to sleep. Now came a long, low, dreary moan, hollow and heartrending, for it seemed like the cry of someone in distress; when I raised myself upon one elbow and listened.

"Old cowl on a chimney," I muttered, letting myself fall back again, now thoroughly determined to sleep, but the moaning continued, the wind whistled and howled, while now came a gentle *tap, tap, tapping* at my window, as if someone was signalling to be admitted.

"*Tap, tap, tap*;" still it kept on, as though whoever tapped was fearful of making too much noise; and at length, nerving myself, I slipped out of bed, crossed the room, and found that the closet door was open, but a vigorous poke inside produced nothing but dust and two or three very sharp sneezes. So, I fastened the door, and listened. All silent: but the next moment began the tapping upon the dirty window-pane again; and, impelled by a mingled sensation of fear and attraction, I crept closer to the sash, and at length made out the shadow of something tapping at the glass.

"Bah! Bah!" I exclaimed the next moment as I shuffled across the room and back to my bed, "strand of ivy and the wind." But I was not to be at peace yet, for now there came a most unmistakable noise behind the wainscot—louder and louder, as if someone were trying to tear a piece of the woodwork down. The place chosen seemed to be the corner beside the cupboard; and at last, having made up my mind that it was the rats, I dropped off to sleep, and slept soundly till morning, when I heard the cheery voice of my host at the door.

"Oh, all right," he said as I answered; "I only came because the girl knocked, and said that something must be the matter, for she could not make you hear."

On descending to breakfast, I found that I was to undergo a rigorous cross-examination as to what I had seen and heard; but one elderly lady present shook her head ominously, freely giving it as her opinion that it was little better than sacrilege to open the haunted chamber, and finishing a very solemn peroration with the words—

"Stop a bit; they don't walk every night."

This was encouraging, certainly; but in the course of the afternoon I went up to my room, and found that it had been well cleaned out, while many little modern appliances had been added to the dingy furniture, so that it wore quite a brightened appearance. The insides of the windows had been cleaned, and a man was then upon a ladder polishing away at the exterior, when I drew his attention to a number of loose ivy strands, which he cut off.

In the cupboard I found plenty of traces of rats in the shape of long-gnawed-off fragments of wood pushed beneath the skirting-board; while, upon holding my head against the chimney, the groaning of the cowl was plainly to be heard, as it swung round dolefully upon some neighbouring chimney.

A pleasant day was spent, and then, after a cosy evening, I was once more ushered into the chamber of horrors, this time being escorted by the whole of the visitors, the gentlemen affectionately bidding me farewell, but not one seeming disposed to accept my offer of changing rooms. However, Ned and Mrs Harrington both wished me to go to their room, when I of course refused; and once more I was alone.

It was now about half-past twelve and Christmas-morning, a regular storm was hurrying round the house, and a strange feeling of crepitation came upon me when I had extinguished the light; and then on climbing into bed I sat and listened for a while, laid my head upon my pillow, and the next moment, or what seemed the next moment, I was startled by a strange beating sound, and as I became aware of a dim, peculiar light, penetrating the room, I heard a low, muffled voice cry appealingly—

"Your hot water, sir—quarter to eight!" while I could hardly believe my eyes had been closed.

Christmas-day passed as it generally does in the country, that is to say, in a most jovial, sociable way; and after fun, frolic, sport, pastime, forfeit, dance, and cards, I stood once more within the haunted chamber with the strange sensation upon me, that though I had met with nothing so far to alarm me—this night, a night when, of all nights in the year, spirits might be expected to break loose, I was to suffer for my temerity.

As soon as I entered and secured the door, I felt that something was wrong, but I roused up the fire, lit the wax candles upon the dressing-table, and then looked round the room.

Apparently, I was alone, but upon opening the big closet door, the great cloak fell down with a ghostly rustle, while a peculiar odour seemed to rise from the heap. The long, thin sword too, fell, with a strange clanging noise as I hastily closed the door, and then setting down the candle tried to compose myself to look at matters in a calm, philosophical manner. But things would not be looked at in that way, and now I began to feel that I was being punished for all, since the next moment I could see the eyes of the large portrait between the windows gleam and roll, now showing the whites, now seeming to pierce me, so intense was their gaze. Then the figure seemed to be slowly coming down from the frame nearer and nearer, till it was close to me, when it slowly receded, and a shade passed over the canvas, so that it was gone.

But for shame and the fear of ridicule, I should have opened the door and cried for aid; in fact, I believe I did rise from the chair and try to reach the door, but some invisible power drew me into a corner of the room, where I leaned panting against the wall to gaze upon a fresh phenomenon. I had brought a chamber candlestick into the room, and after igniting the pair of candles upon the toilet table, placed the flat candlestick between them, and left it alight, but now— no—yes—I rubbed my eyes—there was no mistake.

There were six candles burning.

I started, shook myself, muttering that it was deception; but no, there burned six candles, while their flames were big and blurred with a large, ghastly, blue halo round each, that had a strange weird light; and now I tried to recall what I had read in old ghost stories about corpse candles, for I felt that these three must be of that character.

In an agony of fear I tried to run up to the dressing-table to dash the weird lights over, but again the same strange influence guided my steps, so that I curved off to the bed, where I sat down, trembling in every limb—limbs that refused their office—while I gazed upon the candles which now began to float backwards and forwards before me, till I could bear the strange sight no more, and throwing myself back, I buried my face in the bed.

But there was no relief here, for as I threw myself down at full length, the great bedstead gave a crack, a rattle, and a bound, and then in an agony of dread I was clinging to the bedding, for the huge structure began to rise slowly higher—higher—higher—sailing away apparently upon the wings of the wind, and then again sinking lower and lower and lower to interminable depths, so that I involuntarily groaned and closed my eyes. But that was of no avail, for I could feel the great bedstead career, now on one side, now on the other, and ever going onward through space like some vessel upon a vast aerial sea.

The rapid gliding upward, in spite of the dread, seemed attended with somewhat of an exhilarating effect; but the falling was hideous in the extreme—for now it was slowly and gently, but the next moment the speed was fearful, and I lay trembling in expectation of feeling the structure dash upon the ground, while every time I unclosed my eyes I could see the gyrating candles, and turned giddy with confusion.

And now, with one tremendously swift gliding swoop, away we went, faster and faster, more rapidly than swallows upon the wing. Space seemed obliterated; and, by the rushing noise and singing in my ears, I could feel that the bedstead was careering on where the atmosphere was growing more and more attenuated, while soon, from the catching of my breath, I felt sure that we should soon be beyond air altogether. The candles were gone, but there were stars innumerable, past which we sped with inconceivable rapidity, so that their light seemed continued in one long luminous streak, while ever more and more the speed was increasing, till it seemed that we were attached to some mighty cord, and being whirled round and round with frightful velocity, as if at the end of the string; and now I trembled for the moment when the cord should be loosed, and we should fly off into illimitable space, to go on—on—on for ever!

At last it came, and away I went; but now separated from the bedstead, to which I had clung to the last. On—on—on, with something large and undefined in front of me, which I felt that I should strike, though I was powerless to prevent the collision. Nearer—nearer—nearer, but ever darting along like a shooting-star in its course, I was swept on, till, with a fearful crash, I struck what I now found to be the lost bed, and tried to cling to it once more; but, no! I rolled off, and fell slowly and gradually lower—lower, and evidently out of the sphere of the former attraction, so that at last I fell, with only a moderate bump, upon the floor, when, hastily rising, I found all totally dark, and that the bedpost was beside me; when, shudderingly dragging off some of the clothes on to the carpet, I rolled myself in them, and went off into a heavy sleep.

The next morning several of my friends made remarks upon my pale and anxious looks; and soon after breakfast, Ned beckoned me into his study, and begged of me to tell him whether I had been disturbed.

For a few minutes I felt that I could not tell of the horrors of the past night, even though I had vowed to sleep in the haunted room still; but at last I began my recital, and had arrived at the point where the bedstead set sail, when Ned jumped up, crying:

"Why, I thought from your looks that you really had been disturbed. But I say, old boy, I suppose we must look over it, as it's Christmas; but, do you know, judging by my own feelings, I think I'd better make the punch rather less potent tonight."

"Well, really," I said, "I think so too."

"Do you?" said Ned.

"Oh, yes," I said, "for my head aches awfully;" and no wonder, seeing how it had been Haunted by Spirits!

A Strange Goldfield

Guy Boothby

Of course, nine out of every ten intelligent persons will refuse to believe that there could be a grain of truth in the story I am now going to tell you. The tenth may have some small faith in my veracity, but what I think of his intelligence I am going to keep to myself.

In a certain portion of a certain Australian Colony two miners, when out prospecting in what was then, as now, one of the dreariest parts of the Island Continent, chanced upon a rich find.

They applied to Government for the usual reward, and in less than a month three thousand people were settled on the Field. What privations they had to go through to get there, and the miseries they had to endure when they did reach their journey's end, have only a remote bearing on this story, but they would make a big book.

I should explain that between Railhead and the Field was a stretch of country some three hundred miles in extent. It was badly watered, vilely grassed, and execrably timbered. What was even worse, a considerable portion of it was made up of red sand, and everybody who has been compelled to travel over that knows what it means. Yet these enthusiastic seekers after wealth pushed on, some on horseback, some in bullock-waggons, but the majority travelled on foot; the graves, and the skeletons of cattle belonging to those who had preceded them punctuating the route, and telling them what they might expect as they advanced.

That the Field did not prove a success is now a matter of history, but that same history, if you read between the lines, gives one some notion of what the life must have been like while it lasted. The water supply was entirely insufficient, provisions were bad and ruinously expensive; the men themselves were, as a rule, the roughest of the rough, while the less said about the majority of the women the better. Then typhoid stepped in and stalked like the Destroying Angel through the camp.

Its inhabitants went down like sheep in a drought, and for the most part rose no more. Where there had been a lust of gold there was now panic, terror—every man feared that he might be the next to be attacked, and it was only the knowledge of those terrible three hundred miles that separated them from civilisation that kept many of them on the Field. The most thickly populated part was now the cemetery. Drink was the only solace, and under its influence such scenes were enacted as I dare not describe. As they heard of fresh deaths, men shook their fists at Heaven, and cursed the day when they first saw pick or shovel. Some, bolder than the rest, cleared out just as they stood; a few eventually reached civilisation, others perished in the desert. At last the Field was declared abandoned, and the dead were left to take their last long sleep, undisturbed by the clank of windlass or the blow of pick.

It would take too long to tell all the different reasons that combined to draw me out into that 'most distressful country'. Let it suffice that our party consisted of a young Englishman named Spicer, a wily old Australian bushman named Matthews, and myself. We were better off than the unfortunate miners, inasmuch as we were travelling with camels, and our outfits were as perfect as money and experience could make them. The man who travels in any other fashion in that country is neither more nor less than a madman. For a month past we had been having a fairly rough time of it, and were then on our way south, where we had reason to believe rain had fallen, and, in consequence, grass was plentiful. It was towards evening when we came out of a gully in the ranges and had our first view of the deserted camp. We had no idea of its existence, and for this reason we pulled up our animals and stared at it in complete surprise. Then we pushed on again, wondering what on earth place we had chanced upon.

'This is all right,' said Spicer, with a chuckle. 'We're in luck. Grog shanties and stores, a bath, and perhaps girls.'

I shook my head.

'I can't make it out,' I said. 'What's it doing out here?'

Matthews was looking at it under his hand, and, as I knew that he had been out in this direction on a previous occasion, I asked his opinion.

'It beats me,' he replied; 'but if you ask me what I think I should say it's Gurunya, the Field that was deserted some four or five years back.'

'Look here,' cried Spicer, who was riding a bit on our left, 'what are all these things—graves, as I'm a living man. Here, let's get out of this. There are hundreds of them and before I know where I am old Polyphemus here will be on his nose.'

What he said was correct—the ground over which we were riding was literally bestrewn with graves, some of which had rough, tumble-down head boards, others being destitute of all adornment. We turned away and moved on over safer ground in the direction of the Field itself.

Such a pitiful sight I never want to see again. The tents and huts, in numerous cases, were still standing, while the claims gaped at us on every side like new-made graves. A bullock dray, weather-worn but still in excellent condition, stood in the main street outside a grog shanty whose sign-board, strange incongruity, bore the name of 'The Killarney Hotel'. Nothing would suit Spicer but that he must dismount and go in to explore. He was not long away, and when he returned it was with a face as white as a sheet of paper.

'You never saw such a place,' he almost whispered. 'All I want to do is to get out of it. There's a skeleton on the floor in the back room with an empty rum bottle alongside it.'

He mounted, and, when his beast was on its feet once more, we went on our way. Not one of us was sorry when we had left the last claim behind us.

Half a mile or so from the Field the country begins to rise again. There is also a curious cliff away to the left, and, as it looked like being a likely place to find water, we resolved to camp there. We were within a hundred yards or so of this cliff when an exclamation from Spicer attracted my attention.

'Look!' he cried. 'What's that?'

I followed the direction in which he was pointing, and, to my surprise, saw the figure of a man running as if for his life among the rocks. I have said the figure of a man, but, as a matter of fact, had there been baboons in the Australian bush, I should have been inclined to have taken him for one.

'This is a day of surprises,' I said. 'Who can the fellow be? And what makes him act like that?'

We still continued to watch him as he proceeded on his erratic course along the base of the cliff—then he suddenly disappeared.

'Let's get on to camp,' I said, 'and then we'll go after him and en-deavour to settle matters a bit.'

Having selected a place, we off-saddled and prepared our camp. By this time, it was nearly dark, and it was very evident that, if we wanted to discover the man we had seen, it would be wise not to postpone the search too long. We accordingly strolled off in the direction he had taken, keeping a sharp look-out for any sign of him. Our search, however, was not successful. The fellow had disappeared without leaving a trace of his whereabouts behind him, and yet we were all certain that we had seen him. At length we returned to our camp for supper, completely mystified. As we ate our meal, we discussed the problem and vowed that, on the morrow, we would renew the search. Then the full moon rose over the cliff, and the plain immediately became well-nigh as bright as day.

I had lit my pipe and was stretching myself out upon my blankets when something induced me to look across at a big rock, some half-dozen paces from the fire. Peering round it, and evidently taking an absorbing interest in our doings, was the most extraordinary figure I have ever beheld. Shouting something to my companions, I sprang to my feet and dashed across at him. He saw me and fled. Old as he apparently was, he could run like a jack-rabbit, and, though I have the reputation of being fairly quick on my feet, I found that I had all my work cut out to catch him. Indeed, I am rather doubtful as to whether I should have done so at all had he not tripped and measured his length on the ground. Before he could get up, I was on him.

'I've got you at last, my friend,' I said. 'Now you just come along back to the camp, and let us have a look at you.'

In reply he snarled like a dog and I believe would have bitten me had I not held him off. My word, he was a creature, more animal than man, and the reek of him was worse than that of our camels. From what I could tell he must have been about sixty years of age—was below the middle height, had white eyebrows, white hair and a white beard. He was dressed partly in rags and partly in skins, and went barefooted like a black fellow. While I was overhauling him, the others came up—whereupon we escorted him back to the camp.

'What wouldn't Barnum give for him?' said Spicer. 'You're a beauty, my friend, and no mistake. What's your name?'

The fellow only grunted in reply—then, seeing the pipes in our mouths, a curious change came over him, and he muttered something that resembled 'Give me.'

'Wants a smoke,' interrupted Matthew's. 'Poor beggar's been without for a long time, I reckon. Well, I've got an old pipe, so he can have a draw.'

He procured one from his pack saddle, filled it and handed it to the man, who snatched it greedily and began to puff away at it.

'How long have you been out here?' I asked, when he had squatted himself down alongside the fire.

'Don't know,' he answered, this time plainly enough.

'Can't you get back?' continued Matthews, who knew the nature of the country on the other side.

'Don't want to,' was the other's laconic reply. 'Stay here.'

I heard Spicer mutter, 'Mad—mad as a March hare.'

We then tried to get out of him where he hailed from, but he had either forgotten or did not understand. Next, we inquired how he managed to live. To this he answered readily enough, 'Carnies.'

Now the carny is a lizard of the iguana type, and eaten raw would be by no means an appetizing dish. Then came the question that gives me my reason for telling this story. It was Spicer who put it.

'You must have a lonely time of it out here,' said the latter. 'How do you manage for company?'

'There is the Field,' he said, 'as sociable a Field as you'd find.'

'But the Field's deserted, man,' I put in. 'And has been for years.'

The old fellow shook his head.

'As sociable a Field as ever you saw,' he repeated. 'There's Sailor Dick and 'Frisco, Dick Johnson, Cockney Jim, and half a hundred of them. They're taking it out powerful rich on the Golden South, so I heard when I was down at "The Killarney", a while back.'

It was plain to us all that the old man was, as Spicer had said, as mad as a hatter. For some minutes he rambled on about the Field, talking rationally enough, I must confess that is to say, it would have seemed rational enough if we hadn't known the true facts of the case. At last he got on to his feet, saving. 'Well, I must be going—they'll be expecting me. It's my shift on with Cockney Jim.'

'But you don't work at night,' growled Matthews, from the other side of the fire.

'We work always,' the other replied. 'If you don't believe me, come and see for yourselves.'

'I wouldn't go back to that place for anything,' said Spicer.

But I must confess that my curiosity had been aroused, and I determined to go, if only to see what this strange creature did when he got there. Matthews decided to accompany me, and, not wishing to be left alone, Spicer at length agreed to do the same. Without looking round, the old fellow led the way across the plain towards the Field. Of all the nocturnal excursions I have made in my life, that was certainly the most uncanny. Not once did our guide turn his head, but pushed on at a pace that gave us some trouble to keep up with him. It was only when we came to the first claim that he paused.

'Listen,' he said, 'and you can hear the camp at work. Then you'll believe me.'

We did listen, and as I live, we could distinctly hear the rattling of sluice-boxes and cradles, the groaning of windlasses—in fact, the noise you hear on a goldfield at the busiest hour of the day.

We moved a little closer, and, believe me or not, I swear to you I could see, or thought I could see, the shadowy forms of men moving about in that ghostly moonlight. Meanwhile the wind sighed across the plain, flapping what remained of the old tents and giving an additional touch of horror to the general desolation. I could hear Spicer's teeth chattering behind me, and, for my own part, I felt as if my blood were turning to ice.

'That's the claim, the Golden South, away to the right there,' said the old man, 'and if you will come along with me, I'll introduce you to my mates.'

But this was an honour we declined, and without hesitation. I wouldn't have gone any further among those tents for the wealth of all the Indies.

'I've had enough of this,' said Spicer, and I can tell you I hardly recognised his voice. 'Let's get back to camp.'

By this time our guide had left us, and was making his way in the direction he had indicated.

We could plainly hear him addressing imaginary people as he marched along. As for ourselves, we turned about and hurried back to our camp as fast as we could go.

Once there, the grog bottle was produced, and never did three men stand more in need of stimulants. Then we set to work to find some explanation of what we had seen, or had fancied we saw. But it was impossible. The wind might have rattled the old windlasses, but it could not be held accountable for those shadowy grey forms that had moved about among the claims.

'I give it up,' said Spicer, at last. 'I know that I never want to see it again. What's more, I vote that we clear out of here tomorrow morning.'

We all agreed, and then retired to our blankets, but for my part I do not mind confessing I scarcely slept a wink all night. The thought that that hideous old man might be hanging about the camp would alone be sufficient for that.

Next morning, as soon as it was light, we breakfasted, but, before we broke camp, Matthews and I set off along the cliff in an attempt to discover our acquaintance of the previous evening.

Though, however, we searched high and low for upwards of an hour, no success rewarded us. By mutual consent we resolved not to look for him on the Field. When we returned to Spicer, we placed such tobacco and stores as we could spare under the shadow of the big rock, where the Mystery Man would be likely to see them, then mounted our camels and resumed our journey, heartily glad to be on our way once more.

Gurunya Goldfield is a place I never desire to visit again. I don't like its population.

Aylmer Vance and the Vampire

Alice and Claude Askew

Aylmer Vance had rooms in Dover Street, Piccadilly, and now that I had decided to follow in his footsteps and to accept him as my instructor in matters psychic, I found it convenient to lodge in the same house. Aylmer and I quickly became close friends, and he showed me how to develop that faculty of clairvoyance which I had possessed without being aware of it. And I may say at once that this particular faculty of mine proved of service on several important occasions.

At the same time, I made myself useful to Vance in other ways, not the least of which was that of acting as recorder of his many strange adventures. For himself, he never cared much about publicity, and it was some time before I could persuade him, in the interests of science, to allow me to give any detailed account of his experiences to the world.

The incidents which I will now narrate occurred very soon after we had taken up our residence together, and while I was still, so to speak, a novice.

It was about ten o'clock in the morning that a visitor was announced. He sent up a card which bore upon it the name of Paul Davenant.

The name was familiar to me, and I wondered if this could be the same Mr Davenant who was so well known for his polo playing and for his success as an amateur rider, especially over the hurdles? He was a young man of wealth and position, and I recollected that he had married, about a year ago, a girl who was reckoned the greatest beauty of the season. All the illustrated papers had given their portraits at the time, and I remember thinking what a remarkably handsome couple they made.

Mr Davenant was ushered in, and at first, I was uncertain as to whether this could be the individual whom I had in mind, so wan and pale and ill did he appear. A finely-built, upstanding man at the time of his marriage, he had now acquired a languid droop of the shoulders and a shuffling gait, while his face, especially about the lips, was bloodless to an alarming degree.

And yet it was the same man, for behind all this I could recognise the shadow of the good looks that had once distinguished Paul Davenant.

He took the chair which Aylmer offered him—after the usual preliminary civilities had been exchanged—and then glanced doubtfully in my direction. 'I wish to consult you privately, Mr Vance,' he said. 'The matter is of considerable importance to myself, and, if I may say so, of a somewhat delicate nature.'

Of course, I rose immediately to withdraw from the room, but Vance laid his hand upon my arm.

'If the matter is connected with research in my particular line, Mr Davenant,' he said, 'if there is any investigation you wish me to take up on your behalf, I shall be glad if you will include Mr Dexter in your confidence. Mr Dexter assists me in my work. But, of course—'

'Oh, no,' interrupted the other, 'if that is the case, pray let Mr Dexter remain. I think,' he added, glancing at me with a friendly smile, 'that you are an Oxford man, are you not, Mr Dexter? It was before my time, but I have heard of your name in connection with the river. You rowed at Henley, unless I am very much mistaken.'

I admitted the fact, with a pleasurable sensation of pride. I was very keen upon rowing in those days, and a man's prowess at school and college always remain dear to his heart. After this we quickly became on friendly terms, and Paul Davenant proceeded to take Aylmer and myself into his confidence.

He began by calling attention to his personal appearance. 'You would hardly recognise me for the same man! was a year ago,' he said. 'I've been losing flesh steadily for the last six months. I came up from Scotland about a week ago, to consult a London doctor. I've seen two—in fact, they've held a sort of consultation over me—but the result, I may say, is far from satisfactory.

They don't seem to know what is really the matter with me.'

'Anaemia—heart' suggested Vance. He was scrutinising his visitor keenly, and yet without any particular appearance of doing so. 'I believe it not infrequently happens that you athletes overdo yourselves—put too much strain upon the heart—'

'My heart is quite sound,' responded Davenant. 'Physically it is in perfect condition. The trouble seems to be that it hasn't enough blood to pump into my veins. The doctors wanted to know if I had met with an accident involving a great loss of blood—but I haven't. I've had no accident at all, and as for anaemia, well, I don't seem to show the ordinary symptoms of it. The inexplicable thing is that I've lost blood without knowing it, and apparently this has been going on for some time, for I've been getting steadily worse. It was almost imperceptible at first—not a sudden collapse, you understand, but a gradual failure of health.'

'I wonder,' remarked Vance slowly, 'what induced you to consult me? For you know, of course, the direction in which I pursue my investigations. May I ask if you have reason to consider that your state of health is due to some cause which we may describe as super-physical?'

A slight colour came to Davenant's white cheeks.

'There are curious circumstances,' he said in a low and earnest tone of voice. 'I've been turning them over in my mind, trying to see light through them. I daresay it's all the sheerest folly—and I must tell you that I'm not in the least a superstitious sort of man. I don't mean to say that I'm absolutely incredulous, but I've never given thought to such things—I've led too active a life. But, as I have said, there are curious circumstances about my case, and that is why I decided upon consulting you.'

'Will you tell me everything without reserve?' said Vance. I could see that he was interested.

He was sitting up in his chair, his feet supported on a stool, his elbows on his knees, his chin in his hands—a favourite attitude of his. 'Have you,' he suggested, slowly, 'any mark upon your body, anything that you might associate, however remotely, with your present weakness and ill-health?'

'It's a curious thing that you should ask me that question,' returned Davenant, 'because I have got a curious mark, a sort of scar, that I can't account for. But I showed it to the doctors, and they assured me that it could have nothing whatever to do with my condition. In any case, if it had, it was something altogether outside their experience. I think they imagined it to be nothing more than a birthmark, a sort of mole, for they asked me if I'd had it all my life. But that I can swear I haven't. I only noticed it for the first time about six months ago, when my health began to fail. But you can see for yourself.'

He loosened his collar and bared his throat. Vance rose and made a careful scrutiny of the suspicious mark. It was situated a very little to the left of the central line, just above the clavicle, and, as Vance pointed out, directly over the big vessels of the throat. My friend called to me so that I might examine it, too. Whatever the opinion of the doctors may have been, Aylmer was obviously deeply interested. And yet there was very little to show. The skin was quite intact, and there was no sign of inflammation. There were two red marks, about an inch apart, each of which was inclined to be crescent in shape. They were more visible than they might otherwise have been owing to the peculiar whiteness of Davenant's skin.

'It can't be anything of importance,' said Davenant, with a slightly uneasy laugh. 'I'm inclined to think the marks are dying away.'

'Have you ever noticed them more inflamed than they are at present?' inquired Vance. 'If so, was it at any special time?'

Davenant reflected. 'Yes,' he replied slowly, 'there have been times, usually, I think perhaps invariably, when I wake up in the morning, that I've noticed them larger and more angry looking. And I've felt a slight sensation of pain—a tingling—oh, very slight, and I've never worried about it. Only now you suggest it to my mind, I believe that those same mornings I have felt particularly tired and done up—a sensation of lassitude absolutely unusual to me. And once, Mr Vance, I remember quite distinctly that there was a stain of blood close to the mark. I didn't think anything of it at the time, and just wiped it away.'

'I see.' Aylmer Vance resumed his seat and invited his visitor to do the same. 'And now,' he resumed, 'you said, Mr Davenant, that there are certain peculiar circumstances you wish to acquaint me with. Will you do so?'

And so Davenant readjusted his collar and proceeded to tell his story. I will tell it as far as I can, without any reference to the occasional interruptions of Vance and myself.

Paul Davenant, as I have said, was a man of wealth and position, and so, in every sense of the word, he was a suitable husband for Miss Jessica MacThane, the young lady who eventually became his wife. Before coming to the incidents attending his loss of health, he had a great deal to recount about Miss MacThane and her family history.

She was of Scottish descent, and although she had certain characteristic features of her race, she was not really Scotch in appearance. Hers was the beauty of the far South rather than that of the Highlands from which she had her origin. Names are not always suited to their owners, and Miss MacThane's was peculiarly inappropriate. She had, in fact, been christened Jessica in a sort of pathetic effort to counteract her obvious departure from normal type. There was a reason for this which we were soon to learn.

Miss MacThane was especially remarkable for her wonderful red hair, hair such as one hardly ever sees outside of Italy—not the Celtic red—and it was so long that it reached to her feet, and it had an extraordinary gloss upon it so that it seemed almost to have individual life of its own.

Then she had just the complexion that one would expect with such hair, the purest ivory white, and not in the least marred by freckles, as is so often the case with red-haired girls. Her beauty was derived from an ancestress who had been brought to Scotland from some foreign shore—no one knew exactly whence.

Davenant fell in love with her almost at once and he had every reason to believe, in spite of her many admirers, that his love was returned. At this time, he knew very little about her personal history. He was aware only that she was very wealthy in her own right, an orphan, and the last representative of a race that had once been famous in the annals of history—or rather infamous, for the MacThanes had distinguished themselves more by cruelty and lust of blood than by deeds of chivalry. A clan of turbulent robbers in the past, they had helped to add many a blood-stained page to the history of their country.

Jessica had lived with her father, who owned a house in London, until his death when she was about fifteen years of age. Her mother had died in Scotland when Jessica was still a tiny child. Mr MacThane had been so affected by his wife's death that, with his little daughter, he had abandoned his Scotch estate altogether—or so it was believed—leaving it to the management of a bailiff—though, indeed, there was but little work for the bailiff to do, since there were practically no tenants left. Blackwick Castle had borne for many years a most unenviable reputation.

After the death of her father, Miss MacThane had gone to live with a certain Mrs Meredith, who was a connection of her mother's—on her father's side she had not a single relation left.

Jessica was absolutely the last of a clan once so extensive that intermarriage had been a tradition of the family, but for which the last two hundred years had been gradually dwindling to extinction.

Mrs Meredith took Jessica into Society—which would never have been her privilege had Mr MacThane lived, for he was a moody, self-absorbed man, and prematurely old—one who seemed worn down by the weight of a great grief.

Well, I have said that Paul Davenant quickly fell in love with Jessica, and it was not long before he proposed for her hand. To his great surprise, for he had good reason to believe that she cared for him, he met with a refusal; nor would she give any explanation, though she burst into a flood of pitiful tears.

Bewildered and bitterly disappointed, he consulted Mrs Meredith, with whom he happened to be on friendly terms, and from her he learnt that Jessica had already had several proposals, all from quite desirable men, but that one after another had been rejected.

Paul consoled himself with the reflection that perhaps Jessica did not love them, whereas he was quite sure that she cared for himself. Under these circumstances he determined to try again.

He did so, and with better result. Jessica admitted her love, but at the same time she repeated that she would not marry him. Love and marriage were not for her. Then, to his utter amazement, she declared that she had been born under a curse—a curse which, sooner or later was bound to show itself in her, and which, moreover, must react cruelly, perhaps fatally, upon anyone with whom she linked her life. How could she allow a man she loved to take such a risk? Above all, since the evil was hereditary, there was one point upon which she had quite made up her mind: no child should ever call her mother—she must be the last of her race indeed.

Of course, Davenant was amazed and inclined to think that Jessica had got some absurd idea into her head which a little reasoning on his part would dispel. There was only one other possible explanation. Was it lunacy she was afraid of? But Jessica shook her head. She did not know of any lunacy in her family. The ill was deeper, more subtle than that. And then she told him all that she knew.

The curse—she made us of that word for want of a better—was attached to the ancient race from which she had her origin. Her father had suffered from it, and his father and grandfather before him. All three had taken to themselves young wives who had died mysteriously, of some wasting disease, within a few years. Had they observed the ancient family tradition of intermarriage this might possibly not have happened, but in their case, since the family was so near extinction, this had not been possible.

For the curse—or whatever it was—did not kill those who bore the name of MacThane. It only rendered them a danger to others. It was as if they absorbed from the blood-soaked walls of their fatal castle a deadly taint which reacted terribly upon those with whom they were brought into contact, especially their nearest and dearest.

'Do you know what my father said we have it in us to become?' said Jessica with a shudder.

'He used the word vampires. Paul, think of it—vampires—preying upon the life blood of others.' And then, when Davenant was inclined to laugh, she checked him. 'No,' she cried out, 'it is not impossible. Think. We are a decadent race. From the earliest times our history has been marked by bloodshed and cruelty. The walls of Blackwick Castle are impregnated with evil—every stone could tell its tale, of violence, pain, lust, and murder. What can one expect of those who have spent their lifetime between its walls?'

'But you have not done so,' exclaimed Paul. 'You have been spared that, Jessica. You were taken away after your mother died, and you have no recollection of Blackwick Castle, none at all. And you need never set foot in it again.'

'I'm afraid the evil is in my blood,' she replied sadly, 'although I am unconscious of it now.

And as for not returning to Blackwick—I'm not sure I can help myself. At least, that is what my father warned me of. He said there is something there, some compelling force, that will call me to it in spite of myself. But, oh, I don't know—I don't know, and that is what makes it so difficult. If I could only believe that all this is nothing but an idle superstition, I might be happy again, for I have it in me to enjoy life, and I'm young, very young, but my father told me these things when he was on his deathbed.' She added the last words in a low, awe-stricken tone.

Paul pressed her to tell him all that she knew, and eventually she revealed another fragment of family history which seemed to have some bearing upon the case. It dealt with her own astonishing likeness to that ancestress of a couple of hundred years ago, whose existence seemed to have presaged the gradual downfall of the clan of the MacThanes.

A certain Robert MacThane, departing from the traditions of his family, which demanded that he should not marry outside his clan, brought home a wife from foreign shores, a woman of wonderful beauty, who was possessed of glowing masses of red hair and a complexion of ivory whiteness—such as had more or less distinguished since then every female of the race born in the direct line.

It was not long before this woman came to be regarded in the neighbourhood as a witch. Queer stories were circulated abroad as to her doings, and the reputation of Blackwick Castle became worse than ever before.

And then one day she disappeared. Robert MacThane had been absent upon some business for twenty-four hours, and it was upon his return that he found her gone. The neighbourhood was searched, but without avail, and then Robert, who was a violent man and who had adored his foreign wife, called together certain of his tenants whom he suspected, rightly or wrongly, of foul play, and had them murdered in cold blood. Murder was easy in those days, yet such an outcry was raised that Robert had to take to flight, leaving his two children in the care of their nurse, and for a long while Blackwick Castle was without a master.

But its evil reputation persisted. It was said that Zaida, the witch, though dead, still made her presence felt. Many children of the tenantry and young people of the neighbourhood sickened and died—possibly of quite natural causes; but this did not prevent a mantle of terror settling upon the countryside, for it was said that Zaida had been seen—a pale woman clad in white—flitting about the cottages at night, and where she passed sickness and death were sure to supervene.

And from that time the fortune of the family gradually declined. Heir succeeded heir, but no sooner was he installed at Blackwick Castle than his nature, whatever it may previously have been, seemed to undergo a change. It was as if he absorbed into himself all the weight of evil that had stained his family name—as if he did, indeed, become a vampire, bringing blight upon any not directly connected with his own house. And so, by degrees, Blackwick was deserted of its tenantry. The land around it was left uncultivated—the farms stood empty. This had persisted to the present day, for the superstitious peasantry still told their tales of the mysterious white woman who hovered about the neighbourhood, and whose appearance betokened death—and possibly worse than death.

And yet it seemed that the last representatives of the MacThanes could not desert their ancestral home. Riches they had, sufficient to live happily upon elsewhere, but drawn by some power they could not contend against, they had preferred to spend their lives in the solitude of the now half-ruined castle, shunned by their neighbours, feared and execrated by the few tenants that still clung to their soil.

So, it had been with Jessica's grandfather and great-grandfather. Each of them had married a young wife, and in each case their love story had been all too brief. The vampire spirit was still abroad, expressing itself—or so it seemed—through the living representatives of bygone generations of evil, and young blood had been demanded as the sacrifice.

And to them had succeeded Jessica's father. He had not profited by their example, but had followed directly in their footsteps. And the same fate had befallen the wife whom he passionately adored. She had died of pernicious anaemia—so the doctors said—but he had regarded himself as her murderer.

But, unlike his predecessors, he had torn himself away from Blackwick—and this for the sake of his child. Unknown to her, however, he had returned year after year, for there were times when the passionate longing for the gloomy, mysterious halls and corridors of the old castle, for the wild stretches of moorland, and the dark pinewoods, would come upon him too strongly to be resisted. And so, he knew that for his daughter, as for himself, there was no escape, and he warned her, when the relief of death was at last granted to him, of what her fate must be.

This was the tale that Jessica told the man who wished to make her his wife, and he made light of it, as such a man would, regarding it all as foolish superstition, the delusion of a mind overwrought. And at last—perhaps it was not very difficult, for she loved him with all her heart and soul—he succeeded in inducing Jessica to think as he did, to banish morbid ideas, as he called them from her brain, and to consent to marry him at an early date.

'I'll take any risk you like,' he declared. 'I'll even go and live at Blackwick if you should desire it. To think of you, my lovely Jessica, a vampire! Why, I never heard such nonsense in my life.'

'Father said I'm very like Zaida, the witch,' she protested, but he silenced her with a kiss.

And so, they were married and spent their honeymoon abroad, and in the autumn Paul accepted an invitation to a house party in Scotland for the grouse shooting, a sport to which he was absolutely devoted, and Jessica agreed with him that there was no reason why he should forgo his pleasure.

Perhaps it was an unwise thing to do, to venture to Scotland, but by this time the young couple, more deeply in love with each other than ever, had got quite over their fears. Jessica was redolent with health and spirits, and more than once she declared that if they should be anywhere in the neighbourhood of Blackwick she would like to see the old castle out of curiosity, and just to show how absolutely she had got over the foolish terrors that used to assail her.

This seemed to Paul to be quite a wise plan, and so one day, since they were actually staying at no great distance, they motored over to Blackwick, and finding the bailiff, got him to show them over the castle.

It was a great castellated pile, grey with age, and in places falling into ruin. It stood on a steep hillside, with the rock of which it seemed to form part, and on one side of it there was a precipitous drop to a mountain stream a hundred feet below. The robber MacThanes of the old days could not have desired a better stronghold.

At the back, climbing up the mountainside were dark pinewoods, from which, here and there, rugged crags protruded, and these were fantastically shaped, some like gigantic and misshapen human forms, which stood up as if they mounted guard over the castle and the narrow gorge, by which alone it could be approached.

This gorge was always full of weird, uncanny sounds. It might have been a storehouse for the wind, which, even on calm days, rushed up and down as if seeking an escape, and it moaned among the pines and whistled in the crags and shouted derisive laughter as it was tossed from side to side of the rocky heights. It was like the plaint of lost souls—that is the expression Davenant made use of—the plaint of lost souls.

The road, little more than a track now, passed through this gorge, and then, after skirting a small but deep lake, which hardly knew the light of the sun so shut in was it by overhanging trees, climbed the hill to the castle.

And the castle! Davenant used but a few words to describe it, yet somehow, I could see the gloomy edifice in my mind's eye, and something of the lurking horror that it contained communicated itself to my brain. Perhaps my clairvoyant sense assisted me, for when he spoke of them I seemed already acquainted with the great stone halls, the long corridors, gloomy and cold even on the brightest and warmest of days, the dark, oak-panelled rooms, and the broad central staircase up which one of the early MacThanes had once led a dozen men on horseback in pursuit of a stag which had taken refuge within the precincts of the castle. There was the keep, too, its walls so thick that the ravages of time had made no impression upon them, and beneath the keep were dungeons which could tell terrible tales of ancient wrong and lingering pain.

Well, Mr and Mrs Davenant visited as much as the bailiff could show them of this ill-omened edifice, and Paul, for his part, thought pleasantly of his own Derbyshire home, the fine Georgian mansion, replete with every modern comfort, where he proposed to settle with his wife. And so, he received something of a shock when, as they drove away, she slipped her hand into his and whispered:

'Paul, you promised, didn't you, that you would refuse me nothing?'

She had been strangely silent till she spoke those words. Paul, slightly apprehensive, assured her that she only had to ask—but the speech did not come from his heart, for he guessed vaguely what she desired.

She wanted to go and live at the castle—oh, only for a little while, for she was sure she would soon tire of it. But the bailiff had told her that there were papers, documents, which she ought to examine, since the property was now hers—and, besides, she was interested in this home of her ancestors, and wanted to explore it more thoroughly. Oh, no, she wasn't in the least influenced by the old superstition—that wasn't the attraction—she had quite got over those silly ideas. Paul had cured her, and since he himself was so convinced that they were without foundation he ought not to mind granting her, her whim.

This was a plausible argument, not easy to controvert. In the end Paul yielded, though it was not without a struggle. He suggested amendments. Let him at least have the place done up for her—that would take time; or let them postpone their visit till next year—in the summer—not move in just as the winter was upon them.

But Jessica did not want to delay longer than she could help, and she hated the idea of redecoration. Why, it would spoil the illusion of the old place, and, besides, it would be a waste of money since she only wished to remain there for a week or two. The Derbyshire house was not quite ready yet; they must allow time for the paper to dry on the walls.

And so, a week later, when their stay with their friends was concluded, they went to Blackwick, the bailiff having engaged a few raw servants and generally made things as comfortable for them as possible. Paul was worried and apprehensive, but he could not admit this to his wife after having so loudly proclaimed his theories on the subject of superstition.

They had been married three months at this time—nine had passed since then, and they had never left Blackwick for more than a few hours—till now Paul had come to London—alone.

'Over and over again,' he declared, 'my wife has begged me to go. With tears in her eyes, almost upon her knees, she has entreated me to leave her, but I have steadily refused unless she will accompany me. But that is the trouble, Mr Vance, she cannot; there is something, some mysterious horror, that holds her there as surely as if she were bound with fetters. It holds her more strongly even than it held her father— we found out that he used to spend six months at least of every year at Blackwick—months when he pretended that he was travelling abroad. You see the spell—or whatever the accursed thing may be—never really relaxed its grip of him.'

'Did you never attempt to take your wife away?' asked Vance.

'Yes, several times; but it was hopeless. She would become so ill as soon as we were beyond the limit of the estate that I invariably had to take her back. Once we got as far as Dorekirk—that is the nearest town, you know—and I thought I should be successful if only I could get through the night. But she escaped me; she climbed out of a window—she meant to go back on foot, at night, all those long miles. Then I have had doctors down; but it is I who wanted the doctors, not she. They have ordered me away, but I have refused to obey them till now.'

'Is your wife changed at all—physically?' interrupted Vance.

Davenant reflected. 'Changed,' he said, 'yes, but so subtly that I hardly know how to describe it. She is more beautiful than ever—and yet it isn't the same beauty, if you can understand me. I have spoken of her white complexion, well, one is more than ever conscious of it now, because her lips have become so red—they are almost like a splash of blood upon her face. And the upper one has a peculiar curve that I don't think it had before, and when she laughs, she doesn't smile—

Do you know what I mean? Then her hair—it has lost its wonderful gloss. Of course, I know she is fretting about me; but that is so peculiar, too, for at times, as I have told you, she will implore me to go and leave her, and then perhaps only a few minutes later, she will wreathe her arms round my neck and say she cannot live without me. And I feel that there is a struggle going on within her, that she is only yielding slowly to the horrible influence—whatever it is—that she is herself when she begs me to go, but when she entreats me to stay—and it is then that her fascination is most intense—oh, I can't help remembering what she told me before we were married, and that word'—he lowered his voice-'the word "vampire"—'

He passed his hand over his brow that was wet with perspiration. 'But that's absurd, ridiculous,' he muttered; 'these fantastic beliefs have been exploded years ago. We live in the twentieth century.'

A pause ensued, then Vance said quietly, 'Mr Davenant, since you have taken me into your confidence, since you have found doctors of no avail, will you let me try to help you? I think I may be of some use—if it is not already too late. Should you agree, Mr Dexter and I will accompany you, as you have suggested, to Blackwick Castle as early as possible—by tonight's mail North. Under ordinary circumstances I should tell you as you value your life, not to return—'. Davenant shook his head. 'That is advice which I should never take,' he declared. 'I had already decided, under any circumstances, to travel North tonight. I am glad that you both will accompany me.'

And so, it was decided. We settled to meet at the station, and presently Paul Davenant took his departure. Any other details that remained to be told he would put us in possession of during the course of the journey.

'A curious and most interesting case,' remarked Vance when we were alone. 'What do you make of it, Dexter?'

'I suppose,' I replied cautiously, 'that there is such a thing as vampirism even in these days of advanced civilization? I can understand the evil influence that a very old person may have upon a young one if they happen to be in constant intercourse—the worn-out tissue sapping healthy vitality for their own support. And there are certain people—I could think of several myself—who seem to depress one and undermine one's energies, quite unconsciously, of course, but one feels somehow that vitality has passed from oneself to them. And in this case, when the force is centuries old, expressing itself, in some mysterious way, through Davenant's wife, is it not feasible to believe that he may be physically affected by it, even though the whole thing is sheerly mental?'

'You think, then,' demanded Vance, 'that it is sheerly mental? Tell me, if that is so, how do you account for the marks on Davenant's throat?'

This was a question to which I found no reply, and though I pressed him for his views, Vance would not commit himself further just then.

Of our long journey to Scotland I need say nothing. We did not reach Blackwick Castle till late in the afternoon of the following day. The place was just as I had conceived it—as I have already described it. And a sense of gloom settled upon me as our car jolted us over the rough road that led through the Gorge of the Winds—a gloom that deepened when we penetrated into the vast cold hall of the castle.

Mrs Davenant, who had been informed by telegram of our arrival, received us cordially. She knew nothing of our actual mission, regarding us merely as friends of her husband's. She was most solicitous on his behalf, but there was something strained about her tone, and it made me feel vaguely uneasy. The impression that I got was that the woman was impelled to everything that she said or did by some force outside herself—but, of course, this was a conclusion that the circumstances I was aware of might easily have conduced to. In every other aspect she was charming, and she had an extraordinary fascination of appearance and manner that made me readily understand the force of a remark made by Davenant during our journey.

'I want to live for Jessica's sake. Get her away from Blackwick, Vance, and I feel that all will be well. I'd go through hell to have her restored to me—as she was.'

And now that I had seen Mrs Davenant, I realised what he meant by those last words. Her fascination was stronger than ever, but it was not a natural fascination—not that of a normal woman, such as she had been. It was the fascination of a Circe, of a witch, of an enchantress—and as such was irresistible.

We had a strong proof of the evil within her soon after our arrival. It was a test that Vance had quietly prepared. Davenant had mentioned that no flowers grew at Blackwick, and Vance declared that we must take some with us as a present for the lady of the house. He purchased a bouquet of pure white roses at the little town where we left the train, for the motorcar for has been sent to meet us. Soon after our arrival he presented these to Mrs Davenant. She took them it seemed to me nervously, and hardly had her hand touched them before they fell to pieces, in a shower of crumpled petals, to the floor.

'We must act at once,' said Vance to me when we were descending to dinner that night. 'There must be no delay.'

'What are you afraid of?' I whispered.

'Davenant has been absent a week,' he replied grimly. 'He is stronger than when he went away, but not strong enough to survive the loss of more blood. He must be protected. There is danger tonight.'

'You mean from his wife?' I shuddered at the ghastliness of the suggestion.

'That is what time will show.' Vance turned to me and added a few words with intense earnestness. 'Mrs Davenant, Dexter, is at present hovering between two conditions. The evil thing has not yet completely mastered her—you remember what Davenant said, how she would beg him to go away and the next moment entreat him to stay? She has made a struggle, but she is gradually succumbing, and this last week, spent here alone, has strengthened the evil. And that is what I have got to fight, Dexter—it is to be a contest of will, a contest that will go on silently till one or the other obtains the mastery. If you watch, you may see. Should a change show itself in Mrs Davenant you will know that I have won.'

Thus, I knew the direction in which my friend proposed to act. It was to be a war of his will against the mysterious power that had laid its curse upon the house of MacThane. Mrs Davenant must be released from the fatal charm that held her.

And I, knowing what was going on, was able to watch and understand. I realised that the silent contest had begun even while we ate dinner. Mrs Davenant ate practically nothing and seemed ill at ease; she fidgeted in her chair, talked a great deal, and laughed—it was the laugh without a smile, as Davenant had described it. And as soon as she was able to, she withdrew.

Later, as we sat in the drawing-room, I could feel the clash of wills. The air in the room felt electric and heavy, charged with tremendous but invisible forces. And outside, round the castle, the wind whistled and shrieked and moaned—it was as if all the dead and gone MacThanes, a grim army, had collected to fight the battle of their race.

And all this while we four in the drawing-room were sitting and talking the ordinary commonplaces of after—dinner conversation! That was the extraordinary part of it—Paul Davenant suspected nothing, and I, who knew, had to play my part. But I hardly took my eyes from Jessica's face. When would the change come, or was it, indeed, too late!

At last Davenant rose and remarked that he was tired and would go to bed. There was no need for Jessica to hurry. We would sleep that night in his dressing-room and did not want to be disturbed.

And it was at that moment, as his lips met hers in a goodnight kiss, as she wreathed her enchantress arms about him, careless of our presence, her eyes gleaming hungrily, that the change came.

It came with a fierce and threatening shriek of wind, and a rattling of the casement, as if the horde of ghosts without was about to break in upon us. A long, quivering sigh escaped from Jessica's lips, her arms fell from her husband's shoulders, and she drew back, swaying a little

169

from side to side.

'Paul,' she cried, and somehow the whole timbre of her voice was changed, 'what a wretch I've been to bring you back to Blackwick, ill as you are! But we'll go away, dear; yes, I'll go, too. Oh, will you take me away—take me away tomorrow?' She spoke with an intense earnestness—unconscious all the time of what had been happening to her. Long shudders were convulsing her frame. 'I don't know why I've wanted to stay here,' she kept repeating. 'I hate the place, really—it's evil—evil.'

Having heard these words I exulted, for surely Vance's success was assured. But I was to learn that the danger was not yet past.

Husband and wife separated, each going to their own room. I noticed the grateful, if mystified glance that Davenant threw at Vance, vaguely aware, as he must have been, that my friend was somehow responsible for what had happened. It was settled that plans for departure were to be discussed on the morrow.

'I have succeeded,' Vance said hurriedly, when we were alone, 'but the change may be a transitory. I must keep watch tonight. Go you to bed, Dexter, there is nothing that you can do.'

I obeyed—though I would sooner have kept watch, too—watch against a danger of which I had no understanding. I went to my room, a gloomy and sparsely furnished apartment, but I knew that it was quite impossible for me to think of sleeping. And so, dressed as I was, I went and sat by the open window, for now the wind that had raged round the castle had died down to a low moaning in the pine-trees—a whimpering of time-worn agony.

And it was as I sat thus that I became aware of a white figure that stole out from the castle by a door that I could not see, and, with hands clasped, ran swiftly across the terrace to the wood. I had but a momentary glance, but I felt convinced that the figure was that of Jessica Davenant.

And instinctively I knew that some great danger was imminent. It was, I think, the suggestion of despair conveyed by those clasped hands. At any rate, I did not hesitate. My window was some height from the ground, but the wall below was ivy-clad and afforded good foothold. The descent was quite easy. I achieved it, and was just in time to take up the pursuit in the right direction, which was into the thickness of the wood that clung to the slope of the hill.

I shall never forget that wild chase. There was just sufficient room to enable me to follow the rough path, which, luckily, since I had now lost sight of my quarry, was the only possible way that she could have taken; there were no intersecting tracks, and the wood was too thick on either side to permit of deviation.

And the wood seemed full of dreadful sounds—moaning and wailing and hideous laughter.

The wind, of course, and the screaming of night birds—once I felt the fluttering of wings in close proximity to my face. But I could not rid myself of the thought that I, in my turn, was being pursued, that the forces of hell were combined against me.

The path came to an abrupt end on the border of the sombre lake that I have already mentioned. And now I realised that I was indeed only just in time, for before me, plunging knee deep in the water, I recognized the white-clad figure of the woman I had been pursuing. Hearing my footsteps, she turned her head, and then threw up her arms and screamed. Her red hair fell in heavy masses about her shoulders, and her face, as I saw it in that moment, was hardly human for the agony of remorse that it depicted.

'Go!' she screamed. 'For God's sake let me die!'

But I was by her side almost as she spoke. She struggled with me—sought vainly to tear herself from my clasp—implored me, with panting breath, to let her drown.

'It's the only way to save him!' she gasped. 'Don't you understand that I am a thing accursed? For it is I—I—who have sapped his life blood! I know it now, the truth has been revealed to me tonight! I am a vampire, without hope in this world or the next, so for his sake—for the sake of his unborn child—let me die—let me die!' Was ever so terrible an appeal made? Yet I—what could I do? Gently I overcame her resistance and drew her back to shore. By the time I reached it she was lying a dead weight upon my arm. I laid her down upon a mossy bank, and, kneeling by her side, gazed intently into her face.

And then I knew that I had done well. For the face I looked upon was not that of Jessica the vampire, as I had seen it that afternoon, it was the face of Jessica, the woman whom Paul Davenant had loved.

And later Aylmer Vance had his tale to tell.

'I waited', he said, 'until I knew that Davenant was asleep, and then I stole into his room to watch by his bedside. And presently she came, as I guessed she would, the vampire, the accursed thing that has preyed upon the souls of her kin, making them like to herself when they too have passed into Shadowland, and gathering sustenance for her horrid task from the blood of those who are alien to her race. Paul's body and

Jessica's soul—it is for one and the other, Dexter, that we have fought.'

'You mean,' I hesitated, 'Zaida the witch?'

'Even so,' he agreed. 'Hers is the evil spirit that has fallen like a blight upon the house of MacThane. But now I think she may be exorcized for ever.'

'Tell me.'

'She came to Paul Davenant last night, as she must have done before, in the guise of his wife.

You know that Jessica bears a strong resemblance to her ancestress. He opened his arms, but she was foiled of her prey, for I had taken my precautions; I had placed That upon Davenant's breast while he slept which robbed the vampire of her power of ill. She sped wailing from the room—a shadow—she who a minute before had looked at him with Jessica's eyes and spoken to him with Jessica's voice. Her red lips were Jessica's lips, and they were close to his when his eyes were opened and he saw her as she was—a hideous phantom of the corruption of the ages. And so, the spell was removed, and she fled away to the place whence she had come—'

He paused. 'And now?' I inquired.

'Blackwick Castle must be razed to the ground,' he replied. 'That is the only way. Every stone of it, every brick, must be ground to powder and burnt with fire, for therein is the cause of all the evil. Davenant has consented.'

'And Mrs Davenant?'

'I think,' Vance answered cautiously, 'that all may be well with her. The curse will be removed with the destruction of the castle. She has not—thanks to you—perished under its influence. She was less guilty than she imagined—herself preyed upon rather than preying. But can't you understand her remorse when she realised, as she was bound to realise, the part she had played? And the knowledge of the child to come—its fatal inheritance—'

'I understand.' I muttered with a shudder. And then, under my breath, I whispered, 'Thank God!'

Ken's Mystery

Julian Hawthorne

One cool October evening—it was the last day of the month, and unusually cool for the time of year—I made up my mind to go and spend an hour or two with my friend Keningale. Keningale was an artist (as well as a musical amateur and poet), and had a very delightful studio built onto his house, in which he was wont to sit of an evening. The studio had a cavernous fireplace, designed in imitation of the old-fashioned fireplaces of Elizabethan manor-houses, and in it, when the temperature outdoors warranted, he would build up a cheerful fire of dry logs. It would suit me particularly well, I thought, to go and have a quiet pipe and chat in front of that fire with my friend.

I had not had such a chat for a very long time—not, in fact, since Keningale (or Ken, as his friends called him) had returned from his visit to Europe the year before. He went abroad, as he affirmed at the time, "for purposes of study," whereat we all smiled, for Ken, so far as we knew him, was more likely to do anything else than to study. He was a young fellow of buoyant temperament, lively and social in his habits, of a brilliant and versatile mind, and possessing an income of twelve or fifteen thousand dollars a year; he could sing, play, scribble, and paint very cleverly, and some of his heads and figure—pieces were really well done, considering that he never had any regular training in art; but he was not a worker.

Personally, he was fine-looking, of good height and figure, active, healthy, and with a remarkably fine brow, and clear, full-gazing eye. Nobody was surprised at his going to Europe, nobody expected him to do anything there except amuse himself, and few anticipated that he would be soon again seen in New York. He was one of the sort that find Europe agree with them. Off he went, therefore; and in the course of a few months the rumour reached us that he was engaged to a handsome and wealthy New York girl whom he had met in London. This was nearly all we did hear of him until, not very long afterward, he turned up again on Fifth Avenue, to every one's astonishment; made no satisfactory answer to those who wanted to know how he happened to tire so soon of the Old World; while, as to the reported engagement, he cut short all allusion to that in so peremptory a manner as to show that it was not a permissible topic of conversation with him. It was surmised that the lady had jilted him; but, on the other hand, she herself returned home not a great while after, and, though she had plenty of opportunities, she has never married to this day.

Be the rights of that matter what they may, it was soon remarked that Ken was no longer the careless and merry fellow he used to be; on the contrary, he appeared grave, moody, averse from general society, and habitually taciturn and undemonstrative even in the company of his most intimate friends. Evidently something had happened to him, or he had done something. What? Had he committed a murder? or joined the Nihilists? or was his unsuccessful love affair at the bottom of it? Some declared that the cloud was only temporary, and would soon pass away.

Nevertheless, up to the period of which I am writing, it had not passed away, but had rather gathered additional gloom, and threatened to become permanent.

Meanwhile I had met him twice or thrice at the club, at the opera, or in the street, but had as yet had no opportunity of regularly renewing my acquaintance with him. We had been on a footing of more than common intimacy in the old days, and I was not disposed to think that he would refuse to renew the former relations now. But what I had heard and myself seen of his changed condition imparted a stimulating tinge of suspense or curiosity to the pleasure with which I looked forward to the prospects of this evening. His house stood at a distance of two or three miles beyond the general range of habitations in New York at this time, and as I walked briskly along in the clear twilight air I had leisure to go over in my mind all that I had known of Ken and had divined of his character.

After all, had there not always been something in his nature—deep down, and held in abeyance by the activity of his animal spirits—but something strange and separate, and capable of developing under suitable conditions into—into what? As I asked myself this question I arrived at his door; and it was with a feeling of relief that I felt the next moment the cordial grasp of his hand, and his voice bidding me welcome in a tone that indicated unaffected gratification at my presence. He drew me at once into the studio, relieved me of my hat and cane, and then put his hand on my shoulder.

"I am glad to see you," be repeated, with singular earnestness— "glad to see you and to feel you; and tonight of all nights in the year."

"Why tonight especially?"

"Oh, never mind. It's just as well, too, you didn't let me know beforehand you were coming; the unreadiness is all, to paraphrase the poet. Now, with you to help me, I can drink a glass of whisky and water and take a bit draw of the pipe. This would have been a grim night for me if I'd been left to myself."

"In such a lap of luxury as this, too!" said I, looking round at the glowing fire-place, the low, luxurious chairs, and all the rich and sumptuous fittings of the room. "I should have thought a condemned murderer might make himself comfortable here."

"Perhaps; but that's not exactly my category at present. But have you forgotten what night this is? This is November-eve, when, as tradition asserts, the dead arise and walk about, and fairies, goblins, and spiritual beings of all kinds have more freedom and power than on any other day of the year. One can see you've never been in Ireland."

"I wasn't aware till now that you had been there, either."

"Yes, I have been in Ireland. Yes—" He paused, sighed, and fell into a reverie, from which, however, he soon roused himself by an effort, and went to a cabinet in a corner of the room for the liquor and tobacco. While he was thus employed, I sauntered about the studio, taking note of the various beauties, grotesquenesses, and curiosities that it contained. Many things were there to repay study and arouse admiration; for Ken was a good collector, having excellent taste as well as means to back it. But, upon the whole, nothing interested me more than some studies of a female head, roughly done in oils, and, judging from the sequestered positions in which I found them, not intended by the artist for exhibition or criticism.

There were three or four of these studies, all of the same face, but in different poses and costumes. In one the head was enveloped in a dark hood, overshadowing and partly concealing the features; in another she seemed to be peering duskily through a latticed casement, lit by a faint moonlight; a third showed her splendidly attired in evening costume, with jewels in her hair and ears, and sparkling on her snowy bosom. The expressions were as various as the poses; now it was demure penetration, now a subtle inviting glance, now burning

175

passion, and again a look of elfish and elusive mockery. In whatever phase, the countenance possessed a singular and poignant fascination, not of beauty merely, though that was very striking, but of character and quality likewise.

"Did you find this model abroad?" I inquired at length. "She has evidently inspired you, and I don't wonder at it."

Ken, who had been mixing the punch, and had not noticed my movements, now looked up, and said: "I didn't mean those to be seen. They don't satisfy me, and I am going to destroy them; but I couldn't rest till I'd made some attempts to reproduce—What was it you asked? Abroad? Yes—or no. They were all painted here within the last six weeks."

"Whether they satisfy you or not, they are by far the best things of yours I have ever seen."

"Well, let them alone, and tell me what you think of this beverage. To my thinking, it goes to the right spot. It owes its existence to your coming here. I can't drink alone, and those portraits are not company, though, for aught I know, she might have come out of the canvas tonight and sat down in that chair." Then, seeing my inquiring look, he added, with a hasty laugh, "It's November-eve, you know, when anything may happen, provided its strange enough. Well, here's to ourselves."

We each swallowed a deep draught of the smoking and aromatic liquor, and set down our glasses with approval. The punch was excellent. Ken now opened a box of cigars, and we seated ourselves before the fireplace.

"All we need now," I remarked, after a short silence, "is a little music. By-the-by, Ken, have you still got the banjo I gave you before you went abroad?"

He paused so long before replying that I supposed he had not heard my question. "I have got it," he said, at length, "but it will never make any more music."

"Got broken, eh? Can't it be mended? It was a fine instrument."

"It's not broken, but it's past mending. You shall see for yourself."

He arose as he spoke, and going to another part of the studio, opened a black oak coffer, and took out of it a long object wrapped up in a piece of faded yellow silk. He handed it to me, and when I had unwrapped it, there appeared a thing that might once have been a banjo, but had little resemblance to one now. It bore every sign of extreme age. The wood of the handle was honey-combed with the

176

gnawings of worms, and dusty with dry-rot. The parchment head was green with mould, and hung in shrivelled tatters. The hoop, which was of solid silver, was so blackened and tarnished that it looked like dilapidated iron. The strings were gone, and most of the tuning-screws had dropped out of their decayed sockets. Altogether it had the appearance of having been made before the Flood, and been forgotten in the forecastle of Noah's Ark ever since.

"It is a curious relic, certainly," I said. "Where did you come across it? I had no idea that the banjo was invented so long ago as this. It certainly can't be less than two hundred years old, and may be much older than that."

Ken smiled gloomily. "You are quite right," he said; "it is at least two hundred years old, and yet it is the very same banjo that you gave me a year ago."

"Hardly," I returned, smiling in my turn, "since that was made to my order with a view to presenting it to you."

"I know that; but the two hundred years have passed since then. Yes; it is absurd and impossible, I know, but nothing is truer. That banjo, which was made last year, existed in the sixteenth century, and has been rotting ever since. Stay. Give it to me a moment, and I'll convince you. You recollect that your name and mine, with the date, were engraved on the silver hoop?"

"Yes; and there was a private mark of my own there, also."

"Very well," said Ken, who had been rubbing a place on the hoop with a corner of the yellow silk wrapper; "look at that."

I took the decrepit instrument from him, and examined the spot which he had rubbed. It was incredible, sure enough; but there were the names and the date precisely as I had caused them to be engraved; and there, moreover, was my own private mark, which I had idly made with an old etching point not more than eighteen months before. After convincing myself that there was no mistake, I laid the banjo across my knees, and stared at my friend in bewilderment. He sat smoking with a kind of grim composure, his eyes fixed upon the blazing logs.

"I'm mystified, I confess," said I. "Come; what is the joke? What method have you discovered of producing the decay of centuries on this unfortunate banjo in a few months? And why did you do it? I have heard of an elixir to counteract the effects of time, but your recipe seems to work the other way—to make time rush forward at two hundred times his usual rate, in one place, while he jogs on at his usual gait elsewhere. Unfold your mystery, magician. Seriously, Ken,

177

how on earth did the thing happen?"

"I know no more about it than you do," was his reply. "Either you and I and all the rest of the living world are insane, or else there has been wrought a miracle as strange as any in tradition.

"How can I explain it? It is a common saying—a common experience, if you will—that we may, on certain trying or tremendous occasions, live years in one moment. But that's a mental experience, not a physical one, and one that applies, at all events, only to human beings, not to senseless things of wood and metal. You imagine the thing is some trick or jugglery. If it be, I don't know the secret of it. There's no chemical appliance that I ever heard of that will get a piece of solid wood into that condition in a few months, or a few years. And it wasn't done in a few years, or a few months either. A year ago, today at this very hour that banjo was as sound as when it left the maker's hands, and twenty-four hours afterward—I'm telling you the simple truth—it was as you see it now."

The gravity and earnestness with which Ken made this astounding statement were evidently not assumed. He believed every word that he uttered. I knew not what to think. Of course, my friend might be insane, though he betrayed none of the ordinary symptoms of mania; but however that might be, there was the banjo, a witness whose silent testimony there was no gain-saying. The more I meditated on the matter the more inconceivable did it appear. Two hundred years— twenty-four hours; these were the terms of the proposed equation. Ken and the banjo both affirmed that the equation had been made; all worldly knowledge and experience affirmed it to be impossible. What was the explanation? What is time? What is life? I felt myself beginning to doubt the reality of all things. And so this was the mystery which my friend had been brooding over since his return from abroad. No wonder it had changed him. More to be wondered at was it that it had not changed him more.

"Can you tell me the whole story?" I demanded at length.

Ken quaffed another draught from his glass of whisky and water and rubbed his hand through his thick brown beard. "I have never spoken to any one of it heretofore," he said, "and I had never meant to speak of it. But I'll try and give you some idea of what it was. You know me better than anyone else; you'll understand the thing as far as it can ever be understood, and perhaps I may be relieved of some of the oppression it has caused me. For it is rather a ghastly memory to grapple with alone, I can tell you."

Hereupon, without further preface, Ken related the following tale. He was, I may observe in passing, a naturally fine narrator. There were deep, lingering tones in his voice, and he could strikingly enhance the comic or pathetic effect of a sentence by dwelling here and there upon some syllable. His features were equally susceptible of humorous and of solemn expressions, and his eyes were in form and hue wonderfully adapted to showing great varieties of emotion. Their mournful aspect was extremely earnest and affecting; and when Ken was giving utterance to some mysterious passage of the tale, they had a doubtful, melancholy, exploring look which appealed irresistibly to the imagination. But the interest of his story was too pressing to allow of noticing these incidental embellishments at the time, though they doubtless had their influence upon me all the same.

"I left New York on an Inman Line steamer, you remember," began Ken, "and landed at Havre. I went the usual round of sight-seeing on the Continent, and got round to London in July, at the height of the season. I had good introductions, and met any number of agreeable and famous people. Among others was a young lady, a countrywoman of my own—you know whom I mean—who interested me very much, and before her family left London she and I were engaged. We parted there for the time, because she had the Continental trip still to make, while I wanted to take the opportunity to visit the north of England and Ireland. I landed at Dublin about the 1st of October, and, zigzagging about the country, I found myself in County Cork about two weeks later.

"There is in that region some of the most lovely scenery that human eyes ever rested on, and it seems to be less known to tourists than many places of infinitely less picturesque value. A lonely region too: during my rambles I met not a single stranger like myself, and few enough natives. It seems incredible that so beautiful a country should be so deserted. After walking a dozen Irish miles, you come across a group of two or three one-roomed cottages, and, like as not, one or more of those will have the roof off and the walls in ruins. The few peasants whom one sees, however, are affable and hospitable, especially when they hear you are from that terrestrial heaven whither most of their friends and relatives have gone before them.

"They seem simple and primitive enough at first sight, and yet they are as strange and incomprehensible a race as any in the world. They are as superstitious, as credulous of marvels, fairies, magicians, and omens, as the men whom St. Patrick preached to, and at the same time they are shrewd, sceptical, sensible, and bottomless liars. Upon the whole, I met with no nation on my travels whose company I enjoyed so much, or who inspired me with so much kindliness, curiosity, and repugnance.

"At length I got to a place on the sea-coast, which I will not further specify than to say that it is not many miles from Ballymacheen, on the south shore. I have seen Venice and Naples, I have driven along the Cornice Road, I have spent a month at our own Mount Desert, and I say that all of them together are not so beautiful as this glowing, deep-hued, soft-gleaming, silvery-lighted, ancient harbour and town, with the tall hills crowding round it and the black cliffs and headlands planting their iron feet in the blue, transparent sea. It is a very old place, and has had a history which it has outlived ages since. It may once have had two or three thousand inhabitants; it has scarce five or six hundred today. Half the houses are in ruins or have disappeared; many of the remainder are standing empty.

"All the people are poor, most of them abjectly so; they saunter about with bare feet and uncovered heads, the women in quaint black or dark-blue cloaks, the men in such anomalous attire as only an Irishman knows how to get together, the children half naked. The only comfortable-looking people are the monks and the priests, and the soldiers in the fort. For there is a fort there, constructed on the huge ruins of one which may have done duty in the reign of Edward the Black Prince, or earlier, in whose mossy embrasures are mounted a couple of cannon, which occasionally sent a practice-shot or two at the cliff on the other side of the harbour. The garrison consists of a dozen men and three or four officers and non-commissioned officers. I suppose they are relieved occasionally, but those I saw seemed to have become component parts of their surroundings.

"I put up at a wonderful little old inn, the only one in the place, and took my meals in a dining-saloon fifteen feet by nine, with a portrait of George I (a print varnished to preserve it) hanging over the mantelpiece. On the second evening after dinner a young gentleman came in—the dining-saloon being public property of course—and ordered some bread and cheese and a bottle of Dublin stout. We presently fell into talk; he turned out to be an officer from the fort, Lieutenant O'Connor, and a fine young specimen of the Irish soldier he was. After telling me all he knew about the town, the surrounding country, his friends, and himself, he intimated a readiness to sympathize with whatever tale I might choose to pour into his ear; and I had pleasure in trying to rival his own outspokenness. We became excellent friends; we had up a half-pint of Kinahan's whisky, and the lieutenant expressed himself in terms of high praise of my countrymen, my country, and my own particular cigars. When it became time for him to depart, I accompanied him—for there was a splendid moon abroad—and bade him farewell at the fort entrance, having promised to come over the next day and make the acquaintance of the other fellows. 'And mind your eye, now, going back, my dear boy,' he called out, as I turned my face homeward. 'Faith, 'tis a spooky place, that graveyard, and you'll as likely meet the black woman there as anywhere else!'

"The graveyard was a forlorn and barren spot on the hill-side, just the hither side of the fort: thirty or forty rough head-stones, few of which retained any semblance of the perpendicular, while many were so shattered and decayed as to seem nothing more than irregular natural projections from the ground. Who the black woman might be I knew not, and did not stay to inquire. I had never been subject to ghostly apprehensions, and as a matter of fact, though the path I had to follow was in places very bad going, not to mention a haphazard scramble over a ruined bridge that covered a deep-lying brook. I reached my inn without any adventure whatever.

"The next day I kept my appointment at the fort, and found no reason to regret it; and my friendly sentiments were abundantly reciprocated, thanks more especially, perhaps, to the success of my banjo, which I carried with me, and which was as novel as it was popular with those who listened to it. The chief personages in the social circle besides my friend the lieutenant were Major Molloy, who was in command, a racy and juicy old campaigner, with a face like a sunset, and the surgeon, Dr. Dudeen, a long, dry, humorous genius, with a wealth of anecdotical and traditional lore at his command that I have never seen surpassed. We had a jolly time of it, and it was the precursor of many more like it. The remains of October slipped away rapidly, and I was obliged to remember that I was a traveller in Europe, and not a resident in Ireland. The major, the surgeon, and the lieutenant all protested cordially against my proposed departure, but, as there was no help for it, they arranged a farewell dinner to take place in the fort on All-Halloween.

"I wish you could have been at that dinner with me! It was the essence of Irish good-fellowship. Dr. Dudeen was in great force; the major was better than the best of Lever's novels; the lieutenant was

181

overflowing with hearty good-humour, merry chaff, and sentimental rhapsodies about this or the other pretty girl of the neighbourhood. For my part I made the banjo ring as it had never rung before, and the others joined in the chorus with a mellow strength of lungs such as you don't often hear outside of Ireland. Among the stories that Dr. Dudeen regaled us with was one about the Kern of Querin and his wife, Ethelind Fionguala—which being interpreted signified 'the white-shouldered.' The lady, it appears, was originally betrothed to one O'Connor (here the lieutenant smacked his lips), but was stolen away on the wedding night by a party of vampires, who, it would seem, where at that period a prominent feature among the troubles of Ireland.

"But as they were bearing her along—she being unconscious—to that supper where she was not to eat but to be eaten, the young Kern of Querin, who happened to be out duck-shooting, met the party, and emptied his gun at it. The vampires fled, and the Kern carried the fair lady, still in a state of insensibility, to his house. 'And by the same token, Mr. Keningale,' observed the doctor, knocking the ashes out of his pipe, 'ye're after passing that very house on your way here. The one with the dark archway underneath it, and the big mullioned window at the corner. ye recollect, hanging over the street as I might say—'

"'Go 'long wid the house, Dr. Dudeen, dear,' interrupted the lieutenant; 'sure can't you see we're all dying to know what happened to sweet Miss Fionguala, God be good to her, when I was after getting her safe upstairs—'

"'Faith, then, I can tell ye that myself, Mr. O'Connor,' exclaimed the major, imparting a rotary motion to the remnants of whisky in his tumbler.'

"''Tis a question to be solved on general principles, as Colonel O'Halloran said that time he was asked what he'd do if he'd been the Dook O'Wellington, and the Prussians hadn't come up in the nick o' time at Waterloo. 'Faith,' says the colonel, 'I'll tell ye—'

"'Arrah, then, major, why would ye be interruptin' the doctor, and Mr. Keningale there lettin' his glass stay empty till he hears—The Lord save us! the bottle's empty!'

"In the excitement consequent upon this discovery, the thread of the doctor's story was lost; and before it could be recovered the evening had advanced so far that I felt obliged to withdraw. It took some time to make my proposition heard and comprehended; and a still longer time to put it in execution; so that it was fully midnight before

I found myself standing in the cool pure air outside the fort, with the farewells of my boon companions ringing in my ears.

"Considering that it had been rather a wet evening indoors, I was in a remarkably good state of preservation, and I therefore ascribed it rather to the roughness of the road than to the smoothness of the liquor, when, after advancing a few rods, I stumbled and fell. As I picked myself up I fancied I had heard a laugh, and supposed that the lieutenant, who had accompanied me to the gate, was making merry over my mishap; but on looking round I saw that the gate was closed and no one was visible. The laugh, moreover, had seemed to be close at hand, and to be even pitched in a key that was rather feminine than masculine. Of course, I must have been deceived; nobody was near me: my imagination had played me a trick, or else there was more truth than poetry in the tradition that Halloween is the carnival-time of disembodied spirits. It did not occur to me at the time that a stumble is held by the superstitious Irish to be an evil omen, and had I remembered it it would only have been to laugh at it. At all events, I was physically none the worse for my fall, and I resumed my way immediately.

"But the path was singularly difficult to find, or rather the path I was following did not seem to be the right one. I did not recognise it; I could have sworn (except I knew the contrary) that I had never seen it before. The moon had risen, though her light was as yet obscured by clouds, but neither my immediate surroundings nor the general aspect of the region appeared familiar. Dark, silent hill-sides mounted up on either hand, and the road, for the most part, plunged down-ward, as if to conduct me into the bowels of the earth. The place was alive with strange echoes, so that at times I seemed to be walking through the midst of muttering voices and mysterious whispers, and a wild, faint sound of laughter seemed ever and anon to reverberate among the passes of the hills.

"Currents of colder air sighing up through narrow defiles and dark crevices touched my face as with airy fingers. A certain feeling of anxiety and insecurity began to take possession of me, though there was no definable cause for it, unless that I might be belated in getting home. With the perverse instinct of those who are lost I hastened my steps, but was impelled now and then to glance back over my shoulder, with a sensation of being pursued. But no living creature was in sight. The moon, however, had now risen higher, and the clouds that were drifting slowly across the sky flung into the naked valley dusky shadows, which occasionally assumed shapes that looked like the vague semblance of gigantic human forms.

"How long I had been hurrying onward I know not, when, with a kind of suddenness, I found myself approaching a graveyard. It was situated on the spur of a hill, and there was no fence around it, nor anything to protect it from the incursions of passers-by. There was something in the general appearance of this spot that made me half fancy I had seen it before; and I should have taken it to be the same that I had often noticed on my way to the fort, but that the latter was only a few hundred yards distant therefrom, whereas I must have traversed several miles at least. As I drew near, moreover, I observed that the head-stones did not appear so ancient and decayed as those of the other. But what chiefly attracted my attention was the figure that was leaning or half sitting upon one of the largest of the upright slabs near the road. It was a female figure draped in black, and a closer inspection—for I was soon within a few yards of her—showed that she wore the *calla*, or long hooded cloak, the most common as well as the most ancient garment of Irish women, and doubtless of Spanish origin.

"I was a trifle startled by this apparition, so unexpected as it was, and so strange did it seem that any human creature should be at that hour of the night in so desolate and sinister a place. Involuntarily I paused as I came opposite her, and gazed at her intently. But the moonlight fell behind her, and the deep hood of her cloak so completely shadowed her face that I was unable to discern anything but the sparkle of a pair of eyes, which appeared to be returning my gaze with much vivacity.

"'You seem to be at home here,' I said, at length. 'Can you tell me where I am?'

"Hereupon the mysterious personage broke into a light laugh, which, though in itself musical and agreeable, was of a timbre and intonation that caused my heart to beat rather faster than my late pedestrian exertions warranted; for it was the identical laugh (or so my imagination persuaded me) that had echoed in my ears as I arose from my tumble an hour or two ago. For the rest, it was the laugh of a young woman, and presumably of a pretty one; and yet it had a wild, airy, mocking quality, that seemed hardly human at all, or not, at any rate, characteristic of a being of affections and limitations like unto ours. But this impression of mine was fostered, no doubt, by the unusual and uncanny circumstances of the occasion.

"'Sure, sir,' said she, 'you're at the grave of Ethelind Fionguala.'

"As she spoke, she rose to her feet, and pointed to the inscription on the stone. I bent forward, and was able, without much difficulty, to decipher the name, and a date which indicated that the occupant of the grave must have entered the disembodied state between two and three centuries ago.

"'And who are you?' was my next question.

"'I'm called Elsie,' she replied. 'But where would your honour be going November-eve?'

"I mentioned my destination, and asked her whether she could direct me thither.

"'Indeed, then, 'tis there I'm going myself,' Elsie replied; 'and if your honour'll follow me, and play me a tune on the pretty instrument, 'tisn't long we'll be on the road.'

"She pointed to the banjo which I carried wrapped up under my arm. How she knew that it was a musical instrument I could not imagine; possibly, I thought, she may have seen me playing on it as I strolled about the environs of the town. Be that as it may, I offered no opposition to the bargain, and further intimated that I would reward her more substantially on our arrival. At that she laughed again, and made a peculiar gesture with her hand above her head. I uncovered my banjo, swept my fingers across the strings, and struck into a fantastic dance-measure, to the music of which we proceeded along the path, Elsie slightly in advance, her feet keeping time to the airy measure. In fact, she trod so lightly, with an elastic, undulating movement, that with a little more it seemed as if she might float onward like a spirit. The extreme whiteness of her feet attracted my eye, and I was surprised to find that instead of being bare, as I had supposed, these were encased in white satin slippers quaintly embroidered with gold thread.

"'Elsie,' said I, lengthening my steps so as to come up with her, 'where do you live, and what do you do for a living?'

"'Sure, I live by myself,' she answered; 'and if you'd be after knowing how, you must come and see for yourself.'

"'Are you in the habit of walking over the hills at night in shoes like that?'

"'And why would I not?' she asked, in her turn. 'And where did your honour get the pretty gold ring on your finger?'

"The ring, which was of no great intrinsic value, had struck my eye in an old curiosity-shop in Cork. It was an antique of very old-fashioned design, and might have belonged (as the vender assured me was the case) to one of the early kings or queens of Ireland.

"'Do you like it?' said I.

"'Will your honour be after making a present of it to Elsie?' she returned, with an insinuating tone and turn of the head.

"'Maybe I will, Elsie, on one condition. I am an artist; I make pictures of people. If you will promise to come to my studio and let me paint your portrait, I'll give you the ring, and some money besides.'

"'And will you give me the ring now?' said Elsie.

"'Yes, if you'll promise.'

"'And will you play the music to me?' she continued.

"'As much as you like.'

"'But maybe I'll not be handsome enough for ye,' said she, with a glance of her eyes beneath the dark hood.

"'I'll take the risk of that,' I answered, laughing, 'though, all the same, I don't mind taking a peep beforehand to remember you by.' So saying, I put forth a hand to draw back the concealing hood. But Elsie eluded me, I scarce know how, and laughed a third time, with the same airy, mocking cadence.

"'Give me the ring first, and then you shall see me,' she said, coaxingly.

"'Stretch out your hand, then,' returned I, removing the ring from my finger. 'When we are better acquainted, Elsie, you won't be so suspicious.'

"She held out a slender, delicate hand, on the forefinger of which I slipped the ring. As I did so, the folds of her cloak fell a little apart, affording me a glimpse of a white shoulder and of a dress that seemed in that deceptive semi-darkness to be wrought of rich and costly material; and I caught, too, or so I fancied, the frosty sparkle of precious stones.

"'Arrah, mind where ye tread!' said Elsie, in a sudden, sharp tone.

"I looked round, and became aware for the first time that we were standing near the middle of a ruined bridge which spanned a rapid stream that flowed at a considerable depth below. The parapet of the bridge on one side was broken down, and I must have been, in fact, in imminent danger of stepping over into empty air. I made my way cautiously across the decaying structure; but, when I turned to assist Elsie, she was nowhere to be seen.

"What had become of the girl? I called, but no answer came. I gazed about on every side, but no trace of her was visible. Unless she had plunged into the narrow abyss at my feet, there was no place where she could have concealed herself—none at least that I could discover. She had vanished, nevertheless; and since her disappearance must have been premeditated, I finally came to the conclusion that it was useless to attempt to find her. She would present herself again in her own good time, or not at all. She had given me the slip very cleverly, and I must make the best of it. The adventure was perhaps worth the ring.

"On resuming my way, I was not a little relieved to find that I once more knew where I was. The bridge that I had just crossed was none other than the one I mentioned some time back; I was within a mile of the town, and my way lay clear before me. The moon, moreover, had now quite dispersed the clouds, and shone down with exquisite brilliance. Whatever her other failings, Elsie had been a trustworthy guide; she had brought me out of the depth of elf-land into the material world again. It had been a singular adventure, certainly; and I mused over it with a sense of mysterious pleasure as I sauntered along, humming snatches of airs, and accompanying myself on the strings. Hark! what light step was that behind me? It sounded like Elsie's; but no, Elsie was not there. The same impression or hallucination, however, recurred several times before I reached the outskirts of the town—the tread of an airy foot behind or beside my own. The fancy did not make me nervous; on the contrary, I was pleased with the notion of being thus haunted, and gave myself up to a romantic and genial vein of reverie.

"After passing one or two roofless and moss-grown cottages, I entered the narrow and rambling street which leads through the town. This street a short distance down widens a little, as if to afford the wayfarer space to observe a remarkable old house that stands on the northern side.

"The house was built of stone, and in a noble style of architecture; it reminded me somewhat of certain palaces of the old Italian nobility that I had seen on the Continent, and it may very probably have been built by one of the Italian or Spanish immigrants of the sixteenth or seventeenth century. The moulding of the projecting windows and arched doorway was richly carved, and upon the front of the building was an escutcheon wrought in high relief, though I could not make out the purport of the device. The moonlight failing upon this picturesque pile enhanced all its beauties, and at the same time made it seem like a vision that might dissolve away when the light ceased to shine. I must often have seen the house before, and yet I retained no definite recollection of it; I had never until now examined it with my eyes open, so to speak.

"Leaning against the wall on the opposite side of the street, I contemplated it for a long while at my leisure. The window at the corner was really a very fine and massive affair. It projected over the pavement below, throwing a heavy shadow aslant; the frames of the diamond-paned lattices were heavily mullioned. How often in past ages had that lattice been pushed open by some fair hand, revealing to a lover waiting beneath in the moonlight the charming countenance of his high-born mistress! Those were brave days. They had passed away long since. The great house had stood empty for who could tell how many years; only bats and vermin were its inhabitants.

"Where now were those who had built it? and who were they? Probably the very name of them was forgotten.

"As I continued to stare upward, however, a conjecture presented itself to my mind which rapidly ripened into a conviction. Was not this the house that Dr. Dudeen had described that very evening as having been formerly the abode of the Kern of Querin and his mysterious bride? There was the projecting window, the arched doorway. Yes, beyond a doubt this was the very house. I emitted a low exclamation of renewed interest and pleasure, and my speculations took a still more imaginative, but also a more definite turn.

"What had been the fate of that lovely lady after the Kern had brought her home insensible in his arms? Did she recover, and were they married and made happy ever after; or had the sequel been a tragic one? I remembered to have read that the victims of vampires generally became vampires themselves. Then my thoughts went back to that grave on the hill-side. Surely that was unconsecrated ground. Why had they buried her there? Ethelind of the white shoulder! Ah! why had not I lived in those days; or why might not some magic cause them to live again for me? Then would I seek this street at midnight, and standing here beneath her window, I would lightly touch the strings of my bandore until the casement opened cautiously and she looked down. A sweet vision indeed! And what prevented my realizing it? Only a matter of a couple of centuries or so. And was time, then, at which poets and philosophers sneer, so rigid and real a matter that a little faith and imagination might not overcome it? At all events, I had my banjo, the bandore's legitimate and lineal descendant, and the memory of Fionguala should have the love-ditty.

"Hereupon, having retuned the instrument, I launched forth into an old Spanish love-song, which I had met with in some mouldy library during my travels, and had set to music of my own. I sang low, for the deserted street re-echoed the lightest sound, and what I sang must reach only my lady's ears. The words were warm with the fire of the ancient Spanish chivalry, and I threw into their expression all the passion of the lovers of romance. Surely Fionguala, the white-shouldered, would hear, and awaken from her sleep of centuries, and come to the latticed casement and look down! Hist! see yonder! What light—what shadow is that that seems to flit from room to room within the abandoned house, and now approaches the mullioned window? Are my eyes dazzled by the play of the moonlight, or does the casement move—does it open? Nay, this is no delusion; there is no error of the senses here. There is simply a woman, young, beautiful, and richly attired, bending forward from the window, and silently beckoning me to approach.

"Too much amazed to be conscious of amazement, I advanced until I stood directly beneath the casement, and the lady's face, as she stooped toward me, was not more than twice a man's height from my own. She smiled and kissed her fingertips; something white fluttered in her hand, then fell through the air to the ground at my feet. The next moment she had withdrawn, and I heard the lattice close.

"I picked up what she had let fall; it was a delicate lace handkerchief, tied to the handle of an elaborately wrought bronze key. It was evidently the key of the house, and invited me to enter. I loosened it from the handkerchief, which bore a faint, delicious perfume, like the aroma of flowers in an ancient garden, and turned to the arched doorway. I felt no misgiving, and scarcely any sense of strangeness. All was as I had wished it to be, and as it should be; the medieval age was alive once more, and as for myself, I almost felt the velvet cloak hanging from my shoulder and the long rapier dangling at my belt. Standing in front of the door I thrust the key into the lock, turned it, and felt the bolt yield. The next instant the door was opened, apparently from within; I stepped across the threshold, the door closed again, and I was alone in the house, and in darkness.

"Not alone, however! As I extended my hand to grope my way it was met by another hand, soft, slender, and cold, which insinuated itself gently into mine and drew me forward. Forward I went, nothing loath; the darkness was impenetrable, but I could hear the light rustle of a dress close to me, and the same delicious perfume that had emanated from the handkerchief enriched the air that I breathed, while the little hand that clasped and was clasped by my own alternately tightened and half relaxed the hold of its soft cold fingers. In this manner, and treading lightly, we traversed what I presumed to be a long, irregular passageway, and ascended a staircase. Then another corridor, until finally we paused, a door opened, emitting a flood of soft light, into which we entered, still hand in hand. The darkness and the doubt were at an end.

"The room was of imposing dimensions, and was furnished and decorated in a style of antique splendour. The walls were draped with mellow hues of tapestry; clusters of candles burned in polished silver sconces, and were reflected and multiplied in tall mirrors placed in the four corners of the room. The heavy beams of the dark oaken ceiling crossed each other in squares, and were laboriously carved; the curtains and the drapery of the chairs were of heavy-figured damask. At one end of the room was a broad ottoman, and in front of it a table, on which was set forth, in massive silver dishes, a sumptuous repast, with wines in crystal beakers. At the side was a vast and deep fire-place, with space enough on the broad hearth to burn whole trunks of trees. No fire, however, was there, but only a great heap of dead embers; and the room, for all its magnificence, was cold—cold as a tomb, or as my lady's hand—and it sent a subtle chill creeping to my heart.

"But my lady! how fair she was! I gave but a passing glance at the room; my eyes and my thoughts were all for her. She was dressed in white, like a bride; diamonds sparkled in her dark hair and on her snowy bosom; her lovely face and slender lips were pale, and all the paler for the dusky glow of her eyes. She gazed at me with a strange, elusive smile; and yet there was, in her aspect and bearing, something familiar in the midst of strangeness, like the burden of a song heard long ago and recalled among other conditions and surroundings. It seemed to me that something in me recognized her and knew her, had known her always. She was the woman of whom I had dreamed, whom I had beheld in visions, whose voice and face had haunted me from boyhood up. Whether we had ever met before, as human beings meet, I knew not; perhaps I had been blindly seeking her all over the world, and she had been awaiting me in this splendid room, sitting by those dead embers until all the warmth had gone out of her blood, only to be restored by the heat with which my love might supply her.

"'I thought you had forgotten me,' she said, nodding as if in answer to my thought. 'The night was so late—our one night of the year! How my heart rejoiced when I heard your dear voice singing the song, I know so well! Kiss me—my lips are cold!'

190

"Cold indeed they were—cold as the lips of death. But the warmth of my own seemed to revive them. They were now tinged with a faint colour, and in her cheeks also appeared a delicate shade of pink. She drew fuller breath, as one who recovers from a long lethargy. Was it my life that was feeding her? I was ready to give her all. She drew me to the table and pointed to the viands and the wine.

"'Eat and drink,' she said. 'You have travelled far, and you need food.'

"'Will you eat and drink with me?' said I, pouring out the wine.

"'You are the only nourishment I want,' was her answer. 'This wine is thin and cold. Give me wine as red as your blood and as warm, and I will drain a goblet to the dregs.'

"At these words, I know not why, a slight shiver passed through me. She seemed to gain vitality and strength at every instant, but the chill of the great room struck into me more and more.

"She broke into a fantastic flow of spirits, clapping her hands, and dancing about me like a child. Who was she? And was I myself, or was she mocking me when she implied that we had belonged to each other of old? At length she stood still before me, crossing her hands over her breast. I saw upon the forefinger of her right hand the gleam of an antique ring.

"'Where did you get that ring?' I demanded.

"She shook her head and laughed. 'Have you been faithful?' she asked. 'It is my ring; it is the ring that unites us; it is the ring you gave me when you loved me first. It is the ring of the Kern—the fairy ring, and I am your Ethelind—Ethelind Fionguala.'

"'So be it,' I said, casting aside all doubt and fear, and yielding myself wholly to the spell of her inscrutable eyes and wooing lips. 'You are mine, and I am yours, and let us be happy while the hours last.'

"'You are mine, and I am yours,' she repeated, nodding her head with an elfish smile. 'Come and sit beside me, and sing that sweet song again that you sang to me so long ago. Ah, now I shall live a hundred years.'

"We seated ourselves on the ottoman, and while she nestled luxuriously among the cushions, I took my banjo and sang to her. The song and the music resounded through the lofty room, and came back in throbbing echoes. And before me as I sang, I saw the face and form of Ethelind Fionguala, in her jewelled bridal dress, gazing at me with burning eyes. She was pale no longer, but ruddy and warm, and life was like a flame within her. It was I who had become cold and bloodless, yet with the last life that was in me I would have sung to her of love that can never die. But at length my eyes grew dim, the room seemed to darken, the form of Ethelind alternately brightened and waxed indistinct, like the last flickerings of a fire; I swayed toward her, and felt myself lapsing into unconsciousness, with my head resting on her white shoulder."

Here Keningale paused a few moments in his story, flung a fresh log upon the fire, and then continued:

"I awoke, I know not how long afterward. I was in a vast, empty room in a ruined building. Rotten shreds of drapery depended from the walls, and heavy festoons of spiders' webs grey with dust covered the windows, which were destitute of glass or sash; they had been boarded up with rough planks which had themselves become rotten with age, and admitted through their holes and crevices pallid rays of light and chilly draughts of air. A bat, disturbed by these rays or by my own movement, detached himself from his hold on a remnant of mouldy tapestry near me, and after circling dizzily around my head, wheeled the flickering noiselessness of his flight into a darker corner. As I arose unsteadily from the heap of miscellaneous rubbish on which I had been lying, something which had been resting across my knees fell to the floor with a rattle. I picked it up, and found it to be my banjo—as you see it now.

"Well, that is all I have to tell. My health was seriously impaired; all the blood seemed to have been drawn out of my veins; I was pale and haggard, and the chill—Ah, that chill," murmured Keningale, drawing nearer to the fire, and spreading out his hands to catch the warmth—"I shall never get over it; I shall carry it to my grave."

The Vampire Maid

Hume Nisbet

It was the exact kind of abode that I had been looking after for weeks, for I was in that condition of mind when absolute renunciation of society was a necessity. I had become diffident of myself, and wearied of my kind. A strange unrest was in my blood; a barren dearth in my brains. Familiar objects and faces had grown distasteful to me. I wanted to be alone.

This is the mood which comes upon every sensitive and artistic mind when the possessor has been overworked or living too long in one groove. It is Nature's hint for him to seek pastures new; the sign that a retreat has become needful.

If he does not yield, he breaks down and becomes whimsical and hypochondriacal, as well as hypercritical. It is always a bad sign when a man becomes over-critical and censorious about his own or other people's work, for it means that he is losing the vital portions of work, freshness and enthusiasm.

Before I arrived at the dismal stage of criticism, I hastily packed up my knapsack, and taking the train to Westmorland, I began my tramp in search of solitude, bracing air and romantic surroundings.

Many places I came upon during that early summer wandering that appeared to have almost the required conditions, yet some petty drawback prevented me from deciding. Sometimes it was the scenery that I did not take kindly to. At other places I took sudden antipathies to the landlady or landlord, and felt I would abhor them before a week was spent under their charge. Other places which might have suited me I could not have, as they did not want a lodger. Fate was driving me to this Cottage on the Moor, and no one can resist destiny.

One day I found myself on a wide and pathless moor near the sea. I had slept the night before at a small hamlet, but that was already eight miles in my rear, and since I had turned my back upon it I had not seen any signs of humanity; I was alone with a fair sky above me, a balmy ozone-filled wind blowing over the stony and heather-clad mounds, and nothing to disturb my meditations.

How far the moor stretched I had no knowledge; I only knew that by keeping in a straight line I would come to the ocean cliffs, then perhaps after a time arrive at some fishing village.

I had provisions in my knapsack, and being young did not fear a night under the stars. I was inhaling the delicious summer air and once more getting back the vigour and happiness I had lost; my city-dried brains were again becoming juicy.

Thus, hour after hour slid past me, with the paces, until I had covered about fifteen miles since morning, when I saw before me in the distance a solitary stone-built cottage with roughly slated roof. 'I'll camp there if possible,' I said to myself as I quickened my steps towards it.

To one in search of a quiet, free life, nothing could have possibly been more suitable than this cottage. It stood on the edge of lofty cliffs, with its front door facing the moor and the back-yard wall over-looking the ocean. The sound of the dancing waves struck upon my ears like a lullaby as I drew near; how they would thunder when the autumn gales came on and the seabirds fled shrieking to the shelter of the sedges.

A small garden spread in front, surrounded by a dry-stone wall just high enough for one to lean lazily upon when inclined. This garden was a flame of colour, scarlet predominating, with those other soft shades that cultivated poppies take on in their blooming, for this was all that the garden grew.

As I approached, taking notice of this singular assortment of pop-pies, and the orderly cleanness of the windows, the front door opened and a woman appeared who impressed me at once favourably as she leisurely came along the pathway to the gate, and drew it back as if to welcome me.

She was of middle age, and when young must have been remark-ably good-looking. She was tall and still shapely, with smooth clear skin, regular features and a calm expression that at once gave me a sensation of rest.

To my inquiries she said that she could give me both a sitting and bedroom, and invited me inside to see them. As I looked at her smooth black hair, and cool brown eyes, I felt that I would not be too particular about the accommodation. With such a landlady, I was sure to find what I was after here.

The rooms surpassed my expectation, dainty white curtains and bedding with the perfume of lavender about them, a sitting-room homely yet cosy without being crowded. With a sigh of infinite relief, I flung down my knapsack and clinched the bargain.

She was a widow with one daughter, whom I did not see the first day, as she was unwell and confined to her own room, but on the next day she was somewhat better, and then we met.

The fare was simple, yet it suited me exactly for the time, delicious milk and butter with home-made scones, fresh eggs and bacon; after a hearty tea I went early to bed in a condition of perfect content with my quarters.

Yet happy and tired out as I was, I had by no means a comfortable night. This I put down to the strange bed. I slept certainly, but my sleep was filled with dreams so that I woke late and unrefreshed; a good walk on the moor, however, restored me, and I returned with a fine appetite for breakfast.

Certain conditions of mind, with aggravating circumstances, are required before even a young man can fall in love at first sight, as Shakespeare has shown in his *Romeo and Juliet*. In the city, where many fair faces passed me every hour, I had remained like a stoic, yet no sooner did I enter the cottage after that morning walk than I succumbed instantly before the weird charms of my landlady's daughter, Ariadne Brunnell.

She was somewhat better this morning and able to meet me at breakfast, for we had our meals together while I was their lodger. Ariadne was not beautiful in the strictly classical sense, her complexion being too lividly white and her expression too set to be quite pleasant at first sight; yet, as her mother had informed me, she had been ill for some time, which accounted for that defect. Her features were not regular, her hair and eyes seemed too black with that strangely white skin, and her lips too red for any except the decadent harmonies of an Aubrey Beardsley.

Yet my fantastic dreams of the preceding night, with my morning walk, had prepared me to be enthralled by this modern poster-like invalid.

The loneliness of the moor, with the singing of the ocean, had gripped my heart with a wistful longing. The incongruity of those flaunting and evanescent poppy flowers, dashing the giddy tints in the face of that sober heath, touched me with a shiver as I approached the cottage, and lastly that weird embodiment of startling contrasts completed my subjugation.

She rose from her chair as her mother introduced her, and smiled while she held out her hand. I clasped that soft snowflake, and as I did so a faint thrill tingled over me and rested on my heart, stopping for the moment its beating.

This contact seemed also to have affected her as it did me; a clear flush, like a white flame, lighted up her face, so that it glowed as if an alabaster lamp had been lit; her black eyes became softer and more humid as our glances crossed, and her scarlet lips grew moist. She was a living woman now, while before she had seemed half a corpse.

She permitted her white slender hand to remain in mine longer than most people do at an introduction, and then she slowly withdrew it, still regarding me with steadfast eyes for a second or two afterwards.

Fathomless velvety eyes these were, yet before they were shifted from mine, they appeared to have absorbed all my willpower and made me her abject slave. They looked like deep dark pools of clear water, yet they filled me with fire and deprived me of strength. I sank into my chair almost as languidly as I had risen from my bed that morning.

Yet I made a good breakfast, and although she hardly tasted anything, this strange girl rose much refreshed and with a slight glow of colour on her cheeks, which improved her so greatly that she appeared younger and almost beautiful.

I had come here seeking solitude, but since I had seen Ariadne it seemed as if I had come for her only. She was not very lively; indeed, thinking back, I cannot recall any spontaneous remark of hers; she answered my questions by monosyllables and left me to lead in words; yet she was insinuating and appeared to lead my thoughts in her direction and speak to me with her eyes. I cannot describe her minutely, I only know that from the first glance and touch she gave me I was bewitched and could think of nothing else.

It was a rapid, distracting, and devouring infatuation that possessed me; all day long I followed her about like a dog, every night I dreamed of that white glowing face, those steadfast black eyes, those moist scarlet lips, and each morning I rose more languid than I had been the day before. Sometimes I dreamt that she was kissing me with those red lips, while I shivered at the contact of her silky black tresses as they covered my throat; sometimes that we were floating in the air, her arms about me and her long hair enveloping us both like an inky cloud, while I lay supine and helpless.

She went with me after breakfast on that first day to the moor, and before we came back, I had spoken my love and received her assent. I held her in my arms and had taken her kisses in answer to mine, nor did I think it strange that all this had happened so quickly. She was mine, or rather I was hers, without a pause. I told her it was fate that had sent me to her, for I had no doubts about my love, and she replied that I had restored her to life.

Acting upon Ariadne's advice, and also from a natural shyness, I did not inform her mother how quickly matters had progressed between us, yet although we both acted as circumspectly as possible, I had no doubt Mrs Brunnell could see how engrossed we were in each other. Lovers are not unlike ostriches in their modes of concealment. I was not afraid of asking Mrs Brunnell for her daughter, for she already showed her partiality towards me, and had bestowed upon me some confidences regarding her own position in life, and I therefore knew that, so far as social position was concerned, there could be no real objection to our marriage. They lived in this lonely spot for the sake of their health, and kept no servant because they could not get any to take service so far away from other humanity. My coming had been opportune and welcome to both mother and daughter.

For the sake of decorum, however, I resolved to delay my confession for a week or two and trust to some favourable opportunity of doing it discreetly.

Meantime Ariadne and I passed our time in a thoroughly idle and lotus-eating style. Each night I retired to bed meditating starting work next day, each morning I rose languid from those disturbing dreams with no thought for anything outside my love. She grew stronger every day, while I appeared to be taking her place as the invalid, yet I was more frantically in love than ever, and only happy when with her. She was my lone-star, my only joy--my life.

We did not go great distances, for I liked best to lie on the dry heath and watch her glowing face and intense eyes while I listened to the surging of the distant waves. It was love made me lazy, I thought, for unless a man has all he longs for beside him, he is apt to copy the domestic cat and bask in the sunshine.

I had been enchanted quickly. My disenchantment came as rapidly, although it was long before the poison left my blood.

One night, about a couple of weeks after my coming to the cottage, I had returned after a delicious moonlight walk with Ariadne.

The night was warm and the moon at the full, therefore I left my bedroom window open to let in what little air there was.

I was more than usually fagged out, so that I had only strength enough to remove my boots and coat before I flung myself wearily on the coverlet and fell almost instantly asleep without tasting the night-cap draught that was constantly placed on the table, and which I had always drained thirstily.

I had a ghastly dream this night. I thought I saw a monster bat, with the face and tresses of Ariadne, fly into the open window and fasten its white teeth and scarlet lips on my arm. I tried to beat the horror away, but could not, for I seemed chained down and thralled also with drowsy delight as the beast sucked my blood with a gruesome rapture.

I looked out dreamily and saw a line of dead bodies of young men lying on the floor, each with a red mark on their arms, on the same part where the vampire was then sucking me, and I remembered having seen and wondered at such a mark on my own arm for the past fortnight. In a flash I understood the reason for my strange weakness, and at the same moment a sudden prick of pain roused me from my dreamy pleasure.

The vampire in her eagerness had bitten a little too deeply that night, unaware that I had not tasted the drugged draught. As I woke, I saw her fully revealed by the midnight moon, with her black tresses flowing loosely, and with her red lips glued to my arm. With a shriek of horror I dashed her backwards, getting one last glimpse of her savage eyes, glowing white face and blood-stained red lips; then I rushed out to the night, moved on by my fear and hatred, nor did I pause in my mad flight until I had left miles between me and that accursed Cottage on the Moor.

When I Was Dead

Vincent James O'Sullivan

"And yet my heart
Will not confess he owes the malady
That doth my life besiege."
—*All's Well that Ends Well.*

That was the worst of Ravenel Hall. The passages were long and gloomy, the rooms were musty and dull, even the pictures were sombre and their subjects dire. On an autumn evening, when the wind soughed and wailed through the trees in the park, and the dead leaves whistled and chattered, while the rain clamoured at the windows, small wonder that folk with gentle nerves went a-straying in their wits! An acute nervous system is a grievous burthen on the deck of a yacht under sunlit skies: at Ravenel the chain of nerves was prone to clash and jangle a funeral march. Nerves must be pampered in a tea-drinking community; and the ghost that your grandfather, with a skinful of port, could face and never tremble, sets you, in your sobriety, sweating and shivering; or, becoming scared (poor ghost!) of your bulged eyes and dropped jaw, he quenches expectation by not appearing at all.

So, I am left to conclude that it was tea which made my acquaintance afraid to stay at Ravenel. Even Wilvern gave over; and as he is in the Guards, and a polo player, his nerves ought to be strong enough. On the night before he went, I was explaining to him my theory, that if you place some drops of human blood near you, and then concentrate your thoughts, you will after a while see before you a man or a woman who will stay with you during long hours of the night, and even meet you at unexpected places during the day, I was explaining this theory, I repeat, when he interrupted me with words, senseless enough, which sent me fencing and parrying strangers,—on my guard,

"I say, Alistair, my dear chap!" he began, "you ought to get out of this place, and go up to town and knock about a bit—you really ought, you know."

"Yes," I replied, "and get poisoned at the hotels by bad food, and at the clubs by bad talk, I suppose. No, thank you: and let me say that your care for my health enervates me."

"Well, you can do as you like," says he, rapping with his feet on the floor; "I'm hanged if I stay here after tomorrow—I'll be staring mad if I do!"

He was my last visitor. Some weeks after his departure I was sitting in the library with my drops of blood by me. I had got my theory nearly perfect by this time; but there was one difficulty.

The figure which I had ever before me, was a figure of an old woman with her hair divided in the middle; and her hair fell to her shoulders, white on one side and black on the other. She was a very complete old woman; but, alas! she was eyeless, and when I tried to construct the eyes she would shrivel and rot in my sight. But tonight, I was thinking, thinking, as I had never thought before, and the eyes were just creeping into the head, when I heard a terrible crash outside as if some heavy substance had fallen. Of a sudden the door was flung open, and two maid-servants entered. They glanced at the rug under my chair, and at that they turned a sick white, cried on God, and huddled out.

"How dare you enter the library in this manner?" I demanded, sternly. No answer came back from them, so I started in pursuit. I found all the servants of the house gathered in a knot at the end of the passage.

"Mrs. Pebble," I said smartly, to the housekeeper, "I want those two women discharged tomorrow. It's an outrage! You ought to be more careful."

But she was not attending to me. Her face was distorted with terror.

"Ah dear, ah dear!" she went, "We had better all go to the library together," says she to the others.

"Am I still master of my own house, Mrs. Pebble?" I inquired, bringing my knuckles down with a bang on a table.

None of them seemed to see me or hear me: I might as well have been shrieking in a desert. I followed them down the passage, and forbade them with strong words to enter the library. But they trooped past me, and stood with a clutter round the hearth-rug. Then three or four of them began dragging and lifting, as if they were lifting a helpless body, and stumbled with their imaginary burthen over to a sofa. Old Soames, the butler, stood near.

"Poor young gentleman!" he said, with a sob; "I've knowed him since he was a baby. And to think of him being dead like this—and so young too!"

I crossed the room. "What's all this, Soames?" I cried, shaking him roughly by the shoulders. "I'm not dead, I'm here—here!"

As he did not stir, I got a little scared. "Soames, old friend," I called, "don't you know me? Don't you know the little boy you used to play with? Say I'm not dead, Soames, please, Soames!"

He stooped down and kissed the sofa. "I think one of the men ought to ride over to the village for the doctor, Mr. Soames," says Mrs. Pebble, and he shuffled out to give the order.

Now, this doctor was an ignorant dog, whom I had been forced to exclude from the house, because he went about proclaiming his belief in a saving God, at the same time that he proclaimed himself a man of science. He, I was resolved, should never cross my threshold, and I followed Mrs. Pebble through the house, screaming out prohibition. But I did not catch even a groan from her, not a nod of the head nor cast of the eye, to shew that she had heard.

I met the doctor at the door of the library. "Well!" I sneered, throwing my hand in his face, "have you come to teach me some new prayers?"

He brushed by me as if he had not felt the blow, and knelt down by the sofa.

"Rupture of a vessel on the brain, I think," he says to Soames and Mrs. Pebble after a moment. "He has been dead some hours. Poor fellow! You had better telegraph for his sister, and I will send up the undertaker to arrange the body."

"You liar!" I yelled, "You whining liar! How have you the insolence to tell my servants that I am dead, when you see me here face to face?"

He was far in the passage, with Soames and Mrs. Pebble at his heels, ere I had ended, and not one of the three turned round.

All that night I sat in the library. Strangely enough, I had no wish to sleep, nor, during the time that followed, had I any craving to eat. In the morning the men came, and although I ordered them out, they proceeded to minister about something I could not see. So, all day I stayed in the library or wandered about the house, and at night the men came again, bringing with them a coffin. Then, in my humour, thinking it shame that so fine a coffin should be empty, I lay the night in it, and slept a soft, dreamless sleep—the softest sleep I have ever slept. And when the men came the next day, I rested still, and the undertaker shaved me. A strange valet!

On the evening after that, I was coming downstairs, when I noted some luggage in the hall, and so learned that my sister had arrived. I had not seen this woman since her marriage, and I loathed her more than I loathed any creature in this ill-organised world. She was very beautiful I think—tall, and dark, and straight as a ram-rod—and she had an unruly passion for scandal and dress. I suppose the reason I disliked her so intensely was, that she had a habit of making one aware of her presence when she was several yards off. At half-past nine o'clock my sister came down to the library in a very charming wrap, and I soon found that she was as insensible to my presence as the others. I trembled with rage to see her kneel down by the coffin—my coffin; but when she bent over to kiss the pillow, I threw away control.

A knife which had been used to cut string was lying on a table: I seized it and drove it into her neck. She fled from the room screaming.

"Come, come!" she cried, her voice quivering with anguish, "the corpse is bleeding from the nose."

Then I cursed her.

On the morning of the third day there was a heavy fall of snow. About eleven o'clock I observed that the house was filled with blacks, and mutes, and folk of the county, who came for the obsequies. I went into the library and sat still, and waited. Soon came the men, and they closed the lid of the coffin and bore it out on their shoulders. And yet I sat, feeling rather sadly that something of mine had been taken away: I could not quite think what. For half an hour perhaps—dreaming—dreaming: and then I glided to the hall door. There was no trace left of the funeral but after a while I sighted a black thread winding slowly across the white plain.

"I'm not dead," I moaned, and rubbed my face in the pure snow and tossed it on my neck and hair, "Sweet God, I am not dead."

A Mystery of the Campagna

Von Degen (Anne Crawford)

Martin Detaille's Account of What Happened at the Vigna
Marziali

Marcello's voice is pleading with me now, perhaps because after years of separation I have met an old acquaintance who had a part in his strange story. I have a longing to tell it, and have asked Monsieur Sutton to help me. He noted down the circumstances at the time, and he is willing to join his share to mine, that Marcello may be remembered.

One day, it was in spring, he appeared in my little studio among the laurels and green alleys of the Villa Medici. "Come, *mon enfant*," he said, "put up your paints;" and he unceremoniously took my palette out of my hand. "I have a cab waiting outside, and we are going in search of a hermitage." He was already washing my brushes as he spoke, and this softened my heart, for I hate to do it myself. Then he pulled off my velvet jacket and took down my respectable coat from a nail on the wall. I let him dress me like a child. We always did his will, and he knew it, and in a moment, we were sitting in the cab, driving through the Via Sistina on our way to the Porta San Giovanni, whither he had directed the coachman to go.

I must tell my story as I can, for though I have been told by my comrades, who cannot know very well, that I can speak good English, writing it is another thing. Monsieur Sutton has asked me to use his tongue, because he has so far forgotten mine that he will not trust himself in it, though he has promised to correct my mistakes, that what I have to tell you may not seem ridiculous, and make people laugh when they read of Marcello. I tell him I wish to write this for my countrymen, not his; but he reminds me that Marcello had many English friends who still live, and that the English do not forget as we do. It is of no use to reason with him, for neither do they yield as we do, and so I have consented to his wish. I think he has a reason which he does not tell me, but let it go. I will translate it all into my own language for my own people. Your English phrases seem to me to be always walking sideways, or trying to look round the corner or stand upon their heads, and they have as many little tails as a kite. I will try not to have recourse to my own language, but he must pardon me if I forget myself. He may be sure I do not do it to offend him. How that I have explained so much, let me go on.

When we had passed out of the Porta San Giovanni, the coachman drove as slowly as he liked. The pay is more outside the gates, and they always pretend then that their horses are tired, and creep as slowly as possible; but Marcello was never practical How could he be, I ask you, with an opera in his head? So, we crawled along, and he gazed dreamily before him. At last, when we had reached the part where the little villas and vineyards begin, he began to look about him.

You all know how it is out there; iron gates with rusty names or initials over them, and beyond them straight walks bordered with roses and lavender leading up to a forlorn little casino, with trees and a wilderness behind it sloping down to the Campagna, lonely enough to be murdered in and no one to hear you cry. We stopped at several of these gates and Marcello stood looking in, but none of the places were to his taste. He seemed not to doubt that he might have whatever pleased him, but nothing did so. He would jump out and run to the gate, and return saying, "The shape of those windows would disturb my inspiration," or, "That yellow paint would make me fail my duet in the second Act;" and once he liked the air of the house well enough, but there were marigolds growing in the walk, and he hated them.

So, we drove on and on, until I thought we should find nothing more to reject. At last we came to one which suited him, though it was terribly lonely, and I should have fancied it very *agaçant* to live so far away from the world with nothing but those melancholy olives and green oaks—ilexes, you call them—for company.

"I shall live here and become famous!" he said decidedly, as he pulled the iron rod which rang a great bell inside. We waited, and then he rang again very impatiently and stamped his foot.

"No one lives here, *mon vieux!* Come, it is getting late, and it is so damp out here, and you know that the damp for a tenor voice—" He stamped his foot again and interrupted me angrily.

"Why, then, have you got a tenor? You are stupid! a bass would be more sensible; nothing hurts it. But you have not got one, and you call yourself my friend! Go home without me." How could I, so far on foot? "Go and sing your lovesick songs to your lean English misses! They will thank you with a cup of abominable tea, and you will be in Paradise! This is *my* Paradise, and I shall stay until the angel comes to open it!"

He was very cross and unreasonable, and those were just the times when one loved him most, so I waited and enveloped my throat in my pocket-handkerchief and sang a passage or two just to prevent my voice from becoming stiff in that damp air.

"Be still! silence yourself!" he cried. "I cannot hear if anyone is coming."

Someone came at last, a rough-looking sort of keeper, or *guardiano* as they are called there, who looked at us as though he thought we were mad. One of us certainly was, but it was not I. Marcello spoke pretty good Italian, with a French accent, it is true, but the man understood him, especially as he held his purse in his hand. I heard him say a great many impetuously persuasive things all in a breath, then he slipped a gold piece into the *guardiano's* horny hand, and the two turned toward the house, the man shrugging his shoulders in a resigned sort of way, and Marcello called out to me over his shoulder—

"Go home in the cab, or you will be late for your horrible English party! I am going to stay here tonight." *Ma foi!* I took his permission and left him; for a tenor voice is as tyrannical as a jealous woman. Besides, I was furious, and yet I laughed. His was the artist temperament, and appeared to us by turns absurd, sublime, and intensely irritating; but this last never for long, and we all felt that were we more like him our pictures would be worth more. I had not got as far as the city gate when my temper had cooled, and I began to reproach myself for leaving him in that lonely place with his purse full of money, for he was not poor at all, and tempting the dark *guardiano* to murder him.

Nothing could be easier than to kill him in his sleep and bury him away somewhere under the olive trees or in some old vault of a ruined catacomb, so common on the borders of the Campagna. There were sure to be a hundred such convenient places. I stopped the coachman and told him to turn back, but be shook his head and said something about having to be in the *piazza* of St. Peter at eight o'clock. His horse began to go lame, as though he had understood his master and were his accomplice. What could I do? I said to myself that it was fate, and let him take me back to the Villa Medici, where I had to pay him a pretty sum for our crazy expedition, and then he rattled off, the horse not lame at all, leaving me bewildered at this strange afternoon.

I did not sleep well that night, though my tenor song had been applauded, and the English misses had caressed me much. I tried not to think of Marcello, and he did not trouble me much until I went to bed; but then I could not sleep, as I have told you. I fancied him already murdered, and being buried in the darkness by the *guardiano*. I saw the man dragging his body, with the beautiful head thumping against the stones, down dark passages, and at last leaving it all bloody and covered with earth under a black arch in a recess, and coming back to count the gold pieces.

But then again, I fell asleep, and dreamed that Marcello was standing at the gate and stamping his foot; and then I slept no more, but got up as soon as the dawn came, and dressed myself and went to my studio at the end of the laurel walk. I took down my painting-jacket, and remembered how he had pulled it off my shoulders. I took up the brushes he had washed for me; they were only half cleaned after all, and stiff with paint and soap. I felt glad to be angry with him, and *sacré'd* a little, for it made me sure that he was yet alive if I could scold at him. Then I pulled out my study of his head for my picture of Mucius Scaevola holding his hand in the flame, and then I forgave him; for who could look upon that face and not love it?

I worked with the fire of friendship in my brush, and did my best to endow the features with the expression of scorn and obstinacy I had seen at the gate. It could not have been more suitable to my subject! Had I seen it for the last time? You will ask me why I did not leave my work and go to see if anything had happened to him, but against this there were several reasons. Our yearly exhibition was not far off and my picture was barely painted in, and my comrades had sworn that it would not be ready. I was expecting a model for the King of the Etruscans; a man who cooked chestnuts in the Piazza Montanara, and who had consented to stoop to sit to me as a great favour; and then, to tell the truth, the morning was beginning to dispel my fancies.

I had a good northern light to work by, with nothing sentimental about it, and I was not fanciful by nature; so when I sat down to my easel I told myself that I had been a fool, and that Marcello was perfectly safe: the smell of the paints helping me to feel practical again. Indeed, I thought every moment that he would come in, tired of his caprice already, and even was preparing and practising a little lecture for him. Someone knocked at my door, and I cried "*Entre!*" thinking it was he at last; but no, it was Pierre Magnin.

"There is a curious man, a man of the country, who wants you," he said. "He has your address on a dirty piece of paper in Marcello's handwriting, and a letter for you, but he won't give it up. He says he must see 'il Signor Martino.' He'd make a superb model for a murderer! Come and speak to him, and keep him while I get a sketch of his head."

I followed Magnin through the garden, and outside—for the porter had not allowed him to enter—I found the *guardiano* of yesterday. He showed his white teeth, and said "Good day, *signore*," like a Christian; and here in Rome he did not look half so murderous, only a stupid, brown, country fellow. He had a rough peasant-cart waiting, and he had tied up his shaggy horse to a ring in the walk I held out my hand for the letter and pretended to find it difficult to read, for I saw Magnin standing with his sketch-book in the shadow of the entrance-hall. The note said this—I have it still, and I will copy it. It was written in pencil on a leaf tom from his pocket-book:

> *Mon vieux!* I have passed a good night here, and the man will keep me as long as I like. Nothing will happen to me, except that I shall be divinely quiet, and I have already a famous *motif* in my head. Go to my lodgings and pack up some clothes and all my manuscripts, with plenty of music paper and a few bottles of Bordeaux, and give them to my messenger. Be quick about it!
>
> Fame is preparing to descend upon me! If you care to see me, do not come before eight days. The gate will not be opened if you come sooner. The *guardiano* is my slave, and he has instructions to kill any intruder who in the guise of a friend tries to get in uninvited. He will do it, for he has confessed to me that he has murdered three men already.

(Of course, this was a joke. I knew Marcello's way.)

> When you come, go to the *poste restante* and fetch my letters. Here is my card to legitimate you. Don't forget pens and a bottle of ink! Your
>
> Marcello.

There was nothing for it but to jump into the cart, tell Magnin, who had finished his sketch, to lock up my studio, and go bumping off to obey these commands. We drove to his lodgings in the Via del Governo Vecchio, and there I made a bundle of all that I could think of; the landlady hindering me by a thousand questions about when the *signore* would return. He had paid for the rooms in advance, so she had no need to be anxious about her rent. When I told her where he was, she shook her head, and talked a good deal about the bad air out there, and said "Poor *signorino!*" in a melancholy way, as though he were already buried, and looked mournfully after us from the window when we drove away. She irritated me, and made me feel superstitious. At the corner of the Via del Tritone I jumped down and gave the man a *franc* out of pure sentimentality, and cried after him, "Greet the *signore!*" but he did not hear me, and jogged away stupidly while I was longing to be with him. Marcello was a cross to us sometimes, but we loved him always.

The eight days went by sooner than I had thought they would, and Thursday came, bright and sunny, for my expedition. At one o'clock I descended into the Piazza di Spagna, and made a bargain with a man who had a well-fed horse, remembering how dearly Marcello's want of good sense had cost me a week ago, and we drove off at a good pace to the Vigna Marziali, as I was almost forgetting to say that it was called. My heart was beating, though I did not know why I should feel so much emotion. When we reached the iron gate the *guardiano* answered my ring directly, and I had no sooner set foot in the long flower-walk than I saw Marcello hastening to meet me.

"I knew you would come," he said, drawing my arm within his, and so we walked toward the little grey house, which had a sort of portico and several balconies, and a sun-dial on its front. There were grated windows down to the ground floor, and the place, to my relief, looked safe and habitable. He told me that the man did not sleep there, but in a little hut down toward the Campagna, and that he, Marcello, locked himself in safely every night, which I was also relieved to know.

"What do you get to eat?" said I.

"Oh, I have goat's flesh, and dried beans and polenta, with pecorino cheese, and there is plenty of black bread and sour wine," he answered smilingly. "You see, I am not starved."

"Do not overwork yourself, *mon vieux*" I said; "you are worth more than your opera ever will be."

"Do I look overworked?" he said, turning his face to me in the broad, outdoor light. He seemed a little offended at my saying that about his opera, and I was foolish to do it.

I examined his face critically, and he looked at me half defiantly. "No, not yet," I answered rather unwillingly, for I could not say that he did; but there was a restless, inward look in his eyes, and an almost imperceptible shadow lay around them. It seemed to me as though the full temples had grown slightly hollow, and a sort of faint mist lay over his beauty, making it seem strange and far off. We were standing before the door, and he pushed it open, the *guardiano* following us with slow, loud-resounding steps.

"Here is my Paradise," said Marcello, and we entered the house, which was like all the others of its kind. A hall, with *stucco* bas-reliefs, and a stairway adorned with antique fragments, gave access to the upper rooms. Marcello ran up the steps lightly, and I heard him lock a door somewhere above and draw out the key, then he came and met me on the landing.

"This," he said, "is my work-room," and he threw open a low door. The key was in the lock, so this room could not be the one I heard him close. "Tell me I shall not write like an angel here!" he cried. I was so dazzled by the flood of bright sunshine after the dusk of the passage, that I blinked like an owl at first, and then I saw a large room, quite bare except for a rough table and chair, the chair covered with manuscript music.

"You are looking for the furniture," he said, laughing; "it is outside. Look here!" and he drew me to a rickety door of worm-eaten wood and coarse greenish glass, and flung it open on to a rusty iron balcony. He was right; the furniture was outside: that is to say, a divine view met my eyes. The Sabine Mountains, the Alban Hills, the broad Campagna, with its mediaeval towers and ruined aqueducts, and the open plain to the sea. All this glowing and yet calm in the sunlight. No wonder he could write there! The balcony ran round the corner of the house, and to the right I looked down upon an alley of ilexes, ending in a grove of tall laurel trees—very old, apparently. There were bits of sculpture and some ancient *sarcophagi* standing gleaming among them, and even from so high I could hear a little stream of water pouring from an antique mask into a long, rough trough.

I saw the brown *guardiano* digging at his cabbages and onions, and I laughed to think that I could fancy him a murderer! He had a little bag of relics, which dangled to and fro over his sun-burned breast, and he looked very innocent when he sat down upon an old column to eat a piece of black bread with an onion which he had just pulled out of the ground, dicing it with a knife not at all like a dagger. But I kept my thoughts to myself, for Marcello would have laughed at them. We were standing together, looking down at the man as he drank from his hands at the running fountain, and Marcello now leaned down over the balcony, and called out a long "*Ohé!*" The lazy *guardiano* looked up, nodded, and then got up slowly from the stone where he had been half-kneeling to reach the jet of water.

"We are going to dine," Marcello explained. "I have been waiting for you." Presently we heard the man's heavy tread upon the stairs, and he entered bearing a strange meal in a basket.

There came to light pecorino cheese made from ewe's milk, black bread of the consistency of a stone, a great bowl of salad apparently composed of weeds, and a sausage which filled the room with a strong smell of garlic. Then he disappeared and came back with a dish full of ragged-looking goat's flesh cooked together with a mass of smoking polenta, and I am not sure that there was not oil in it.

"I told you I lived well, and now you see!" said Marcello. It was a terrible meal, but I had to eat it, and was glad to have some rough, sour wine to help me, which tasted of earth and roots.

When we had finished, I said, "And your opera! How are you getting on?"

"Not a word about that!" he cried. "You see how I have written!" and he turned over a heap of manuscript; "but do not talk to me about it. I will not lose my ideas in words." This was not like Marcello, who loved to discuss his work, and I looked at him astonished.

"Come," he said, "we will go down into the garden, and you shall tell me about the comrades. What are they doing? Has Magnin found a model for his Clytemnestra?"

I humoured him, as I always did, and we sat upon a stone bench behind the house, looking toward the laurel grove, talking of the pictures and the students. I wanted to walk down the ilex alley, but he stopped me.

"If you are afraid of the damp, don't go down there," he said; "the place is like a vault. Let us stay here and be thankful for this heavenly view."

"Well, let us stay here," I answered, resigned as ever. He lit a cigar and offered me one in silence. If he did not care to talk, I could be still too. From time to time he made some indifferent observation, and I answered it in the same tone. It almost seemed to me as though we, the old heart-comrades, had become strangers who had not known each other a week, or as though we had been so long apart that we had grown away from each other. There was something about him which escaped me. Yes, the few days of solitude had indeed put years and a sort of shyness, or rather ceremony, between us! It did not seem natural to me now to clap him on the back, and make the old, harmless jokes at him. He must have felt the constraint, too, for we were like children who had looked forward to a game and did not know what to play at.

At six o'clock I left him. It was not like parting with Marcello. I felt rather as though I should find my old friend in Home that evening, and here only left a shadowy likeness of him. He accompanied me to the gate, and pressed my hand, and for a moment the true Marcello looked out of his eyes; but we called out no last words to each other as I drove away. I had only said, "Let me know when you want me;" and he had said, "*Merci!*" and all the way back to Rome I felt a chill upon me, his hand had been so cold, and I thought and thought what could be the matter with him.

That evening I spoke out my anxiety to Pierre Magnin, who shook his head and declared that malaria fever must be taking hold of him, and that people often began to show it by being a little odd.

"He must not stay there! We must get him away as soon as possible," I cried.

"We know Marcello, and that nothing can make him stir against his will," said Pierre. "Let him alone, and he will get tired of his whim. It will not kill him to have a touch of malaria, and some evening he will turn up among us merry as ever."

But he did not. I worked hard at my picture and finished it, but for a few touches, and he had not yet appeared. Perhaps it was the extreme application, perhaps the sitting out in that damp place, for I insist upon tracing it to something more material than emotion. Well, whatever it was, I fell ill; more ill than I had ever been in my life. It was almost twilight when it overtook me, and I remember it distinctly, though I forget what happened afterward, or, rather, I never knew, for I was found by Magnin quite unconscious, and he has told me that I remained so for some time, and then became delirious, and talked of nothing but Marcello. I have told you that it was very nearly twilight; but just at the moment when the sun is gone the colours show in their true value. Artists know this, and I was putting last touches here and there to my picture, and especially to my head of Mucius Scaevola, or, rather, Marcello.

211

The rest of the picture came out well enough; but that head, which should have been the principal one, seemed faded and sunk in. The face appeared to grow paler and paler, and to recede from me; a strange veil spread over it, and the eyes seemed to close. I am not easily frightened, and I know what tricks some peculiar methods of colour will play by certain lights, for the moment I spoke of had gone, and the twilight greyness had set in; so, I stepped back to look well at it. Just then the lips, which had become almost white, opened a little, and sighed! An illusion, of course. I must have been very ill and quite delirious already, for to my imagination it was a real sigh, or, rather, a sort of exhausted gasp. Then it was that I fainted, I suppose, and when I came to myself, I was in my bed, with Magnin and Monsieur Sutton standing by me, and a *Soeur de Charité* moving softly about among medicine bottles, and speaking in whispers. I stretched out my hands, and they were thin and yellow, with long, pale nails; and I heard Magnin's voice, which sounded very far away, say, "*Dieu merci!*" And now Monsieur Sutton will tell you what I did not know until long afterward.

Martin Detaille.

2

ROBERT SUTTON'S ACCOUNT OF WHAT HAPPENED AT THE VIGNA
MARZIALI.

I am attached to Detaille, and was very glad to be of use to him, but I never fully shared his admiration for Marcello Souvestre, though I appreciated his good points. He was certainly very promising—I must say that. But he was an odd, flighty sort of fellow, not of the kind which we English care to take the trouble to understand. It is my business to write stories, but not having need of such characters I have never particularly studied them. As I say, I was glad to be of use to Detaille, who is a thorough good fellow, and I willingly gave up my work to go and sit by his bedside. Magnin knew that I was a friend of his, and very properly came to me when he found that Detaille's illness was a serious one and likely to last for a long time. I found him perfectly delirious, and raving about Marcello.

"Tell me what the *motif* is! I know it is a *Marche Funèbre!*" And here he would sing a peculiar melody, which, as I have a knack at music, I noted down, it being like nothing I had heard before. The Sister of Charity looked at me with severe eyes; but how could she know that all is grist for our mill, and that observation becomes with us a mechanical habit? Poor Detaille kept repeating this curious melody over and over, and then would stop and seem to be looking at his picture, crying that it was fading away.

"Marcello! Marcello! You are fading too! Let me come to you!" He was as weak as a baby, and could not have moved from his bed unless in the strength of delirium.

"I cannot come!" he went on; "they have tied me down." And here he made as though he were trying to gnaw through a rope at his wrists, and then burst into tears. "Will no one go for me and bring me a word from you? Ah! if I could know that you are alive!"

Magnin looked at me. I knew what he was thinking. He would not leave his comrade, but I must go. I don't mind acknowledging that I did not undertake this unwillingly. To sit by Detaille's bedside and listen to his ravings enervated me, and what Magnin wanted struck me as troublesome but not uninteresting to one of my craft, so I agreed to go. I had heard all about Marcello's strange seclusion from Magnin and Detaille himself, who lamented over it openly in his simple way at supper at the Academy, where I was a frequent guest.

I knew that it would be useless to ring at the gate of the Vigna Marziali. Not only should I not be admitted, but I should arouse Marcello's anger and suspicion, for I did not for a moment believe that he was not alive, though I thought it very possible that he was becoming a little crazy, as his countrymen are so easily put off their balance. Now, odd people are oddest late in the day and at evening-time. Their nerves lose the power of resistance then, and the real man gets the better of them. So, I determined to try to discover something at night, reflecting also that I should be safer from detection then. I knew his liking for wandering about when he ought to be in his bed, and I did not doubt that I should get a glimpse of him, and that was really all I needed.

My first step was to take a long walk out of the Porta San Giovanni, and this I did in the early morning, tramping along steadily until I came to an iron gate on the right of the road with "Vigna Marziali" over it; and then I walked straight on, never stopping until I had reached a little bushy lane running down toward the Campagna to the right. It was pebbly, and quite shut in by luxuriant ivy and elder bushes, and it bore deep traces of the last heavy rains. These had evidently been effaced by no footprints, so I concluded that it was little used. Down this path I made my way cautiously, looking behind and before me, from a habit contracted in my lonely wanderings in the

Abruzzi. I had a capital revolver with me—an old friend—and I feared no man; but I began to feel a dramatic interest in my undertaking, and determined that it should not be crossed by any disagreeable surprises.

The lane led me further down the plain than I had reckoned upon, for the bushy edge shut out the view; and when I had got to the bottom and faced round, the Vigna Marziali was lying quite far to my left. I saw at a glance that behind the grey casino an alley of ilexes ended in a laurel grove; then there were plantations of kitchen-stuff, with a sort of thatched cabin in their midst, probably that of the gardener. I looked about for a kennel, but saw none, so there was no watch-dog. At the end of this primitive kitchen garden was a broad patch of grass, hounded by a fence, which I could take at a spring. Now, I knew my way, but I could not resist tracing it out a little farther. It was well that I did so, for I found just within the fence a sunken stream, rather full at the time, in consequence of the rains, too deep to wade and too broad to jump. It struck me that it would be easy enough to take a board from the fence and lay it over for a bridge. I measured the breadth with my eye, and decided that the board would span it; then I went back as I had come, and returned to find Detaille still raving.

As he could understand nothing, it seemed to me rather a fool's errand to go off in search of comfort for him; but a conscious moment might come, and, moreover, I began to be interested in my undertaking; and so I agreed with Magnin that I should go and take some food and rest and return to the Vigna that night. I told my landlady that I was going into the country and should return the next day, and I went to Nazarri's and laid in a stock of sandwiches and filled my flask with something they called sherry, for, though I was no great wine-drinker, I feared the night-chill.

It was about seven o'clock when I started, and I retraced my morning's steps exactly. As I reached the lane, it occurred to me that it was still too light for me to pass unobserved over the stream, and I made a place for myself under the hedge and lay down, quite screened by the thick curtain of tangled overhanging ivy.

I must have been out of training, and tired by the morning's walk, for I fell asleep. When I awoke it was night; the stars were shining, a dank mist made its way down my throat, and I felt stiff and cold. I took a pull at my flask, finding it nasty stuff, but it warmed me. Then I rang my repeater, which struck a quarter to eleven, got up and shook myself free of the leaves and brambles, and went on down the lane. When I got to the fence I sat down and thought the thing over. What did

I expect to discover? What was there to discover? Nothing! Nothing but that Marcello was alive; and that was no discovery at all, for I felt sure of it. I was a fool, and had let myself be allured by the mere stage nonsense and mystery of the business, and a mouse would creep out of this mountain of precautions!

Well, at least, I could turn it to account by describing my own absurd behaviour in some story yet to be written, and, as it was not enough for a chapter, I would add to it by further experience. "Come along!" I said to myself. "You're an ass, but it may prove instructive." I raised the top board from the fence noiselessly. There was a stile just there, and the boards were easily moved. I laid down my bridge with some difficulty and stepped carefully across, and made my way to the laurel grove as quickly and noiselessly as possible.

There all was thick darkness, and my eyes only grew slowly accustomed to it. After all there was not much to see; some stone seats in a semicircle, and some fragments of columns set upright with antique busts upon them. Then a little to the right a sort of arch, with apparently some steps descending into the ground, probably the entrance to some discovered branch of a catacomb. In the midst of the enclosure, not a very large one, stood a stone table, deeply fixed in the earth. No one was there; of that I felt certain, and I sat down, having now got used to the gloom, and fell to eat my sandwiches, for I was desperately hungry.

Now that I had come so far, was nothing to take place to repay me for my trouble? It suddenly struck me that it was absurd to expect Marcello to come out to meet me and perform any mad antics he might be meditating there before my eyes for my especial satisfaction. Why I had supposed that something would take place in the grove I do not know, except that this seemed a fit place for it. I would go and watch the house, and if I saw a light anywhere, I might be sure that he was within. Any fool might have thought of that, but a novelist lays the scene of his drama and expects his characters to slide about in the grooves like puppets. It is only when mine surprise me that I feel they are alive.

When I reached the end of the ilex alley, I saw the house before me. There were more cabbages and onions after I had left the trees, and I saw that in this open space I could easily be perceived by any one standing on the balcony above. As I drew back again under the ilexes, a window above, not the one on the balcony, was suddenly lighted up; but the light did not remain long, and presently a gleam shone through the glass oval over the door below.

I had just time to spring behind the thickest trunk near me when the door opened. I took advantage of its creaking to creep up the slanting tree like a cat, and lie out upon a projecting branch.

As I expected, Marcello came out. He was very pale, and moved mechanically like a sleep-walker. I was shocked to see how hollow his face had become, as he held the candle still lighted in his hand, and it cast deep shadows on his sunken cheeks and fixed eyes, which burned wildly and seemed to see nothing. His lips were quite white, and so drawn that I could see his gleaming teeth. Then the candle fell from his hand, and he came slowly and with a curiously regular step on into the darkness of the ilexes, I watching him from above. But I scarcely think he would have noticed me had I been standing in his path. When he had passed, I let myself down and followed him. I had taken off my shoes, and my tread was absolutely noiseless; moreover, I felt sure he would not turn round.

On he went with the same mechanical step until he reached the grove. There I knelt behind an old *sarcophagus* at the entrance, and waited. What would he do? He stood perfectly still, not looking about him, but as though the clock-work within him had suddenly stopped. I felt that he was becoming psychologically interesting, after all. Suddenly he threw up his arms as men do when they are mortally wounded on the battlefield, and I expected to see him fall at full length. Instead of this, he made a step forward.

I looked in the same direction and saw a woman, who must have concealed herself there while I was waiting before the house, come from out of the gloom, and as she slowly approached and laid her head upon his shoulder, the outstretched arms clasped themselves closely around her, so that her face was hidden upon his neck.

So, this was the whole matter, and I had been sent off on a wild-goose chase to spy out a common love-affair! His opera and his seclusion for the sake of work, his tyrannical refusal to see Detaille unless he sent for him—all this was but a mask to a vulgar intrigue which, for reasons best known to himself, could not be indulged in in the city. I was thoroughly angry! If Marcello passed his time mooning about in that damp hole all night, no wonder that he looked so wretchedly ill, and seemed half mad! I knew very well that Marcello was no saint Why should he be? But I had not taken him for a fool! He had had plenty of romantic episodes, and as he was discreet without being uselessly mysterious no one had ever unduly pried into them, nor should we have done so now.

I said to myself that that mixture of French and Italian blood was at the bottom of it; French flimsiness and light-headedness and Italian love of cunning! I looked back upon all the details of my mysterious expedition. I suppose at the root or my anger lay a certain dramatic disappointment at not finding him lying murdered, and I despised myself for all the trouble I had taken to this ridiculous end: just to see him holding a woman in his arms. I could not see her face, and her figure was enveloped from head to foot in something long and dark; but I could make out that she was tall and slender, and that a pair of white hands gleamed from her drapery. As I was looking intently, for all my indignation, the couple moved on, and still clinging to one another descended the steps.

So even the solitude of the lonely laurel grove could not satisfy Marcello's insane love of secrecy! I kept still awhile; then I stole to where they had disappeared, and listened; but all was silent, and I cautiously struck a match and peered down. I could see the steps for a short distance below me, and then the darkness seemed to rise and swallow them. It must be a catacomb, as I had imagined, or an old Roman bath, perhaps, which Marcello had made comfortable enough, no doubt, and as likely as not they were having a nice little cold supper there. My empty stomach told me that I could have forgiven him even then could I have shared it. I was in truth frightfully hungry as well as angry, and sat down on one of the stone benches to finish my sandwiches.

The thought of waiting to see this love-sick pair return to upper earth never for a moment occurred to me. I had found out the whole thing, and a great humbug it was! Now I wanted to get back to Home before my temper had cooled, and to tell Magnin on what a fool's errand he had sent me. If he liked to quarrel with me, all the better!

All the way home I composed cutting French speeches, but they suddenly cooled and petrified like a gust of lava from a volcano when I discovered that the gate was closed. I had never thought of getting a pass, and Magnin ought to have warned me. Another grievance against the fellow! I enjoyed my resentment, and it kept me warm as I patrolled up and down. There are houses, and even small eating-shops, outside the gate, but no light was visible, and I did not care to attract attention by pounding at the doors in the middle of the night; so I crept behind a bit of wall. I was getting used to hiding by this time, and made myself as comfortable as I could with my ulster, took another pull at my flask, and waited.

At last the gate was opened and I slipped through, trying not to look as though I had been out all night like a bandit. The guard looked at me narrowly, evidently wondering at my lack of luggage. Had I had a knapsack I might have been taken for some innocently mad English tourist indulging in the mistaken pleasure of trudging in from Frascati or Albano; but a man in an ulster, with his hands in his pockets, sauntering in at the gate of the city at break of day as though returning from a stroll, naturally puzzled the officials, who looked after me and shrugged their shoulders.

Luckily, I found an early cab in the *piazza* of the Lateran, for I was dead-beat, and was soon at my lodgings in the Via della Croce, where my landlady let me in very speedily. Then at last I had the comfort of throwing off my clothes, all damp with the night dew, and turning in. My wrath had cooled to a certain point, and I did not fear to lower its temperature too greatly by yielding to an overwhelming desire for sleep. An hour or two could make no great difference to Magnin—let him fancy me still hanging about the Vigna Marziali! Sleep I must have, no matter what he thought.

I slept long, and was awakened at last by my landlady, Sora Hanna, standing over me, and saying, "There is a *signore* who wants you."

"It is I, Magnin!" said a voice behind her. "I could not wait for you to come!" He looked haggard with anxiety and watching.

"Detaille is raving still," he went on, "only worse than before. Speak, for Heaven's sake! Why don't you tell me something?" And he shook me by the arm as though he thought I was still asleep.

"Have you nothing to say? You must have seen something! Did you see Marcello?"

"Oh! yes, I saw him."

"Well?"

"Well, he was very comfortable—quite alive. He had a woman's arms around him."

I heard my door violently slammed to, a ferocious "*Sacré gamin!*" and then steps springing down the stairs. I felt perfectly happy at having made such an impression, and turned and resumed my broken sleep with almost a kindly feeling toward Magma, who was at that moment probably tearing up the Spanish Scalinata two steps at a time, and making himself horribly hot. It could not help Detaille, poor fellow! He could not understand my news. When I had slept long enough, I got up, refreshed myself with a bath and something to eat, and went off to see Detaille. It was not his fault that I had been made a fool of, so I felt sorry for him.

I found him raving just as I had left him the day before, only worse, as Magnin said. He persisted in continually crying, "Marcello, take care! no one can save you!" in hoarse, weak tones, but with the regularity of a knell, keeping up a peculiar movement with his feet, as though he were weary with a long road, but must press forward to his goal. Then he would stop and break into childish sobs.

"My feet are so sore," he murmured, piteously, "and I am so tired! But I will come! They are following me, but I am strong!" Then a violent struggle with his invisible pursuers, in which he would break off into that singing of his, alternating with the warning cry. The singing voice was quite another from the speaking one. He went on and on, repeating the singular air which he had himself called a Funeral March, and which had become intensely disagreeable to me. If it was one indeed, it surely was intended for no Christian burial. As he sang, the tears kept trickling down his cheeks, and Magnin sat wiping them away as tenderly as a woman. Between his song he would clasp his hands, feebly enough, for he was very weak when the delirium did not make him violent, and cry in heart-rending tones, "Marcello, I shall never see you again! Why did you leave us?" At last, when he stopped for a moment, Magnin left his side, beckoning the Sister to take it, and drew me into the other room, closing the door behind him.

"Now tell me exactly how you saw Marcello," said he; so, I related my whole absurd experience—forgetting, however, my personal irritation, for he looked too wretched and worn for anybody to be angry with him. He made me repeat several times my description of Marcello's face and manner as he had come out of the house. That seemed to make more impression upon him than the love business.

"Sick people have strange intuitions," he said, gravely; "and I persist in thinking that Marcello is very ill and in danger. *Tenez!*" And here he broke off, went to the door, and called "*Ma soeur!*" under his breath. She understood, and after having drawn the bedclothes straight, and once more dried the trickling tears, she came noiselessly to where we stood, the wet handkerchief still in her hand. She was a singularly tall and strong-looking woman, with piercing black eyes and a self-controlled manner. Strange to say, she bore the adopted name of Claudius, instead of a more feminine one.

"*Ma soeur,*" said Magnin, "at what o'clock was it that he sprang out of bed and we had to hold him for so long?"

"Half-past eleven and a few minutes," she answered promptly. Then he turned to me.

"At what time did Marcello come out into the garden?"

"Well, it might have been half-past eleven," I answered, unwillingly. "I should say that three quarters of an hour might possibly have passed since I rang my repeater. Mind you, I won't swear it!" I hate to have people try to prove mysterious coincidences, and this was just what they were attempting.

"Are you sure of the hour, *ma soeur?*" I asked, a little tartly. She looked at me calmly with her great, black eyes, and said:

"I heard the Trinità de' Monti strike the half-hour just before it happened."

"Be so good as to tell Monsieur Sutton exactly what took place," said Magnin.

"One moment, *monsieur,*" and she went swiftly and softly to Detaille, raised him on her strong arm, and held a glass to his lips, from which he drank mechanically. Then she came and stood where she could watch him through the open door.

"He hears nothing," she said, as she hung the handkerchief to dry over a chair; and then she went on. "It was half-past eleven, and my patient had been very uneasy—that is to say, more so even than before. It might have been four or five minutes after the clock had finished striking that he became suddenly quite still and then began to tremble all over, so that the bed shook with him." She spoke admirable English, as many of the Sisters do, so I need not translate, but will give her own words.

"He went on trembling until I thought he was going to have a fit, and told Monsieur Magnin to be ready to go for the doctor, when just then the trembling stopped, he became perfectly stiff, his hair stood up upon his head, and his eyes seemed coming out of their sockets, though he could see nothing, for I passed the candle before them. All at once he sprang out of his bed and rushed to the door. I did not know he was so strong. Before he got there, I had him in my arms, for he has become very light, and I carried him back to bed again, though he was struggling like a child. Monsieur Magnin came in from the next room just as he was trying to get up again, and we held him down until it was past, but he screamed Monsieur Souvestre's name for a long time after that. Afterward he was very cold and exhausted, of course, and I gave him some beef-tea, though it was not the hour for it."

"I think you had better tell the Sister all about it," said Magnin, turning to me. "It is best that the nurse should know everything."

"Very well," said I; "though I do not think it's much in her line." She answered me herself: "Everything which concerns our patients is our business. Nothing shocks us." Thereupon she sat down and thrust her hands into her long sleeves, prepared to listen. I repeated the whole affair as I had done to Magnin. She never took her brilliant eyes from off my face, and listened as coolly as though she had been a doctor hearing an account of a difficult case, though to me it seemed almost sacrilege to be describing the behaviour of a love-stricken youth to a Sister of Charity.

"What do you say to that, *ma soeur?*" asked Magnin, when I had done.

"I say nothing, *monsieur*. It is sufficient that I know it;" and she withdrew her hands from her sleeves, took up the handkerchief, which was dry by this time, and returned quietly to her place at the bedside.

"I wonder if I have shocked her, after all?" I said to Magnin.

"Oh, no," he answered. "They see many things, and a *soeur* is as abstract as a confessor; they do not allow themselves any personal feelings. I have seen Soeur Claudius listen perfectly unmoved to the most abominable ravings, only crossing herself beneath her cape at the most hideous blasphemies. It was last summer when poor Justin Revol died. You were not here." Magnin put his hand to his forehead.

"You are looking ill yourself," I said. "Go and try to sleep, and I will stay."

"Very well," he answered; "but I cannot rest unless you promise to remember everything he says, that I may hear it when I wake;" and he threw himself down upon the hard sofa like a sack, and was asleep in a moment; and I, who had felt so angry with him but a few hours ago, put a cushion under his head and made him comfortable.

I sat down in the next room and listened to Detaille's monotonous ravings, while Soeur Claudius read in her book of prayers. It was getting dusk, and several of the academicians stole in and stood over the sick man and shook their heads. They looked around for Magnin, but I pointed to the other room with my finger on my lips, and they nodded and went away on tiptoe.

It required no effort of memory to repeat Detaille's words to Magnin when he woke, for they were always the same. We had another Sister that night, and as Soeur Claudius was not to return till the next day at midday, I offered to share the watch with Magnin, who was getting very nervous and exhausted, and who seemed to think that some such attack might be expected as had occurred the night before. The new Sister was a gentle, delicate-looking little woman, with tears in her soft brown eyes as she bent over the sick man, and crossed herself from time to time, grasping the crucifix which hung from the beads at her waist. Nevertheless, she was calm and useful, and as punctual as Soeur Claudius herself in giving the medicines.

The doctor had come in the evening, and prescribed a change in these. He would not say what he thought of his patient, but only declared that it was necessary to wait for a crisis. Magnin sent for some supper, and we sat over it together in silence, neither of us hungry. He kept looking at his watch.

"If the same thing happens tonight, he will die!" said he, and laid his head on his arms.

"He will die in a most foolish cause, then," I said, angrily, for I thought he was going to cry, as those Frenchmen have a way of doing, and I wanted to irritate him by way of a tonic; so, I went on—

"It would be dying for a *vaurien* who is making an ass of himself in a ridiculous business which will be over in a week! Souvestre may get as much fever as he likes! only don't ask me to come and nurse him."

"It is not the fever," said he slowly, "it is a horrible nameless dread that I have; I suppose it is listening to Detaille that makes me nervous. Hark!" he added, "it strikes eleven. "We must watch!"

"If you really expect another attack you had better warn the Sister," I said; so he told her in a few words what might happen.

"Very well, *monsieur*," she answered, and sat down quietly near the bed, Magnin at the pillow, and I near him. No sound was to be heard but Detaille's ceaseless lament.

And now, before I tell you more, I must stop to entreat you to believe me. It will be almost impossible for you to do so, I know, for I have laughed myself at such tales, and no assurances would have made me credit them. But I, Robert Sutton, swear that this thing happened. More I cannot do. It is the truth.

We had been watching Detaille intently. He was lying with closed eyes, and had been very restless. Suddenly he became quite still, and then began to tremble, exactly as Soeur Claudius had described. It was a curious, uniform trembling, apparently in every fibre, and his iron bedstead shook as though strong hands were at its head and foot. Then came the absolute rigidity she had also described, and I do not exaggerate when I say that not only did his short-cropped hair seem to stand erect, but that it literally did so. A lamp cast the shadow of his profile against the wall to the left of his bed, and as I looked at the immovable outline which seemed painted on the wall, I saw the hair slowly rise until the line where it joined the forehead was quite a different one—abrupt instead of a smooth sweep. His eyes opened wide and were frightfully fixed, then as frightfully strained, but they certainly did not see us.

We waited breathlessly for what might follow. The little Sister was standing close to him, her lips pressed together and a little pale, but very calm. "Do not be frightened, *ma soeur* ," whispered Magnin; and she answered in a business-like tone, "No, *monsieur*," and drew still nearer to her patient, and took his hands, which were stiff as those of a corpse, between her own to warm them. I laid mine upon his heart; it was beating so imperceptibly that I almost thought it had stopped, and as I leaned my face to his lips I could feel no breath issue from them. It seemed as though the rigor would last forever.

Suddenly, without any transition, he hurled himself with enormous force, and literally at one bound, almost into the middle of the room, scattering us aside like leaves in the wind. I was upon him in a moment, grappling with him with all my strength, to prevent him from reaching the door. Magnin had been thrown backward against the table, and I heard the medicine bottles crash with his fall. He had flung back his hand to save himself, and rushed to help me with the blood dropping from a cut in his wrist. The little Sister sprang to us, Detaille had thrown her violently back upon her knees, and now, with a nurse's instinct, she tried to throw a shawl over his bare breast. We four must have made a strange group!

Four? We were five! Marcello Souvestre stood before us, just within the door! We all saw him, for he was there. His bloodless face was turned toward us unmoved; his hands hung by his side as white as his face; only his eyes had life in them; they were fixed on Detaille.

"Thank God, you have come at last!" I cried. "Don't stand there like a fool! Help us, can't you?" But he never moved. I was furiously angry, and, leaving my hold, sprang upon him to drag him forward. My outstretched hands struck hard against the door, and I felt a thing like a spider's web envelop me. It seemed to draw itself over my mouth and eyes, and to blind and choke me, and then to flutter and tear and float from me.

Marcello was gone!

Detaille had slipped from Magnin's hold, and lay in a heap upon the floor, as though his limbs were broken. The Sister was trembling violently as she knelt over him and tried to raise his head. We gazed at one another, stooped and lifted him in our arms, and carried him back to his bed, while Soeur Marie quietly collected the broken phials.

"You saw it, *ma soeur?*" I heard Magnin whisper hoarsely.

"Yes, *monsieur!*" she only answered, in a trembling voice, holding on to her crucifix. Then she said, in a professional tone:

"Will *monsieur* let me bind up his wrist?" And though her fingers trembled and his hand was shaking, the bandage was an irreproachable one.

Magnin went into the next room, and I heard him throw himself heavily into a chair. Detaille seemed to be sleeping. His breath came regularly; his eyes were closed with a look of peace about the lids, his hands lying in a natural way upon the quilt. He had not moved since we laid him there. I went softly to where Magnin was sitting in the dark. He did not move, but only said, "Marcello is dead!"

"He is either dead or dying," I answered, "and we must go to him."

"Yes," Magnin whispered, "we must go to him, but we shall not reach him."

"We will go as soon as it is light," I said, and then we were still again.

When the morning came at last, he went and found a comrade to take his place, and only said to Soeur Marie, "It is not necessary to speak of this night;" and at her quiet "You are right, *monsieur*," we felt that we could trust her. Detaille was still sleeping. Was this the crisis the doctor had expected? Perhaps; but surely not in such fearful form. I insisted upon my companion having some breakfast before we started, and I breakfasted myself, but I cannot say I tasted what passed between my lips.

We engaged a closed carriage, for we did not know what we might bring home with us, though neither of us spoke out his thoughts. It was early morning still when we reached the Vigna Marziali, and we had not exchanged a word all the way. I rang at the bell, while the coachman looked on curiously. It was answered promptly by the *guardiano*, of whom Detaille has already told you."

"Where is the *signore?*" I asked through the gate.

"*Chi lo sa?*" he answered. "He is here, of course; he has not left the Vigna. Shall I call him?"

"*Call him?*" I knew that no mortal voice could reach Marcello now, but I tried to fancy he was still alive.

"No," I said. "Let us in. We want to surprise him; he will be pleased."

The man hesitated, but he finally opened the gate, and we entered, leaving the carriage to wait outside. We went straight to the house; the door at the back was wide open. There had been a gale in the night, and it had torn some leaves and bits of twigs from the trees and blown them into the entrance-hall. They lay scattered across the threshold, and were evidence that the door had remained open ever since they had fallen. The *guardiano* left us, probably to escape Marcello's anger at having let us in, and we went up the stairs unhindered, Magnin foremost, for he knew the house better than I, from Detaille's description. He had told him about the corner room with the balcony, and we pretended that Marcello might be there, absorbed betimes in his work, but we did not call him.

He was not there. His papers were strewn over the table as though he had been writing, but the ink-stand was dry and full of dust; he could not have used it for days. We went silently into the other chambers. Perhaps he was still asleep? But, no! We found his bed untouched, so he could not have lain in it that night. The rooms were all unlocked but one, and this closed door made our hearts beat. Marcello could scarcely be there, however, for there was no key in the lock; I saw the daylight shining through the keyhole. We called his name, but there came no answer. We knocked loudly, still no sign from within; so, I put my shoulder to the door, which was old and cracked in several places, and succeeded in bursting it open.

Nothing was there but a sculptor's modelling-stand, with something upon it covered with a white cloth, and the modelling-tools on the floor. At the sight of the cloth, still damp, we drew a deep breath. It could not have hung there for many hours, certainly not for twenty-four. We did not raise it.

"He would be vexed," said Magnin, and I nodded, for it is accounted almost a crime in the artist's world to unveil a sculptor's work behind his back. We expressed no surprise at the fact of his modelling; a ban seemed to lie upon our tongues. The cloth hung tightly to the object beneath it, and showed us the outline of a woman's head and rounded bust, and so veiled we left her. There was a little winding stair leading out of the passage, and we climbed it, to find ourselves in a sort of belvedere, commanding a superb view. It was a small, open terrace, on the roof of the house, and we saw at a glance that no one was there.

We had now been all over the casino, which was small and simply built, being evidently intended only for short summer use. As we stood leaning over the balustrade we could look down into the garden. No one was there but the *guardiano*, lying among his cabbages with his arms behind his head, half asleep. The laurel grove had been in my mind from the beginning, only it had seemed more natural to go to the house first. Now we descended the stairs silently and directed our steps thither.

As we approached it, the *guardiano* came toward us lazily.

"Have you seen the *signore?*" he asked, and his stupidly placid face showed me that he, at least, had no hand in his disappearance.

"No, not yet," I answered, "but we shall come across him somewhere, no doubt. Perhaps he has gone to take a walk, and we will wait for him. What is this?" I went on, trying to seem careless. We were standing now by the little arch, of which you know.

"This?" said he; "I have never been down there, but they say it is something old. Do the *signori* want to see it? I will fetch a lantern."

I nodded, and he went off to his cabin. I had a couple of candles in my pocket, for I had intended to explore the place, should we not find Marcello. It was there that he had disappeared that night, and my thoughts had been busy with it; but I kept my candles concealed, reflecting that they would give our search an air of premeditation which would excite curiosity.

"When did you see the *signore* last?" I asked, when he had returned with the lantern.

"I brought him his supper yesterday evening."

"At what o'clock?"

"It was the *Ave Maria, signore*," he replied. "He always sups then."

It would be useless to put any further questions. He was evidently utterly unobserving, and would lie to please us.

"Let me go first," said Magnin, taking the lantern. We set our feet upon the steps; a cold air seemed to fill our lungs and yet to choke us, and a thick darkness lay beneath. The steps, as I could see by the light of my candle, were modern, as well as the vaulting above them. A tablet was let into the wall, and in spite of my excitement I paused to read it, perhaps because I was glad to delay whatever awaited us below. It ran thus:

"*Questo antico sepolcro Romano scopri il Conte Marziali nell' anno 1853, e piamente conservo.*" In plain English:

"Count Marziali discovered this ancient Homan sepulchre in the year 1853, and piously preserved it."

I read it more quickly than it has taken time to write here, and hurried after Magnin, whose footsteps sounded faintly below me. As I hastened, a draught of cold air extinguished my candle, and I was trying to make my way down by feeling along the wall, which was horribly dark and clammy, when my heart stood still at a cry from far beneath me—a cry of horror!

"Where are you?" I shouted; but Magnin was calling my name, and could not hear me. "I am here. I am in the dark!"

I was making haste as fast as I could, but there were several turnings.

"I have found him!" came up from below.

"Alive?" I shouted. No answer.

One last short flight brought me face to face with the gleam of the lantern. It came from a low doorway, and within stood Magnin, peering into the darkness. I knew by his face, as he held the light high above him, that our fears were realised.

Yes, Marcello was there. He was lying stretched upon the floor, staring at the ceiling, dead, and already stiff, as I could see at a glance. We stood over him saying not a word, then I knelt down and felt of him, for mere form's sake, and said, as though I had not known it before, "He has been dead for some hours."

"Since yesterday evening," said Magnin, in a horror-stricken voice, yet with a certain satisfaction in it, as though to say, "You see, I was right."

Marcello was lying with his head slightly thrown back, no contortions in his handsome features; rather the look of a person who has quietly died of exhaustion—who has slipped unconsciously from life to death. His collar was thrown open and a part of his breast, of a ghastly white, was visible. Just over the heart was a small spot.

"Give me the lantern," I whispered, as I stooped over it. It was a very little spot, of a faint purplish-brown, and must have changed colour within the night.

I examined it intently, and should say that the blood had been sucked to the surface, and then a small prick or incision made. The slight subcutaneous effusion led me to this conclusion. One tiny drop of coagulated blood closed the almost imperceptible wound. I probed it with the end of one of Magnin's matches. It was scarcely more than skin-deep, so it could not be the stab of a stiletto, however slender, or the track of a bullet. Still, it was strange, and with one impulse we turned to see if no one were concealed there, or if there were no second exit. It would be madness to suppose that the murderer, if there was one, would remain by his victim. Had Marcello been making love to a pretty *contadina*, and was this some jealous lover's vengeance? But it was not a stab. Had one drop of poison in the little wound done this deadly work?

We peered about the place, and I saw that Magnin's eyes were blinded by tears and his face as pale as that upturned one on the floor, whose lids I had vainly tried to close. The chamber was low, and beautifully ornamented with *stucco bas-reliefs,* in the manner of the well-known one not far from there upon the same road. Winged *genii*, griffins, and arabesques, modelled with marvellous lightness, covered the walls and ceiling. There was no other door than the one we had entered by. In the centre stood a marble *sarcophagus*, with the usual subjects sculptured upon it, on the one side Hercules conducting a veiled figure, on the other a dance of nymphs and fauns. A space in the middle contained the following inscription, deeply cut in the stone, and still partially filled with red pigment:

D. M.
VESPERTILIAE·THC·AIMATOΠΩTIΔOC·
Q · FLAVIVS · VIX · IPSE · SOSPES ·
MON · POSVIT.

"What is this?" whispered Magnin. It was only a pickaxe and a long crowbar, such as the country people use in hewing out their blocks of "*tufa,*" and his foot had struck against them. Who could have brought them here? They must belong to the *guardiano* above, but he said that he had never come here, and I believed him, knowing the Italian horror of darkness and lonely places; but what had Marcello wanted with them? It did not occur to as that archaeological curiosity could have led him to attempt to open the *sarcophagus*, the lid of which had evidently never been raised, thus justifying the expression, "piously preserved."

As I rose from examining the tools my eyes fell upon the line of mortar where the cover joined to the stone below, and I noticed that some of it had been removed, perhaps with the pickaxe which lay at my feet. I tried it with my nails and found that it was very crumbly. Without a word I took the tool in my hand, Magnin instinctively following my movements with the lantern. What impelled us I do not know. I had myself no thought, only an irresistible desire to see what was within. I saw that much of the mortar had been broken away, and lay in small fragments upon the ground, which I had not noticed

228

before. It did not take long to complete the work. I snatched the lantern from Magnin's hand and set it upon the ground, where it shone full upon Marcello's dead face, and by its light I found a little break between the two masses of stone and managed to insert the end of my crowbar, driving it in with a blow of the pickaxe. The stone chipped and then cracked a little. Magnin was shivering.

"What are you going to do?" he said, looking around at where Marcello lay.

"Help me!" I cried, and we two bore with all our might upon the crowbar. I am a strong man, and I felt a sort of blind fury as the stone refused to yield. What if the bar should snap? With another blow I drove it in still further, then using it as a lever, we weighed upon it with our outstretched arms until every muscle was at its highest tension. The stone moved a little, and, almost fainting, we stopped to rest.

From the ceiling hung the rusty remnant of an iron chain which must once have held a lamp. To this, by scrambling upon the *sarcophagus*, I contrived to make fast the lantern.

"Now!" said I, and we heaved again at the lid. It rose, and we alternately heaved and pushed until it lost its balance and fell with a thundering crash upon the other side; such a crash that the walls seemed to shake, and I was for a moment utterly deafened, while little pieces of stucco rained upon us from the ceiling. When we had paused to recover from the shock we leaned over the *sarcophagus* and looked in.

The light shone full upon it, and we saw—how is it possible to tell? We saw lying there, amid folds of mouldering rags, the body of a woman, perfect as in life, with faintly rosy face, soft crimson lips, and a breast of living pearl, which seemed to heave as though stirred by some delicious dream. The rotten stuff swathed about her was in ghastly contrast to this lovely form, fresh as the morning! Her hands lay stretched at her side, the pink palms were turned a little outward, her eyes were closed as peacefully as those of a sleeping child, and her long hair, which shone red-golden in the dim light from above, was wound around her head in numberless finely plaited tresses, beneath which little locks escaped in rings upon her brow. I could have sworn that the blue veins on that divinely perfect bosom held living blood! We were absolutely paralyzed, and Magnin leaned gasping over the edge as pale as death, paler by far than this living, almost smiling face to which his eyes were glued. I do not doubt that I was as pale as he at this inexplicable vision.

As I looked, the red lips seemed to grow redder. They *were* redder!

The little pearly teeth showed between them. I had not seen them before, and now a clear ruby drop trickled down to her rounded chin and from there slipped sideways and fell upon her neck. Horror-struck I gazed upon the living corpse, till my eyes could not bear the sight any longer. As I looked away my glance fell once more upon the mysterious inscription, half Latin, half Greek, and the awful meaning of the words flashed upon me suddenly as I read them this second time. "To *Vespertilia*"—that was in Latin, and even the Latin name of the woman suggested a thing of evil flitting in the dusk. But the full horror of the nature of that thing had been veiled to Roman eyes un-der the Greek translated as "The blood-drinker, the vampire woman." And Flavius—her lover—*vix ipse sospes*, "himself hardly saved" from that deadly embrace, had buried her here, and set a seal upon her sepulchre, trusting to the weight of stone and the strength of clinging mortar to imprison for ever the beautiful monster he had loved.

"Infamous murderess!" I cried, "you have killed Marcello!" and a sudden, vengeful calm came over me.

"Give me the pickaxe," I said to Magnin. I can hear myself saying it still. He picked it up and handed it to me as in a dream; he seemed little better than an idiot, and the beads of sweat were shining on his forehead. I took my knife, and from the long wooden handle of the pickaxe I cut a fine, sharp stake. Then I clambered, scarcely feeling any repugnance, over the side of the *sarcophagus*, my feet among the folds of Vespertilia's decaying winding-sheet, which crushed like ashes beneath my boot.

I looked for one moment at that white breast, but only to choose the loveliest spot, where the network of azure veins shimmered like veiled turquoises, and then with one blow I drove the pointed stake deep down through the breathing snow and stamped it in with my heel.

An awful shriek, so ringing and horrible that I thought my ears must have burst; but even then, I felt neither fear nor horror. There are times when these cannot touch us. I stooped and gazed once again at the face, now undergoing a fearful change—fearful and final!

"Foul vampire!" I said quietly in my concentrated rage. "You will do no more harm now!" And then, without looking back upon her cursed face, I clambered out of the horrible tomb.

We raised Marcello, and slowly carried him up the steep stairs—a difficult task, for the way was narrow and he was so stiff. I noticed that the steps were ancient up to the end of the second flight; above, the modern passage was somewhat broader. When we reached the top, the *guardiano* was lying upon one of the stone benches; he did not mean us to cheat him out of his fee. I gave him a couple of *francs*.

"You see that we have found the *signore*," I tried to say in a natural voice. "He is very weak, and we will carry him to the carriage." I had thrown my handkerchief over Marcello's face, but the man knew as well as I that he was dead. Those stiff feet told their own story, but Italians are timid of being involved in such affairs. They have a childish dread of the police, and he only answered, "Poor *signorino!* He is very ill; it is better to take him to Rome," and kept cautiously clear of us as we went up to the ilex alley with our icy burden, and he did not go to the gate with us, not liking to be observed by the coachman, who was dozing on his box. With difficulty we got Marcello's corpse into the carriage, the driver turning to look at us suspiciously. I explained we had found our friend very ill, and at the same time slipped a gold piece into his hand, telling him to drive to the Via del Governo Vecchio. He pocketed the money, and whipped his horses into a trot, while we sat supporting the stiff body, which swayed like a broken doll at every pebble in the road.

When we reached the Via del Governo Vecchio at last, no one saw us carry him into the house. There was no step before the door, and we drew up so close to it that it was possible to screen our burden from sight. When we had brought him into his room and laid him upon his bed, we noticed that his eyes were closed; from the movement of the carriage, perhaps, though that was scarcely possible. The landlady behaved very much as I had expected her to do, for, as I told you, I know the Italians. She pretended, too, that the *signore* was very ill, and made a pretence of offering to fetch a doctor, and when I thought it best to tell her that he was dead, declared that it must have happened that very moment, for she had seen him look at us and close his eyes again. She had always told him that he ate too little and that he would be ill. Yes, it was weakness and that bad air out there which had killed him; and then he worked too hard. When she had successfully established this fiction, which we were glad enough to agree to—for neither did we wish for the publicity of an inquest—she ran out and fetched a gossip to come and keep her company.

So died Marcello Souvestre, and so died Vespertilia the blood-drinker at last.

There is not much more to tell. Marcello lay calm and beautiful upon his bed, and the students came and stood silently looking at him, then knelt down for a moment to say a prayer, crossed themselves, and left him for ever.

We hastened to the Villa Medici, where Detaille was sleeping, and Sister Claudius watching him with a satisfied look on her strong face. She rose noiselessly at our entrance, and came to us at the threshold. "He will recover," said she, softly. She was right. When he awoke and opened his eyes, he knew us directly, and Magnin breathed a devout "Thank God!"

"Have I been ill, Magnin?" he asked very feebly.

"You have had a little fever," answered Magnin, promptly; "but it is over now. Here is Monsieur Sutton come to see you."

"Has Marcello been here?" was the next question. Magnin looked at him very steadily.

"No," he only said, letting his face tell the rest.

"Is he dead, then?" Magnin only bowed his head. "Poor friend!" Detaille murmured to himself, then closed his heavy eyes and slept again.

A few days after Marcello's funeral we went to the fatal Vigna Marziali to bring back the objects which had belonged to him. As I laid the manuscript score of the opera carefully together, my eye fell upon a passage which struck me as the identical one which Detaille had so constantly sung in his delirium, and which I had noted down. Strange to say, when I reminded him of it later, it was perfectly new to him, and he declared that Marcello had not let him examine his manuscript. As for the veiled bust in the other room, we left it undisturbed, and to crumble away unseen.

The Red Hand

Arthur Machen

The Problem of the Fish-Hooks

'There can be no doubt whatever,' said Mr. Phillipps, 'that my theory is the true one; these flints are prehistoric fish-hooks.'

'I dare say; but you know that in all probability the things were forged the other day with a door-key.'

'Stuff!' said Phillipps; 'I have some respect, Dyson, for your literary abilities, but your knowledge of ethnology is insignificant, or rather non-existent. These fish-hooks satisfy every test; they are perfectly genuine.'

'Possibly, but as I said just now, you go to work at the wrong end. You neglect the opportunities that confront you and await you, obvious, at every corner; you positively shrink from the chance of encountering primitive man in this whirling and mysterious city, and you pass the weary hours in your agreeable retirement of Red Lion Square fumbling with bits of flint, which are, as I said, in all probability, rank forgeries.'

Phillipps took one of the little objects, and held it up in exasperation.

'Look at that ridge,' he said. 'Did you ever see such a ridge as that on a forgery?'

Dyson merely grunted and lit his pipe and the two sat smoking in rich silence, watching through the open window the children in the square as they flitted to and fro in the twilight of the lamps, as elusive as bats flying on the verge of a dark wood.

'Well,' said Phillipps at last, 'it is really a long time since you have been round. I suppose you have been working at your old task.'

'Yes,' said Dyson, 'always the chase of the phrase. I shall grow old in the hunt. But it is a great consolation to meditate on the fact that there are not a dozen people in England who know what style means.'

'I suppose not; for the matter of that, the study of ethnology is far from popular. And the difficulties! Primitive man stands dim and very far off across the great bridge of years.'

'By the way,' he went on after a pause, 'what was that stuff you were talking just now about shrinking from the chance of encountering primitive man at the corner, or something of the kind? There are certainly people about here whose ideas are very primitive.'

'I wish, Phillipps, you would not rationalise my remarks. If, I recollect the phrases correctly, I hinted that you shrank from the chance of encountering primitive man in this whirling and mysterious city, and I meant exactly what I said. Who can limit the age of survival? The troglodyte and the lake-dweller, perhaps representatives of yet darker races, may very probably be lurking in our midst, rubbing shoulders with frock-coated and finely draped humanity, ravening like wolves at heart and boiling with the foul passions of the swamp and the black cave. Now and then as I walk in Holborn or Fleet Street, I see a face which I pronounce abhorred, and yet I could not give a reason for the thrill of loathing that stirs within me.'

'My dear Dyson, I refuse to enter myself in your literary "trying-on" department. I know that survivals do exist, but all things have a limit, and your speculations are absurd. You must catch me your troglodyte before I will believe in him.'

'I agree to that with all my heart,' said Dyson, chuckling at the ease with which he had succeeded in 'drawing' Phillipps. 'Nothing could be better. It's a fine night for a walk,' he added taking up his hat.

'What nonsense you are talking, Dyson!' said Phillipps. 'However, I have no objection to taking a walk with you: as you say, it is a pleasant night.'

'Come along then,' said Dyson, grinning, 'but remember our bargain.'

The two men went out into the square, and threading one of the narrow passages that serve as exits, struck towards the north-east. As they passed along a flaring causeway they could hear at intervals between the clamour of the children and the triumphant *Gloria* played on a piano-organ the long deep hum and roll of the traffic in Holborn, a sound so persistent that it echoed like the turning of everlasting wheels. Dyson looked to the right and left and conned the way, and presently they were passing through a more peaceful quarter, touching on deserted squares and silent streets black as midnight. Phillipps had lost all count of direction, and as by degrees the region of faded respectability gave place to the squalid, and dirty stucco offended the eye of the artistic observer, he merely ventured the remark that he had never seen a neighbourhood more unpleasant or more commonplace.

'More mysterious, you mean,' said Dyson. 'I warn you, Phillipps, we are now hot upon the scent.'

They dived yet deeper into the maze of brickwork; some time before they had crossed a noisy thoroughfare running east and west, and now the quarter seemed all amorphous, without character; here a decent house with sufficient garden, here a faded square, and here factories surrounded by high, blank walls, with blind passages and dark corners; but all ill-lighted and unfrequented and heavy with silence.

Presently, as they paced down a forlorn street of two-storey houses, Dyson caught sight of a dark and obscure turning.

'I like the look of that,' he said; 'it seems to me promising.' There was a street lamp at the entrance, and another, a mere glimmer, at the further end. Beneath the lamp, on the pavement, an artist had evidently established his academy in the daytime, for the stones were all a blur of crude colours rubbed into each other, and a few broken fragments of chalk lay in a little heap beneath the wall.

'You see people do occasionally pass this way,' said Dyson, pointing to the ruins of the screever's work. 'I confess I should not have thought it possible. Come, let us explore.'

On one side of this byway of communication was a great timber-yard, with vague piles of wood looming shapeless above the enclosing wall; and on the other side of the road a wall still higher seemed to enclose a garden, for there were shadows like trees, and a faint murmur of rustling leaves broke the silence. It was a moonless night, and clouds that had gathered after sunset had blackened, and midway between the feeble lamps the passage lay all dark and formless, and when one stopped and listened, and the sharp echo of reverberant footsteps ceased, there came from far away, as from beyond the hills, a faint roll of the noise of London. Phillipps was bolstering up his courage to declare that he had had enough of the excursion, when a loud cry from Dyson broke in upon his thoughts.

'Stop, stop, for Heaven's sake, or you will tread on it! There! almost under your feet!' Phillipps looked down, and saw a vague shape, dark, and framed in surrounding darkness, dropped strangely on the pavement, and then a white cuff glimmered for a moment as Dyson lit a match, which went out directly.

'It's a drunken man,' said Phillipps very coolly.

'It's a murdered man,' said Dyson, and he began to call for police with all his might, and soon from the distance running footsteps echoed and grew louder, and cries sounded.

A policeman was the first to come up.

'What's the matter?' he said, as he drew to a stand, panting. 'Anything amiss here?' for he had not seen what was on the pavement.

'Look!' said Dyson, speaking out of the gloom. 'Look there! My friend and I came down this place three minutes ago, and that is what we found.'

The man flashed his light on the dark shape and cried out.

'Why, it's murder,' he said; 'there's blood all about him, and a puddle of it in the gutter there. He's not dead long, either. Ah! there's the wound! It's in the neck.'

Dyson bent over what was lying there. He saw a prosperous gentleman, dressed in smooth, well-cut clothes. The neat whiskers were beginning to grizzle a little; he might have been forty-five an hour before; and a handsome gold watch had half slipped out of his waistcoat pocket. And there in the flesh of the neck, between chin and ear, gaped a great wound, clean cut, but all clotted with drying blood, and the white of the cheeks shone like a lighted lamp above the red.

Dyson turned, and looked curiously about him; the dead man lay across the path with his head inclined towards the wall, and the blood from the wound streamed away across the pavement, and lay a dark puddle, as the policeman had said, in the gutter. Two more policemen had come up, the crowd gathered, humming from all quarters, and the officers had as much as they could do to keep the curious at a distance. The three lanterns were flashing here and there, searching for more evidence, and in the gleam of one of them Dyson caught sight of an object in the road, to which he called the attention of the policeman nearest to him.

'Look, Phillipps,' he said, when the man had secured it and held it up. 'Look, that should be something in your way!'

It was a dark flinty stone, gleaming like obsidian, and shaped to a broad edge something after the manner of an adze. One end was rough, and easily grasped in the hand, and the whole thing was hardly five inches long. The edge was thick with blood.

'What is that, Phillipps?' said Dyson; and Phillipps looked hard at it.

'It's a primitive flint knife,' he said. 'It was made about ten thousand years ago. One exactly like this was found near Abury, in Wiltshire, and all the authorities gave it that age.'

The policeman stared astonished at such a development of the case; and Phillipps himself was all aghast at his own words. But Mr. Dyson did not notice him. An inspector who had just come up and was listening to the outlines of the case, was holding a lantern to the dead man's head. Dyson, for his part, was staring with a white heat of curiosity at something he saw on the wall, just above where the man was lying; there were a few rude marks done in red chalk.

'This is a black business,' said the inspector at length: 'does anybody know who it is?'

A man stepped forward from the crowd. 'I do, governor,' he said, 'he's a big doctor, his name's Sir Thomas Vivian; I was in the 'orspital abart six months ago, and he used to come round; he was a very kind man.'

'Lord,' cried the inspector, 'this is a bad job indeed. Why, Sir Thomas Vivian goes to the Royal Family. And there's a watch worth a hundred guineas in his pocket, so it isn't robbery.'

Dyson and Phillipps gave their cards to the authority, and moved off, pushing with difficulty through the crowd that was still gathering, gathering fast; and the alley that had been lonely and desolate now swarmed with white staring faces and hummed with the buzz of rumour and horror, and rang with the commands of the officers of police. The two men once free from this swarming curiosity stepped out briskly, but for twenty minutes neither spoke a word.

'Phillipps,' said Dyson, as they came into a small but cheerful street, clean and brightly lit, 'Phillipps, I owe you an apology. I was wrong to have spoken as I did tonight. Such infernal jesting,' he went on, with heat, 'as if there were no wholesome subjects for a joke. I feel as if I had raised an evil spirit.'

'For Heaven's sake say nothing more,' said Phillipps, choking down horror with visible effort. 'You told the truth to me in my room; the troglodyte, as you said, is still lurking about the earth, and in these very streets around us, slaying for mere lust of blood.'

'I will come up for a moment,' said Dyson, when they reached Red Lion Square, 'I have something to ask you. I think there should be nothing hidden between us at all events.'

Phillipps nodded gloomily, and they went up to the room, where everything hovered indistinct in the uncertain glimmer of the light from without.

When the candle was lighted and the two men sat facing each other, Dyson spoke.

'Perhaps,' he began, 'you did not notice me peering at the wall just above the place where the head lay. The light from the inspector's lantern was shining full on it, and I saw something that looked queer to me, and I examined it closely. I found that someone had drawn in red chalk a rough outline of a hand—a human hand—upon the wall. But it was the curious position of the fingers that struck me; it was like this'; and he took a pencil and a piece of paper and drew rapidly, and then handed what he had done to Phillipps. It was a rough sketch of a hand seen from the back, with the fingers clenched, and the top of the thumb protruded between the first and second fingers, and pointed downwards, as if to something below.

'It was just like that,' said Dyson, as he saw Phillipps's face grow still whiter. 'The thumb pointed down as if to the body; it seemed almost a live hand in ghastly gesture. And just beneath there was a small mark with the powder of the chalk lying on it—as if someone had commenced a stroke and had broken the chalk in his hand. I saw the bit of chalk lying on the ground. But what do you make of it?'

'It's a horrible old sign,' said Phillipps—'one of the most horrible signs connected with the theory of the evil eye. It is used still in Italy, but there can be no doubt that it has been known for ages. It is one of the survivals; you must look for the origin of it in the black swamp whence man first came.'

Dyson took up his hat to go.

'I think, jesting apart,' said he, 'that I kept my promise, and that we were and are hot on the scent, as I said. It seems as if I had really shown you primitive man, or his handiwork at all events.'

INCIDENT OF THE LETTER

About a month after the extraordinary and mysterious murder of Sir Thomas Vivian, the well-known and universally respected specialist in heart disease, Mr. Dyson called again on his friend Mr. Phillipps, whom he found, not as usual, sunk deep in painful study, but reclining in his easy-chair in an attitude of relaxation. He welcomed Dyson with cordiality.

'I am very glad you have come,' he began; 'I was thinking of looking you up. There is no longer the shadow of a doubt about the matter.'

'You mean the case of Sir Thomas Vivian?'

'Oh, no, not at all. I was referring to the problem of the fish-hooks. Between ourselves, I was a little too confident when you were here last, but since then other facts have turned up; and only yesterday I had a letter from a distinguished F.R.S. which quite settles the affair. I have been thinking what I should tackle next; and I am inclined to believe that there is a good deal to be done in the way of so-called undecipherable inscriptions.'

'Your line of study pleases me,' said Dyson, 'I think it may prove useful. But in the meantime, there was surely something extremely mysterious about the case of Sir Thomas Vivian.'

'Hardly, I think. I allowed myself to be frightened that night; but there can be no doubt that the facts are patient of a comparatively commonplace explanation.'

'Really! What is your theory then?'

'Well, I imagine that Vivian must have been mixed up at some period of his life in an adventure of a not very creditable description, and that he was murdered out of revenge by some Italian whom he had wronged.'

'Why Italian?'

'Because of the hand, the sign of the *mano in fica*. That gesture is now only used by Italians. So, you see that what appeared the most obscure feature in the case turns out to be illuminant.'

'Yes, quite so. And the flint knife?'

'That is very simple. The man found the thing in Italy, or possibly stole it from some museum. Follow the line of least resistance, my dear fellow, and you will see there is no need to bring up primitive man from his secular grave beneath the hills.'

'There is some justice in what you say,' said Dyson. 'As I understand you, then, you think that your Italian, having murdered, Vivian, kindly chalked up that hand as a guide to Scotland Yard?'

'Why not? Remember a murderer is always a madman. He may plot and contrive nine-tenths of his scheme with the acuteness and the grasp of a chess-player or a pure mathematician; but somewhere or other his wits leave him and he behaves like a fool. Then you must take into account the insane pride or vanity of the criminal; he likes to leave his mark, as it were, upon his handiwork.'

'Yes, it is all very ingenious; but have you read the reports of the inquest?'

'No, not a word. I simply gave my evidence, left the court, and dismissed the subject from my mind.'

'Quite so. Then if you don't object, I should like to give you an account of the case. I have studied it rather deeply, and I confess it interests me extremely.'

'Very good. But I warn you I have done with mystery. We are to deal with facts now.'

'Yes, it is fact that I wish to put before you. And this is fact the first. When the police moved Sir Thomas Vivian's body, they found an open knife beneath him. It was an ugly-looking thing such as sailors carry, with a blade that the mere opening rendered rigid, and there the blade was all ready, bare and gleaming, but without a trace of blood on it, and the knife was found to be quite new; it had never been used. Now, at the first glance it looks as if your imaginary Italian were just the man to have such a tool. But consider a moment. Would he be likely to buy a new knife expressly to commit murder? And, secondly, if he had such a knife, why didn't he use it, instead of that very odd flint instrument?

'And I want to put this to you. You think the murderer chalked up the hand after the murder as a sort of "melodramatic Italian assassin his mark" touch. Passing over the question as to whether the real criminal ever does such a thing, I would point out that, on the medical evidence, Sir Thomas Vivian hadn't been dead for more than an hour; That would place the stroke at about a quarter to ten, and you know it was perfectly dark when we went out at 9.30. And that passage was singularly gloomy and ill-lighted, and the hand was drawn roughly, it is true, but correctly and without the bungling of strokes and the bad shots that are inevitable when one tries to draw in the dark or with shut eyes.

'Just try to draw such a simple figure as a square without looking at the paper, and then ask me to conceive that your Italian, with the rope waiting for his neck, could draw the hand on the wall so firmly and truly, in the black shadow of that alley. It is absurd. By consequence, then, the hand was drawn early in the evening, long before any murder was committed; or else—mark this, Phillipps—it was drawn by someone to whom darkness and gloom were familiar and habitual; by someone to whom the common dread of the rope was unknown!

'Again: a curious note was found in Sir Thomas Vivian's pocket. Envelope and paper were of a common make, and the stamp bore the West Central postmark. I will come to the nature of the contents later on, but it is the question of the handwriting that is so remarkable. The address on the outside was neatly written in a small clear hand, but the letter itself might have been written by a Persian who had learnt the English script. It was upright, and the letters were curiously contorted, with an affectation of dashes and backward curves which really reminded me of an Oriental manuscript, though it was all perfectly legible. But—and here comes the poser—on searching the dead man's waistcoat pockets a small memorandum book was found; it was almost filled with pencil jottings. These memoranda related chiefly to matters of a private as distinct from a professional nature; there were appointments to meet friends, notes of theatrical first-nights, the address of a good hotel in Tours, and the title of a new novel—nothing in any way intimate.

'And the whole of these jottings were written in a hand nearly identical with the writing of the note found in the dead man's coat pocket! There was just enough difference between them to enable the expert to swear that the two were not written by the same person. I will just read you so much of Lady Vivian's evidence as bears on this point of the writing; I have the printed slip with me. Here you see she says: "I was married to my late husband seven years ago; I never saw any letter addressed to him in a hand at all resembling that on the envelope produced, nor have I ever seen writing like that in the letter before me. I never saw my late husband using the memorandum book, but I am sure he did write everything in it; I am certain of that because we stayed last May at the Hotel du Faisan, Rue Royale, Tours, the address of which is given in the book; I remember his getting the novel *A Sentinel* about six weeks ago. Sir Thomas Vivian never liked to miss the first-nights at the theatres. His usual hand was perfectly different from that used in the note-book."

'And now, last of all, we come back to the note itself. Here it is in facsimile. My possession of it is due to the kindness of Inspector Cleeve, who is pleased to be amused at my amateur inquisitiveness. Read it, Phillipps; you tell me you are interested in obscure inscriptions; here is something for you to decipher.'

Mr. Phillipps, absorbed in spite of himself in the strange circumstances Dyson had related, took the piece of paper, and scrutinised it closely. The handwriting was indeed bizarre in the extreme, and, as Dyson had noted, not unlike the Persian character in its general effect, but it was perfectly legible.

'Read it aloud,' said Dyson, and Phillipps obeyed.

'"Hand did not point in vain. The meaning of the stars is no longer obscure. Strangely enough, the black heaven vanished, or was stolen yesterday, but that does not matter in the least, as I have a celestial globe.

Our old orbit remains unchanged; you have not forgotten the number of my sign, or will you appoint some other house? I have been on the other side of the moon, and can bring something to show you."'

'And what do you make of that?' said Dyson.

'It seems to me mere gibberish,' said Phillipps; 'you suppose it has a meaning?'

'Oh, surely; it was posted three days before the murder; it was found in the murdered man's pocket; it is written in a fantastic hand which the murdered man himself used for his private memoranda. There must be purpose under all this, and to my mind there is something ugly enough hidden under the circumstances of this case of Sir Thomas Vivian.'

'But what theory have you formed?'

'Oh, as to theories, I am still in a very early stage; it is too soon to state conclusions. But I think I have demolished your Italian. I tell you, Phillipps, again the whole thing has an ugly look to my eyes. I cannot do as you do, and fortify myself with cast-iron propositions to the effect that this or that doesn't happen, and never has happened. You note that the first word in the letter is "hand". That seems to me, taken with what we know about the hand on the wall, significant enough, and what you yourself told me of the history and meaning of the symbol, its connection with a world-old belief and faiths of dim far-off years, all this speaks of mischief, for me at all events. No; I stand pretty well to what I said to you, half in joke that night before we went out. There are sacraments of evil as well as of good about us, and we live and move to my belief in an unknown world, a place where there are caves and shadows and dwellers in twilight. It is possible that man may sometimes return on the track of evolution, and it is my belief that an awful lore is not yet dead.'

'I cannot follow you in all this,' said Phillipps; 'it seems to interest you strangely. What do you propose to do?'

'My dear, Phillipps,' replied Dyson, speaking in a lighter tone, 'I am afraid I shall have to go down a little in the world. I have a prospect of visits to the pawnbrokers before me, and the publicans must not be neglected. I must cultivate a taste for four ale; shag tobacco I already love and esteem with all my heart.'

Search for the Vanished Heaven

For many days after the discussion with Phillipps. Mr. Dyson was resolute in the line of research he had marked out for himself. A fervent curiosity and an innate liking for the obscure were great incentives, but especially in this case of Sir Thomas Vivian's death (for Dyson began to boggle a little at the word 'murder') there seemed to him an element that was more than curious. The sign of the red hand upon the wall, the tool of flint that had given death, the almost identity between the handwriting of the note and the fantastic script reserved religiously, as it appeared, by the doctor for trifling jottings, all these diverse and variegated threads joined to weave in his mind a strange and shadowy picture, with ghastly shapes dominant and deadly, and yet ill-defined, like the giant figures wavering in an ancient tapestry. He thought he had a clue to the meaning of the note, and in his resolute search for the 'black heaven', which had vanished, he beat furiously about the alleys and obscure streets of central London, making himself a familiar figure to the pawnbroker, and a frequent guest at the more squalid pot-houses.

For a long time, he was unsuccessful, and he trembled at the thought that the 'black heaven' might be hid in the coy retirements of Peckham, or lurk perchance in distant Willesden, but finally, improbability, in which he put his trust, came to the rescue. It was a dark and rainy night, with something in the unquiet and stirring gusts that savoured of approaching winter, and Dyson, beating up a narrow street not far from the Gray's Inn Road, took shelter in an extremely dirty 'public', and called for beer, forgetting for the moment his preoccupations, and only thinking of the sweep of the wind about the tiles and the hissing of the rain through the black and troubled air.

At the bar there gathered the usual company: the frowsy women and the men in shiny black, those who appeared to mumble secretly together, others who wrangled in interminable argument, and a few shy drinkers who stood apart, each relishing his dose, and the rank and biting flavour of cheap spirit. Dyson was wondering at the enjoyment of it all, when suddenly there came a sharper accent. The folding-doors swayed open, and a middle-aged woman staggered towards the bar, and clutched the pewter rim as if she stepped a deck in a roaring gale.

Dyson glanced at her attentively as a pleasing specimen of her class; she was decently dressed in black, and carried a black bag of somewhat rusty leather, and her intoxication was apparent and far advanced. As she swayed at the bar, it was evidently all she could do to stand upright, and the barman, who had looked at her with disfavour, shook his head in reply to her thick-voiced demand for a drink. The woman glared at him, transformed in a moment to a fury, with bloodshot eyes, and poured forth a torrent of execration, a stream of blasphemies and early English phraseology.

'Get out of this,' said the man; 'shut up and be off, or I'll send for the police.'

'Police, you —— ' bawled the woman 'I'll —— well give you something to fetch the police for!' and with a rapid dive into her bag she pulled out some object which she hurled furiously at the barman's head.

The man ducked down, and the missile flew over his head and smashed a bottle to fragments, while the woman with a peal of horrible laughter rushed to the door, and they could hear her steps pattering fast over the wet stones.

The barman looked ruefully about him.

'Not much good going after her,' he said, 'and I'm afraid what she's left won't pay for that bottle of whisky.' He fumbled amongst the fragments of broken glass, and drew out something dark, a kind of square stone it seemed, which he held up.

'Valuable cur'osity,' he said, 'any gent like to bid?'

The *habitués* had scarcely turned from their pots and glasses during these exciting incidents; they gazed a moment, fishily, when the bottle smashed, and that was all, and the mumble of the confidential was resumed and the jangle of the quarrelsome, and the shy and solitary sucked in their lips and relished again the rank flavour of the spirit.

Dyson looked quickly at what the barman held before him.

'Would you mind letting me see it?' he said; 'it's a queer-looking old thing, isn't it?'

It was a small black tablet, apparently of stone, about four inches long by two and a half broad, and as Dyson took it he felt rather than saw that he touched the secular with his flesh. There was some kind of carving on the surface, and, most conspicuous, a sign that made Dyson's heart leap.

'I don't mind taking it,' he said quietly. 'Would two shillings be enough?'

'Say half a dollar,' said the man, and the bargain was concluded. Dyson drained his pot of beer, finding it delicious, and lit his pipe, and went out deliberately soon after. When he reached his apartment, he locked the door, and placed the tablet on his desk, and then fixed himself in his chair, as resolute as an army in its trenches before a beleaguered city. The tablet was full under the light of the shaded candle, and scrutinising it closely, Dyson saw first the sign of the hand with the thumb protruding between the fingers; it was cut finely and firmly on the dully black surface of the stone, and the thumb pointed downward to what was beneath.

'It is mere ornament,' said Dyson to himself, 'perhaps symbolical ornament, but surely not an inscription, or the signs of any words ever spoken.'

The hand pointed at a series of fantastic figures, spirals and whorls of the finest, most delicate lines, spaced at intervals over the remaining surface of the tablet. The marks were as intricate and seemed almost as much without design as the pattern of a thumb impressed upon a pane of glass.

'Is it some natural marking?' thought Dyson; 'there have been queer designs, likenesses of beasts and flowers, in stones with which man's hand had nothing to do'; and he bent over the stone with a magnifier, only to be convinced that no hazard of nature could have delineated these varied labyrinths of line. The whorls were of different sizes; some were less than the twelfth of an inch in diameter, and the largest was a little smaller than a sixpence, and under the glass the regularity and accuracy of the cutting were evident, and in the smaller spirals the lines were graduated at intervals of a hundredth of an inch. The whole thing had a marvellous and fantastic look, and gazing at the mystic whorls beneath the hand, Dyson became subdued with an impression of vast and far-off ages, and of a living being that had touched the stone with enigmas before the hills were formed, when the hard rocks still boiled with fervent heat.

'The "black heaven" is found again,' he said, 'but the meaning of the stars is likely to be obscure for everlasting so far as I am concerned.'

London stilled without, and a chill breath came into the room as Dyson sat gazing at the tablet shining duskily under the candle-light; and at last as he closed the desk over the ancient stone, all his wonder at the case of Sir Thomas Vivian increased tenfold, and he thought of the well-dressed prosperous gentleman lying dead mystically beneath the sign of the hand, and the insupportable conviction seized him that between the death of this fashionable West End doctor and the weird spirals of the tablet there were most secret and unimaginable links.

For days he sat before his desk gazing at the tablet, unable to resist its lodestone fascination, and yet quite helpless, without even the hope of solving the symbols so secretly inscribed. At last, desperate he called in Mr. Phillipps in consultation, and told in brief the story of the finding the stone.

'Dear me!' said Phillipps, 'this is extremely curious; you have had a find indeed. Why, it looks to me even more ancient than the Hittite seal. I confess the character, if it is a character, is entirely strange to me. These whorls are really very quaint.'

'Yes, but I want to know what they mean. You must remember this tablet is the "black heaven" of the letter found in Sir Thomas Vivian's pocket; it bears directly on his death.'

'Oh, no, that is nonsense! This is, no doubt, an extremely ancient tablet, which has been stolen from some collection. Yes, the hand makes an odd coincidence, but only a coincidence after all.'

'My dear Phillipps, you are a living example of the truth of the axiom that extreme scepticism is mere credulity. But can you decipher the inscription?'

'I undertake to decipher anything,' said Phillipps. 'I do not believe in the insoluble. These characters are curious, but I cannot fancy them to be inscrutable.'

'Then take the thing away with you and make what you can of it. It has begun to haunt me; I feel as if I had gazed too long into the eyes of the Sphinx.'

Phillipps departed with the tablet in an inner pocket. He had not much doubt of success, for he had evolved thirty-seven rules for the solution of inscriptions. Yet when a week had passed and he called to see Dyson there was no vestige of triumph on his features. He found his friend in a state of extreme irritation, pacing up and down in the room like a man in a passion. He turned with a start as the door opened.

'Well,' said Dyson, 'you have got it? What is it all about?'

'My dear fellow, I am sorry to say I have completely failed. I have tried every known device in vain. I have even been so officious as to submit it to a friend at the Museum, but he, though a man of prime authority on the subject, tells me he is quite at fault. It must be some wreckage of a vanished race, almost, I think—a fragment of another world than ours. I am not a superstitious man, Dyson, and you know that I have no truck with even the noble delusions, but I confess I yearn to be rid of this small square of blackish stone. Frankly, it has given me an ill week; it seems to me troglodytic and abhorred.'

Phillipps drew out the tablet and laid it on the desk before Dyson.

'By the way,' he went on, 'I was right at all events in one particular; it has formed part of some collection. There is a piece of grimy paper on the back that must have been a label.'

'Yes, I noticed that,' said Dyson, who had fallen into deepest disappointment; 'no doubt the paper is a label. But as I don't much care where the tablet originally came from, and only wish to know what the inscription means, I paid no attention to the paper. The thing is a hopeless riddle, I suppose, and yet it must surely be of the greatest importance.'

Phillipps left soon after, and Dyson, still despondent, took the tablet in his hand and carelessly turned it over. The label had so grimed that it seemed merely a dull stain, but as Dyson looked at it idly, and yet attentively, he could see pencil-marks, and he bent over it eagerly, with his glass to his eye. To his annoyance, he found that part of the paper had been torn away, and he could only with difficulty make out odd words and pieces of words. First, he read something that looked like 'inroad', and then beneath, 'stony-hearted step——' and a tear cut off the rest. But in an instant a solution suggested itself, and he chuckled with huge delight.

'Certainly,' he said out loud, 'this is not only the most charming but the most convenient quarter in all London; here I am, allowing for the accidents of side streets, perched on a tower of observation.'

He glanced triumphant out of the window across the street to the gate of the British Museum. Sheltered by the boundary wall of that agreeable institution, a 'screever', or artist in chalks, displayed his brilliant impressions on the pavement, soliciting the approval and the coppers of the gay and serious.

'This,' said Dyson, 'is more than delightful! An artist is provided to my hand.'

The Artist of the Pavement

Mr. Phillipps, in spite of all disavowals—in spite of the wall of sense of whose enclosure and limit he was wont to make his boast—yet felt in his heart profoundly curious as to the case of Sir Thomas Vivian. Though he kept a brave face for his friend, his reason could not decently resist the conclusion that Dyson had enunciated, namely, that the whole affair had a look both ugly and mysterious. There was the weapon of a vanished race that had pierced the great arteries; the red hand, the symbol of a hideous faith, that pointed to the slain man; and then the tablet which Dyson declared he had expected to find, and had certainly found, bearing the ancient impress of the hand of malediction, and a legend written beneath in a character compared with which the most antique cuneiform was a thing of yesterday. Besides all this, there were other points that tortured and perplexed. How to account for the bare knife found unstained beneath the body? And the hint that the red hand upon the wall must have been drawn by someone whose life was passed in darkness thrilled him with a suggestion of dim and infinite horror. Hence, he was in truth not a little curious as to what was to come, and some ten days after he had returned the tablet he again visited the 'mystery-man', as he privately named his friend.

Arrived in the grave and airy chambers in Great Russell Street, he found the moral atmosphere of the place had been transformed. All Dyson's irritation had disappeared, his brow was smoothed with complacency, and he sat at a table by the window gazing out into the street with an expression of grim enjoyment, a pile of books and papers lying unheeded before him.

'My dear Phillipps, I am delighted to see you! Pray excuse my moving. Draw your chair up here to the table, and try this admirable shag tobacco.'

'Thank you,' said Phillipps, 'judging by the flavour of the smoke, I should think it is a little strong. But what on earth is all this? What are you looking at?'

'I am on my watch-tower. I assure you that the time seems short while I contemplate this agreeable street and the classic grace of the Museum portico.'

'Your capacity for nonsense is amazing,' replied Phillipps, 'but have you succeeded in deciphering the tablet? It interests me.'

'I have not paid much attention to the tablet recently,' said Dyson. 'I believe the spiral character may wait.'

'Really! And how about the Vivian murder?'

'Ah, you do take an interest in that case? Well, after all, we cannot deny that it was a queer business. But is not "murder" rather a coarse word? It smacks a little, surely, of the police poster. Perhaps I am a trifle decadent, but I cannot help believing in the splendid word; "sacrifice", for example, is surely far finer than "murder".'

'I am all in the dark,' said Phillipps. 'I cannot even imagine by what track you are moving in this labyrinth.'

'I think that before very long the whole matter will be a good deal clearer for us both, but I doubt whether you will like hearing the story.'

Dyson lit his pipe afresh and leant back, not relaxing, however, in his scrutiny of the street. After a somewhat lengthy pause, he startled Phillipps by a loud breath of relief as he rose from the chair by the window and began to pace the floor.

'It's over for the day,' he said, 'and, after all, one gets a little tired.'

Phillipps looked with inquiry into the street. The evening was darkening, and the pile of the museum was beginning to loom indistinct before the lighting of the lamps, but the pavements were thronged and busy. The artist in chalks across the way was gathering together his materials, and blurring all the brilliance of his designs, and a little lower down there was the clang of shutters being placed in position. Phillipps could see nothing to justify Mr. Dyson's sudden abandonment of his attitude of surveillance, and grew a little irritated by all these thorny enigmas.

'Do you know, Phillipps,' said Dyson, as he strolled at ease up and down the room, 'I will tell you how I work. I go upon the theory of improbability. The theory is unknown to you? I will explain. Suppose I stand on the steps of St. Paul's and look out for a blind man lame of the left leg to pass me, it is evidently highly improbable that I shall see such a person by waiting for an hour. If I wait two hours the improbability is diminished, but is still enormous, and a watch of a whole day would give little expectation of success. But suppose I take up the same position day after day, and week after week, don't you perceive that the improbability is lessening constantly—growing smaller day after day. Don't you see that two lines which are not parallel are gradually approaching one another, drawing nearer and nearer to a point of meeting, till at last they do meet, and improbability has vanished altogether. That is how I found the black tablet: I acted on the theory of improbability. It is the only scientific principle I know of which can enable one to pick out an unknown man from amongst five million.'

'And you expect to find the interpreter of the black tablet by this method?'

'Certainly.'

'And the murderer of Sir Thomas Vivian also?'

'Yes, I expect to lay my hands on the person concerned in the death of Sir Thomas Vivian in exactly the same way.'

The rest of the evening after Phillipps had left was devoted by Dyson to sauntering in the streets, and afterwards, when the night grew late, to his literary labours, or the chase of the phrase, as he called it. The next morning the station by the window was again resumed. His meals were brought to him at the table, and he ate with his eyes on the street. With briefest intervals, snatched reluctantly from time to time, he persisted in his survey throughout the day, and only at dusk, when the shutters were put up and the 'screever' ruthlessly deleted all his labour of the day, just before the gas-lamps began to star the shadows, did he feel at liberty to quit his post. Day after day this ceaseless glance upon the street continued, till the landlady grew puzzled and aghast at such a profitless pertinacity.

But at last, one evening, when the play of lights and shadows was scarce beginning, and the clear cloudless air left all distinct and shining, there came the moment. A man of middle age, bearded and bowed, with a touch of grey about the ears, was strolling slowly along the northern pavement of Great Russell Street from the eastern end. He looked up at the Museum as he went by, and then glanced involuntarily at the art of the 'screever', and at the artist himself, who sat beside his pictures, hat in hand. The man with the beard stood still an instant, swaying slightly to and fro as if in thought, and Dyson saw his fists shut tight, and his back quivering, and the one side of his face in view twitched and grew contorted with the indescribable torment of approaching epilepsy. Dyson drew a soft hat from his pocket, and dashed the door open, taking the stair with a run.

When he reached the street, the person he had seen so agitated had turned about, and, regardless of observation, was racing wildly towards Bloomsbury Square, with his back to his former course. Mr. Dyson went up to the artist of the pavement and gave him some money, observing quietly, 'You needn't trouble to draw that thing again.'

Then he, too, turned about, and strolled idly down the street in the opposite direction to that taken by the fugitive. So, the distance between Dyson and the man with the bowed head grew steadily greater.

STORY OF THE TREASURE-HOUSE

'There are many reasons why I chose your rooms for the meeting in preference to my own. Chiefly, perhaps because I thought the man would be more at his ease on neutral ground.'

'I confess, Dyson,' said Phillipps, 'that I feel both impatient and uneasy. You know my standpoint: hard matter of fact, materialism if you like, in its crudest form. But there is something about all this affair of Vivian that makes me a little restless. And how did you induce the man to come?'

'He has an exaggerated opinion of my powers. You remember what I said about the doctrine of improbability? When it does work out, it gives results which seem very amazing to a person who is not in the secret. That is eight striking, isn't it? And there goes the bell.'

They heard footsteps on the stair, and presently the door opened, and a middle-aged man, with a bowed head, bearded, and with a good deal of grizzling hair about his ears, came into the room. Phillipps glanced at his features, and recognised the lineaments of terror.

'Come in, Mr. Selby,' said Dyson. 'This is Mr. Phillipps, my intimate friend and our host for this evening. Will you take anything? Then perhaps we had better hear your story—a very singular one, I am sure.'

The man spoke in a voice hollow and a little quavering, and a fixed stare that never left his eyes seemed directed to something awful that was to remain before him by day and night for the rest of his life.

'You will, I am sure, excuse preliminaries,' he began; 'what I have to tell is best told quickly. I will say, then, that I was born in a remote part of the west of England, where the very outlines of the woods and hills, and the winding of the streams in the valleys, are apt to suggest the mystical to any one strongly gifted with imagination.

'When I was quite a boy there were certain huge and rounded hills, certain depths of hanging wood, and secret valleys bastioned round on every side that filled me with fancies beyond the bourne of rational expression, and as I grew older and began to dip into my father's books, I went by instinct, like the bee, to all that would nourish fantasy. Thus, from a course of obsolete and occult reading, and from listening to certain wild legends in which the older people still secretly believed, I grew firmly convinced of the existence of treasure, the hoard of a race extinct for ages, still hidden beneath the hills, and my every thought was directed to the discovery of the golden heaps that lay, as I fancied within a few feet of the green turf.

'To one spot, in especial, I was drawn as if by enchantment; it was a tumulus, the domed memorial of some forgotten people, crowning the crest of a vast mountain range; and I have often lingered there on summer evenings, sitting on the great block of limestone at the summit, and looking out, far over the yellow sea towards the Devonshire coast. One day as I dug heedlessly with the ferrule of my stick at the mosses and lichens which grew rank over the stone, my eye was caught by what seemed a pattern beneath the growth of green; there was a curving line, and marks that did not look altogether the work of nature.

'At first, I thought I had bared some rarer fossil, and I took out my knife and scraped away at the moss till a square foot was uncovered.

Then I saw two signs which startled me; first, a closed hand, pointing downwards, the thumb protruding between the fingers, and beneath the hand a whorl or spiral, traced with exquisite accuracy in the hard surface of the rock.

'Here I persuaded myself, was an index to the great secret, but I chilled at the recollection of the fact that some antiquarians had tunnelled the tumulus through and through, and had been a good deal surprised at not finding so much as an arrowhead within. Clearly, then, the signs on the limestone had no local significance; and I made up my mind that I must search abroad. By sheer accident I was in a measure successful in my quest. Strolling by a cottage, I saw some children playing by the roadside; one was holding up some object in his hand, and the rest were going through one of the many forms of elaborate pretence which make up a great part of the mystery of a child's life.

'Something in the object held by the little boy attracted me, and I asked him to let me see it. The plaything of these children consisted of an oblong tablet of black stone; and on it was inscribed the hand pointing downwards, just as I had seen it on the rock, while beneath, spaced over the tablet, were a number of whorls and spirals, cut, as it seemed to me, with the utmost care and nicety.

'I bought the toy for a couple of shillings; the woman of the house told me it had been lying about for years; she thought her husband had found it one day in the brook which ran in front of the cottage: it was a very hot summer, and the stream was almost dry, and he saw it amongst the stones. That day I tracked the brook to a well of water gushing up cold and clear at the head of a lonely glen in the mountain. That was twenty years ago, and I only succeeded in deciphering the mysterious inscription last August. I must not trouble you with irrelevant details of my life; it is enough for me to say that I was forced, like many another man, to leave my old home and come to London. Of money I had very little, and I was glad to find a cheap room in a squalid street off the Gray's Inn Road. The late Sir Thomas Vivian, then far poorer and more wretched than myself, had a garret in the same house, and before many months we became intimate friends, and I had confided to him the object of my life.

'I had at first great difficulty in persuading him that I was not giving my days and my nights to an inquiry altogether hopeless and chimerical; but when he was convinced, he grew keener than myself, and glowed at the thought of the riches which were to be the prize of some ingenuity and patience. I liked the man intensely, and pitied his case; he had a strong desire to enter the medical profession, but he lacked the means to pay the smallest fees, and indeed he was, not once or twice, but often reduced to the very verge of starvation. I freely and solemnly promised, that under whatever chances, he should share in my heaped fortune when it came, and this promise to one who had always been poor, and yet thirsted for wealth and pleasure in a manner unknown to me, was the strongest incentive. He threw himself into the task with eager interest, and applied a very acute intellect and un-wearied patience to the solution of the characters on the tablet.

'I, like other ingenious young men, was curious in the matter of handwriting, and I had invented or adapted a fantastic script which I used occasionally, and which took Vivian so strongly that he was at the pains to imitate it. It was arranged between us that if we were ever parted, and had occasion to write on the affair that was so close to our hearts, this queer hand of my invention was to be used, and we also contrived a semi-cypher for the same purpose.

'Meanwhile we exhausted ourselves in efforts to get at the heart of the mystery, and after a couple of years had gone by I could see that Vivian began to sicken a little of the adventure, and one night he told me with some emotion that he feared both our lives were being passed away in idle and hopeless endeavour. Not many months after-wards he was so happy as to receive a considerable legacy from an aged and distant relative whose very existence had been almost forgotten by him; and with money at the bank, he became at once a stranger to me. He had passed his preliminary examination many years before, and forthwith decided to enter at St. Thomas's Hospital, and he told me that he must look out for a more convenient lodging.

'As we said goodbye, I reminded him of the promise I had given, and solemnly renewed it; but Vivian laughed with something between pity and contempt in his voice and expression as he thanked me. I need not dwell on the long struggle and misery of my existence, now doubly lonely; I never wearied or despaired of final success, and every day saw me at work, the tablet before me, and only at dusk would I go out and take my daily walk along Oxford Street, which attracted me, I think, by the noise and motion and glitter of lamps.

'This walk grew with me to a habit; every night, and in all weath-ers, I crossed the Gray's Inn Road and struck westward, sometimes choosing a northern track, by the Euston Road and Tottenham Court Road, sometimes I went by Holborn, and I sometimes by way of

Great Russell Street. Every night I walked for an hour to and fro on the northern pavement of Oxford Street, and the tale of De Quincey and his name for the Street, 'Stony-hearted step mother', often recurred to my memory. Then I would return to my grimy den and spend hours more in endless analysis of the riddle before me.

'The answer came to me one night a few weeks; ago; it flashed into my brain in a moment, and I read the inscription, and saw that after all I had not wasted my days. "The place of the treasure-house of them that dwell below," were the first words I read, and then followed minute indications of the spot in my own country where the great works of gold were to be kept for ever. Such a track was to be followed, such a pitfall avoided; here the way narrowed almost to a fox's hole, and there it broadened, and so at last the chamber would be reached. I determined to lose no time in verifying my discovery—not that I doubted at that great moment, but I would not risk even the smallest chance of disappointing my old friend Vivian, now a rich and prosperous man.

'I took the train for the West, and one night, with chart in hand, traced out the passage of the hills, and went so far that I saw the gleam of gold before me. I would not go on; I resolved that Vivian must be with me; and I only brought away a strange knife of flint which lay on the path, as confirmation of what I had to tell. I returned to London, and was a good deal vexed to find the stone tablet had disappeared from my rooms. My landlady, an inveterate drunkard, denied all knowledge of the fact, but I have little doubt she had stolen the thing for the sake of the glass of whisky it might fetch.

'However, I knew what was written on the tablet by heart, and I had also made an exact facsimile of the characters, so the loss was not severe. Only one thing annoyed me: when I first came into possession of the stone, I had pasted a piece of paper on the back and had written down the date and place of finding, and later on I had scribbled a word or two, a trivial sentiment, the name of my street, and such-like idle pencillings on the paper; and these memories of days that had seemed so hopeless were dear to me: I had thought they would help to remind me in the future of the hours when I had hoped against despair.

'However, I wrote at once to Sir Thomas Vivian, using the handwriting I have mentioned and also the quasi-cypher. I told him of my success, and after mentioning the loss of the tablet and the fact that I had a copy of the inscription, I reminded him once more of my promise, and asked him either to write or call. He replied that he would see me in a certain obscure passage in Clerkenwell well known to us both in the old days, and at seven o'clock one evening I went to meet him. At the corner of this by way, as I was walking to and fro, I noticed the blurred pictures of some street artist, and I picked up a piece of chalk he had left behind him, not much thinking what I was doing. I paced up and down the passage, wondering a good deal, as you may imagine, as to what manner of man I was to meet after so many years of parting, and the thoughts of the buried time coming thick upon me, I walked mechanically without raising my eyes from the ground.

'I was startled out of my reverie by an angry voice and a rough inquiry why I didn't keep to the right side of the pavement, and looking up I found I had confronted a prosperous and important gentleman, who eyed my poor appearance with a look of great dislike and contempt. I knew directly it was my old comrade, and when I recalled myself to him, he apologised with some show of regret, and began to thank me for my kindness, doubtfully, as if he hesitated to commit himself, and, as I could see, with the hint of a suspicion as to my sanity. I would have engaged him at first in reminiscences of our friendship, but I found Sir Thomas viewed those days with a good deal of distaste, and replying politely to my remarks, continually edged in "business matters", as he called them. I changed my topics, and told him in greater detail what I have told you.

'Then I saw his manner suddenly change; as I pulled out the flint knife to prove my journey "to the other side of the moon", as we called it in our jargon, there came over him a kind of choking eagerness, his features were somewhat discomposed, and I thought I detected a shuddering horror, a clenched resolution, and the effort to keep quiet succeed one another in a manner that puzzled me. I had occasion to be a little precise in my particulars, and it being still light enough, I remembered the red chalk in my pocket, and drew the hand on the wall. "Here, you see, is the hand", I said, as I explained its true meaning, "note where the thumb issues from between the first and second fingers", and I would have gone on, and had applied the chalk to the wall to continue my diagram, when he struck my hand down much to my surprise.

'"No, no," he said, "I do not want all that. And this place is not retired enough; let us walk on, and do you explain everything to me minutely." I complied readily enough, and he led me away choosing the most unfrequented by-ways, while I drove in the plan of the hidden house word by word. Once or twice as I raised my eyes, I caught Vivian looking strangely about him; he seemed to give a quick glint up and down, and glance at the houses; and there was a furtive and anxious air about him that displeased me. "Let us walk on to the north," he said at length, "we shall come to some pleasant lanes where we can discuss these matters, quietly; my night's rest is at your service." I declined, on the pretext that I could not dispense with my visit to Oxford Street, and went on till he understood every turning and winding and the minutest detail as well as myself. We had returned on our footsteps, and stood again in the dark passage, just where I had drawn the red hand on the wall, for I recognised the vague shape of the trees whose branches hung above us.

"'We have come back to our starting-point,' I said; "I almost think I could put my finger on the wall where I drew the hand. And I am sure you could put your finger on the mystic hand in the hills as well as I. Remember between stream and stone."

'I was bending down, peering at what I thought must be my drawing, when I heard a sharp hiss of breath, and started up, and saw Vivian with his arm uplifted and a bare blade in his hand, and death threatening in his eyes. In sheer self-defence I caught at the flint weapon in my pocket, and dashed at him in blind fear of my life, and the next instant he lay dead upon the stones.

'I think that is all,' Mr. Selby continued after a pause, 'and it only remains for me to say to you, Mr. Dyson, that I cannot conceive what means enabled you to run me down.'

'I followed many indications,' said Dyson, 'and I am bound to disclaim all credit for acuteness, as I have made several gross blunders. Your celestial cypher did not, I confess, give me much trouble; I saw at once that terms of astronomy were substituted for common words and phrases. You had lost something black, or something black had been stolen from you; a celestial globe is a copy of the heavens, so I knew you meant you had a copy of what you had lost.

'Obviously, then, I came to the conclusion that you had lost a black object with characters or symbols written or inscribed on it, since the object in question certainly contained valuable information and all information must be written or pictured. "Our old orbit remains unchanged"; evidently our old course or arrangement. "The number of my sign" must mean the number of my house, the allusion being to the signs of the zodiac. I need not say that "the other side of the moon" can stand for nothing but some place where no one else has been; and "some other house" is some other place of meeting, the "house" being the old term "house of the heavens." Then my next step was to find the "black heaven" that had been stolen, and by a process of exhaustion I did so.'

'You have got the tablet?'

'Certainly. And on the back of it, on the slip of paper you have mentioned, I read 'inroad,' which puzzled me a good deal, till I thought of Grey's Inn Road; you forgot the second *n*. "Stony-hearted step——" immediately suggested the phrase of De Quincey you have alluded to; and I made the wild but correct shot, that you were a man who lived in or near the Gray's Inn Road, and had the habit of walking in Oxford Street, for you remember how the opium-eater dwells on his wearying promenades along that thoroughfare. On the theory of improbability, which I have explained to my friend here, I concluded that occasionally, at all events, you would choose the way by Guildford Street, Russell Square, and Great Russell Street, and I knew that if I watched long enough, I should see you. But how was I to recognise my man? I noticed the screever opposite my rooms, and got him to draw every day a large hand, in the gesture so familiar to us all, upon the wall behind him.

'I thought that when the unknown person did pass, he would certainly betray some emotion at the sudden vision of the sign, to him the most terrible of symbols. You know the rest. Ah, as to catching you an hour later, that was, I confess, a refinement. From the fact of your having occupied the same rooms for so many years, in a neighbourhood moreover where lodgers are migratory to excess, I drew the conclusion that you were a man of fixed habit, and I was sure that after you had got over your fright you would return for the walk down Oxford Street. You did, by way of New Oxford Street, and I was waiting at the corner.'

'Your conclusions are admirable,' said Mr. Selby. 'I may tell you that I had my stroll down Oxford Street the night Sir Thomas Vivian died. And I think that is all I have to say.'

'Scarcely,' said Dyson. 'How about the treasure?'

'I had rather we did not speak of that,' said Mr. Selby, with a whitening of the skin about the temples.

'Oh, nonsense, sir, we are not blackmailers. Besides, you know you are in our power.'

'Then, as you put it like that, Mr. Dyson, I must tell you I returned to the place. I went on a little farther than before.'

The man stopped short; his mouth began to twitch, his lips moved apart, and he drew in quick breaths, sobbing.

'Well, well,' said Dyson, 'I dare say you have done comfortably.'

'Comfortably,' Selby went on, constraining himself with an effort, 'yes, so comfortably that hell burns hot within me for ever. I only brought one thing away from that awful house within the hills; it was lying just beyond the spot where I found the flint knife.'

'Why did you not bring more?'

The whole bodily frame of the wretched man visibly shrank and wasted; his face grew yellow as tallow, and the sweat dropped from his brows. The spectacle was both revolting and terrible, and when the voice came it sounded like the hissing of a snake.

'Because the keepers are still there, and I saw them, and because of this,' and he pulled out a small piece of curious gold-work and held it up.

'There,' he said, 'that is the Pain of the Goat.'

Phillipps and Dyson cried out together in horror at the revolting obscenity of the thing.

'Put it away, man; hide it, for Heaven's sake, hide it!'

'I brought that with me; that is all,' he said. 'You do not wonder that I did not stay long in a place where those who live are a little higher than the beasts, and where what you have seen is surpassed a thousandfold?'

'Take this,' said Dyson, 'I brought it with me in case it might be useful'; and he drew out the black tablet, and handed it to the shaking, horrible man.

'And now,' said Dyson, 'will you go out?'

The two friends sat silent a little while, facing one another with restless eyes and lips that quivered.

'I wish to say that I believe him,' said Phillipps.

'My dear Phillipps,' said Dyson as he threw the windows wide open, 'I do not know that, after all, my blunders in this queer case were so very absurd.'